The Bridal Canopy

Library of Modern Jewish Literature

Other titles in the Library of Modern Jewish Literature

The Bridal Canopy

S. Y. AGNON

Translated by I. M. Lask

SYRACUSE UNIVERSITY PRESS

First Syracuse University Press Edition 2000

10   11   12   6   5   4   3

Originally published in 1967. Reprinted by arrangement with Schocken Books, Inc.

The paper used in this publication meets the minimum requirements of
American National Standard for Information Sciences—Permanence of
Paper for Printed Library Materials, ANSI Z39.48-1984. ∞™

Library of Congress Cataloging-in-Publication Data

Agnon, Shmuel Yosef, 1888-1970.

[Hakhnasat kalah. English]

The bridal canopy / S.Y. Agnon : translated by I. M. Lask.—1st Syracuse University Press ed.

p.   cm. — (Library of modern Jewish literature)

Previously published: New York : Schocken Books, c1967.

ISBN 0-8156-0640-0 (pbk. : alk. paper)

I. Lask, I. M. (Israel Meir), 1905– II. Title.   III. Series.

PJ5053.A4 H313 2000

892.4'35—dc21   99-089763

Manufactured in the United States of America

Contents

BOOK ONE

CONTENTS

BOOK TWO

[vi]

Book One

CAST THY BURDEN UPON THE LORD AND HE SHALL SUSTAIN THEE

CHAPTER ONE: THERE ONCE WAS A HASSID · THREE SISTERS · WISDOM OF WOMEN · TEXT OF A LETTER : AND FEAR SHALL NOT PASS O'ER HIS HEAD ✺ The following story deals with a devout man, a Hassid, who was so poor as to be overborne by his poverty, may Mercy deliver us, but who always sat at the holy toil of the Torah, because he kept his distance from the current affairs of the world; so he had no commerce nor traffickings nor dealings like other folk, but found his entire delight in God's Torah, both the generally revealed and that which is held secret, to wit, the lore of Kabbala. He served The Name in awe and fear and love and never thought of acquiring honor through study or of being esteemed a scholar by himself or others; nor yet of his own advantage in assuring himself a portion of the World to Come. He studied to fashion a seat for the Divine Presence, and to no other end whatsoever.

His dwelling was underground in a damp, narrow, gloomy cellar lacking seat upon which to sit and table at which to sit, bed upon which to lie and all other household furniture save a straw mat spread out on the ground; upon it his folk would lie, never moving thence by night or day so that their garments might not spoil even more. And so poverty-stricken was he that his only property was one cock called Reb Reveille, who used to rouse him to serve the Creator. And he had been named Reb Reveille because of the verse in Psalms, "He rallied light through the darkness for the upright."

Ere his cock was done crowing this poor Hassid would speed to the House of Study in order to fashion a link 'twixt the night and the day, by means of Torah and prayer uttered with sweet sound and pleasant voice, till his spirit would mount to the Universe of Intelligence as though it were freed of the senses and the things known of the senses. And he had a fine custom of prolonging his entreaties until midday, in order that his prayers might accompany all those of Israel; since men are sometimes in no mood for prayer early in the day, and may delay for an hour or so.

His prayers ended, he never dashed away, as do the gluttons, to fill his frame with perishables and corruptible things which increase the flesh and the worms that later feed thereon; but he would sustain his intellectual self on the Story of the Manna and the like.

[3]

When his desires rebelled and turned too strongly toward matters of food and drink he would subdue them with a page of Gemara according to the prescription of the verse in Proverbs, "Come break of my bread", and therein he would find a sufficient breakfast; all the more was this so at the third meal of the day, in which words of Torah are a regular part of the menu. At noon, when folk are accustomed to eat meat, he would say to himself, Is it meat you want? Well, what am I to do when our sages of blessed memory said that the ignorant may not eat meat; so let us study first; maybe the Holy and Blest One will light your eyes so that you discover some new point in the Law, and you'll be entitled to a flesh meal. Then, thinking it over, this Hassid would grieve himself for fear he was making his Torah a pickax to delve with, against all the injunctions of the sages, thereby consuming his portion of Paradise in his present life.

Now this Hassid was burdened with daughters, each older than the next by a year or more; that is, Gittele, the youngest, was about seventeen; then came Blume, her sister, who was about nineteen; and oldest of all was Pessele, the first-born, about twenty; ragged and barefoot they went, without proper clothing or garments, so they stayed at home perforce and never showed their faces in the street. And they all were charming, graceful and fair, with well-grown breasts and well-grown hair, but within their hearts, alas, fluttered despair at the days of their youth that were almost done; but redeemers from their maidenhood there were none.

When the youngest reached the age at which a virgin should be wed, Frummet, the wife of the Hassid in question, began to address herself to her husband. How much longer, said she to him, will you be as unfeeling as a raven toward your children? Have you no pity for your hapless, hopeless daughters who sit sighing and weeping like wives whose husbands have vanished, and who know not whether they are widowed or not? Why, the girls have all but wept their eyes away and the hair on their head is turning white, yet here you sit like a lump of clay in form of a man, without lifting a finger to marry them off. Come, look at their old-time playmates, and see how many babies are nestling at their teats, while these maidens shrivel and wither away, suffering with never a word to say, just because there is no bridegroom to make an end of shame and gloom.

The words went to the heart of the Hassid and aroused within him his fatherly pity. He sighed a bitter sigh, then turned his gaze back upon the Gemara, putting his trust in the Lord, since all things accord with His Will and Word.

What did Frummet do? She went to the saintly Rabbi of Apta, who was a true lover of Israel and who was wont to say, I can boast even in the presence of the Court on High that the love of Israel is embedded in my heart. And she cried out to him, did Frummet, Rabbi, aid me. My daughters have reached a fitting age for marriage, but I lack the wherewithal to wed them off, while their father is too far from worldly matters to concern himself. Not enough that we eke out the scantiest living plucking feathers for cushions; now there are ripe and ready maidens with none to cover their heads and lead them under the Bridal Canopy.

The saint took the end of his beard in his hand, combing his white hair with his fingers, and said, Go and borrow some fine garments for your husband. I and my acquaintances will hire him a covered waggon so that he can make the round of the villages and hamlets for money, to carry out the commandment of bringing a maiden under the Bridal Canopy, until such time as His Blessed Name prepares a suitable match for him.

Frummet's heart overflowed with joy, and she asked, Rabbi, what portion shall he promise his daughter? Whatever sum the bridegroom's father may promise for his son, he answered, let your husband promise as much for your daughter. And he gave her his blessing, and she departed.

Returning home, Frummet said to her husband, Yudel, do you know where I now come from?—from the house of the holy Rabbi of Apta. Do you know what he said? This is what he said, Long life to him. And she told him all the details.

The Hassid hesitated whether to take the road, since travel diminishes the study of the Torah and prayer with the congregation, as well as disturbing a man's customary ways. Nonetheless he did not dismiss the matter, for it is a duty to hearken to the words of the wise. So he applied to himself the saying of the sage, When your daughter attains puberty free your slave; that is, free yourself, for you are one of the slaves of the Blessed Creator. So he went to good men, God-fearing and true, such as do not hold back their workers' hire or fail through any kind of ill faith; and they lent him fine garments, a long coat of silk, a satin robe, a broad-woven girdle, silver-buckled shoes, a sable hat and a handsome stick; and fellow Hassidim hired him a waggon with a canopy.

And the holy Rabbi, that lover of Israel, took pen in hand, soared on the wings of lofty speech and wrote a letter for Rabbi Yudel to en-flame the hearts of all good people who love charity and deeds of loving-kindness; and blessed him, that The Name might prosper his way. And this is a copy of the text:

Hear, O Israel, my people, give ear, gather all ye who hold wisdom dear, look around with discerning eye, lend ear to these my words concerning this Hassid and pious one, Rabbi Yudel Nathanson, re-garding a dowry for his daughter, the bride (who shall be exalted) to give the maiden a marriage portion, and the needs of the wedding in proportion. Now the bridegroom comes to wed, but wealth and prosperity are fled; yet lad and lass wed not unless cash be paid, so let him come singing with the sheaves of his mead.

Rabbi Yudel took the letter of commendation, folded it, put it away, took his leave of the Rabbi and returned home to his wife and daughters. They brought him the fine garments and he did them on, setting a small cushion over his belly after the fashion of worthies who have not been blessed with a paunch. Then they brought him a light meal which he ate and followed with Grace; after which he rose and recited the Prayer for a Journey.

His neighbor entered to bid him God speed, took a coin, pressed it against the mezuzah on the doorpost, gave it to Rabbi Yudel and said, Rabbi Yudel, I give you this coin so that you may serve as my emissary. When you reach the place to which you journey, offer it for charity in my name, so that you may fall under the rule that those who are sent to carry out a commandment come to no harm.

Then Nuta, the waggoner, arrived with his two horses, one named Ivory, the other Peacock, which matched one another in points and looks and were familiar with all the roads; there was no inn which they could not smell a full Sabbath day's journey away. A pair of horses was required because the holy Rabbi of Apta had remarked, Two are better than one since they add to the importance of the traveler.

Nuta pulled up in front of Rabbi Yudel's dwelling and cracked his whip so that the sound could be heard far and wide. Peacock raised his hoofs, kicked the ground and started tugging at the waggon. Not so fast, brother Peacock, says Ivory to him; give your legs a rest; sure as you're standing here you don't need to shake them yet a while. And he smiled at his partner who always forgot one of the rules of travel; namely, that even when the traveler has already mounted the waggon it is no sign that he will start out, if the waggon is still near his home; therefore a much-traveled horse is always ready to stand waiting a while.

But Rabbi Yudel would not start out until he had finished reciting the account of the Offering of Isaac and added, Lord of the Universe, as Father Abraham offered his son Isaac, so mayst Thou offer up all my foes and those that hate me; and mayst Thou treat me with the qualities of loving-kindness and of mercy; and mayst Thou fulfil, O Lord our God, the verse which says, let all these Thy servants descend and bow down before me saying, Go thou forth and all the people at thy feet, and afterward I shall go forth; and send me Thy holy Princes and Angels who derive from this verse, to accompany me in all my ways; and deliver me from all foes and robbers and every manner of trouble; and let them seal up all those that hate me and trouble me so that they may possess no power against me for ill; and make Thou my way prosper. Amen, selah.

Now the neighbors came, men and women, when they heard that Rabbi Yudel was starting out. And Rabbi Yudel took three of his friends and said in front of them, A Song of Degrees, I shall lift up mine eyes unto the hills; whence shall my help come? My help cometh from the Lord who maketh heaven and earth. And after him they responded, The Lord shall preserve thy going out and thy coming in now and evermore. And his three gentle daughters repeated each verse in a whisper, and wiped their eyes so that their sleeves became sopping wet.

Here Nuta entered in a fury and seized Rabbi Yudel by the cloak, for he feared that that Hassid might suddenly decide to finish the whole Book of Psalms with all the following prayers before he started out; so he urged him to mount the waggon. Rabbi Yudel moved a short pace, said, Right away, set his lips to the mezuzah, kissed it three times and said, The Lord is my guardian, the Lord is my keeper; He shall guard my going out and my coming in. And his wife and daughters said, For life and peace, now and henceforth evermore. And then he mounted the waggon.

To cut a long story short, Rabbi Yudel sat on the waggon and turned his face to all the four quarters, while his family called after him, Go to life and blessing and success, and all his neighbors, men and women, called, And to joy and to peace without ill meetings, and may you merit to return home speedily to life and peace, amen. And when he sat down he twirled his stick three times in the air and prayed the Short Prayers, including the waggoner in his prayers, that he might be delivered from any manner of foe or robber or despoiler or highwayman, also from every fashion of weapon. Having completed his prayer he began to sing "Mighty, Awesome and Dread." Nuta took the whip, cracked it over the horses' heads, and up came their hoofs happily, raising a dust which covered the waggon.

The city of Brod spins away; fine big houses pass in the twinkling of an eye; huts sprout up from the ground, folk standing by them with their hands above their eyes gazing after the waggon.

Within a few moments they were out of the town and its dust, and the face of the world was revealed, with the heavens a half-globe above the earth, as though land and sky were akissing one another. Rabbi Yudel crossed his legs, gazed about him, sang, "Lord of the World", nodded to the passers-by, whether circumcised or, saving your presence, uncircumcised, and marveled at the great light which the Holy and Blest One had, by His loving-kindness, spread over the entire Universe; as though the Holy and Blest One had brought out sparks and gleams of His hidden store of light in order to deck and array the world.

Then Rabbi Yudel began to perfume the air with holy words for a great and special purpose. Many are the souls which had no time to repent before death and so cannot come to their rest. These wander wide in the world, some floating on the waters, some hanging in the trees. And whenever a Jew utters a holy word or thought they hasten thereto, array themselves therein and mount aloft; and the Masters of Wrath and the Masters of Judgment have no dominion over them.

After the Hassid had done his good deed for the dead, he bestirred him to do a good deed for the living, moved toward the waggoner, condescended to everyday speech and began conversing with him of the world's affairs, in order to cheer and liven him up. He began to ask him how business was, and all those other questions with which people filled with the milk of human kindness try to do good with their words when they cannot do good with their money. He let his face give light on the whole world. When they passed a man he

[8]

greeted him. If a non-Jew greeted him he answered, Amen, according to the advice of Rabbi Tanhuma in the Jerusalem Talmud who said, when a non-Jew greets you respond, Amen, as is written in Deuteronomy, "Blest shalt thou be by all the nations."

They journeyed southwest amid woods arrayed in trees and treacherous with robbers; they passed through the gentile villages, Hotnik and Kuzmir, also the village, New Smolensk, where little urchins came out and began throwing stones after them. Reb Yudel, says Nuta to him, keep your head inside the waggon under cover so the stones won't hit you. I have no fear of them, responds Reb Yudel, I've already said the Prayer for a Journey, so I'm safe.

Thereupon Nuta whipped up his horses, thinking to himself that folk really have little sense if they go giving Ivory and Peacock all this trouble for such a donkey. And Rabbi Yudel, hovering on the wings of the intellect, said, The devout Rabbi Behaya wrote in his book, *The Duties of the Heart,* that Man is composed of spirit and body, both being the goodness of the Creator toward us. Now that the soul's armed, it clearly protects the Man's limbs, for it's impossible that it should forsake them at a time of danger.

And a few minutes later they reached the village of Pinkevitz.

CHAPTER TWO: IN THE VILLAGES TO LODGE Nuta tugged the reins, pulled up the waggon in front of the inn, descended and helped Rabbi Yudel down; then unharnessed the horses and gave them their oats, while Reb Yudel entered the inn and prayed the Afternoon and Evening Prayers. The innkeeper stared at Reb Yudel and said, It seems to me that I have seen your honor before, though I don't know where. Of course you have, nodded Reb Yudel, since all the souls of Israel were present at Mount Sinai when the Torah was given us; so now that our two souls meet again you recognize me. And maybe your honor has recognized me in the way of nature, for I come from Brod and I'm Yudel Student and I pray in the southwest corner of the old House of Study.

Then give me to wit my master, says Paltiel, the innkeeper, to Reb Yudel, what blessing I should say on seeing you— Who doth clothe the naked, or Who doth make the creatures strange? For I've never before seen your honor dressed in such fine clothes.

Rabbi Yudel raised his two hands on high and replied, His Name knows and can be witness that it isn't for my own honor I wear these clothes, nor yet to deceive folk; I was ordered to put them on by the holy Rabbi of Apta, when my wife went to beseech mercy from him for the sake of my three daughters, who've reached a marriageable age, and I haven't anything to wed them off with; so he told me to go out to the countryside to seek for a dowry. And so as the Children of Israel should turn a charitable eye on me they made me dress like well-off folk do, because anybody who wears fine clothes is given a fine alms; only as soon as The Name has me find my daughter a bridegroom I'll do off these fine clothes; and I trust that He, may He be blest, won't hold that I've done something sinful; for all I do I'm only doing in order to bring the bride to the Bridal Canopy.

The moment Paltiel heard that Rabbi Yudel was traveling to fulfill the commandment of the Bridal Canopy, he brought brandy tinctured with wormwood, and glasses, and a sort of cake; and they sat down at the table in front of the oven, and he filled the glasses, and they said a blessing and drank. Paltiel seized Reb Yudel's hand, shook it and blessed him with the wish that he might find fine bridegrooms for all three of his gentle daughters and have the merit of seeing an upright generation from them. Reb Yudel answered,

Amen, to the blessings, adding, And may we merit to hear salvations
and comforts together with All Israel our brethren, amen; and may
we merit to see the Redeemer revealing himself speedily, amen. They
tasted some crumbs of cake and took another sip. In came Nuta, put
down his whip, gazed at the bottle and poured himself out a glass.
Once started he did not stop, since bitter brandy is a choice drink,
and one you do not meet with at all hours of the day.

And why is it such a specialty? Because it's made with wormwood.
How, you ask? Like this. A man goes and plucks wormwood, puts
them in a bottle of brandy and leaves the bottle tight closed until
the liquor is green as the herb and the herb is sopping with brandy.
Once the liquor is green and the herbs have sucked up the brandy
they are removed, squeezed out and the liquor is absorbed. And
what should be done until you get as far as that? Drink plain brandy,
of course.

Meanwhile Sarah, Paltiel's wife, was kneading and pressing and
rolling and cutting up a dough of barley meal; then she stuffed
onions and pepper in meat, and meat in the pieces of dough, folded
the dough into pancakes, put them in the pot, put the pot on to
cook until they were done, garnished them with onions cooked in
fat and brought them to the table.

And they ate and ate again until their spoons dropped from their
hands. Then Nuta moaned and said, Sarah, you have cooked fine
pancakes, but we haven't the strength to eat; while Reb Yudel put
his hands on his belly and said, Oh dear, oh dear.

That night there were no strangers at the inn, and Paltiel and his
wife made much of their guests, and fulfilled the commandment of
hospitality joyfully, after the fashion of our brethren who dwell in
hamlets and villages, plying them with food and drink and gladness;
and they addressed themselves to Reb Yudel's heart with good words
and comfortable. See here, said Paltiel to Reb Yudel, I'll go bail that
you'll soon be giving your daughters out; and you and I will dance
before the bride so that the dust mounts to the very ceiling. Come
and have a look at His blessed power and love, and how He does
not overlook even the last and the least of Israel. See, I'm precious
poor in commandments fulfilled and the doing of good deeds, but
all the same there's never yet been a time or an occasion when He
hasn't treated me with loving-kindness. While yet I dwelt within
my mother's vitals He treated me with favor; when I came out into

the air of the world He treated me with favor; when it was my time to serve in the army He treated me with favor; and when it was my time to make a match He again treated me with favor. And once his tongue was set a wagging he began to relate

THE GENERATIONS OF A MAN.

It was at this spot and in this very house that my fathers and fore-fathers dwelt, and it was here that I too was born. Not in the house, truth to tell, but next to it. As to how I came to be born next to the house—well, it was like this. My father, may he rest in peace, was highly thought of by the Lord of the Manor because he always used to pay the yearly rent on the inn before it fell due. But the time came when his affairs went badly, may Mercy deliver us, and he wasn't able to pay even when it fell due, let alone beforehand. So he asked him to wait. Says the Lord of the Manor to him, You know I won't do that for any Jew. And he sent his men along and they ejected the furniture and put my mother out of the house. At that time my mother, may she rest in peace, was in the family way, and when this trouble came her birth pangs began, and she gave birth.

But, when trouble came, salvation came with it. The Almighty may wound with one hand, but with the other He heals. You knew Reb Yerahmeel; if you didn't learn from him your fathers learnt from him. All his life Reb Yerahmeel was a veritable pauper, with daughters every one of them older than her sisters and unluckier. When the youngest one was old enough to marry, the whole town began to boil up. Was it possible? Here was a man who had taught so much Torah and set up so many pupils to wed wives and have sons and daughters born to them, and now were his own daughters to sit and wait till their hair turned white?

They took counsel and decided to buy him a cow, for they said, A cow gives milk, so let his daughters sell the milk and they'll earn themselves their dowries. Two of Reb Yerahmeel's former pupils made the round of the town, but they didn't collect enough to buy a cow. What did they do? They said, We'll take a money box and hang it up in Rabbi Yerahmeel's house; and anybody who comes along will drop in a coin or two. Israel is merciful and we are the children of the merciful ones; there have been collecting boxes for charity all these ages, and we've never found any spider webs over the slots. As long as there's no other way there's no better way. So they took a money box and hung it up in Reb Yerahmeel's house. If a woman came to her son in the class she'd slip a coin in. If a man came to pick himself a bridegroom for his daughter he'd slip a coin in. In a little while the box was full and had to be emptied, and Reb Yerahmeel's wife put the coins in a stocking, which she kept in a chest. When she came to take out the stockings one Eve of Passover, in honor of the festival, she found all the stockings filled with coins to a value of two hundred thalers. Says Reb Yerahmeel, That's enough, and put the box away.

Then they began to get busy about the cow and the best way to make it yield a lot of milk; and Reb Yerahmeel found a charm against witchcraft. Before ever they had purchased the cow Reb Yerahmeel's daughters were renowned all over the town. And what was their renown? A milch cow. Only as yet Rabbi Yerahmeel had not been able to turn his attention to buying one.

When the thirty-third day of the Omer came round his wife said to him, Today you're taking your pupils to the village of Pinkevitz to play in the countryside; please drop in on the innkeeper while you're there, and maybe he can advise you or go and buy a cow with you. So he took his stick and his money in hand and set off for Pinkevitz.

There he found a woman lying in the open, and the innkeeper weeping and wailing. What are you crying for, Yehiel? Reb Yerahmeel asks him. What can I do but weep, answers the innkeeper; here's my wife has just borne a son and the Lord of the Manor has put us out of doors. Reb Yerahmeel seized him by the coat and said, Quick, go and pay the Lord of the Manor what's coming to him. Said the innkeeper, Reb Yerahmeel, you're making mock of me. How can I pay the Lord of the Manor when I haven't a doit?

Thereupon Rabbi Yerahmeel takes out his money bag, saying, Take all my cash and pay him. They put the furniture back in the inn, put the mother to bed and congratulated the father that a son had been given him. But the father sighed and said, If only the mother lives.

The innkeeper went back to the beginning and said, Well, and neither died. My mother used to tell me that then the midwife took the child and raised it to its mother. When the mother saw her son she kissed him and said, Lord of the World, such tiny ears, and wept for joy. The children who had come with Reb Yerahmeel opened their wallets, took out all kinds of dainties and gave her to eat and drink, stayed there until it grew dark and repeated the Hear O Israel at her bedside. On the eighth day from the birth Reb Yerahmeel came with a congregation of ten Jews to the village, and they brought the child into the Covenant of Father Abraham and called his name Paltiel. Paltiel, that's me.

Paltiel grew like yeasty dough, long and broad; and his father and mother dwelt in peace. The villagers were fond of Father Yehiel, and whatever trouble mightn't come, they would always be asking his advice about it. If the priest drank a drop too much and sold the church vessels Father would redeem them and return them. If the head of the village went wrong and was in danger of his life Father would give him a tip how to get out of the hands of the law. He was a good advocate for them before the Lord of the Manor as well. And since he hadn't been able to make a good enough living out of the inn he began to go in for business. How? If a fox pelt happened to come his way, or the skin of a hare or a bushel of wheat or a cake of wax, he used to buy it for sale in the town.

Before long he began to make the round of the neighboring hamlets, and went into partnership with Peretz, the grocer. When two Jews in a village live at peace the Holy and Blest One gives them both bread. Peretz was a widower with a daughter and a little shop, a sort of shed jutting out of the house. He used to say, did Peretz, In any case I buy my own household requirements in town, so I'll also buy for the villagers who have their own work to do, and I'll get paid for my trouble. But he lost as much as he earned, because he used to give credit on the strength of goods they promised to bring and didn't bring. In brief, Father and Peretz used to go about their business on Mondays, each in his own direction; and sometimes they would meet somewhere and come home together.

One Thursday a Jew came to town and told how he had seen Yehiel, the innkeeper, lying murdered in the forest; and the whole congregation mourned and brought him to town. The rabbi sent to us to tell us not to mourn, nor was I to say the Mourner's Prayer, until it had been proven by reliable and decisive evidence who the slain man was. But it was not simple to identify; the head had been hacked off the body. So my mother was left a widow, and not only a widow but also a desolate, forsaken wife; while I was not even permitted to repeat the Mourner's Prayer. But Brod is a city of scholars, sages and scribes; they began to exchange questions and responses and finally decided that in this special case the possibly forsaken woman might remarry. But truth to tell that permission served no practical purpose save to magnify the Torah and glorify it; for my mother had taken sick with grief and pain.

And what happened to Father happened to his partner as well. Once a farmer summoned Peretz to sell him honey. They went down into the cellar together to examine the honey, and there the farmer turned a cauldron of boiling pitch on him. Some time later his body was found, but nobody could recognize him. And they brought him to a Jewish grave, burying him next to Father among all the others martyred to hallow The Name.

Mother didn't live long after Father was dead. But The Blessed Name did not permit her to depart from the world until he had brought fresh troubles upon her. At that time I had to go to serve the Kaiser, and I was in the bloom of strength. I did all I could to weaken myself. The amount of vinegar I drank! And the number of nights I did without sleep! And in case I might begin to fall asleep I had someone standing over me to wake me up again, and I didn't spare my strength trying to lose it.

When the appointed day came I went to the Rabbi of Ziditshov to ask him to beseech mercy on my account, so that I might be discharged from the Kaiser's service. He saw that my earlocks were cut off and my beard was kept impiously short and my clothes weren't those of the youngsters who sit in the Houses of Study, and he says to me, Lout, and who *should* go to the army then if not you and the likes of you?

Rabbi, said I to him, if I am taken to the army my mother will die of hunger. Wait a while, says he to me, and went out. I stood waiting for half an hour or an hour or so, and he didn't return. Where is the Rabbi? I asked. In the privy, they told me. Woe's me, I thought, whether I go or don't go. If I go the Rabbi will be vexed, and if I don't go I lose the fifty thalers I sent to the army physician so that he should exempt me from the Kaiser's service; and now he's waiting for me at his house so as to know me at the examination and let me go. And if I come late he won't be there.

At last the Rabbi came in. When he saw me he said, Are you still standing there? Bring the basin and ewer so that I may wash

[15]

my hands. You can do that much service to a disciple of the wise. I brought them and poured water from the ewer over his hands. He chanted the blessing, Who hast formed man in wisdom and created in him many orifices and cavities; and he groaned so that my blood curdled for fear. Then he sat down on his seat, turned his two holy eyes aloft and said, A fine new generation without earlocks or beard. Lovely Jews you have in your world, Lord of the Universe. Then he turned to me and said, May it be His will that they may like the look of you just as much as I like the look of you. Now let me see your back.

I went off and found the doctor at his door. Said I to him, I'm Paltiel from the village of Pinkevitz. He looked at me but had nothing to say. I followed him to the Town Hall. When I entered, the officers looked up and said, Here's a lion from the village. And I began wondering to myself what I would be able to tell Mother if they didn't let me go, and I stood all startled and upset. The recruiting sergeant put his hand on me, said, Strip, and stood me against the measuring rod; and I stood a full head and shoulders above him and the rod together. Why, I already saw myself with a sword hanging on my thigh agoing to the wars. But then the doctor gets up, passes his hands over my body, raps round about my heart with his fingers and sends me away. The recruiting sergeant took a kick at me for luck, and I departed in peace.

Home I rushed to tell Mother. When I got there I found her lying on the bed in the open, like the day she had borne me, when the servants of the Lord of the Manor had turned her and my father out of the inn; for just then they were putting the house in order for the Passover. And what do you suppose Mother was doing? Holding a cushion in her arms like a mother holds her baby to her; with her lips she was twittering to it, calling it all manner of loving names. Before I could say a word to her she raised the cushion toward me and said, See, Yehiel, the child's alive as well. And so she remained all the time she was ill, not recognizing me; and when I stood by her she thought it was my father Yehiel, nor did her queer smile leave her blackish lips until she gave up the ghost and passed away.

When a man's rich he can devote himself to mourning, may Mercy deliver us; but a poor man has no opportunity of weeping his dead even at the very hour of death. The Passover was at the door; I had to prepare all the requirements of the festival, scalding the vessels with tears running from my eyes. May such a Passover befall all foes of Zion.

After the festival I returned to my work. The compassion with which His Blessed Name has stamped His creatures was suddenly aroused in the villagers. If anybody had anything to sell, he sold it to me in a friendly way; if anybody had anything to buy, he bought it from me in a friendly way. What they drank they paid for. And on Sabbaths and festivals I even had Jews for company.

Matchmakers began to propose matches to me. Take up the tambour, lad, and the fife; wed a wife and enjoy your life. But I sent them away. I told them that as long as I was saying the Mourner's Prayer I would not take a wife. And The Name was of the same mind, and I had the merit of getting what I merited.

It happened one morning that coming out of the synagogue I thought to myself, Village homes are tombstones. My mother has died, and I can say the Mourner's Prayer for her only once a day, since I haven't time to go to town twice in twenty-four hours to pray both morning and evening prayers with the congregation. Suddenly my heart felt drawn to the cemetery. I began thinking that I must get back to the village and that a mourner is forbidden to visit the cemetery during the first twelve months. All the same I never turned back but went there.

While I stood over my father's grave I observed a girl standing over the grave of Peretz and weeping, Father, Father. Turning my eyes on her, I saw she was Sarah, my neighbor. I remembered her father's death and how she had no relation or person to stand for her; I clean forgot that I must go back to the village; and she and I remained standing in the graveyard.

As we stood there, the sky became covered with clouds and rain fell. Come under cover with me, I said to her. We entered the deadhouse, and I said to her, Sarah, you and I are orphans without either father or mother except the Great Father in Heaven; will He not take pity upon us both? While we were standing, a flash of lightning from the clouds lit up the tombstones of our two fathers. Said I, Sarah, our fathers let their faces shine on us; by your life the in-laws approve of the match.

When the rains stopped and the sun began shining again, the sexton and his wife came out. Wish us good luck and *mazal tov*, I

[17]

said to them; we have plighted our troth today. Says the sexton's wife, All the world comes here to die and these two come to get married, *mazal tov, mazal tov.* Thereupon the sexton brought out a bottle of brandy and drank long life to us, and seized his pick and shovel and began dancing and shouting, Jews, I rejoice. And he took us to Reb Yerahmeel in town. Reb Yerahmeel wept for joy and laughed through his tears and said, Happy am I to have merited this, and woe's me that your parents never merited this. After I stopped saying the Mourner's Prayer I took Sarah to be my wife after the faith of Moses and Israel, may it be till we are a hundred and twenty years old.

The innkeeper ended with a sigh, drinking a glass of blessing thereby; while each guest with address did his best, you may guess, that thirsty he might not die.

Paltiel, seeing that his guests enjoyed listening to him, wanted to continue, but his wife tapped him gently over the lips, saying, These folk are tired out, and he goes filling their ears with foolishness and triflings as though the end of the whole world had come and he was afraid he might leave it, God forbid, before he has a chance of telling them all his secrets. Tomorrow the Holy and Blest One will make His sun shine as well and bring day. You had all better go to sleep. Paltiel, I'm ashamed of you, sitting and telling stories and having no pity on the candle and the wick. Even in Brod all the world's asleep by now, and this fellow's still wide awake.

Paltiel smiled and wiped his mouth, saying, They didn't invent when they said that ten measures of chatter descended to the world and womenfolk grabbed nine. Did you hear how she rattled on? As I'm a Jew I'm prepared to give up the other measure as well, if only they shut up. If you please, Reb Yudel, climb up on top of the stove and turn your attention to sleeping; while as for you, Nuta, don't be afraid you'll have to sleep in the air. Here's the table at your service. Stretch yourself out and go to sleep, and, The Name willing, tomorrow we'll recount the deeds of God.

So Rabbi Yudel mounted the stove and covered himself over with his cloak, while Nuta stretched out on the table, covered himself with a sheepfell and lay there. Ere they had completed the blessing, "Who maketh sleep to fall upon my eyes," their lids were closed in slumber and they slept until the sun shone; then they arose, prayed and ate their breakfast.

[18]

It was a bright fine day and the time had come for digging the potatoes up; so Paltiel was about to go to the fields and did not delay the Hassid but gave him a generous alms, while his wife gave him those sorts of cakes which do not need the washing of the hands before eating. Also she gave him a hot-water bottle to tie to his belly, for what with so much eating and drinking his bowels were out of order.

Said Paltiel to his wife, If you give a Jew trouble and must load him with a stone hot-water bottle, see at least that he doesn't have all his trouble for nothing. And he filled a measure of brandy, held it up to the light, emptied the water from the bottle, poured in the brandy and tied it to the belly of Rabbi Yudel underneath his little tallith. And they took leave of each other affectionately. The innkeeper returned to his barrels and flagons and to serving the pagans, while the Hassid mounted the cart without stumbling or hurt.

CHAPTER THREE: THEY THAT DID FEED ON DAIN-
TIES ✧ They left Pinkevitz in order to go to the village of
Yanovki; but on the way Nuta turned off in another direction.
If Paltiel, argued Nuta, is in the fields today, although he doesn't
make his living on the land, the Yanovki Jews who do make their
living on the land will certainly not be found at home; so instead
we'll go to Zabletitz, since Zabletitz is a fair-sized place, and if we
don't find Reuben we'll find Simeon, and if we don't find Simeon
we'll find Levi or Judah. So Nuta tugged his hat down on his forehead, filled his nostrils with snuff tobacco and signaled his horses to
start. Although we are going somewhere else, said Nuta to his
horses, I'm not troubling you overmuch, for in an hour and a half
we'll be there and eat our lunch; by your life there's no better road
than that.

Said Rabbi Yudel, And is there a good road or a bad? Only when
a man enters a town let him say I'm happy to have come here, since
had it seemed evil to Him, may He be blessed, would He have
brought me here? Similarly with all the other imagined needs; no
man knows what is good or what is not good; and only after the
thing is finished with can he say, I did well, for if it hadn't been well
in the sight of the All-Present He would not have permitted me to
do it.

Here Nuta interrupted and said, Ask the horses and don't ask Reb
Yudel. Then the horses began lifting their legs, running fast, dragging the waggon; they shook up the Hassid until he got all mixed
up, his bowels began turning upside down within him and he was
taken with the chills as though a cold-water pipe had been run
through his bones.

Now this was not the fever described in the learned commentary on
the Sabbath Laws, which begins cold and ends hot, but a sort of ache
coming from the stomach that makes you feel as though a huge
ponderous stone must be lying there. In addition, the hot-water
bottle which the innkeeper had tied round his belly to cure him was
no longer hot, but added one chill to the other. His face turned
green, and his tongue began knocking against his teeth; if it had not
been for his teeth his tongue would have flown away like a bird from
its nest.

THE BRIDAL CANOPY

So Reb Yudel wrapped himself up in his overcoat and began to sing the Song of Songs, since all remedies are contained in the Song of Songs, as our sages of blessed memory taught in the books of the Kabbala. Beginning with an ulterior motive he went on to chant it for its own sake, feeling ashamed that he had any personal aim and object in saying the Song of Songs; all his members began trembling with fear, and his face burnt as a torch and he went on singing till his soul found itself in the Universe of Intelligence. Remonstrating with his pains, he raised his voice in song, and the worse the pain the louder he sang.

When Nuta heard Reb Yudel singing the Song of Songs he turned his head round and stared at him. At that very moment Reb Yudel's mouth opened and he brought up everything he had inside him; and Nuta in turn began to look all but dead, as though his own afterbirth had been clapped over his face. And right away his mouth too burst open, and lumps and bundles and tufts of all kinds of food which need not be detailed here began to empty out. Although Nuta was not a spiritual man like that Hassid, and his bowels were thick as waggon ropes, he too was suffering from the pancakes. So overcome were they both that Hassid could not be told from waggoner.

Finally they rose, wiped their faces, descended from the waggon, cleansed themselves of their earthiness, climbed up again and drew together like brethren in trouble. Said Reb Yudel to Nuta, Brother Nuta, how I sympathize with that innkeeper who eats pancakes every day and drinks lots and lots of brandy, and fills his paunch with pain and his head with all kind of whirlings. How much our sages of blessed memory spoke against eating; yet the world still goes wrong and folk eat and drink every day of their lives and crush themselves with suffering. And they counseled so many measures that a man's eating might not harm him; for instance, he should busy himself with the Torah while eating, and chew the food with his teeth, since it is the nature of the body to swallow ere the teeth have ground, whereby the belly is filled with more than satisfies it, and when he gets up from the table he feels heavy and swollen; but if he chews with his teeth his food digests itself and he does not need to eat much; and if he meditates on the Torah as well between one course and the next he does not burden his thought with the lust for food and drink. But what do we see? When a man sits down to eat he at once forgets all such good advice and stuffs his body and fills his paunch and dulls his heart and besots his understanding and finally drives himself out of the world. I remember when I used to pray in Reb Koppel's prayer book—before I changed it for the prayer book of the holy Sheloh, Rabbi Isaiah Hurwitz, who wrote the *Two Tablets of the Covenant*—when I used to read the Laws of Feasts I used to say, Rejoice, rejoice, oh bowels mine, that ye have not transgressed the words of the sages; and now I have to yell for pain, Oh my belly, oh my belly.

Said the waggoner to him, Reb Yudel, does your honor know whom you resemble? The man I met in Hungary. Once I took wares to Hungary and Hungary is blessed with wealth and has inhabitants fat as stuffed calves who eat and drink all their lives long; what the whole of Brod eats on the Eve of Atonement wouldn't be enough even for the dessert of a single one of them. There I found a man writhing in a muddy pool, his behind upwards, asking your pardon; and he was throwing his arms and his legs about and yelling in his pain, Oh, oh, oh, my belly, my belly. Says I to him, What are you yelling for so much? Says he to me, And why shouldn't I yell, seeing I'm dying and my wife will have to remain single all her life long, as though I had deserted her, and my children will be orphans, and I don't even know whether I'll be brought to a Jewish grave.

Says I to him, Friend, how do you come to this? Says he, I'm a poor man and not used to rich foods. Today I entered the house of a hospitable Jew who gave me white bread and a dish of cream. I dipped my bread into the cream till all the cream had gone; he went and brought me more cream; I dipped my bread in cream until the bread had gone; he went and brought me more bread; I dipped my bread in cream until the cream had gone and he went and brought me some more cream. In short, before the bread was finished he brought me cream and before the cream was finished he brought me bread and before I could manage to stop and make a break, my belly was full fit to burst.

Said Reb Yudel, That fellow told the truth, for we have heard tell the like about the saintly Reb Raphael of Bershad who used to love truth and pursue truth and was wont to keep his distance from any utterance which might contain even the very dust of falsehood; and on that account he was very careful, when speaking, not to utter a yes or a no for fear it might not be truth. On one occasion he came to Ruzhin and the holy Rabbi of Ruzhin offered him some preserves.

When he had finished the holy Rabbi of Ruzhin said, If you like I'll give you some more. Now the saint was afraid to say no in case it might not be true, so he went on eating. When he had finished, the holy Rabbi of Ruzhin said, If you like I'll give you some more. The saint was still afraid to say no for fear it would not be the truth, so he went on eating. When he had finished the holy Rabbi of Ruzhin said, If you like I will give you some more. The saint was still afraid to say no in case it might not be true, so he went on eating until there was nothing left in the pot. And then the holy Rabbi of Ruzhin said, It's worth a man's while to stick to the truth if he eats a full pot of preserves.

Nuta had mentioned cream and bread, and Reb Yudel had added the story of the preserves, so Nuta's bowels revolted within him; and whatsoever had been left over from the last night's feast in his belly was spewed out by his mouth and nose and so forth. In a little while Nuta said to Reb Yudel, You said well, Reb Yudel, that no trouble comes save from eating and drinking. I can tell you that all the trouble into which I walked, I walked into either through eating or through drinking. I had the trouble of the robbers because of drinking and the trouble of my wife because of eating. When you see a man getting into trouble, take a look at his paunch. And if you should ask me, But Nuta, where is your paunch, I will answer that trouble has eaten it away.

To which Reb Yudel said, The words deserve to be graven upon the heart, since profitable conduct and good come from them. Said Nuta, What profitable conduct and good can you get out of them when the fellow to whom they happened never learnt anything from them? But since your honor wants to listen I am ready to tell. And Nuta began to tell

A POT STORY.

For all that folk have the habit of calling me the Brod waggoner, I don't come from Brod and I wasn't born in Brod; but it's Bisk I come from and in Bisk I was born, seeing no man's born in two different places at the same time. And since that's the case, they only call me the Brod Waggoner because it's the way of the world to hold fast to what's false, falsehood being a thing they're fonder of than truth; seeing that if they preferred truth they'd be calling me the Bisk waggoner instead of the Brod waggoner.

THE BRIDAL CANOPY

Now this Bisk is a little town like a Polish pancake. And what's the difference between their pancakes and our Jewish ones? Like this. Our pancakes are filled with meat or cheese or potatoes or grain grits or fruit, while their pancakes have neither meat nor cheese nor potatoes nor grain grits nor fruit, and nothing in them at all except a double layer of dough. Go bite into them all day long and you won't get anything out of them more than dough. And that's how Bisk is, one lot of houses in, another lot of houses out, and go where you like you get nowhere except from one lot of houses to another.

It's on a river, is Bisk, with a lot of bridges crossing and keeping the town together, and it drives a big trade in boards and earthenware and flax; and there's a huge palace there, as old as old, but never a Jew makes anything out of it.

Now let's leave the palace to itself with the river and the bridges and all the folk of Bisk except one only, and he's the fountainhead and source of all my troubles, and please God an end should come to him and my troubles together; for instance, that that palace should tumble down on him and bury him beneath it and bring some sort of benefit to two Jews at once.

And who's that fellow? Well, I told you before that the Bisk folk sell earthenware and flax, and in Bisk it's their habit, when they send a load of flax, that they cover it over with broken shards of earthenware so as the highwaymen shouldn't pay too much attention to the goods. And once this fellow hired me to take a load of goods to Brod, not telling me the stuff was flax; and since the waggon was piled up with earthenware I was sure it *was* earthenware. I harnessed the horses to the waggon, took the reins in my hand, and off we went. The countryside was yellow with standing corn, and the trees were full of fruit; and the sun shone bright, and my heart was at ease, and the horses took their way without dashing off like Peacock here and without dragging and crawling like Ivory there, but like real horses should; and I sat up above at my ease, singing, "For behold as the clay in the potter's hand," with the earthenware joining in the responses to the hymn.

Passersby greeted me and I greeted them back; some of them clodhoppers big as giants with long hair like wild beasts and eyes starting out of their heads, who glanced at the waggon and went their way. And if it hadn't been for a couple of drops of water I drank, I'd have got to Brod and been back at Bisk without any trouble or mishaps; only on the way I noticed a fountain with water direct from the hills, and I got down to drink. When I'd finished I reckoned I might as well have some water with me for the way. I took one vessel and found it broken; I took another and that was broken as well; whatever I took in hand was broken. When a flax-man sends his wares he takes care not to cover them with whole jars but with broken ones which cost him nothing.

I'd shifted all the earthenware and the flax could be seen. Along came a robber, hit me over the head and knocked my hat off. But he didn't want me to go bareheaded and have a sin on my conscience, God forbid, for he immediately clapped a pot over my napper; what's more, he slipped a cord between its two handles so as it shouldn't tumble off, and tied both my hands to a tree. To finish off with he landed me another blow as a parting gift and went his way; and it goes without saying that he took my horses with him, for horses are useful when you're in a hurry.

And where did he leave Nuta? May the like never befall another wayfarer, Nuta was standing and slipping alternately, for rain began to fall and turned the whole soil into a morass. So there I was dancing up and down in all the queerest imaginable ways, trying to drag myself out of the mud; and my head would knock against the top of the pot and I'd fall back even deeper. But the Holy and Blest One sends the remedy before the blow, for if it hadn't been for that pot I'd have sunk into the ground head and all, like Korah in the bible. But while I was standing dancing, along came a waggonload of Hassidim, and seeing a pot doing a jig they asked, Do you reckon that pot's doing a jig all on its own? Then I yelled through the pot, I'm Nuta tied up under the pot. They took a look at me, let me out, gave me something to cover my head, sat me down on the waggon along with them and took me into Brod. Well, and all that trouble came upon me only because of drinking; but it's scarcely worth mentioning against what happened to me because of eating.

I'm really astonished at your story, said Reb Yudel, for we find the Midrash says, It's a custom all the world over that a man doesn't pass by a river without swallowing a few mouthfuls of water; now you did just what the Midrash says, and why should you have been punished for it? Said Nuta in reply, For the two drops of water I drank I had myself knocked about and had my money stolen and my horses taken and was left like an empty vessel; and because of what I ate afterwards I had a wife added me on top of everything. As people say, one trouble calls in its friend and as folk also say, your later troubles make you forget the early ones.

Reb Nuta, says Reb Yudel, you know as much as all that? Yes, says Nuta, I've got lots and lots of troubles. Reb Nuta, says Reb Yudel to him, there's never a man without his trouble, only I was referring to the way you casually quoted the Babylonian Talmud and the Jerusalem Talmud and the Tosephta and Rashi; for in his commentary on Psalms Rashi quotes "One trouble calls in the other," while you find "the later troubles make you forget the first ones" in the Gemara of the Babylonian Talmud as well as in the Jerusalem Talmud and Tosephta, and all at the end of the first chapter of the treatise on Blessings. And Reb Yudel was about to jump out of the waggon in order not to make use of this disciple of the sages. But Nuta answered, Reb Yudel, you're talking nonsense; these are things every man learns for himself. And I wish I hadn't learnt them, for if a man learns things on his own body he doesn't let them slip from his heart any more. And now if you don't interrupt me I'm prepared to go on with my story.

Nuta, my dear man, said Reb Yudel, and why should I interrupt you? I enjoy listening to you; for every word a man utters is itself of the Holy and Blest One. When a Jew relates his troubles how does he do it? He says, The Blessed Name aided me, The Blessed Name never forsook me; and so you find the praise of the All-Present mounting aloft in every utterance. And further, as long as Israel is in trouble it is as though the trouble were before Him, as we find Isaiah saying "in all their trouble He is troubled," and as it also says in Psalms, "I shall be with Him in time of trouble"; and so if the All-Present grieves isn't it proper that we should bear His grief in our hearts?

And since we've come round as far as this I'll tell you something. The tale is told that a certain saint was once put in prison, and his disciples found him weeping. Said they to him, Master, why are you weeping? My sons, he answered them, God grieves with me, so ought not I weep? As David said, "Yea though I walk through the valley of the shadow of death I shall not fear," since why should I grumble, "for thou art with me" and my suffering reaches the Presence. And so it is regarding benefits, as King David, may he rest in peace, said, "That I may relate all Thy praises," and soon "I shall rejoice in Thy salvation," through having been saved I tell Thy praises. And now I've said all that to you, start off and I'll listen. Where was I? said Nuta. You were on the waggon, said Reb Yudel, together with the Hassidim who found you on the road.

That's right, said Nuta. So they set me on their waggon and brought me into Brod and set me down at an inn. It happened to be Friday, and the mistress of the house stood at the oven taking out all manner of bakings. And I thought to myself, Well, Nuta, and if some of those dainty dishes were set in front of you maybe you wouldn't be able to eat, eh? Why, since you left Bisk you've had nothing more to get on with than water and a whacking. If my cash hadn't been taken from me I'd ask for something to eat, but, now I haven't a doit, I haven't even the face to ask.

But since my inside was standing up for its rights I said to it, Evildoer, I said, have you ever seen anybody eating before he says his prayers? Instead of calling for grub call for tefillin and do what you have to do.

I did so, and the master of the house offered me his praying shawl as well. When he saw that I didn't put on the praying shawl he asked me, Are you a single man? Yes, I answered. Straightaway he made his wife a sign and said, Give this young man something to eat. And before I finished saying my prayers they brought me a pot with something cooked in it. At that time I was a modest youngster who never looked at women, so I don't rightly know who brought it to me, the mistress or her daughter. And he even invited me to eat at his table during the Sabbath.

During the day he asked me what he had to ask and I told him what I had to tell. Then he set his hand on my shoulder and said, Nuta, don't worry, and he pointed with his other hand and said, Do you see her? By your life she'll be the making of you. At the same time they brought me something cooked in a pot and I told myself, Eat before you go into what he said. So I nodded my head to him out of politeness and went on eating.

After the Sabbath his kinsfolk and relatives came in and wanted to hear the story of the pot. When I'd told them all about it they burst out laughing and said, We never heard a better tale than that all our lives. By your life there's none like it even in the book of the Brod Community, for what has a pot to do with a top? Then they clapped me on the shoulder and said, All the evil leads to good and joy will come out of this.

Meanwhile, there I was offering up praise and thanksgiving to The Blessed Name, Who had been so good to me in my trouble, and had brought me to the house of this man whom I blessed with all the good blessings I could think of. And I wasn't satisfied until I had prayed, Lord of the Universe, what other blessing can I wish him now I've wished him everything I had in my heart to wish; but You know full well that there's never a man without his trouble, so if this fellow has some trouble at home which he can't get rid of, may it be Your will that You with Your great mercies should deliver him from that trouble because of his hospitality toward me.

And I saw at once that my blessing was fulfilled, for they wrote an engagement contract for his daughter the same evening. How glad I was then, and how happy to be present at that rejoicing! Everybody who was there looked to me as though he might be the bridegroom. When they saw how happy I was they grew even fonder of me than before and sat me at the head. Then the master of the house stood up and said to me *mazal tov,* good luck, Nuta. And I nod my head back at him and respond, *Mazal tov,* good luck, in-law.

Straightaway everybody present stood up and said to me, *Mazal tov, mazal tov,* and the women began smashing pots and plates and yelling, *Mazal tov, mazal tov.* I went into all the corners searching for the bridegroom to congratulate him and wish him *mazal tov;* and wherever I turned I found a hand stuck out at me and grabbing mine and shaking it, and somebody saying *mazal tov,* bridegroom, *mazal tov,* Nuta.

And so I learnt that the bridegroom was none other than me myself, though I hadn't so much as thought whether I wanted to marry her; but after the business with the pots I could hardly turn round and declare that I didn't want her, particularly as I had had so much out of the pots myself. So I said to myself, There you are, glutton; if that pot had been smashed and you hadn't eaten out of it on Sabbath eve they wouldn't be asmashing so many pots and plates after the Sabbath.

But I could see that once the thing was done it was over and done with, so I submitted and accepted what was coming, saying to myself, Nuta, if you're a horse put on your reins. I suppose they decreed so above—that you would take a load of flax, thinking it pots, and have a pot clapped on your head, and be brought to a man who would give you grub out of a pot, and finish up by having many a pot smashed. And there is never a day that I don't remember my pot story. Reb Yudel, what are all those pots against the ones which my wife smashes over me when she gets into her tantrums? Though God forbid that I should complain against my wife; before I complain against her I ought to complain about myself being in such a hurry to eat.

And that was one of the things which Reb Yudel learnt from the waggoner and by which he was able to explain a verse in the Torah. It is written in the Torah, "and Noah awoke from his wine." Why does the verse have to read "from his wine", when it ought to read "and Noah awakened from the wine"; after all, what difference does it make whether the wine on which Noah got drunk was his own? Why then is it written so definitely "his wine"? To teach you that the righteous Noah did not blame his drunkenness on other people saying, They gave me wine and I became drunk; but he put the blame on himself and on his wine.

While he had been speaking Nuta sat like Alexei, excuse my mentioning them together, when the latter went ajourneying with the holy Rabbi, Israel Baal Shem Tov, of blessed memory. It was Alexei's custom, when he traveled with the Baal Shem Tov, that he sat with his back to the horses and his face toward the Baal Shem Tov out of respect for the Baal Shem Tov of blessed memory. But the horses of the Baal Shem Tov of blessed memory used to go at a word and required no driver, while as for Nuta's horses—the moment he took his eyes off them they left the king's highway and went by the roundabout routes which are called Polish roads. Where they should have gone to Zabletitz they went toward Tzech and Tshisk; that was not sufficient, for they grazed as they went until their bellies were full; they found their loads heavy and began to look for a way of getting out of their harness. What did Nuta do? He tightened the reins and led them towards Pedhoretz, which is a big village where Jews live, some of them stockdealers and others forest leasers who cut down the trees and take them to Zlotshov, where wood is expensive.

They began mounting to Pedhoretz and could see the whole village, but it disappeared right away, for the road to Pedhoretz climbs up and runs down, and the descent follows sharp on the ascent. Great was Nuta's fury, for he had intended to eat the noon meal at

Zabletitz, and now his horses had gone the wrong way and spoilt his
day; and, since he could not let his anger out on the horses for fear
they would grow obstinate and bring them all into danger, his anger
doubled and more. Such is the quality of flesh and blood; even when
he had nothing to grumble about he grumbled, seeing that if he had
reached Zabletitz he would not have eaten anything, since he was
tired out because of Paltiel's pancakes. Nor was Reb Yudel in good
condition; at every jolt he caught hold of his belly and said, If I hadn't
taken the road I could have been going over a chapter of the Mishnah
now and I would have learnt a page of Gemara; but now I am reft
from all good, and hang between heaven and earth, rocks and mountains on the one side, rushing torrents on the other, the waggon
shaking up all my body, and my bowels being crushed within me.

The horses took tiny steps and pulled the waggon gently, each
wheel turning forward and back but the waggon scarcely appearing
to move. At last Nuta took the whip in hand and cracked it over the
heads of the horses; but he found his hands weak with all the vapors
that had mounted from his stomach to his brain. Reb Yudel sat
swathed in his greatcoat, his hands on his belly, calling to mind the
names of all the sages of the Mishnah who are said to have suffered
the like pains; such as Rabbi Judah the Prince who suffered with his
bowels; and Ulla who had the cramps because of dates; and the
Priests in the Temple who, as the Mishnah tells us, had Ben Ahia
appointed over those who suffered with their bowels; and Rabbi
Obadiah of Bertinoro of blessed memory explains in that connection,
in the course of his commentary, that because the priests ate much
meat and drank water their bowels were disturbed and they always
required physicians. And so Reb Yudel sat there wondering how he
merited to suffer the same aches as those righteous ones; and he
conceived a very high opinion of Nuta, who had also merited the
aches of the righteous; and he began sauntering with him among
matters that are over and above the ordinary courses of nature; such
as the reason for which King Hezekiah suppressed the Book of
Remedies, and why he was thanked for having done so.

Come, said Reb Yudel, and you'll see that the Holy and Blest One
has arranged all His works with wisdom, understanding and knowledge; He arranged the generations with wisdom by not creating us
in the generation of Hezekiah nor creating Hezekiah in our generation, for had we been alive in Hezekiah's times or had he been alive

nowadays, who knows whether we would have thanked him and praised him; for had Hezekiah not suppressed the Book of Remedies I'd have had a look at it and found a remedy and cured myself.

And Reb Yudel went on, Brother Nuta, if somebody were to bring me some citron conserve I'd give him the whole world for it. Then Nuta yelled at him, All he requires is some citron conserve; he hasn't had enough with the cakes and the pancakes and the cookies he ate yesterday. Answers Reb Yudel, Nuta, my dear, and is it with my gullet I'm concerned? I need a remedy. Know you that citron is excellent as a remedy; for we find in the Midrash the story of a man who fulfilled many commandments and sold his house and all his possessions for the sake of the commandments. On the last day but one of the Feast of Tabernacles his wife gave him ten shekels and said, Go and buy your children something in the market. When he reached the market he was met by the Charity Wardens, who called on him to give his contribution for their act of charity, as they had to clothe a certain orphan girl. He took the money he had and gave it to them; but then he was ashamed to go home.

So he went to the synagogue instead, and there he saw the citrons which the children throw away on the last day but one of the festival (as we learn in the Treatise on Tabernacles "thereupon the children break up their palm fronds and eat their citrons"). He took enough of those discarded citrons to fill a sack, and took sail over the Great Sea until he reached the city of the king. At that time the king was suffering in his bowels, and in dream he had been told, to cure yourself take and eat of the citrons which the Jews throw away at the end of the Feast of Tabernacles; then you will be made whole. But though they searched throughout the city and the land and all the ships in port, none could they find. As they went their way they found that Jew seated on his sack; and they asked him, What have you for sale? He replied, I am a poor man and have nothing with me. Nevertheless they opened his sack and found it filled with citrons; they took them and brought them to the king, who ate of them and became whole. Then they filled his sack with gold and he went his way.

Yes, said Nuta, the citron has many a good quality, for a conserve can be made of it, and if a woman eats its upper tip she has an easy conception. True, added Reb Yudel, and the books say that whoever buys a fine citron merits—— But before he could finish the vapors

[31]

THE BRIDAL CANOPY

mounted to his head again, and he remained like an inn during a gentile festival. In an inn during a gentile festival the floor dances underneath, the ceiling is sooty, the walls of the room sweat, and the house is full of smoke; and correspondingly Reb Yudel's legs went dancing on their own, his head was sooty, his body sweated, and his bowels were drying up inside him.

He began to urge Nuta to stop the horses. When he stopped he urged him to continue driving, saying, When I reach a town I'll go to a wise man and have some blood let. Yet though he was suffering so greatly of the journey, he bore no ill will against the saint of Apta who had caused him to undertake his travels, but thought to himself in the words of Numbers, "Now these are the journeys of Israel by the commandment of the Lord"; since all the travels of the Israelite accord with His blessed Word.

It was then that he seemed to see the likeness of the saint as though he were standing before him. And then Reb Yudel felt the truth of the world's words that a man should feel linked with the saint on whom he depends, even when he is not in his presence. Despite all the great sufferings that Reb Yudel had undergone through eating and drinking, the moment he thought of that saintly one his pains vanished. They used to tell of that saint that his eating and drinking were beyond the ways of nature, so that thereby he might mend all that his age blemished through food and drink. On the Eve of Atonement he would eat so much that his belly became like an ark, and he would rest his prayer book upon it as does the cantor when he rests his prayer book on the lectern and prays for All Israel.

Once his pains had eased, Reb Yudel called on Nuta to speed up the horses, in order that they might reach town and pray the Afternoon Prayers with the congregation; for he had not prayed with the congregation during the whole of the day.

CHAPTER FOUR: WITCHCRAFT · A GREAT WONDER HAPPENED THERE ✍ Many are the thoughts in a man's heart. Reb Yudel desired to reach the town and repeat the Afternoon Prayers with the congregation before they had as much as reached the shadow of the town bounds. The forest went and fields came by with mud huts half swallowed in the earth, thatch roofs covering the other half, tiny windows peeping out like blind eyes that see nothing, smoke coming out at the roof and all the cracks in the house walls, and children filthy with tar and dung dancing half naked and barefoot on the dunghills. There live the peasantry, who are serfs to the lords of the gentiles.

The waggon reached the village of Pedhoretz when day was beginning to fade from the sky, and the universes were a confusion of light and dark. Reb Yudel, longing to repeat the Afternoon Prayers with the congregation, urged Nuta to whip up the horses so as to fulfill the words of Hosea, "Let us pursue the knowledge of the Lord." But at this place Reb Yudel underwent many trials; for Nuta stopped the horses, descended and entered a house even more outlandish than all the others in the village, and never a one there as rank as that one; for in that house was a gentile woman famed for her witcheries.

Nuta found her sitting on her bed, her arms folded on her breast and in her bosom a black cock whose comb touched her chin; with her chin she was stroking the comb until it doubled over on the cock's head. Nuta stood in front of her, greeted her and said, Come and listen to what happened to a fellow like me. Yesterday I visited Paltiel the innkeeper with a certain Jew, and he made a huge spread in our honor and we ate fat cakes, and onion wafers, and fat pancakes filled with meat and onions and pepper and oil, and before and after we drank off our glasses of brandy. We stayed there all night long until it became light, happy to find so many good things in the world. But when we started out again my grub went topsy-turvy inside as though all the devils had got into my belly; and they never left inside me as much as the mother's milk I sucked as a baby. What can I say or what can I tell you, His Blessed Name created all kinds of fine victuals and liquor and if it weren't for the evil spirits of the belly a man might eat and drink and get some pleasure out of it. So

[33]

life of me, soul mine, apple of my eye, give me a hand and reprove the evil spirits so that they may leave me alone.

The woman remained silent and made no answer; it is the way of all warlocks and witches that they remain silent before they set about their works; for were the demons to hear their voice they would forsake the body in order to return and damage it later. Nuta placed his two arms on his belly and stood facing her, turning his eyes to her for aid. She arose and went to a corner, whence she took earth of tombs which she had ready; she put the earth in water, whispered over it, sprinkled Nuta with it and whispered again. And she conjured the spirits in the belly and the space round the heart in peace to depart without ache, pain or smart, not in his swollen belly to dart or to fly, nor be obdurate, but depart staid and still lest she grind them to dust in the stones of her mill and destroy them on high and under the sky. And Nuta in turn conjured her not to make the sign of the cross with either her right hand or her left, neither with the water nor with the earth, neither on his body nor near his body, neither on his backbone nor upon his chest; for it is their way of healing to make the sign of the cross, so that the sickness finally returns still more strongly. Lower your mouth, said she to him; he lowered his mouth. Open your mouth, said she to him, and stick your tongue out; he opened his mouth and poked out his tongue. Roll up your tongue, said she to him; and up he rolled his tongue. Then she gave him water to drink in which she had boiled herbs full of witchcraft, saying, Your body is in order. Then he gave her her pay and promised her to bring some brandy out of the bottle which Paltiel had tied round his companion's belly.

Meanwhile Reb Yudel sat on the waggon staring round about him in every direction, and saw that day was departing and the little light left was swallowed by a great deal of darkness, while legions of clouds were seizing the light till it could no longer separate itself but was swallowed up. Placing his hand in his pocket in order to pay the waggoner his wages before praying, he descended from the waggon and entered the house so as to wash his hands for prayer. As soon as he entered a black cock met him. No sooner was he done with the cock than he found before him a great terrifying dog which bayed at him until the Hassid all but felt his soul flee thence for fear. And on account of his fear he completely forgot the fifty-two charms, according to the numerical value of the word "dog" in Hebrew, whereby we silence curs; and he forgot that secret which King David, may he rest in peace, revealed to us in the verse "Dogs were round about us"; and he forgot the detailed explanation given in the Zohar, the holy book of the Kabbala; and he made a great and doleful outcry. Out came Nuta calling him by name, Reb Yudel, God be with you, don't be afraid, Reb Yudel; and he delivered him from peril.

One transgression leads to another. Nuta had been cured through a transgression, so the joy of transgressing entered into him. He began to crow like a cock and bark like a dog, until the dog and the cock became confused so that the cock entered the dog's quarters without the dog noticing. What did Nuta do but set the dog on him, and it drove the cock away. When it drew near him he drove it away, and when he drove it away it cried cock-a-doodle-doo. Now he made his voice sound like a cock and now like a dog so that they should attack one another, like the gentile nobles who amuse themselves by animal baiting.

Reb Yudel, recognizing that this must be a sort of abiding place for wanton spirits, rebuked him and called upon him to let the dog be and turn away from the cock; because he who hunts with dogs will never partake of the joyous feast of Leviathan in the afterlife. Nuta at once repented absolutely and entirely, stopped stirring up the quarrel and wishing to do the Hassid a friendly turn said to him, There is a gentile woman in this house who can perform cures. Reb Yudel, understanding whither matters were tending, cried out with all his might, Is there no God in Israel? And the power of his cry was such that it led to the veritable hallowing of The Name; for Nuta was so startled at his voice that his aches and pains began again, and he recognized that the Powers of Pollution are only deception. The Hassid tugged Nuta saying, Catch hold of my girdle so that we can flee from the shadow of this house and pray. So Nuta started his horses off until they were at a distance from the house; then they stopped to pray and repeated the Eighteen Blessings twice, once for the Afternoon Service and once for the Evening Service; for the daylight had gone before they had managed to say the full Afternoon Prayers. And when Reb Yudel came to the words, "Who hath not made our portion like to them," he spat full and free, and if Nuta had not got away in good time he might have been well-nigh drowned. And when he came to the further words, "Therefore we hope in thee, oh Lord our God," he lifted himself from upon the ground, raised his two hands high above his head and began clapping his hands and crying out with great devotion and awesome yearning, "That we may speedily behold the glory of Thy might"; and his voice could be heard in the distance.

Nehemiah, the dairyman, coming along and seeing Reb Yudel the Hassid praying and dancing and clapping his hands, said to himself, This must be a great saint; for in those times the country was chockfull of saints. Said he to him, Rabbi, you will sup with me. He answered, I am not a rabbi nor yet a "Good Jew"; but if a Jew desires to observe the commandment of hospitality I am ready and prepared to aid him with my body. And he said to the waggoner, Reb Nuta, now I'll take the reins.

The villager was happy to fulfill the commandment of hospitality, Reb Yudel rejoiced to aid another in fulfilling a commandment, Nuta was glad to give his horses a breather, and the horses were most delighted of all to rest their bones. Nuta took the reins in hand and began driving in silence, the horses stretched their necks, jerked their heads and lowered them toward the earth, and the sound of their hoofs began to mount through the darkness. The sky was full of stars, the ground went on like a black spool and a cold breeze stirred the trees of the forest. Now and again the cry of an animal could be heard, or a stone grating under the waggon wheels.

Reb Yudel walked along with the villager, never uttering a word. When he saw the heavens and the stars he began to gaze at them in order to see the handiwork of the Holy and Blest One; which is a great commandment to fulfill, as Isaiah said, "Lift up your eyes on high and see who created these, these heavens and their hosts." And so they reached the house surrounded by a fence of trees and stones.

The master of the house entered, kissed the mezuzah on the doorpost and said, Sima, light the lamp and spread a cloth on the table; worthy folk have come to our parts. The mistress of the house filled a dish with oil, lit the wick and spread a sort of tablecloth on a barrel of butter. And why not on the table? Because that was covered with a great number of dishes; and not only the table, but every nook and cranny in the house was covered by all kinds of jugs and tins filled with milk and milk products. And there was a kind of box standing there filled with square cheeses laid side by side, like books in a bookcase. Reb Yudel, thinking they really were books, said to himself, Israel is no widower nor the Torah a widow. And he applied to himself that verse in Psalms, "It is good for me that I suffered, that I may learn Thy statutes." I'll sit a while, rest a while, and take a book out of the case.

Meanwhile the mistress of the house brought bread and butter and cheese and milk. Reb Yudel washed his hands, dipped his bread in the milk and broke off a piece of cheese the size of an olive. Although he was not in proper health he compelled himself to eat in order to carry out the Talmudic injunction, "Do whatever the Master of the house tells you." Nuta immediately joined them in order to eat, it being human nature that even if you are not hungry, no sooner do you see your companions eating than you want to join them. During the meal Reb Yudel told Nehemiah and his wife of his three daughters who had reached marriageable age and he had nothing on which to wed them off; and so he was journeying for the sake of bringing the bride under the canopy.

Meanwhile three lads came in whose heads scraped the ceiling. Reb Yudel sat wondering to himself, I wonder whether the Holy and Blest One hasn't brought before me the matches for my daughters, as it says in Samuel, "Man looketh at that which the eye sees." Scarcely had they greeted him when they stretched out their hands at the table; straightway the table was cleared and their mother served them with a fresh helping; and they stuffed huge mouthfuls so that not as much was left as a crumb for the poor.

They did not wash their hands beforehand, nor did they say the grace after food. And thereupon the Hassid felt great grief for them and he sighed within himself, Lord of the Universe, these are the children of Thy chosen and tested ones to whom Thou didst descend upon Mount Sinai to give them the Torah and the commandments. And he began rebuking himself, saying, Yudel, Yudel, the offspring of Abraham, Isaac and Jacob do grow without Torah and without commandments, while you eat and drink and are satisfied and say, All is well, my soul; isn't it your duty to seat them upon your knees and teach them a section of the Torah?

At this point Nehemiah brought straw for his guests to sleep on and put out the light. Reb Yudel removed his shoes, took his cushion from off his belly and set it at his head, stretched himself on his couch and repeated the Night Prayer. Thereupon his members began contending one with another. Said the hands, Can a Jew lie down without studying before he sleeps? Said the legs, We haven't the strength to stand. Interrupted the eyes, And even if you could stand what would be the use of your standing when there's no light? Said the tongue, And are you exempt from the study of the Torah when there is no light? Then all the members answered at once, Who's as well off as you are in your dark place; you'd better be still and not let the Hassid loose on us. And Reb Yudel lay wondering that, though he was lying, his body should still be wandering wide in the world; for even when they lie down, that is, people who are not used to traveling, it seems to them that they are still rolling along the road.

Suddenly he saw a house filled with books, one of which was gleaming strongly. He wished to have a look at it, when a hand suddenly snatched it and disappeared with it through a window. And in the dream he was told that all the other books were but commentaries on that one book. Then Reb Yudel awoke to hear the master and mistress of the house quarreling. The master yelled, Woe to you for leaving the door open so that the cat entered and ate up all the cheese, and she yelled, No, it was you who left the door open so that the cat came in and ate up all the cheese, and now our enemies will raise their heads and take our place with the customers and we can go abegging.

Somebody got up and struck a light; and they saw that the cat had stolen only one cheese, while all the others were safe in their places in the box. Sima stopped yelling about the cheese and began wailing with shame for being disheveled and half dressed. Her husband threw her her clothes and she covered herself, got up, closed the door and asked pardon of the Hassid for disturbing his rest. But once their sleep was interrupted they did not lie down; and since they did not lie down they rose to set about their work.

The Hassid applied the argument to himself, If they are rising who toil for themselves, how much more should I do so. So at once he took the book *The Gates of Zion,* sat himself on the ground and began weeping and lamenting the burning of the House of our God after the fashion of those pious ones who rise for that purpose at the midnight hour; but the housefolk thought he had collapsed and cried, Water, water. Said Nuta to them, Leave him alone, for he is bewailing the destruction of Jerusalem. They stood staring in astonishment; then they went out to their work. Nehemiah went to the squire's cattle while his wife and sons went to the cows of the other gentiles; Nuta went off to give his horses their feed, and Reb Yudel was left alone with a half-wit lass named Zipporah.

Now the lass had been sane and sound to begin with. But one night she had left the house to empty a bucket of dirty water, and Those who dwell Without had seized her and she had vanished with them. For many a day her parents mourned and finally gave up all hope. When at length she returned she no longer possessed the Image of God, and could not be accounted properly human. Her mother and father asked her, Where have you been? She gave no answer. What have you been doing? She gave no answer, but stretched herself out on the straw and never shifted thence. But sometimes she would cry out in the peasant tongue and sometimes would moan like an animal.

Reb Yudel finished the Midnight Service and his heart mourned and shook because of the removal of the Divine Presence and the disunion of hearts. And he began singing in the spoken Yiddish-Teutsch, *Kalle, wie bistie? Chusen, wie gehstie?* meaning, Bride, where art thou? Bridegroom, whither goest thou? This was the song of the holy Rabbi of Kalov who used to herd geese in his childhood, and all of whose movements reflected the music of the Union of the Holy and Blest One and the Divine Presence after the fashion of bridegroom and bride.

As he sang the lass rose from the straw and began weeping so that her voice could be heard all through the village. Thereupon her mother and father returned at once and in great joy, and offered him all they could in the way of hospitality. Before an hour was out the report had gone through the entire neighborhood, and folk came running to see the wonder and to beg a blessing from the mouth of that Hassid, in order that God might bless them; and they invited the Hassid to their homes to say a blessing over the bread, in order that thereby their bread might be blest.

In brief the whole countryside grew bright for him, and his feet grew familiar with many places; for he spent several days in Razhenev and Zabletitz, in Tshech, Tshisk and Zahoretz, all of them villages in the neighborhood of Pedhoretz. He released many a cow from spells and gave the village folk all manner of charms and remedies, such as how to stop a nose bleeding or how to bring bees back to their hive, as well as how to rid the body of lice. How? You take a thread of wool, dip it in oil and place it on your clothes; all the lice will gather together there and you can kill them all together at the same time. God forbid that Rabbi Yudel should spend his time preparing charms and remedies; only it happened that he had written them down for his own use. Now where do you suppose he wrote them down if not in the margins of his prayer book; and in order to fulfill the commandment, "Thou shalt love thy neighbor as thyself," he made them known to other folk as well.

Nor did he forget that lass. Until he arrived she did not know as much as even a single blessing; but he even taught her to say the blessing over the Sabbath and Festival lights. On the Sabbath eve he said to her, Kindle the lights. Now in the lands of His Majesty the Kaiser of Austria it is not customary for a maiden to light the candles and say the blessing over them, so why did she have to do so? But there was a purpose. When she lit the candles her tears were flowing; and a great wonder happened there, for the flame did not go out nor the wick fall, and indeed the light gleamed all through the house. Said the dairyman, D'you see my daughter's candle? By your life it doesn't need to be ashamed before her mother's.

When they had eaten and said grace he sat the three sons of the master of the house before him, opened the Pentateuch and began teaching them the Portion of the Week, taking every word to pieces for them and veritably putting it into their mouths. Those who did not see the joy of their mother, with her daughter hale and healthy and her three sons sitting like rabbis learning Torah, have never seen a mother rejoicing. And so Reb Yudel went on reading with them until they fell asleep. And you can judge for yourselves how great was Reb Yudel's love for the Torah, if the noise of their snoring never upset him.

But to return to the daughter. On the Sabbath morning the dairyman had a *minyan* of ten Jews for prayer at his house. Reb Yudel had them bring Zipporah to the place of prayer when they were praying and reciting the Torah, in order that the holy words might enter her ears. And within a few days she was quite well.

Thereupon her father gathered all his friends and made a thanksgiving feast. Reb Yudel sat at the head of the table, with Nuta beside him gladdening the guests with the songs of the Brod singers. And it is something hard to grasp that those songs were composed in waggery, but the villagers sang them as poesy and praise. Some had spread far and wide because their daughters used to serve in the houses of the well to do, and their mistresses used to make them toil hard; so they used to sing these songs for annoyance and hard work. Sometimes the wandering cantors heard the tunes and garbed the prayers in them. For such is the power of good deeds; even though they are mocked at, the illumination within them brings them back to the good way.

During the feast the daughter sat beside her mother with her hand on her brow saying, Give back to me the joy of Thy salvation, as Reb Yudel had taught her so that she should be admired. A certain widower, seeing the girl, had the love of her enter his heart; her father proposed a dowry of two hundred Rhenish gulden and they wrote the engagement contract. And who should receive match money saving the abovementioned Reb Yudel, who received two gulden and twenty kreuzers; and Reb Yudel took the match money and put it away toward the dowry for his own daughters' matches.

As long as Reb Yudel stayed with the dairyman he was not short of meat; for a man does not esteem what he has in plenty, and therefore Sima cooked him meat, milk produce being of no account in her eyes, and she thinking that only meat makes a meal; like the tale of the slaughterer and the dairyman. Once upon a time a certain slaughterer had to go to a village. Said his wife to him, Eat plenty of meat, for you are going where there's nothing but milk and butter and cheese. So he eats meat at morn, meat at noon and meat at night till the meat all but runs out at the nose. Said he to his wife, Blest be His Name that I'm going to the dairyman in the village where I shan't see any meat. But when he came to the dairyman's house the dairyman said to his wife, Will we have a slaughterer come to our house and let him go away again without meat? So they brought him chicken. He took as much chicken as would cover a finger tip and left the rest. They said to themselves, This was a chicken and not good enough for a slaughterer; so they fed him with goose. He took as much goose as would cover a finger tip and left the rest. Said they, Poultry isn't meat; and brought him veal. They did this morning and evening, weekday and Sabbath.

Some time later the dairyman had to visit the slaughterer. Said his wife to him, Beloved husband, eat as much butter and cheese as you can, and drink plenty of milk, for in town they'll stuff you with meat. So he drank milk in all its forms and ate butter and cheese, morning, evening, weekday and Sabbath, and at last he said to his wife, Blest be the All-Present that I'm going to the slaughterer where I shan't see milk. When he came to town the slaughterer said to his wife, Here's the dairyman come, and will he be satisfied with meat? So she went out and bought a gallon of milk, a barrel of butter and a whole cheese. Today she treated him to milk in the morning, milk at noon and milk at night; tomorrow she treated him to a milk feast at morn, another at noon and a third at night. The one who wanted milk got meat and the one who wanted meat got milk.

And so it was with Reb Yudel till almost Hanuka, when the rabbis began to visit the villages to collect Hanuka money from the villagers and didn't leave behind them as much as an egg for a woman in childbed. All the time Reb Yudel spent in Pedhoretz, Nuta was taking wheat and barley to town and bringing back all kinds of goods to the village; he ate and drank and had a good time and fed Ivory and Peacock on oats without any mixture of straw and chaff; and the horses grew fat as two wardens of charity.

CHAPTER FIVE: AN INHABITED LAND ✧ Trees and fields stood bare, and the winds blew and blew. The greater part of Kislev was over but snow had not yet fallen. If the prophecy of the almanac were to be depended on there would be none that year. And what difference did it make? It made a difference regarding snow sleighs. The farmers make simple snow sleighs by bending wood when it is damp, and make seats of twigs and branches and fix them together with wooden pegs; and when the horses fall you tumble into the snow with all the passengers; a sleigh like that cost three or four Rhenish thalers. One with iron runners and prepared by a smith costs seven to eight Rhenish. A zlebikel costs from seven to ten Rhenish. What's the difference between a zlebikel and a snow sleigh? A snow sleigh can be made by anybody, while a zlebikel can be made only by a craftsman; it has a soft seat and is comfortable for travel. Likewise it is covered with a sort of booth. But Nuta didn't have the money for a winter sleigh. All the same he did not worry. What's the difference? If the almanac could be depended on he wouldn't need any winter sleigh and if the almanac couldn't be depended on he was traveling with Reb Yudel. If Reb Yudel was satisfied he was satisfied.

All along the road they met waggon after waggon in which were seated rabbis who came from the villages; some of them were loaded with cabbages and potatoes, and some with eggs and poultry. Now Reb Yudel had never been sluggish in greeting the disciples of the wise, so whenever he saw a well-garbed man he stopped the waggon, descended to greet him and stood ready to hear him uttering words of Torah; for wherever the disciples of the wise may go there is Torah to be found with them. And Reb Yudel likewise made the place glad with words of Torah. And Reb Yudel could then be compared to nothing better than a gold bell with a pearl clapper, he being all meek and modest and his mouth full of wisdom. How greatly he rejoiced, did Reb Yudel, to be come into an inhabited land full of the great ones of the Torah.

They were not all of equal merit. Sometimes he met scholars who turned up new points in the Torah that were really of no point, or preachers who cursed the householders for not having paid them for their sermons. As one wise man has said about these, they are far

worse than Balaam, the wicked; for Balaam demanded his full house
of gold and silver to curse Israel but gave them his blessings free of
charge; but these folk demand to be paid for their blessings while
they throw in their curses gratis. More than this; they speak their
worst of Israel, saying, Israel deserves all the troubles that befall
him, God forbid. Had they been alive in the days of Titus, the
wicked, they would have said, Titus did well to burn the Temple.
Now what answer did Reb Yudel make to one such sermonizer
whom he heard cursing and reviling because his sermons had not
been paid for? Said Reb Yudel to him, Master so-and-so, I'm not a
sermonizer nor the son of a sermonizer, and I can't open my mouth
in parables; but for your honor's sake, since you find all manner of
reproach in the actions of Israel, I'll tell you

THE STORY OF THE TWO–EYED RABBI AND THE
STORY OF THE ONE–EYED PREACHER.

It is told that a certain saint was on the road and saw a Jew in a
carriage; so he hurried to greet him. He found him a fine figure of a
man, dressed in silk with a sable hat on his head and silver-buckled
shoes on his feet and a red handkerchief hanging out of his pocket
and a fine stick by him and his face furious, with one eye swollen
up as big as his fist; and he was covering the swelling with his dribble
and dabbing it with a handkerchief and cursing and reviling and
railing at Israel's foes. He greeted him and was greeted in return.

Said the man to the saint, Where do you come from? Answered
he, From a great city of saints and Hassidim do I come. Said the
man, It astonishes me to hear that there is any such city. Said the
saint, By your life, every man there is meek and humble of spirit
and God-fearing, and does deeds of loving-kindness to all mankind,
taking as much trouble over the most unworthy man in Israel as
though he were the king's messenger. The other covered his swollen
eye with his hand, looked at him with his hale eye and groaned. Now
why did he groan seeing he should have been glad; only this man
was a preacher who traveled from place to place preaching sermons
in public and being paid; and that day he had not been paid for one
of his sermons.

And now the saint asked him, And your honor, from which spot
do you come? Said he, From a town of transgressors and sinners,

men of wrath and evil thoughts, who derive pleasure from the shame
of the disciples of the wise, and despise the Torah and despise those
who study the Torah and contemn reproof and mock at words of
admonition and have no decent behavior, woe to them that they left
their mothers' wombs only to aggravate their Creator.

Said the other, I wonder that there should be such men. Said the
preacher, May their bones rot for a pack of unparalleled shameless
evildoers and heretics and profaners of the name of Heaven, and
scoffers and haters of reproof, who mock the words of the wise and
pride themselves on the degradation of the scholar. Would they had
all been burnt ere I ventured among them. Lord of the Universe, as
I'm a Jew I swear You'd have no loss. How I reproved them, how I
rebuked them, how many tears I shed for their evil courses; and did
they give me the pay I asked, or treat me with respect? No, what
did they do, those sinners, but sling all sorts of stuff at me till me
eye swelled up.

Only one eye? asks the saint. Maybe it wasn't good enough for
those evildoers, answers the other, that they let me go with one hale
eye. Said the saint, Evildoers are you calling them; by your life
they're nothing but saints. Said the preacher, Those folk kept back
my pay and knocked out my eye and you go calling them saints!
Then you can't be other than as bad as they are. Said the saint to him,
Israel is not suspected of executing justice unless judgment has
been passed, so they must certainly have done it for the sake of
Heaven; and as for you, before you blaspheme and revile and curse
Israel's foes I'll ask you something, seeing you're a preacher.

Ask, said the other. Said he, Why was Man created with two eyes
when it's possible to see with one; look how many people there are
in the world with one eye who see all they require; and it's well
known that nothing's wasted, so what are two eyes for? Said the
other, If you ask it shows you have an answer. The answer's straight-
forward, said he. Man was created with two eyes so that with one
eye he might see the greatness of the Holy and Blest One, and with
the other contemplate his own lowliness. I'll give you an instance. I
came to a town and they greeted me; and straightway I beheld the
greatness of the Holy and Blest One.

For all that I'm a petty creature of no importance He led a son of
Abraham His beloved to trouble himself and be hospitable and treat
me with such respect. And so with one eye I observe the greatness of

the Holy and Blest One, while with the other I contemplate my own lowliness.

My fellow Jew provides me with food and drink, and straightway I see the greatness of the Holy and Blest One. He has so many Universes and so many saints in His Universes, and still the Almighty takes thought to sustain me. When my host offers me a bed, I repeat the Hear O Israel and cover my face in very shame. Lord of the Universe, how many men there are in the world whose very fingernails are worth more than all my body, and yet they're left without food or lodging or couch, while I lie abed on pillows and cushions. Father in Heaven, I know that I have no merits of good deeds, yet the compassion Thou hast with me leads Thee to show me charity and loving-kindness.

And so with one eye I see my own lowliness and with the other the greatness of the Holy and Blest One. Then the following day my host prepares me a meal and gives me a coin; and I think to myself, How much trouble my host has been to on my account, how much food he has set before me, how many cushions and pillows he has prepared for me; and he has been to all this trouble only because I have done wrong by spoiling my living, so that I'm like a sick man being nursed by kind folk. And so with one eye I observe the greatness of the Holy and Blest One, while with the other I contemplate my own unworthiness.

But as for you, who can see nothing but yourself and your importance and your wisdom and your knowledge of the Torah, and who never turn your eyes anywhere except toward yourself, and not only this but you've taken upon yourself the august duty of uttering words of admonition and reproof, and if they don't crown you with gold pieces you rage and fume at once and begin to call down all manner of abominations upon Israel—why do you do so? Only because you don't see anything but yourself and anybody who doesn't see anything more than himself doesn't need more than a single eye.

> *That is the end*   *of the tale of three eyes,*
> *If so be you've a soul*   *may it serve you for eyes.*

Meanwhile Nuta had climbed down from the waggon, unharnessed the horses and taken them to water, saying to himself, You can depend upon Reb Yudel not ending his Torah talk in a hurry, so while he's at his affairs I'll be at mine. Whereupon the waggoners said to Nuta, It looks as though you mean to take possession and squat here. Said he to them, You don't know Reb Yudel. Once Reb Yudel gets going on Torah talk you can roast an ox and be eating it before he stops. Hearing this, they thought the matter over, opened their bundles, drank long life and good health and sweetened the bitter of the spirit with cakes and the like. Having eaten and drunk, they filled their pipes and set up a smoke like an inn after a fairing; then they began chatting of straw and hosses and hoss thieves and the good city of Ropshitz where the thieves really do have some idea how hosses should be stolen. But Reb Yudel and his companions charged the air with words of Torah; and if it hadn't been for the poultry tied in their waggons and beating their wings and clucking and quacking and gobbling and crowing, the voice of the Torah would have been heard all the way to Brod.

But at last Reb Yudel took his leave of his companions and went back to the waggon, while Nuta took leave of his companions and turned the horses' heads to the left; and they made for the village of Medan where they fashion wooden spoons and ladles and shovels, from which the Jews make a good living, and from thence they take blackberries to Tarnapol; for Tarnapol of Podolia has no pines in the neighborhood, so blackberries are precious there, for they grow only in pine forests.

Nonetheless Reb Yudel could not effect anything at Medan, for the Medan folk were weary of the commandment of hospitality; all those days rabbis upon rabbis had come to collect their perquisites, so the folk paid no attention to Reb Yudel and turned their eyes away from the commandment regarding the Bridal Canopy. And when Nuta told them the story of Reb Yudel's powers manifested at Pedhoretz they paid no attention, saying that he had made all of it up to get money from them.

And therefore Reb Yudel's heart became soft as wax and he wished to return home, saying, I have done my share, and if the Holy and Blest One does not desire, why must I meddle in this affair? And he was all ready to do off his fine clothes and remove the cushion from his belly and become like ordinary men. For he did not know that all this was but a trial to see how far he was prepared to go for the sake of that commandment; in the way that those who serve His Name are tried to see how steadfast they are in His Blessed service.

And what did Nuta do? He set off to the village of Virchevish.

Although Virchevish was of no importance as a village it was an important place in Nuta's eyes; this being its importance, that there dwelt Pessel, the aunt of Frummet, Reb Yudel's wife, who had the same name as Pessele, Frummet's daughter. This Pessel was blessed with exceeding wealth, for she had a brownie dwelling in her cellar, and he had brought blessings with him.

Nonetheless she continued to live as though she were poor, and was not to be told in the way of food or clothing or dwelling from all her kinsfolk. As she had behaved before the brownie came, so she behaved after, just as our sages of blessed memory have said, "Though the peasant were to become king he'd keep his reed basket hanging from his neck." When this Pessel would come to Brod to prostrate herself on the graves of her forefathers she would lodge with Frummet, her niece, together with all her poor kinsfolk, and would eat her own food out of her own basket after the fashion of villagers.

There was only one change to be observed in her since the brownie had taken up his lodging in her house; she had become deaf in both her ears, and it was exceedingly difficult to hold conversation with her. Nobody knew whether she had become deaf through the brownie rapping on the walls or for some other reason. Gabriel, her husband, who came from Hasiamur and was blind of one eye, also used to behave as though he were the same pauper as in Hasiamur. When the skies clouded over he would go out into the village street with a knife in his hand which he shook toward the clouds while he said what he had to say; and when the earth brought forth its produce the peasants would bring him the fruit of their soil as they did, saving your grace, to their shave-poll priest.

In brief, Nuta betook himself to Virchevish and to the house of Pessel, where he stopped the horses in front of the windows, descended, opened the door and with cheerful voice cried, The Name aid you, Aunt Pessel, where's my uncle Gabriel? Peace be with you, with you be peace, I'm bringing you something you'll be glad to have. Meanwhile Reb Yudel entered, placed his pack on the table, turned his face cheerily toward the housefolk and said, Blest are those here, and offered his hand in greeting to his uncle, holding it away from his aunt so that she should not seize it as in her affection she might wish to do. And he smiled at Pessel's grandchildren as well, saying to them, For the moment put each your hand in my girdle, and then I'll take your hands one by one and greet you in turn.

But Reb Yudel's kinsfolk did not turn pleasant faces toward him, nor were they glad to see him, nor did they prepare the table or bring him anything over which to say the blessing for food; nor did they say, Sit down Yudel, sit down; instead they looked daggers at the very ground on which he stood. But the Holy and Blest One kept closed the intelligent sight of Reb Yudel so that he never noticed the black looks of the household but acted according to his fashion, that is, with gladness. Now he took hold of one child and said, Tell me what you've learnt today, and now he took another and asked, What's the Portion of the Week?

As for Nuta, once he was in the house, he too behaved like one of the family; seeing a pot on the oven he took off the cover to see what was inside; seeing a string of garlic he broke off a clove to rub on his bread; and but for the children who began scratching him with their nails till they made his hands like a sieve, yelling, Grandpa, Grandma, this Jew here's stealing the garlic, Nuta would have eaten happily with more relish to his appetite. Thereupon Reb Yudel began to feel cold in his very bones, although he had not removed his overcoat since entering; his spirits fell, his tongue grew stiff so that he could say nothing, and he prayed in his heart that the Holy and Blest One might perform a miracle and deliver him from thence.

Meanwhile the day grew short and the room filled with mist. Reb Yudel washed his hands and began to prepare for the Afternoon Service, saying his prayers in a low voice and without a clear mind, moaning so that they should notice him there. He could be compared to a man who had found his way among dumb folk. Now and again Gabriel would look at him with his one eye, but before Reb Yudel had a chance to speak to him he would be looking away. Then Reb Yudel remembered the words of his wife, Frummet, who had said, Yudel, when you come to my aunt Pessel, cry out, Hear ye heavens, my daughter has reached her marriage age and you go turning your eyes away from her, and isn't she flesh of your flesh and bone of your bone, and aren't you both named after the same grandmother? If you don't come to my aid I must needs summon the dead from their graves.

Woe's me for Frummet, said Reb Yudel to himself, and woe's me for Pessel; woe's me if I tell her and woe's me if I don't; and either way, woe's me. However, he thought of the commandment of bringing the bride under the Bridal Canopy, which same is so great a com-

mandment, and said to himself, The merit of performing the commandment shall serve me. And at once he began speaking to Pessel,
saying to her that Pessele, his daughter, had reached marriageable
age and they had not a doit, so he was journeying for the sake of the
Bridal Canopy; and Frummet had told him that when he came to her
aunt Pessel he should tell her all about it, and assuredly she would
not stand over their blood but would support us with a generous
hand; and for the sake of doing so let the Holy and Blest One aid
them with all that was good.

When he began speaking Pessel put her right hand to her ear like
a sort of trumpet and shrilled, Gabriel, Gabriel, what's he saying?
Said Gabriel to her, May it be His will that the mouths of all our
foes and accusers should be stopped up, how should I know what he's
a saying of? Then Pessel put her hand back on her right ear like a
sort of trumpet and shrilled, Yudel, what's he saying? So Reb Yudel
repeated the words of Gabriel to her. Pessel nods her head and says,
Yes, he's right, he's right.

Then Nuta joins them and chimes in, I know an outsider hasn't
got any call to mix in family affairs, but, if I shut up, the very
stones in the wall will cry out aloud; and is this fit and proper and
just? Your kinsman has to marry off a girl who's grown to her term,
and you turn your eyes away from him. You don't need to give him
more than your brownie brings you in a single night and he'd be able
to marry off all his three daughters at one go. Here Gabriel winked at
Nuta with his one eye; Nuta took the hint, understanding that a loud
voice isn't nice for the brownie, and went on in a whisper, I'll say it
once again and I'm asking you why you turn your eyes away from
your poor kinsman; by your lives, if you give him a single night's
goods, he and his wife Frummet and his three daughters can rise from
the earth on which they lie outstretched. I know the brownie tricks;
for all he's such a little fellow he brings in more overnight than ten
Jews or two gentiles, saving your grace, in a twelvemonth.

Pessel put her hand back over her ear again like a kind of trumpet
and asked, Gabriel, what are you all talking about? Said he, Let them
tell you and not me. Then Nuta put his mouth to Pessel's ear and
bawled, Pessel, I'm talking to you both about the brownie in your
house. Pessel pierced him with her eyes and said, What is there in
our house? Rats are there in our house! Set your drunken father
over them to keep 'em from gnawing the soles of your feet. Nuta

quivered all over, while Reb Yudel roused and said, What's that, Reb Nuta? Said Nuta, I wouldn't stay the night here though they gave me the world of riches. Kinsfolk like these are worse than wild beasts. It's with good reason they say that a rich man's a swine. Did you see when I got up to take a clove of garlic how the kids set their nails in me? Like grandmother, like grandchildren. Pessel, may her mother bury her, has been teaching them her tricks.

But Reb Yudel thought of his kinsfolk with respect. Says Reb Yudel, How many good advantages rich folk have who can do charity with their money. Therefore every man must honor the rich, and though a man be great in Torah and commandments as Rabbi Judah the Prince he should still honor the rich. Come, see the greatness and praiseworthiness of the rich whom the Holy and Blest One himself makes His emissary, giving him of His silver and gold; and if he is important in the sight of the Holy and Blest One, he should be even more so in our sight.

Answered Nuta, By my life, Reb Yudel, the Almighty don't know to whom He should give and to whom He shouldn't give. Said Reb Yudel, God forbid, don't say such things; but wealth and property make a man's heart vain, as it says in Deuteronomy, "And thy herds and thy flocks multiply, and thy silver and thy gold is multiplied", and it goes straight on in the next verse, "And thy heart being lifted up thou dost forget"; and Solomon said, in his Proverbs, "Lest I be full and belie and say, who is the Lord?" Indeed, this thing comes under the category of Trial, and if I were to go into it at length, my time would run out long before my words. In the Ethics of the Fathers it was long ago said by Rabbi Akiba, "All things are given on pledge, and a net is spread for all that lives." Happy is he who does not lose his pledge but departs in peace. And what are we to harbor dissatisfaction with the Divine Presence?

Meanwhile they had left the village of Virchevish and turned toward Ushni. But it seems the trouble meted out to them for that day was not yet at an end. They had thought to reach Ushni while yet it was day, but they did not start out along the way until night had fallen. I don't know how far Ushni is from Virchevish, but I know they lie close together. Yet before they had gone far the horses had left the track. When Nuta got off the waggon in order to lead them back to the path he found he didn't know where he was. So he stood with his horses in the dark turning this way and that; he looked aloft but there was no star; he looked below but there was no path. So he began sniffing the way with his nostrils and reaching forward and groping with his hands. As he did so the whip slipped from his hands. He bent to lift it up and the reins fell from his hands. He stood up to catch hold of the reins and the horses ran away.

Thereupon Nuta began yelling, Reb Yudel, catch 'em by the bit. Where are we, Reb Yudel called back, I can't see anything at all. While they stood like that a sort of light began shining. Nuta found his whip, climbed up again, caught hold of the reins and began driving the horses toward the light. As they drew near it moved away from them. Nuta put the horses at a gallop and they began chasing the light, but whenever they approached it moved away. They all but caught the light up three or four times, and each time the light went on shifting ahead.

What do I know about it more than you already know? It was a will-o'-the-wisp; a man may chase it a whole night long and when day comes he finds himself where he began. Nuta recognized that this must be a will-o'-the-wisp, and that the further they went the further they would go astray. Said Nuta, I don't move from here until the dawn comes. For he was not so mad, Nuta, as to let himself be driven mad. He stood looking this way and that. There were no stars in the sky and the night was lightless and a strong wind was blowing, and the horses stood still in their places without moving, as though they didn't know the way either; and Reb Yudel sat moaning in fear.

For a wild beast might come out of the forest all of a sudden; the wolf and the lion and the bear and the leopard and the panther and the snake referred to in one passage of the Talmud came into mind with the lion and the bear and the leopard and the panther and the snake referred to in another passage in the Talmud; and Reb Yudel began to be frightened, and groaned by reason of his heart being emptied of the fear of Heaven so that room was left for him to fear wild beasts.

Reb Yudel was then sorry for two things: for the story of the coward which is told in the book, *Duties of the Heart,* by Behaya, in the section on the Love of God, where a pious one tells how he met the coward sleeping in desert places and asked him, Have you no fear of the lion that you sleep in such a spot? To which he replied, I should be shamed before God were He to see me fearing anything other than Him; and the story of Reb Uri Hassid, the Seraph of Strelisk

They tell of Reb Uri of Strelisk that once he was traveling in the darkness of midnight when the horses stopped in the middle of the way and refused to go on. The waggoner went to see what ailed them and found a bear standing in front of them; so he began to cry out. Said Reb Uri to him, Have no fear. And he descended from the waggon, walked up to the bear, raised his hat from his brow, and away fled the bear at once. Then said Reb Uri, Do not call this a sign or a wonder, for it is written in the Torah in the Book of Genesis, "and the fear of you and the dread of you shall be upon all the beasts of the earth"; if a man does not destroy the image of God which he bears he has no reason to fear any beast; or as it is said in the Ethics of the Fathers, "Whoever is well thought of by the creatures is well thought of by the Omni-Present." Creatures means living creatures, including animals; if they think well of a person and are not his foes it is a sign that the Spirit of the Omni-Present is also satisfied with him.

Here Reb Yudel groaned and said, Yudel, you fabler, you'd better correct your feeble deeds. For it is said that each and every man in Israel needs to know and continually think that in the Universe he is unique of his kind and that none such as he has ever yet been in the Universe; for, had there been such a one as him in the Universe already, there would have been no need for him in the Universe, since every man is something fresh in the Universe and is required to set right his standards in this Universe until all the Universes are set right by means of all Israel, and our righteous Messiah comes with speed and in our days. Or, as Reb Uri said, Uri has no fear that he will be judged for not being like Abraham or like any of the other righteous ones and saints; but I do fear that I shall be judged for not being what Uri has it in him to be.

Meanwhile Nuta was pacing to and fro, clapping his hands together so that they shouldn't freeze in the cold, and growling like a bear, How Gabriel peeped with his one eye, May he be consumed by the rats together with Pessel his wife and all their offspring. Swine that they are, never even letting us breathe in their house. They reckon they've already caught Luck by the foot. And I say the brownie can leave them all of a sudden and take their luck with him. In all my days I've never seen such Jews. By your life, even a gentile would have prepared us a place to stay.

You know, I was once driving through a snowstorm. On the way the horses stopped and wouldn't budge. In my place anybody else would have started thrashing them and beating them within an inch of their lives, but I saw it wasn't the whip they were needing but oxen to get them and the waggon out of the snow. So I got down from the waggon at once and said to my fares, I'm going to look for help, and you, see you don't fall asleep; for if you do you'll finish up dead in the snow. And I turned my eyes in all directions, and what shall I tell you, Reb Yudel, there's never a house nor a sign of a house but a wilderness of snow stretching before me and after. I raised my eyes aloft, and what shall I tell you, Reb Yudel, that snow wouldn't let me raise an eye; when you lifted your head up the flakes of snow would fill your eye sockets; if you didn't keep on the move the snow below would cover your legs and the snow above would cover your head.

So I took to my feet and ran as hard as I was able till I saw a sort of light gleaming across the snow and reached a house. I entered and found gentiles, men and women, standing drinking and making merry because the mistress of the house was in the throes of birth, and as I entered she bore a son. I told them my story and at once the master of the house rose and said, In virtue of the son born to me as this here Jew entered I'm going to give him a hand. And right away he fetched his oxen, and he and his companions went and dragged out the waggon and the horses from the snow and harnessed the oxen to the waggon and brought us to the house and gave us brandy to drink with mead and bear. Well, well, what can I tell you more; that was a night and that was liquor——

But before Nuta could tell all he had to tell in praise of the different kinds of liquor he had drunk that night, they suddenly saw a fresh light gleaming, no will-o'-the-wisp but a fixed and stationary light. Nuta at once mounted the waggon and turned the horses' heads in that direction. The light remained in one place and did not retreat from them, and they came closer and closer until they stopped by a house. Said Nuta, Thank God and thank Him again for having pity on His creatures and bringing us to a place of rest.

But Reb Yudel remembered any number of travelers' tales about wayfarers going astray at midnight in the pitch darkness and suddenly seeing a house in front of them; and when they entered the house they found males and females there dancing and doing all manner of unseemly actions, that house being a meeting place of demons, may the Merciful One deliver us. So Reb Yudel feared to enter lest that should happen to him, God forbid, which had happened to them; and he took his fringes in hand and prepared for battle.

Meanwhile Nuta was groping for the door and said, By your life, Reb Yudel, this is a Jewish house, and I'd like our uncle Gabriel to have a bruise over his eye as big as this mezuzah on the doorpost. Then Nuta knocked at the door, but it was not opened. He knocked again, but it was left closed. So he picked up a stone and began hammering on the door till it was opened in front of them and the master of the house came out with a candle burning in his hand; and they recognized one another, Nuta recognizing Gabriel and Gabriel recognizing Nuta. As people say, where a man goes once he returns a second time.

As soon as it grew light Nuta started out again for Ushni, which they reached before the hour was up. Reb Yudel raised his two hands on high and offered praise and thanksgiving to The Blessed Name Who had brought him out of the house of hard people and set an end and a bound to the illusions of night, and had brought them to an inhabited place. Said Reb Yudel to Nuta, I'm happy that we have reached here. May it be His desire that the Lord our God should show us the truth of the saying, Change your place, change your luck. If you hadn't hung about on the road, answered Nuta, spinning your yarns, we'd have been in Ushni yesterday yet, and wouldn't have needed to go chasing our shadows all night long.

I'm surprised at you, Reb Nuta, said Reb Yudel, calling words of Torah yarn-spinning. Said Nuta, And what was all your talk then but so much empty chatter? See here, you learn Torah and they learn Torah, so what drove all of you to that long confabulation? Have we got two Torahs by any chance so that, where one of you learns one, another studies the other? It's one and the same Torah that you've all been studying. So it turns out that you know what they know, and they know what you know, so why did you need to argue the toss for such a long time? Or maybe the story of the one-eyed preacher you told that fellow along the road can also be reckoned as Torah?

You're right, said Reb Yudel. And for that I've been punished. The Holy and Blest One said, What's this, Yudel, you go sharpening your wits with a story of a one-eyed man; all right, I've got a one-eyed man in pickle for you. And now this is what I'm going to beg of you, Reb Nuta: that you don't remind me of the Virchevish business, and for my part I'll also uproot it from my heart so that I shouldn't harbor any bad thoughts about my kinsfolk.

And it was for that reason that as long as they were on the road neither of them mentioned what happened at Virchevish; which was not like Nuta, who enjoyed telling about past troubles in order to shout and vent his spleen; nor like Reb Yudel, who was fond of relating troubles because they gave him a chance of recounting the salvations of the Lord.

Meanwhile Nuta tightened the reins, clucked with his tongue and stopped the horses, descended and said, Reb Yudel, shift your feet and come down. While they were speaking a man came up to them, greeted them, invited them to his house, gave them some brandy and cake over which to say the blessing on divers kinds of food, and in the evening spread them a table and prepared them beds. This man was named Reb Yom Tov, and for his second wife he had married the daughter of Reb Yerahmeel, the teacher. In his house it was the established custom that a cloth was spread on the table for guests and wayfarers to come in and eat; and the cloth was never removed.

How surprised Nuta was to see the daughter of Reb Yerahmeel, the teacher, happy and content, with her offspring and offspring's offspring filling the house. Having heard the tale how Reb Yerahmeel had given away his money, he had reckoned that his daughters must have died virgins with a black canopy, God forbid, prepared for them at their deaths, as is done for a virgin who was never brought under the canopy. But He, may He be blest, repays those who carry out His commandments according to the scale of the commandment they have performed. That is what is meant by the saying in the Ethics of the Fathers, "The reward of a commandment is a commandment"; the actual commandment itself pays its reward as was the case with Reb Yerahmeel.

Reb Yerahmeel's son-in-law told them, My Father-in-law, Yerahmeel, may he rest in peace, didn't know the value of money, but all the same he prospered more in his affairs than those who turn worlds upside down for cash. You know the beginning of the story;

after all, it's from Paltiel's house you're coming, and it's his habit to tell the tale of Reb Yerahmeel. As that's the case I'll tell you what happened to my father-in-law after he returned from Pinkevitz without either cow or money. To be brief, when he came back home without a cow his wife asked him, Where's the money, Yerahmeel? Said he, Didn't you send me to buy a cow? That's right, says she, and where's the cow? Says he, And if a better piece of business than a cow came my way wasn't I justified in investing my cash in it? What sort of business is it, she asked, in which you've invested all your money? He glossed the matter over with smooth words but didn't tell her anything, like those modest folk who perform charity in secret, and answered all her questions with wisdom, as when she asked him, Have you put out the money at interest? Yes, said he. Have you lent our money to a lord? Yes, he said.

My mother-in-law reckoned he meant the lord of the village, while he meant nobody else than the Lord of Lords. So her imagination set to work and took her from profit to profit until she became all enthusiastic with her fancies. Said the neighbor women to one another, she has a face like a moneylender. And right away the matchmakers began rising betimes to call on them, till they married off their daughters, my wife among them. And in that way my father-in-law, may he rest in peace, saw the reward for his carrying out the commandment in This World. And more than that, Yehiel returned him his money in poultry and eggs and butter and cheese and foxskins enough to make him a fine fur coat. In the long run his sons-in-law found out the truth, but by that time the whole business was over and done with.

To return to our first theme. To make a long story short, he spread them a table and prepared them their beds. Reb Yudel stretched himself out on his bed, covered himself up to his beard, said the Night Prayers and tried to fall asleep, seeing that the night before he had been kept awake all night long. But he could not rest. His eyes were closed, but his body was wide awake, and the more he pressed his eyelids together the more he felt as though his lashes were red-hot needles.

To begin with he lay on his left side, according to the advice of Maimonides of blessed memory; since he was not comfortable he turned over on his right; but being careful not to go against the words of the wise he turned back to his left. And so he rolled and tossed from one side to the other, and taking both sides together he didn't sleep on either. How greatly he desired to sleep, but the Holy and Blest One removed sleep from his eyes, and all night long one-eyed Gabriel was peeping at him with his one eye dancing and twinkling and suddenly fixing itself in the middle of his forehead like the folk in the isles of the sea who have an eye in the middle of their brows; and the eye went on roaming about till there was never a place where it couldn't be found.

Anybody else in Reb Yudel's place might have taken fright, but Reb Yudel conned over to himself all the different things said about eyes, as the passage in the Ethics of the Fathers, "Know what is above thee—a seeing eye," and the story in the Talmud about Alexander of Macedon, who was given a round bone against which he weighed all the silver and gold in his possession without outweighing it. What's this, he asked the sages. Said they, 'Tis the eye socket of a human being, which never knows enough. How do you know it is so, he asked them. Said they, take a fistful of dust and cover it over. He did so, and the beam of the scales went up.

So Reb Yudel tried to imagine a fistful of dust in order to bring thoughts of penitence into his heart, when he suddenly found the whole world covered with snow. The horses stood still in the snow without moving, while the waggoner yelled for aid and his legs sank in the snow; when he dragged one out the other vanished, and when he pulled that one out the other sank again. When he got out of the snow he came to Pessel. Careful as Reb Yudel was not to remind himself of the matter of Pessel, what could he do when his thoughts took their own course? All manner of ideas came into his mind and he said, What can I tell my wife Frummet when she asks whether I have visited Pessel? God forbid I should say anything against her kinswoman. And he tried to think of any manner of thing that would keep him from thinking about that. But seeing he had no power to drive the thoughts of her away, he set himself in the hands of the Holy and Blest One, for those that trust in Him shall ne'er be shamed. And straightaway he rolled his body up in the bed and began slumbering.

How much good Reb Yudel derived from his sleep! His limbs rested, he regained his mental balance and did not enter on unnecessary thoughts, for Reb Yudel was all but questioning, God forbid, the words of the sages who say in the Talmud, "night was created

only for the purpose of sleep", and here was he unable to fall asleep;
also it was hard for him to understand why there are men who stay
in one place all their lives through and the Holy and Blest One
brings what they require to their own place, while he could not find
his necessities in his own place but was compelled to travel foreign
parts; and if he was compelled to travel to foreign parts, why should
he have to trundle on from place to place and from man to man,
staying today with this one and tomorrow with that, some of them
mean people who tugged their hands back hard from deeds of charity.
And then it was certainly a hard question he had to ask of the
prophet Isaiah who bore witness "and the people are all of them
righteous." To be sure, the Torah is a sketch map of the world, and
the world goes its way in accordance with the rules by which the
Torah is expounded; further, all souls do emanate from the letters
of the Torah; there are verses which are in a text with which they
have no connection, and there are verses which stand in a text but
which refer to some other text. Now he whose soul doth emanate
from a verse in its proper place finds his living awaiting him in its
place; while he whose soul emanates from a letter which is out of
place in the verse finds his living awaiting him only at a distance.
And therefore he, Reb Yudel that is, must be one of those souls derived from an out-of-place letter in a verse, and so he had to satisfy
his needs by wandering far and wide; yet even so the difficulty remained as to how Holy Writ could say, "And Thy people are all
righteous." But the two difficulties answered one another, and Thy
people are all righteous, referring to All Israel; and there can be no
all without constituent parts.

Similarly the night has been created only for sleep. Now didn't the
sages know that there are nights when you can't sleep? But the sages
spoke in general. How great are the words of the sages, said Reb
Yudel when he told of the matter, for even that night I slept well and
sweetly. And Reb Yudel went on, His blessed conduct of the world
is with righteousness and justice and mercy, and the Almighty doesn't
need the explanations of flesh and blood, for His conduct will provide all the necessary explanations. Somebody else in Reb Yudel's
place might have forgotten the essential part and gone on complaining next day against the All-Present; but Reb Yudel stored the
matter up in his heart, and if the Holy and Blest One did swing him
from place to place, and apparently there was no explanation, he

never asked why. Never had Reb Yudel been warped and twisted for perversity's sake; and that day he accepted with affection even things that raised all kinds of problems and difficulties, as being conditioned by the conduct of the world.

And so you find that when Nuta took him and sat him on the waggon he never asked, Aren't we comfortable with Reb Yom Tov, but rose and started off.

So Reb Yudel left Ushni and came to Sasov, which is the Sasov where the holy Rabbi, Moshe Leib of Sasov, lies buried; he was the saint who shared the sufferings of all men as though they were his own, and he used to support orphans from his own pocket and cover their heads and cure them of boils.

Were we to begin telling tales of his valor and might we would never be done; but since it's a tale of the Bridal Canopy which we're telling, we'll throw in a story on the same subject. It happened when he was still sitting in the House of Study as a single man that he heard a poor fellow telling his companion how his daughter was mature and adult, but was crazy and ugly and he had no money to marry her off; and he knew that nobody would be able to live with her because she was such an ugly thing, so what did he want? Well, maybe, and if only some man would want to marry her in order to cover her head, since he could not bear the shame because she was over thirty years old. Said the saint to a match maker, Go and tell that fellow I want to marry his daughter. Said the match maker, You're making mock of me; for that saint was the son of worthy folk, came of fine stock and was expert in the Torah as well as very handsome; while that girl was a half-wit, and none so clammy as she. Said he, God forbid; and did not let the matter rest until he married her. When his father heard of it he ordered him to divorce her; and on account of the commandment of filial obedience he had to obey.

This tale put Reb Yudel in mind of his three daughters who had reached marriageable age and had none to cover their heads; and he thought to himself, Our sages of blessed memory said in the Talmud, "The righteous and saintly are greater in their deaths than in their lives"; I shall not remove from his grave until I find salvation. But he felt ashamed of begging for himself from that saint, for they told that he had been wont to say, He who is within four leagues of Sasov on the day of my demise and does not come to my grave will make me wroth with him; and Brod was within four leagues of Sasov, yet until then he had not visited his grave. Said Reb Yudel, I was a fool at the time, to my present loss; that saint, who loved Israel so greatly in his lifetime—how wroth he will be with them after his death.

How careful a man needs to be regarding the things he hears, lest he be included among those of whom the Book of Proverbs writes, "The gullible believeth every word." Consider how great a love that saint bore to the commandment of the Bridal Canopy; once he made a feast for an orphan youth and maiden, and rejoiced exceedingly in the music, honoring bride and bridegroom. In the hour of his rejoicing he said, Would that I may be brought to the grave to this tune. In good time the players went with their instruments to the Holy Congregation of Brod; on the road the horses began galloping with the waggon and could not be stopped till they came to a graveyard. There the players saw a crowd of men bringing a corpse for burial amid weepings and wailings. They asked, What is the town called and who is the departed? Said the folk, Sasov's the town and it's our holy Rabbi of Sasov who has left us behind. Then the players, remembering the words of the saint, reminded themselves of the tune they played at the wedding of the orphan youth and maiden. A session of the Court was held on the spot, which permitted them to play on that spot; and over his grave they played the tune, as he had wished.

When Nuta saw that Reb Yudel had planted himself in the synagogues and Houses of Study in order to hear stories, and was forgetting the object of his journey, Nuta said to himself, I'll just shift Sasov away from him, and he won't worry any more about trifles. So he harnessed the horses, sat Reb Yudel in the waggon, and they went off to a village called Koltov; and it lived up to the meaning of its name in Hebrew (in which tongue it signifies "all good"), for it was full of Jews who treated him well and gave him a lodging and food and money. Nonetheless he complained and moaned continually for having left Sasov. On this occasion Reb Yudel said, It's all right for you now, Reb Nuta, but for me it was better then than now.

Nuta, however, paid no great attention to Reb Yudel's words but took Reb Yudel's stick, put it in Reb Yudel's hand and said, Reb Yudel, come and we'll set about carrying out the commandment of the Bridal Canopy. And he went with Reb Yudel from house to house; and ne'er a house was to be found where they didn't fulfill the commandment of hospitality; while Nuta for his own part carried out the saying of the Midrash, "If it's good for my master it's good for me." From Koltov they next went to Monastrik, which is also full of Jews, no evil eye upon them, so that they can pray in full congregation even on weekdays like the large towns. Reb Yudel stayed there some hours, and they gave him food and money to the best of their powers; and the waggoner, to rhyme, never wasted his time, with here a meal and there a repast, and his team ate their fill and did not need to fast.

From Monastrik they went to Benif village, where there is a famous woman named Deborah who wears leathern stockings and smokes a pipe and has a brandy distillery which is known and famed throughout the land; and she practises hospitality. We have heard tell that Rabbi Meir of Premislein claims that they respect her in Heaven and have declared there aloft that Benif brandy is good; and what they know aloft they know alow.

From Benif they went onto the Holy Congregation of Belkomin, a small town with few folk who go their own righteous way but are rather tight-fisted. From Belkomin they went to Yishkevitz and from Yishkevitz to the Holy Congregation of Alesk, which was formerly a fortified city ruled over by a holy man of God, the righteous Gaon Rabbi Joseph, who left benediction behind him in his book *The Stores of Joseph*. From Alesk they went to Chvatov and from Chvatov to Zahoretz and from Zahoretz to Yeshenev, which is a large village where well-to-do people are to be found. From Yeshenev they made for the village of Wallochei. All that road is one of ups and downs, so that the horses' shoes came off their hoofs. From Wallochei they made for a place called Prelsk. For all the efforts it took them to make Prelsk, when they got there they went empty away. And how was that? Because in the whole of Prelsk there's not a single Jew, but two houses inhabited by two wicked men who keep the forests. Blessed be He who kept Reb Yudel from being torn by the teeth of their dogs.

Peacock had desired to kick them in the belly so that their guts would spill on to the road, but Ivory said to Peacock, Brother Peacock, don't interfere in what's none o' your affair, for fear that what happened to the mouse might happen to you. And what happened to the mouse? asked he. So Ivory began telling him the tale of

THE MOUSE AND THE COCK.

There was a cock that lived with a Jew. He made an easy living and lacked for nothing. Nonetheless he was troubled and worried and never a smile would you catch on his face. When the month of Ellul came round at the end of the summer his troubles were doubled and he'd never crow without bursting into tears. Now a mouse lived there as well. The mouse asks the cock, Choicest of poultry, why dost thou sorrow so? If it be by reason of thy sustenance, 'tis always awaiting thee; and if it be thy dwelling, thou dwellest with human beings; yet despite all this thou 'rt grieved and terrified and quivering and crestfallen like to a helpless and weary cock.

Said he, Hath not Jeremiah said, "Curst be the cock that trusteth in man," while Elihu hath told Job, "Is there an angel over him, a single counselor, one among a thousand, to tell his uprightness to Man?"; all the good things of thy speech are as nought to me when I see the master of the house taking his prayer book in hand. And why? By reason of a certain prayer, in the Order of Prayers, called "Sons of Man"; when he readeth this prayer on the appointed Eve of Atonement he taketh a cock, whirleth it about his head, saith, This cock shall go to death, and handeth it over to the slaughterer. Of me did Jeremiah lament, "I am the cock that have seen affliction."

Said the mouse to the cock, Yet King David, may he rest in peace, hath said in the Psalms, "Which cock shall live and not see death?"; and Job likewise saith, "And cock shall die and waste away." How be it, so long as thy time is not come to be rid of the world, by thy life thou 'rt not yet dead; therefore gird up thy loins as a cock and trust in the Lord; as is said in Jeremiah, "Blest is the cock that trusteth in the Lord", and in Psalms, "Blessed be the cock who hath set his trust in the Lord", and in thee shall be fulfilled the verse of Job, "Thy years as the years of the cock." And if thou dost set thy trust in me, I shall deliver thee from the pitfalls of Mankind, as is written in Job elsewhere, "Deliver him from going down to the pit; I have found a ransom." Said the cock, And how canst thou deliver me from the hand of Man?

Said the mouse, Hast never in thy days heard what my father did to the lion who was bound and captive among Mankind? Father gnawed the ropes and freed the lion. What father did for the king of beasts I can but do for thy cockyness, strongest of birds. But of thee I require that thou shouldst hearken unto me, as Job hath said, "Let a wise cock hearken unto me."

Said the cock to himself, Let the miracle come whence it will, I shall hearken to that which is in his mouth; and to the mouse he said, And how wilt thou act to deliver me?

Said he, Choicest of poultry, the days of the Night Prayers of Penitence that precede the New Year do approach, when men arise betimes to the synagogues; I shall go and eat up the prayer book so that not so much as a single letter shall be left. Said the cock, For Thy salvation have I hoped, O Lord. And when the nights of the Prayers of Penitence came round, the household all went off to the synagogue and left the house without a human being. Out came the mouse from his hole to eat up the prayer book, and thereupon the cat on the watch fell upon him and consumed him.

When Peacock heard the story of the rat and the cock he kept his legs out of the argument and never interfered in what wasn't his own affair. From Prelsk they went on to Zritsh village and from Zritsh to Hiltshitz village and from Hiltshitz to Potshapi. At Potshapi Nuta could have got a new winter sleigh for absolutely the half o' nothing. And how was that? There was a gentile there who was about to wed a wife and needed to buy brandy for the marriage feast, so he was selling his goods and chattels. And why didn't Nuta buy then? Because he depended on the almanac, which prophesied a winter without snow, and did not know that the compiler of the almanac had written expressly, "Yet He who causeth times to change shall do as He will"; so the compiler of the almanac can pardon him his humiliation.

We do not know how the journey continued, for they should have gone on to Kadelbishi and Dubeya; but when we find them again they are on the road to Pedkomin; but the horses had grown accustomed to hasten to town, for in towns it was Reb Yudel's way to spend some time and they could rest; so that they must have gone astray to find themselves where they were.

Nuta stopped them and turned to Podpolni village, and from Podpolni village to Vidri, where there is a big stone house in the middle of the forest, roundish like a sort of hat, without a roof but with very thick walls, and three little houses standing close by: it was called the Round Inn. In that place passers-by and wayfarers would sleep with their eyes open, for no man could be sure that his very teeth wouldn't be stolen from his mouth.

Were we to start telling all that happened to Nuta and his horses at that inn we would never come to an end. During the night, when they were all asleep, thieves came up and blocked the doors of the inn from outside and took the horses out of their stalls. It was a miracle that the building was without a roof; for when Nuta sensed what was happening he climbed up there and jumped down flat on the backs of the thieves, who at once let the horses go and ran away. So Nuta harnessed the horses and betook himself to Tsharnitzi, which is a big village set on a lofty place, and Jews dwell there. They made a stop, drank something hot, went on to Pinkovtsi and from Pinkovtsi made for Pedkomin.

CHAPTER SIX: THE MEN OF THE CITY · A DEBATE UPON WISDOM · A SATISFACTORY INTERPRETATION OF THE FEAST THAT DOES NOT SATISFY THE FEASTERS ⚬ Nuta went off to feed his horses, and Reb Yudel entered the House of Study to pray the Afternoon and Evening Prayers. They greeted him there and asked him whence and whither, in the way of Jewish folk. Reb Yudel opened the letter of the Rabbi of Apta, and it found favor in the eyes of all who saw it, while the garments also stood him in good stead; as Rabbi Yohanan said in the Talmud, "Garments cause esteem." Each one gave his alms, the rich according to his wealth and the poor according to what he could spare. He was especially well treated by a venerable, honored God-fearing man named Reb Manesh Segal, whose heart knew wisdom and who, ever since he had grown to manhood, set aside a tithe of all his profits in a separate box, keeping special account books wherein he reckoned up his Income and Expenditure with his Possessor as one man checks up with another, drawing up a just account year by year and being as exact over a doit as over a hundred gold pieces; for he held that the money was not his own but that of the Holy and Blest One, while he was, as it were, the treasurer in charge of the funds.

Since most of the men of the place were followers of the Rabbi of Apta, they honored Reb Yudel with food and drink, and drew up a list of the wealthy and well to do so that he need not weary his legs calling on men who do not give alms. There was not a wealthy man or well to do whom they did not include in the list; even Heshel, the "enlightened," was not omitted. That same Heshel was to have married the daughter of Reb Manesh, but after he went astray he remained unwedded and unobservant of the commandments.

Said the elders, We are vexed with you, youngsters, for including Heshel on the same page as the God-fearing. Said the youngsters, We are vexed with you elders for desiring to deprive Reb Yudel.

Said the elders, We are vexed with you, youngsters, who are going to a short-coated man that does not trouble regarding commandments. Said the youngsters, His coat may be short, but his pocket is long, and, besides, in the commandments concerning the behavior of

[66]

THE BRIDAL CANOPY

one man toward another he is more observant than many of the
righteous.

Said the elders, And isn't it written clear and plain in the Mishnah,
"You shall not do on a garment composed of mixed materials even
over ten others, and not even to get it past the Customs"; and yet you
want Reb Yudel to go taking money from this man! But we know
that it's not the love of Reb Yudel that takes you to Heshel; it's because you want to see a man learning Gemara with head uncovered.
See to it that no words of heresy enter your ears.

(The elders had found a quotation referring to the Customs,
because Pedkomin is near the frontier and you can find smugglers
there; but most of the inhabitants are God-fearing and whole. I myself knew many householders there who did not as much as touch
anything in the way of business on the day of the New Moon, which
was a festival in days of old.)

Now Heshel, the "enlightened" *maskil,* dwelt outside the town
in a gentile quarter, since to Heshel's mind it was impossible to dwell
in town because of the stench. So he remained without the congregation and without a wife; and he wore a short coat. And although the
coat was short it had in it all the failings in garments classified by
the righteous of the age. Further, he kept company with the "enlightened" or *maskilim* of the period who wrote high-flown and empty
communications; and added his share of vanity and vexation of spirit.

Two youngsters came with Reb Yudel to the maskil. Said the maskil
to them, whose sons are you and what do you seek? Said they, this
Reb Yudel has three daughters of marriageable age and hasn't got
what to marry them off with; and the Rabbi of Apta gave him a
letter of recommendation since he's a fine Jew.

At this Heshel began clapping his hands and calling, Kashi, Kashi.
In came the servant girl dressed in bright colors and with plaits like
waggon ropes. He asked her, *Kashi, tzi to ladni zhid?,* meaning in
the Polish tongue, Is this a fine Jew?

They spoke spiritually and he corporeally. For the Hassid was a
man of fine appearance, beautiful as Joseph, and since he had grown
to manhood no comb had held sway over his beard, while the
hair of his earlocks was clumped and entangled with that of his
beard, in order to conjoin the quality of Judgment symbolized by the
hair of the earlocks with the quality of Mercy symbolized in the
hair of the beard.

THE BRIDAL CANOPY

The servant girl took one look at the Hassid, spat out and left the room. And Reb Yudel already began to fear that he had come among that band of Those that are Without who are called the Foolers, and who attach themselves to a man in order to befool him with mockery.

But Heshel calmed Reb Yudel down, gave him a piece of silver and blessed him with the wish that he would find his daughters bridegrooms healthy as gentiles but with Jewish souls. Reading the rabbi's letter, he praised his sweet style; and here he found an opportunity to presume upon them. Said Heshel to the youngsters, My lads, take care to learn wisdom and style and grammar, for grammar is the foundation of the world. Wherein is a man more than other living creatures? Surely in understanding, in speech and in writing; but if he is not precise and grammatical he might as well be a beast. As the beast in question lows without grammar, so he bellows without grammar. My lads, I tell you every man has to be a man, so that what befell Solomon Jacob should not befall him.

And who was Solomon Jacob, and what befell him? they asked. Said he to them, Before I come to tell you the story of Solomon Jacob I have to tell you the story of Solomon Jacob's bed. Said they, And who's a stopping of you? He shook his finger at them and said, Idle stories you're wanting to hear, eh! And making himself comfortable in his chair, as though his time were all at his own disposal, he began to tell of

SOLOMON JACOB'S BED.

Even if you went from one end of the world to the other, Solomon Jacob used to say when he was in cheerful mood, by your life you won't find any bed like mine. For Solomon Jacob had his couch in the synagogue on the eastern bench, where no seat costs less than two hundred pieces a year; so when he lay down and stretched himself out he would cover five or six places, and five or six places each of them worth two hundred pieces—can you have a more expensive bed?

When does this apply? By day, of course. But at night he would sooner never have been born than make his bed. And how did he make his bed? First Solomon Jacob would take a torn sheet worn out by long use, fold it over, put it under his head and cover himself over with his coat. In the beginning he had used his breeches as a sort of pillow, but when he came to the saying of the sages in the Talmud that the person who places his apparel under his head forgets his studies, he was careful not to do so; but he had to keep his eyes turned away for fear of the temptation. When the beadle was not looking Solomon Jacob would double over the cloth and put it under his head; but miracles don't happen every night; this beadle was as full of eyes as the Angel of Death, and once he had been caught, and his punishment had more than balanced his comfort.

Now, if you suppose that this couch was the property of Solomon Jacob and he could lie down on it whenever he liked, you are mistaken. When the last foot had died away in the market place and men lay stretched on their beds a shopkeeper would suddenly dash into the Close to slake the Holy and Blest One with a page of Gemara, and where should he sit if not on Solomon Jacob's bed? Time and again Solomon Jacob raises his head to see when the man will go, his heart wailing within him, Woe's me, woe's me, when will my bones rest on their couch? And his evil inclinations would be yelling at him, Where is your supper, and troubling him like a snake whose bite in one place is felt in all the limbs. However, Heaven is on his side, for he has already said the prayer before sleep and therefore may not eat. So dust in your eyes to you, Satan.

When the shopkeeper goes out Solomon Jacob does off his vest, pours forth his heart before the merciful God that he may be delivered from thoughts of transgression, stretches himself out comfortably on the bench and closes his eyes. Night being created only for sleep, as we have learnt, let all the kings of east and west come now and he will not move hence.

Thereupon he is overrun by all kinds of bugs and gnats and fleas which rob his eyes of sleep; and in addition unpleasant pains trouble him. The whole world might as well have been stilled and only women left. When Satan comes to the impure the door is open to him, says the Talmud; Satan raises before his eyes the face of that gentile woman who cleans the clothes on the eves of Sabbaths and festivals, with her womb between her teeth, as the Hebrew has it, and her swollen clothes; also the wet nurse at the warden's house who suckles twins at her breast and who once bared a breast and squirted a jet of milk in his face. Alas, where were now those nights when he used to say, "In thy hand I entrust my spirit," and straightway fell asleep?

He knew that he would not be pure again, and that he said in vain the first four Psalms and performed the other corrections of the soul. He was evil, and the Holy and Blest One, as the Midrash tells us, does not desire praise from the evil. But forgetting his suffering and his shame, he would cry out for the shaming of the Divine Presence, and would leap from his bed, wash his hands again and repeat the General Correction of our master, Reb Nachman of blessed memory, or the *Tana Debei Eliyah,* weeping from the overflow of his broken heart, Lord of the Universe, isn't it enough that I remain without a wife and without joy and without blessing and without good, and am not a man? Why must Thou trouble me with evil thoughts and evil imaginings? I know that I am a low and worthless creature and am unworthy of having even a hair's breadth of pleasure from your world; so either take my soul or leave me as a dumb stone lying in its place without sin.

And he would seize his chest with his two hands, pressing his nails into the flesh, and would stand half naked and weeping in the middle of the Close until his blood cooled off. Being thoroughly awakened from his evil inclination he would return to his bed, turn his eyes to the clock on the wall or a soul lamp burning on the anniversary of somebody's death, and would start meditating on his place in the world.

I am twenty-four years old and am still without a wife, so I harm my soul with thoughts of transgression, and harry my bones on this hard bench; and as yet I have not enjoyed a bed. How long? And again and again he would repeat, How long, how long, in a voice sad as the tune of "Oh come my love to meet the bride" on the Sabbath before the Ninth of Ab, when we mourn the Destruction of the Temple; and his body would twist itself up like a question mark in the new-fangled modern books.

How long? Younger than he, who still played at Kid and Wolf, were already married and had children, while he was still single. Was he not a suitable young man? At any rate his spirit was no lower than that of his companions, who existed in the world only in order to permit the execution of the Talmudic Precept, "Take care of the sons of the poor, for from them goeth forth the Torah." Why had they merited to be wed while he, the time for the breaking of his bachelorhood many years overdue, had to have the mercies of the Holy and Blest One turned away from him? And so Solomon Jacob would lie night by night until the footsteps of those who Watch for the Dawn were heard in the courtyard, and he rose, washed his hands, descended from the bench and put away his pillow till the following night.

But the Holy and Blest One does not withhold the reward of any youth. It happened that a village girl, the daughter of a tax collector, had set her eyes on a gentile; so her father desired to marry her off before the whole country talked scandal about her; when he came to town to hear the Book of Esther read he saw Solomon Jacob and found him suitable; they shook hands on it and entered into a match. When the Lord prospers the way of man, says the Book of Proverbs, his enemies also make peace with him; these being, as the Midrash tells us, the fleas and gnats. While even the sheet under his head, on which he had not been able to lie because of its smell, ceased being disgusting from the time the spring sun began shining.

So he lay quietly on the bench as though he were doing it a favor, like a youth who has gone to a distant place of Torah whence he proposes to return. For he was a bridegroom and had a bride; and for the Passover he was invited to the house of his father-in-law-to-be, where they would treat him with honor, give him all kinds of dainties and, above all, prepare him a bed. Not a bed like the one in the Close, but a real, honest-to-goodness bed. So Solomon Jacob lay on the couch in the Close, continually estimating the width of that bed and the number of cushions and pillows it contained, each one marked with the name of his betrothed, as is the custom of the daughters of the rich who embroider their names on their bed linen. Lord of the Universe, in thy great mercies wrinkle up the days that come toward us and speed Passover Eve.

On the Eve of Passover, Solomon Jacob rose early, went down to a warm bath, did on a clean shirt, prayed at sunrise, took a tractate of the Talmud and went out to the village in order to complete the tractate in the presence of his father-in-law-to-be, thereby freeing him from the Fast of the Firstborn. The village was two-hours walk from the town, and those knowing the way used to go skirting the forest by the brook where folk gather willow boughs for the last day of Tabernacles, and save about half an hour. The innkeeper had desired to send a waggon for him, but Solomon Jacob had not wished it, saying, All through the winter I had to frowst in the House of Study; so now I'll walk a while, for there's nothing better for the system after sitting a long time at study than walking along the road; also it's the custom of young men to visit their betrothed afoot. And on the way I'll run over some of the commentaries on tonight's Passover relation so as to spice my father-in-law-to-be's table with them.

In short the sun was shining, the snow was melting away underfoot, gray ooze clung to his legs, the forests remained standing silent and Solomon Jacob went on walking. He knew his father-in-law-to-be was awaiting him, and as soon as he would see him with a Gemara in his hand he would come running toward him and exclaim, Happy is he who comes hither with his Talmud in his hand. And he would answer back, The Talmud permits us the eighth of an eighth of pride.

But it seemed to him that he had already walked more than necessary. He had gone astray, God forbid. The very sun was not so bright in the sky, and evening was beginning to draw near. Solomon Jacob shifted the Gemara from his right hand to his left and reassured himself, quoting, Until the season we begin to pray for dew, which marks the commencement of summer, the sun is no proof of time. Nonetheless he was growing impatient. His legs were quivering and reeling and refused to support his body, while look where he would there was no sign of a house. Who could say when he would reach there?

Why didn't I have a bite before starting out? Because I wanted to finish the tractate in the presence of the tax collector. And if I hadn't gone to the village but stayed in the Close to finish it, some five or six fellows would have joined me, and each would have treated me to some money and a glass of brandy and cake. Arguing that my head couldn't stand six glasses of brandy straight off, still I could have given them to the beadle on condition he returned them to me when called upon to do so after the Passover. Sometimes the heart grows cramped with hunger and a glass of brandy strengthens it. And now all I need is one sip and I can run like a horse. Don't be so clever but forget all your quodlibets, Solomon Jacob, as the Psalmist says, "Commit thy way unto the Lord," etcetera; in a little while you'll be done with all your troubles. A bridegroom in the home of his betrothed—what better can there be?

But maybe he wouldn't get there at all. There's a story of a prince who set out for distant parts. In due time he had to return to his kingdom because of the royal crown and came to a forest filled with all manner of wild beasts—and tomorrow when his father-in-law-to-be goes to pray in town he'll find him lying dead, or gentiles might find him, and he wouldn't even have the last comfort of a Jewish grave.

But while his imagination was terrifying him Solomon Jacob saw a mare tied to the fence of a house and whinnying toward a horse at grass in the meadow, and at once recognized that this was the house of his intended. So Solomon Jacob raised both his eyes on high and offered praise and thanksgiving to The Blessed Name who had led him in the true path; then he looked down in shame and stared at his clothes and boots, which were disgustingly muddy. His betrothed would see him in a few minutes, and what would he have to say for himself? Says the Song of Songs, "Look not upon me that I am dark of hue, that the sun hath made me swart", and the Midrash remarks that these are the disciples of the wise who are ugly as pitch in the present world; but in the hereafter they are radiant as the sun. While another explanation of the phrase, "Look not upon me that I am dark of hue" would have it that these are the disciples of the wise who, though they appear ugly and black in this world, have within them the Torah, the Bible, the Mishnah, the Midrash, the laws of the Talmud, the supplementary Tosephta lore and the legends. Look not upon my misery, "Mine is the silver and Mine is the gold saith the Lord of Hosts", as we find in Haggai.

Out came his father-in-law-to-be, greeted him and showed him the greatest possible affection all the way to the house. For he had already feared that jealous folk might have intervened and seduced the bridegroom to change his mind. Said the father-in-law to Solomon Jacob, If I had known that you would get yourself lost on the way I would have sent the waggon for you; you can't imagine how worried we were for fear some sort of accident might have happened to you. Solomon Jacob nodded his head, entered with the other, kissed the mezuzah, and tears started from his eyes. For his proposed father-in-law had said, How worried we were, as though he were a person about whose well-being people troubled themselves. Had it been good manners he would have swung like an ape from the lintel of the door in praise and thanksgiving.

While he stood so, his betrothed came out of the kitchen and stood before him pink and pretty, her plaits in her right hand and a smile on her lips. Shifting her plaits to her left hand she greeted him, and as her plump hand gripped his a quiver passed through him so that his tongue shriveled up, and he lost his power of speech. He bowed his shoulders even more, bent his hand and gripped the back of the Gemara firmly with his fingers. Said his betrothed, Put away your Bible and sit down; and she took it out of his hands gently and set it on the table.

In came his mother-in-law-to-be, in festival array, veiled and adorned like a dowager, with felt shoes on her feet which had grown swollen during the winter while she stood out in the open to prevent her daughter meeting that gentile. When she saw Solomon Jacob she smiled at him, said, Blest be he who comes, and showed how glad she was at his presence. Said the betrothed of Solomon Jacob to her mother, Mother, maybe he'll eat a little. Her mother rebuked her affectionately, saying, Silly, don't you know it's time for the Afternoon Prayers? And she said to Solomon Jacob, And how should she know seeing she's lived all her life in the village? But now please God, I'm sure you'll teach her, Solomon Jacob.

Solomon Jacob set his right hand on his heart in oath, raised his two eyes and looked into vacancy. Back came the wench, took her plaits in her right hand, took a pin out of her hair, put it between her teeth, flung her hair back behind her and ran away so that nothing was left but the scent of her. Her mother shook her head, called her a hind and indicated her to Solomon Jacob. Meanwhile the father-in-law-to-be returned with two prayer books, one for himself and the other for Solomon Jacob. And they rose to pray the Afternoon and Evening Prayers.

The house was bright with the festival lights; the table was spread with matzos, wine, meat, sheepshank and green parsley. And in the odor from the kitchen were mingled fat and the bride's scent.

The innkeeper did on the shroud in accordance with custom, examined the table to see that everything was prepared according to ritual, and hallowed the wine. Solomon Jacob also took goblet in hand and hallowed to a sweet chant. The bride's mother poured a second glass and the girl began asking the traditional questions, "How does this night differ from all others?" Her plump chin moved on her neck, her teeth blossomed between her red lips and her voice was like matzos being broken. Solomon Jacob took hold of the edge of the table and inhaled her breath. The father-in-law-to-be straightened his apparel, leaned back comfortably, took the Hagada in hand and enthusiastically replied, "Slaves were we in Egypt." And he went on reading with enthusiasm till they reached the meal interval.

And Solomon Jacob read out of the same Hagada as his betrothed, holding his breath so that she shouldn't feel his presence, while she, far from being frightened by him, was actually touching him. And when they ate she passed him all the good portions. Solomon Jacob thrust his fork into the meat, pushed it about on the dish, pressed the pieces with clumsy fingers, felt sad at heart that he had no knowledge of the ways of the world and felt himself out of all place. Said he to himself, Although my lips find it hard to thank her, still my heart is prepared to fulfill in her regard the Talmudic adage, "Hold your wives dear."

The Eve-of-Passover service ended; the father-in-law and mother-in-law-to-be began dozing, while Solomon Jacob and his betrothed remained sitting together reading the Song of Songs, as is done on Passover Eve. Solomon Jacob kept his finger on the place and interpreted for her in accordance with the commentary of Rashi, "Behold thou art beautiful, my love, behold thou art beautiful, thine eyes are doves; as the dove which, once she knows her match and pair, does not permit him to pair with another", and so on.

The candles began guttering. There was a whistle outside. The wench started but immediately went on reading in a sweet and happy voice, " 'Tis the voice of my love; behold he cometh." And Solomon Jacob, keeping his finger on the place, went on interpreting in accordance with Rashi, "The poet returns to the beginning like a man who stops short and returns saying, I never told you the beginning. Behold he standeth behind our wall, peering through the windows, peeping through the lattice chinks." And so they read until they finished the book.

After they ended she rose, kissed the book, took Solomon Jacob by the hand, led him quietly past the sleepers so as not to awaken them, opened a door and led him into a room scented with pillows and cushions, set a candle on the table and said, Here's your bed, Solomon Jacob; lie down in peace and rest upon it in peace. And as she went out she turned her face back, smiled at him, closed the door behind her and vanished. Solomon Jacob straightened his earlocks, made a queer grimace, sat down on the chair, inhaled the fragrance of the pillows and the cushions, did off his clothes and removed his boots. Heaven's aid being heaven's aid, it was a great pity that on this night the Prayer before Slumber included no more than the Hear O Israel. Offering praises and thanksgiving to The Blessed Name he turned back the sheets.

From the pillows was wafted a pleasing and gentle coolness. Stripped of his clothes he stood beside the bed. How many pillows there were here, and how many sheets! Had he not been troubled at the idea of crushing the sheets he would have stretched himself out and fallen asleep at once. The verses of the Song of Songs were still whispered by his lips in couplets, "Behold thou art fair, my love, and our couch is likewise fresh; the voice of my love that knocketh, open to me; they have taken my veil from me, I did not know my mind." Copper bowls and tin dishes gleamed from the wall, smiling at him; it encouraged him and he lifted his foot toward the bed.

But ere he entered the bed he heard the housewife weeping. Had the evil eye gained sway, God forbid, over his betrothed? Solomon Jacob turned his face toward the window and saw the housewife standing with arms outstretched, howling and wailing and weeping, while his father-in-law-to-be ran half naked after a coach which was dashing off as though driven by furies. Suddenly the crack of a whip rent the air. His father-in-law-to-have-been came stumbling back, his hand over his cheek, crying, There's no daughter, no daughter. Solomon Jacob's betrothed had fled with her gentile lover.

Tears welling into Solomon Jacob's eyes stuck his upper and lower eyelashes together. One scalding tear dropped onto his right leg, which was lifted to the edge of the bed; and so he stood.

> *Here ends the story of Solomon Jacob*
> *And all of his power and might.*
> *Sweet youths, may it never fall to your lot*
> *To lie on his bed at night.*

Have you listened, lads? Heshel asked the youngsters. Said they, Lord of Abraham, what astonishing things happen in the world! And what was the end of Solomon Jacob? Said he to them, My sons, what more can I tell you than I have told you? Solomon Jacob, who studied the Bible a great deal and the Talmud a great deal and spent his life in the House of Study, and derived not even as much as his little finger was worth of pleasure out of the world—why was he punished so much? Because he never learnt anything except Torah. My sons, it is a man's duty to know writing and other tongues, and anyone who does not know writing and other tongues is called contemptible; as our sages of blessed memory remark in the Talmud about the verse in Obadiah, "Thou art extremely contemptible", because they know neither writing nor other languages. And they also say elsewhere in the Talmud that a disciple of the wise has to know to write.

Said the lads, But didn't the Maharsho explain there that writing means he should accustom himself to writing scrolls of the Torah, Tefillin and Mezuzoth? Said he to them, I knqw what the Maharsho explains, but I tell you that now we may not refrain from learning the writing and languages of the people among whom we live and from whom we make our living. In the Book of the Covenant it says, He who wishes to make his sons free and to spread his seed wide amid the nations will, when they are small, teach them the writing and language of the peoples; and daily experience testifies to this.

Said Reb Yudel to the youngsters, Leave me to answer him. Then Reb Yudel said to him, And doesn't it say in the *Tana Debei Eliyah* that they shall not learn the language of Egypt, and mean nevermore? Said he, Their reason was because of idolatry, since the writing and language of Egypt were based on their idolatry; but other languages of the peoples have nothing of idolatry in them, and there is no prohibition against their study. And thus we are told that the members of the Sanhedrin of old in Jerusalem knew seventy tongues.

Said he, If you have studied you haven't revised, and if you've revised you haven't descended to the ultimate meaning of the sages. The words of the Torah are sparse in one spot and plentiful elsewhere. What is concealed here is explicitly revealed in the Kabbala-book Zohar, "The Sanhedrin knew seventy tongues, which are seventy aspects of the Torah." In addition the Talmud says, "Petahiah is Mordecai, and he was called Petahiah (the Opener), because he opened matters and expounded them and knew seventy tongues," whence you may know that he used to expound the Torah in seventy aspects.

Happy is he who holds aloof from the wisdom of the world; and he who studies is under a curse, as our rabbis of blessed memory said in the Talmud, "Curst is the man who teaches his son Greek wisdom"; and the numerical value of the letters composing "Greek" amount to two hundred and eighty-one, which is the number of Lilith and her hosts; for all the external wisdoms come from the wisdom of the Greeks, for the ancient philosophers were Greeks who received their wisdom from the Greeks, who inherited it from the Bnei Kedem, the latter having been the sons of the concubines of Abraham who received these wisdoms from him; as we find in the legend that the presents that Abraham gave to the sons of the concubines were the Names of Pollution. But the knowledge of the Blessed Name, which was all he had, he gave to his son, our father, Isaac.

And you know there was nobody greater among the nations of the world than Aristotle, and we find he confessed to Simeon the saintly high priest that the Torah of Moses is true; and he became a convert and wrote a letter to his pupil, Alexander of Macedon, in which he gives praise and thanksgiving to The Blessed Name who delivered him from the foolishness which is philosophy; and had he been able to gather all his books together he would have burnt them so as not to spoil people's minds, philosophy being falsehood and those who have any truck with it going down to the pit; whereas those who hold fast to the Torah shall walk in the light alive.

All Joshua Heshel's arguments were silenced and he couldn't open his mouth, but fulfilled the words of the Ethics of the Fathers, "I have found nothing better for a body than silence." Reb Yudel told us, It was hard for me then, when I stood debating with Heshel, for all that I worsted him; his movements were calm, and as he went about his room he took a pace and stopped, took another and stopped and looked round unconsciously in all directions; or else he turned his head back and sat with his head bent to the left and tears, as it were, gathering in his eyes. And Reb Yudel added, In books I have seen it written that such is the face of those born under the planet Venus; and all their days long they are attracted toward transgression and are affectionately esteemed by all who see them; and these are liable to follow them because of their affection. But the wise man has eyes in his head in order not to stand within their bounds and not look upon their faces.

But meanwhile Reb Yudel said to the youngsters, The beginning of wisdom is the fear of the Lord. The sun is declining and we have not yet said the Afternoon Prayers; and he straightway dragged them to the House of Study, where they prayed the Afternoon and Evening Prayers among the God-fearing who, even if they do something unfit, do it only for the purposes of the commandment, as to pay the wages of the teacher or to buy an extra fine citron for the Tabernacles festival.

Between the Afternoon and Evening Services they related what the "enlightened" *maskil* had said and the answer they had given him. The entire House of Study mocked him, together with the whole Grammar which those "enlightened" *maskilim* had made up out of their heads. Nor should you be surprised at the ancients who grammarized, as we find Rashi of blessed memory doing in many a place; for this matter is akin to that of the high places on which our forefathers used to offer up sacrifices; but when the nations of the world began copying their deeds they were forbidden for Israel.

We mentioned above that that selfsame "enlightened" *maskil,* Joshua Heshel, had studied much Torah and was a prodigy and a Constant Student. Reb Menahem Manesh Segal had already desired to wed him to his daughter; but he went after his eyes and turned these on another woman, and was reft of Torah and reft of greatness. What was in his hand was taken from him, and what he sought was not given him. And this, then, was the tale of

TORAH AND GREATNESS.

Of Reb Menahem Manesh Segal folk said that, had he not feared an evil eye, he would have had both his daughters brought under the Bridal Canopy at one and the same time; for there was a bridegroom ready waiting even for the younger one. When the town judge had gone to test the knowledge of the lads he found two gold vessels, both of them worthy of the daughter of Reb Menahem Manesh; but since it is impossible for two kings to use one crown, and since neither one displaced the other, he made no choice between them. So Reb Menahem Manesh found him silent, and Reb Menahem began to wonder whether he had troubled him in vain.

Said the judge to him, I have found two scabbards for the Torah, both of them equal, but who shall undertake to choose between the two? Reb Menahem Manesh answered, That's what the sages meant when they said in the Talmud that a judge knows nothing more than what his eyes see. I have a second daughter who has also reached her term; let the older be for the older and the younger for the younger. And he applied to himself the saying, While your fire burns cut your pumpkins and roast them.

What did he do but take Abraham Isaac, the older one, for his first daughter and keep an eye on Joshua Heshel for his younger daughter; as it is said, Older for older and younger for younger. Whoever saw the two fine lads could exclaim, Blest is he who has chosen them and their studies. And since everybody knew that Joshua Heshel was going to marry the daughter of Reb Menahem Manesh they began to treat him with respect. The warden of the House of Study used to summon him to read the final section of the Portion of the Week, and the beadle never plagued his life because of the number of candles he used, as is the way of beadles toward ordinary students. While when the young married men, who came from elsewhere, used to speak to him they always used to slur their pronunciation so as not to thou-thee him as young married men do the lads.

And what did Joshua Heshel resemble? A bridegroom, save that no gold chain had yet been hung on his coat. He too began to take care of himself, and when he saw a fleck on his jacket he would remove it. If it was cold without he would cough like a delicate man, while if the sun were shining he would fan himself with the handkerchief in his pocket. And thenceforward his fingers were always at his earlocks to make them into two rings. When the elders went out to chat he would follow them, his left thumb in his girdle and his right finger and thumb curling his earlocks. He stopped playing "kid and wolf" with the boys, and used to play chess with the young married men.

Even the woman who was paid to supply Joshua Heshel's meals began to improve his food. What she gave for breakfast she never gave for supper, and what she gave for supper she never gave for breakfast. She knew that Joshua Heshel was going to marry the daughter of Reb Menahem Manesh, and said to herself, Since he's about to enter the house of a wealthy man, and a bridegroom is petted in his bride's house, I'll accustom him to pleasant dishes so that he may not remember my table for dispraise, nor come to a change of diet which is the commencement of bowel sickness. She too began speaking to him with respect and added the "Master" to his name, calling him *Reb* Joshua Heshel; and she was very grieved that her daughter Hasya had no respect for him but went on calling him Heshel even in front of other people, just as though he were a poor lad, not the person whom Reb Menahem Manesh had chosen for his daughter. And it even happened that once, when she gave him water to wash his hands before the Grace after Meals, she spilled it over a fine coat which he had put on the day the town heard he was to be a bridegroom. But the truth of the matter was that Joshua Heshel's heart did not turn to the daughter of Reb Menahem Manesh, for ever since he ate at the widow's he had his eyes on her daughter, Hasya, and she had hers on him; but the matter had not yet been revealed. The heart had not revealed it to the lips.

Meanwhile the townsfolk began making preparations for the marriage of the daughter of Reb Menahem Manesh, for there was nobody in town that wasn't closely associated with him; one prayed with Reb Menahem Manesh in a certain holy place, another had met Reb Menahem Manesh at a religious feast and had given him advice about painting his fences, a third had borrowed an accommodation loan from Reb Menahem Manesh—not that he had needed to borrow, but in order to establish a friendly footing—while a fourth still owed Reb Menahem Manesh an old debt. And invitations were already beginning to go out from Reb Menahem Manesh's house. The wags took their invitations and sent them on to all the people on bad terms with Reb Menahem Manesh. They would not come but would send wedding presents; they would have no satisfaction of the wedding feast but would give presents. Reb Menahem Manesh being good-humored, there was no fear that he would be angry.

And besides those coming because of Reb Menahem, there were those coming because of the bridegroom, who came from the House of Study where all are kin and brethren. If The Name gives a bride, the relations by marriage come of themselves. And besides those coming in virtue of the bridegroom there were those who came in virtue of Joshua Heshel. As everybody knew, Joshua Heshel was intended for the rich man's younger daughter, so he was like a bridegroom and his friends and kinsfolk were also kinsfolk for the purposes of the wedding.

The lads began making preparations for tripping up the bridegroom in the course of his homily. They used to come to him as he sat studying, and encircle him with questions so as to excogitate, by means of cross-questioning, the law on which he had chosen to speak.

But the wide-awake keep their hearts to themselves, and he would divert them to some other issue. If he were studying the law of the man who marries a gentile woman he would divert them to the law regarding the invalidity or otherwise of the act of *halitza* when performed with the left hand; if he were studying the law of the marriage of a half-slave, half-freeman being no marriage he would jump quickly over to the law regarding the trustworthiness of a man who seizes all his wife has and says that she is rebellious.

And Joshua Heshel also set himself in the House of Study and devoted himself to the entire Six Orders of the Talmud. Now why? Folk said it was because Simeon Phineas was going to try and hunt him down. Simeon Phineas had set his eyes on the younger daughter of Reb Menahem Manesh, and wished to supplant Joshua Heshel. Everybody knew that nothing was behind it. Was it likely that Reb Menahem Manesh would let Joshua Heshel go? Theoretically, of course, it was possible. After all, the match had not yet been made, and things are different beforehand. And further, the thing that makes you say Yes leads me to say No. Why has Reb Menahem Manesh set his eye on Joshua Heshel if not because he stands above the rest? Now if Simeon Phineas should surmount him, what point would there be in keeping Joshua Heshel? So it must be a case of the stronger winning and the winner getting the daughter.

The truth of the matter was that this was so much wordy and worthless disputation; for had Joshua Heshel not been unmarried he would long have had his rabbinical dispensation, permitting him to give instruction and to act as judge. And he had not received it because the rabbi was careful not to give ordination to an unmarried youth; for as long as a man is unmarried he is like snow before Hanuka, lacking permanence. And who was Simeon Phineas, pray, to overwhelm him in law? Joshua Heshel need but bare his arm and Simeon Phineas would lie stretched before him like a corpse. Dwarf that he was, did he suppose that, because the rabbi had given him his old robe for overcoming the slaughterer in regard to questionable conditions in the lungs of slaughtered animals, he was a great man? What did he look like in that robe other than a flea in a slipper?

Nonetheless Joshua Heshel never left the House of Study and was precise to a hair's breadth with those around him. Joshua Heshel knew that his comrade, Simeon Phineas, had the use of books that

are out of general reference, and who knows whose Torah he might
not utter? The matter might be compared, by way of a parable, to the
story of the rich man who arranged a match with a poor one. The
rich man began preparing himself all manner of fine clothes. Folk
said, You're a rich man with lots of fine clothes, so why do you need
fresh? Particularly as your new relation by marriage is a poor man
whose festival garb isn't as good as your Ninth of Ab mourning
array. Said the rich man to them, If my new kinsman by marriage
were wealthy I would know that he would clothe himself in whatever garments he has; but since he's a poor man and will have to
borrow his garments from others, he may go and borrow them from
the prince; so I have to be very particular about my clothes in order
not to be shamed by him.

All the townsfolk came to the wedding of the daughter of Reb
Menahem Manesh, and washed their hands and broke bread and
brought the bride into the big room and sat her beside the bridegroom. When they were all in place and eating, the musicians began
playing. Wine had been poured into the flute, and when the flute
player began to play it squirted out over his face, and those assembled
grew still merrier, began clapping their hands, raised their feet on
high and began dancing before the bride, crying to one another in
the words of the Talmud, How do we dance before the bride? And
they responded to each other, Lovable and pleasing bride. And they
went on dancing and repeating, How do we dance before the bride?
And they went on dancing and responding, Lovable and pleasing
bride.

The bride sat at the bridegroom's right hand, her face red with
shame, moistening her parted lips with the gold broth she ate from
the same dish as the bridegroom; the waiters brought meat and the
guests loosened their girdles, their forks sank into fat and the silence
of eating fell upon the house. High on the wall gleamed the portraits
of the sages of Israel; above them sat Moses our Master with the
two Tables of the Covenant in his hand; and facing him sat King
Solomon composed of the verses of Ecclesiastes, sitting on a high and
lofty chair with lions and leopards couching at his feet; and in large
black letters could be seen the words from his book, "And of mirth,
what doth it achieve?"

The rabbi, who never ate on weekdays and never ate meat outside
his own house, sat twiddling his fingers; when he grew tired he said

to the bridegroom, Bridegroom, say something to us. So the bridegroom rose to his feet and delivered a long homily as to whether a bride may be gazed at to endear her to her husband, and came to the conclusion that it was permissible to look at the adornments she wore on the first day for the sake of endearment. He finished his homily, wiped off the sweat from his brow and sat down like a man who has removed a heavy load he was carrying on his shoulders, and having removed it desires nothing more, the removal being its own reward.

Said the judge to the youngsters, Youngsters, why don't we hear your voices? Said the marriage jester, Rabbi, they're afraid they may startle the poultry in the plates.

Then Joshua Heshel rose to his feet and said, Bridegroom, let your ears hear what your mouth has said. On what authority do you find it permissible to gaze at the bride's adornments if not that of the Rosh in such and such a commentary of his? But even the Rosh only permits her litter to be gazed at for the purposes of evidence, allowing witnesses to testify that such and such a woman went forth in a veil with her head disheveled; and permission was given only because of the necessity; for were it not so who could testify that she was a virgin? But concerning the other adornments regarding which no evidence is taken—in spite of all you say it is prohibited to gaze upon them.

Here Simeon Phineas arose, not quite sure yet with whom he should disagree, whether to argue against the words of the bridegroom or the words of Joshua Heshel. But when he smelt the odor of the furs of which the *streimel* on Joshua Heshel's head was made, he began to cluck behind him like a chicken and cried, Joshua Heshel, before you begin chopping logic with the Rosh, first have a look at the distinction he makes between the matter of the veil on the head of the bride and the matter of gazing at her face. No distinction is ever made between the veil and the remainder of her adornments; and just as you may look at the bridal veil so you may gaze at the remainder of the adornments of the bride, for were it prohibited how could witnesses be permitted to look in order to testify? Do we advise a man to sin in order to acquit his fellow?

Said Joshua Heshel, Simeon Phineas, why must you go confusing one point with another? I was only dealing with the first point of the Rosh which is the essence of the matter; the explanation is that the witnesses had seen the veil beforehand and heard from the guests that the veil was intended for the bride. Hence it follows that so much as looking at the veil when it is upon the head of the bride is prohibited, which must then of necessity follow regarding the other adornments; otherwise you have the Rosh erring with regard to a Mishnaic tradition reported in the Gemara. For in such and such a place we learn as a Mishnaic tradition that a man should not gaze at a beautiful woman and so forth, nor upon the colored garments of a woman. And the Mishnaic tradition makes no distinction between a bride on the first day of marriage and all other women.

Simeon Phineas caught Joshua Heshel by his kaftan and said, Scholard that you are, you've been careful not to have the Rosh erring with regard to a Mishnaic tradition, while you yourself have erred regarding a clearly enunciated law in the Shulchan Aruch, where Rabbi Moses Isserles expressly states, "But it is permissible to gaze upon the adornments she wears!" And if you tell me that the author of the Perisha commentary disagrees with Rabbi Moses Isserles—— When it's a question of master and pupil whom do you listen to if not the master?

Joshua Heshel stretched out his arm, narrowed his gaze upon Simeon Phineas like a huntsman who sees some tiny quarry in front of him, and twisted his pleasant lips in contemptuous mockery. But that moment he saw the face of Hasya pink with jealous despair, and all his argumentations were stopped, and the power of speech left him. The judge looked at him and said, Joshua Heshel, the joy of a man is the response of his mouth, says Holy Writ. Open thy mouth and let thy words shine forth.

But the answering point trembling on Joshua Heshel's lips never came to expression, and the thumb all ready to pounce upon the weak point in his comrade's words hung wearily in the air. And he in turn let his eyes sink into the visage of Hasya, the widow's daughter.

He knew that what he was doing had no sense, but wished to be rid of the disputation with his comrade. The reins counseled, the heart understood, but the tongue came to no expression. His limbs grew weaker, his lids began closing on his eyes, a pleasant forgetfulness putting his whole body to sleep took possession of him. His head was heavy as a stone jar filled with wine, and a loving smile hovered upon his pleasant lips. And the guests shook their heads and said, Joshua Heshel is cut off from his bride, Joshua Heshel is cut off from the household of Reb Menahem Manesh.

> *Such is the tale of Heshel*
> *Who on beauty turned his eyes,*
> *To be tumbled from his greatness,*
> *A warning to the wise.*

Having ended the prayers, Alter, the slaughterer, invited Reb Yudel to eat with him. Now there was a wag there named Hayyim Jonah who said to Alter, Reb Alter, let Reb Yudel go for he has already been invited by Reb Misery. Hayyim Jonah was tricky and brought Reb Misery into it in order to load him with a guest when Reb Misery would have no opportunity of evading the imposition because of all the people present. All the congregation wondered, for they were accustomed to say of Reb Misery that no man had ever broken bread with him, nor had a guest ever kissed the mezuzah at his door; for Reb Misery was a great miser who used to lend money at high interest to poor shopkeepers and would sit at the entrance to the shops; when the shopkeeper measured a quantity of rice or millet or grits or salt, and a grain or two were left in the measure, he would take it and put it in a bag inside his coat. And he carried a bottle, so that when the shopkeeper measured a doit's worth of oil and a drop were left in the measure, he would squeeze the measure to make the drop trickle out into his bottle. And on that feasted he and his household.

The miser had to agree despite himself, tugged the Hassid by his robe and urged him to hasten. And why? Because if he were to loiter he increased his hunger and would finish up by eating double. And so they set out, Reb Misery walking after his fashion, quickly and impetuously, but stopping all of a sudden and looking down at the ground. Often he would turn round and look behind and cower down. The wags used to say that he did so because he wished to spare the ground the full weight of the body upon it. And he would twist his fingers and stare at Reb Yudel, covering his eyes with his lids so that Reb Yudel should not notice.

They went all the way to a dark house. Then Reb Misery asked Reb Yudel, Why did you have to come with me? God forbid that I should be chary of guests, for no house should be closed before any Jew; only what am I sorry for? That elsewhere they'd have fed you on fatlings while with me you fall on grits or millet. And he urged his wife to bring his meal with two spoons. Said his wife, Why do you need two spoons? That's what folk say, When the miser becomes a spendthrift he eats with two spoons. We have a guest, said Reb Misery. What have we? asked Reb Misery's wife of him. Said Reb Misery, A guest. Do you think that my breath lessens his appetite? A guest we have, I tell you, a guest's been thrust my way. Some godless joker put up this here Jew to come and fast with me.

Then Reb Misery's wife raised her voice and cried, May all my evil dreams fall on his head, what can I give this here guest of yours? He had to go searching to find guests. And while still speaking she had to come and take a look at the novelty with her own eyes. Hush, hush, hush, do you think the food's cooking by the Unuttered Name? Wood, wood. May fire burn you, you wicked thing. The wood's a burning, and she has to stand here staring at comedies!

Out she went and brought in a millet dish with two little wooden spoons. Reb Misery took out his bottle, counted in three precise drops of oil to flavor the millet, stuck a wick in the dish and lit it for light. So the light burnt on the one side of the dish and from the other side he ate and advised Reb Yudel not to set his teeth in the spoon but to lick it clean, for teeth are bad for wood. And the Hassid sat with the miser until the moon rose, when the miser puts out the light and the Hassid gets up and goes.

On the morrow he was invited by a decent householder who spread before him a full table that made up for the previous day. Said the householder to Reb Yudel, We knew you'd be sorry for what you'd get, but how could we let something pass, the like of which isn't even reported in the community book? And in the course of the meal he told him how a certain widow had settled a lot of money on Reb Misery so that he should marry her daughter; and because of a pair of woolen-lined slippers, which she had promised him and never gave him, he had given his wife a divorce; and the widow had cursed him to have no pleasure of the world, and her curse had been fulfilled, for there was never a miser so stingy and mean as he.

And on the Holy Sabbath the Gaon and Father of the Court invited Reb Yudel. And the Gaon and Father of the Court was a great and acute mind and a Kabbalist, being one of those Hassidim who never united with the pupils of the Baal Shem Tov of blessed memory; he used to fast from one Sabbath to the next, and said the hallowing over wine in a beer mug and would eat a whole round cake with butter, then drink another mug like the first of grape wine, repeat the rest of the blessings and wash his hands for the meal. They brought him a dish filled with twelve big slices of fish and twelve big Sabbath loaves; he would eat these together with the fish, and drink a glass of brandy big as Elijah's glass in order to fine his tripes; after this they would bring him a huge bowl of broth, and he would drink another glass of grape wine after it and eat a huge quantity of meat, roast and underdone, and seven kinds of dessert; and say grace after meals over a glass of wine. And when midnight came they roused him from Heaven to rise, and he would move his members a little and entreat by reason of the weariness and the fasting and the feasting and would say, Maybe you can get on there without me?

As he did on Sabbath eves, so he did on the Sabbath morn. That Sabbath was the Sabbath of the New Moon which occurs during Hanukah, so at the rabbi's house they had prepared three different kinds of pudding, one for the Holy Sabbath, one for the Sabbath of the New Moon and one for the Sabbath of Hanukah. How much satisfaction he gathered in his quarters!

Reb Yudel remained in the town another few days; one day he ate with Reb Alter, another day with Reb Manesh and a third day with the philanthropic Chief of the District, Reb Samuel, after whom I am named; he was the father of my grandsire, Reb Zvi Aryeh, and Reb Zvi Aryeh was the sire of my father who taught me, Reb Shulem Mordecai, may their righteous memories be a blessing. And he himself acted for the public weal in finding hosts for such a God-fearing disciple of the wise; and he prayed many prayers in many a House of Study and learnt many fine and upright customs from the fine and upright.

And Reb Yudel could already have left Pedkomin, for there was nobody with the means who had not given him alms, the rich according to his riches and the poor according to his need; but he still had something to learn there. One day he stood in the House of Study repeating the Evening Prayers, when there entered a poor man dressed in rags, named Reb Joshua Eleazar. Looking at his face you could see that it wasn't merely after the festivals that he fasted on Mondays and Thursdays; and at home he had a wife sick with all kinds of diseases, may the Merciful One deliver us.

Don't be thinking that a wonder happened to him through Reb Yudel as had happened to Zipporah, the dairyman's daughter; but you can learn the right way, for all the troubles of time did not cause the poor man to stop bearing everything with love, and carrying out the commandment of hospitality. Said the poor man to Reb Yudel, Reb Yudel, come with me to eat supper. Said he, Wait for me until the orphans have ended the Memorial Prayer. I fear, said he, that someone else may precede me. Said Reb Yudel, I go only with you.

They went through dark and narrow alleys till they came to a veritable ruin. There he took Reb Yudel by the arm and said, Be careful not to fall; there are thirteen steps here. And he began descending, counting one, two and three, and warning him not to stumble at the last one; for there's always one step more than you expect.

Together they entered a vault which was damp from within and into which gutter water ran from without; and its walls were cracked, with vermin of different kinds crawling about them. The householder stopped, kissed the mezuzah, held out his arms and said, Blest is he who comes, struck a light, put his hand into the oven, took out a dish filled with potatoes, sprinkled salt over them, said, Let us sit and eat, and said the blessing with great gladness.

Seeing that Reb Yudel did not eat, he said, Why aren't you eating? Reb Yudel gave no answer. Said the other, Do you fear that they haven't been cooked enough and so may harm your system? By your life they've been standing cooked ever since yesterday. I knew that the Holy and Blest One would not withhold his mercies from me but would send me a guest, so I left them over to eat together with my guest.

Said Reb Yudel to him, By my faith I have no fear for my system; but I did fear that I might transgress the words of our sage Maimonides of blessed memory, who said a newcomer should not eat of a meal which is not sufficient for those already there.

Said the other, Reb Yudel, I am astonished that you never penetrated to the full meaning of their blessed saying. What is a meal that is insufficient for those already there? That means a meal in which the victuals themselves do not satisfy them; for instance, they have bread and wish for radish, they have radish and wish for onions, they have onions but long for a drop of oil; it is assuredly impermissible to enjoy a meal with such people, who are not satisfied with what they have; but as for me, recognizing the goodness of His Blessed Name as I do for every crumb He prepares for me, can you possibly withhold your hand from my meal? And still more, even at such times as my very soul goes out with hunger I thrust temptation from me saying, And how do I know that the food would suit me? Maybe it would harm me; so rather than desire to eat it would be better for me to bless in accordance with the words of Deuteronomy, "And ye shall be exceeding heedful to your souls."

Reb Yudel, hearing these words, seized his beard and said, Had I come only to learn this thing of you it would have been sufficient; and he said his blessing and ate. In the course of their meal Reb Joshua Eleazar said to Reb Yudel, come and see how great are the works of the Lord. Although these potatoes are not of the seven kinds of fruit that grow in the Land of Israel, nevertheless the Holy and Blest One put into them strength sufficient to sustain a Jew.

While they were sitting so, a thin cry came from behind a screen, Lazi, Lazi. Joshua Eleazar rose and said, Is all well with you, Feigele? I'm here. The voice came again, Who's there? Joshua Eleazar answered, A Jew named Reb Yudel. Again came the voice, Lazi, and what is he doing here? I invited him, Feigele, answered Joshua Eleazar, to sup with me.

Then came the voice again, May his food be tasty and good. Lazi, Lazi. Joshua Eleazar answered afresh, I'm here close by to you, Feigele. Do you need anything? What shall we give the guest, asked the voice. I'm giving him potatoes, replied her husband.

Where have you potatoes from, asked the voice again. Yesterday, replied Joshua Eleazar, I brought potatoes and boiled them and left them in the oven. Back came the voice, Liar that you are, and yesterday you told me you had eaten enough.

Feigele, answered Joshua Eleazar, by your life I never lied to you; I was quite satisfied then. Said Feigele, But Lazi, how can you say you were satisfied when you never ate anything? Then her husband said, The fact is this: I was just about to eat when I suddenly thought of inviting a guest, and I was so happy at my resolve that I forgot to eat.

You should have told me the truth, said Feigele. I was afraid, confessed Joshua Eleazar, that you might be vexed with me. Then Feigele said, Lazi, Lazi, how could I be vexed with you? And so, said Joshua Eleazar, you're not vexed with me, Feigele? God forbid, she answered, and now don't neglect your guest.

So Joshua Eleazar came back to Reb Yudel. Said Reb Yudel, You look as though something had made you happy. To be sure something has, he answered, since I am among those who merit to be aided by my wife.

When they parted Joshua Eleazar sighed and said, I wish to conjoin myself in that commandment of bringing the bride under the canopy; but what can I do when I have nothing. But before Reb Yudel had gone forth Joshua Eleazar broke off a sort of silver coin which he had hanging on a chain round his neck and said, My mother, may she rest in peace, tied this charm round my neck so that the evil eye might never hold sway over me; Reb Yudel, I beseech you to take it so that I may share in that commandment. He who keeps the commandments shall not know evil, so I have nought to fear.

CHAPTER SEVEN: THE SINCERE IN THE WAY · TWO
REB YUDELS ॐ On the Sabbath following the Sabbath of
Hanukah the Hassid was to be found in the village of Pole-
krif, a league from the town; and in the village was a Jewish leaseholder named Tovya, who was a far-famed doer of charity and who
held open house. He had a big house full of rooms, in each of which
was a bed and a chair and a lamp; and the guests stayed there. Each
wayfarer had the right to stay there a whole week, with the householder satisfying all his requirements; and on the Sabbath they all
ate at his table, save that the men ate with him and the women with
his wife. If anybody came with a wife and children they were sup-
plied a special room, since the householder wished to preserve decency.

And there was a woman's house where poor women stayed, and
it was a distance from the men's house so that nothing untoward
might befall. And the mistress of the house herself kept an eye on
the purity of the dishes. When they departed the leaseholder would
give them an alms; he would give to the men, and his wife to the
women.

And he had a particularly fine custom; he had a horse which was
no longer fit for work, and when a poor man came who collected
rags and bones and his horse was old and weak he would give him
the other horse as a gift. Such was this man's way of performing
charity. May it be His will that we merit the doing of acts of charity
and kindness. And he was dressed in plain clothes, wearing a torn
vest, a floppy cap and clogs; and his arms were long, reaching right
down to his knees as is the way with doers of charity; and his hair
tumbled over his forehead.

When he saw the Hassid and the waggoner he took the Hassid to
the guesthouse and the horses to the stable and began to groom
them. Nuta, thinking him a groom of the household, clapped him
on the shoulder and said, What's-a-name, what are your wages from
your governor? Said he, My food alone.

When he had finished in the stable he joined the guests, and when
he came to Reb Yudel, he asked him, What's your name and where
are you from? Said Reb Yudel, My name's Yudel and I'm journeying with a letter of the Rabbi of Apta, because my daughters have

reached marriageable age and I haven't the wherewithal to wed them off.

Tovya stared at him, then said, Wonder of wonders; for at that very time a man was staying with him who described himself as Reb Yudel Hassid. So Tovya turned round and began shouting, Reb Yudel, Reb Yudel, whereabouts is Reb Yudel Hassid here? Reb Yudel tugged him by the arm and said, Here I am; but the leaseholder paid no attention, and kept on shouting, Reb Yudel, Reb Yudel, whereabouts is Reb Yudel Hassid here?

Thereupon Reb Yudel understood that there must be another Reb Yudel there; said he to the leaseholder, I see he must be a Hassid and humble, and by reason of his humility he hides himself. And he was astonished that The Blessed Name should have made two men identical in name and nickname and requirement, this signifying money; but to prove the words of those of blessed memory, their appearances were different one from the other, the one being dark and the other gingery.

And the leaseholder called to that Reb Yudel who was not really Reb Yudel but who had claimed to be Reb Yudel and said to him, My friend, and did you expect me to do anything against you because you came to me with a falsehood? But to try your words, if Judah is really your name, repeat me your Biblical verse in which each word begins with a consecutive letter of your name. He began stammering and repeating some verse beginning with a letter J, but it was not the verse composing the name Judah, which he would certainly have known had that been his name. And immediately everybody saw clearly that he could not be Reb Yudel.

But Reb Yudel nursed a strong liking for the false Reb Yudel because he had taken upon himself so great a trouble even though he had no daughters who required to be married off; like the righteous of the world who take upon themselves the troubles of the world although they are themselves free from all iniquity.

The false Reb Yudel, however, slipped away and went and found Nuta and said to him, Come along with me, I've something to talk over with you. Said Nuta to him, I can see by your face that it's nothing very decent. Said the other, My friend, a man's face is no evidence as to his character. In any case, replied Nuta, your face is as good as a hundred witnesses that you weren't born under the sign of Jupiter the just. Said the other, If men's faces told their nature,

[93]

never a man would come to market but with iron chains on him.

Said Nuta, Leave me alone. Said the other, I see you're wide awake. So why do you have to go rolling round with a donkey of a Hassid? Wouldn't you be better off if you were in with a saint and ate fish and chicken crops all day long till your belly burst and worms came crawling out of your belly button, and when you'd die of it you'd have enough in hand to buy you a fine place in the cemetery along with all the other saints?

And who's the saint that I can stand in with? asked Nuta. Why, me, said the other.

You? asked Nuta in astonishment. Why, what are you staring at like that? said the other to him. But what sort of saint are you, asked Nuta, when you have a face like a hoss thief? All the better, answered the other. That's a fine advantage, that is. And how? Because folk will say I'm one of those hidden and secret saints who hide themselves in a plain everyday sort of appearance. And what have you been up to till now? asked Nuta. Said the other, I was a wonder-rabbi and showed all sorts of marvels. And where, said Nuta, is your attendant? If my attendant were with me, answered the other, d'you think I'd need a hostler like you? Come on, said Nuta, let's hear where he's gone? Said the other, He's been jailed. They caught him? asked Nuta. They swore false evidence against him, said the other, that he'd stolen a horse, but the fellow who had him run in got his punishment all right. Not only did he not get his horse back, but the judge goes out riding on it of a Sabbath.

While they were speaking they heard the footsteps of somebody approaching; the tramp lifted his head on high, leapt toward the moon and then, turning to the newcomers, cried, Peace be with you, with you be peace, according to the ceremony for hallowing the New Moon; while Nuta went off to make sure his horses were still in place, for fear that the saint had found himself another attendant.

But Reb Yudel held the Reb Yudel who was not Reb Yudel in high esteem and continued to do so; and when the other returned to the guesthouse he stood staring into the face of Reb Yudel who was Reb Yudel but not the true Reb Yudel until the maidservant of the householder arrived and asked, Who's Reb Yudel Hassid here? Who's Reb Yudel Hassid here? He's wanted at the householder's to eat. Thereupon Reb Yudel said to that Reb Yudel who was not Reb Yudel but who pretended to be Reb Yudel, Reb Yudel, your honor's being called for. Said Reb Yudel who was not Reb Yudel to Reb Yudel who was Reb Yudel, Are you the Reb Yudel they call the Hassid? If you're the one may your like never increase in Israel. Said he, And for why? Said the other, Because through you I've lost plenty of money. Reb Yudel felt grieved and commiserated with the Reb Yudel who had lost money through him, even though in Reb Yudel's eyes money wasn't an important thing.

Then the householder entered and invited Reb Yudel to his home in order to hear words of Torah from him, for the very appearance of Reb Yudel attested that he was a disciple of the wise. And he had a big house the roof of which was tiled with blocks of wood like the houses in big cities; and there were many trees round the house to protect it from the wind on rainy days and from the sun on sunny days. Also he had dunghills piled with manure before the windows to manure the fields and always to remind him not to be proud of his wealth. The storehouses were filled with old corn and the magazines with new, and there was a great byre with many an animal for service and milking. All the week round they baked cornbread, but for the Sabbath they made it wheaten. But the householder and his wife ate black bread which was half straw and chaff all the week round like the villagers; for they had been accustomed to it since they were children before they had merited wealth.

In addition he used to tell stories of what had befallen him during his days of poverty, so that his children should not pride themselves on his wealth. Once when he rented a mill a German entered the mill with a sack on his shoulders and said to him, Grind me this wheat. Said I to him, Heave up your sack into the hopper and I'll grind your wheat. Said he, Lend a hand. I went to help him but could not shift the sack; and I said to him, I wonder how you managed to get the sack here. Why? he asked. Now we're together we can't budge it; so how could you have carried it all the way? It came in a waggon, he answered. Then I called to the mill hand, and we heaved at it all together, but still it never shifted. A second one I called, and he heaved with us, but still it wouldn't budge.

Then I stood up and opened the sack to find it filled with snow; and straightaway the winds began to blow, and the entire mill was filled with snow; and that was in the very heat of July. And within the gusts of wind danced and leapt creatures which looked like men but had cocks' legs. Then I understood what my customer must be,

[95]

and I recited the Hear O Israel. And straightaway the snow vanished and the winds stopped, and there was no sack and no German.

In came the millowner and asked me, Jew, why are you a yelling so much? And how shouldn't I yell, I answered him, and told him the whole story. Then the gentleman began mocking and said, Why, that's the former miller whom I dismissed and he came to put the wind up you. Thereafter I was afraid to dwell in the mill, so I took my wife and children and went away from there, and came to my last loaf, may the Merciful One deliver us; and in my shoulders I can still feel the weight of that snow.

And now, said the mistress of the house, everybody says my good man's clearheaded and there's never a tenant who doesn't come to him for advice; and where was all his wisdom when he was poor? Once when he was bringing flour for the Passover matzoth in a waggon, he found the river in flood so that the water reached the waggon and the flour and spoilt it; and he could well have carried the flour on his shoulder and saved it.

When Reb Yudel took his leave Tovya gave him a measure full of copper coins. Reb Yudel loaded the coins on the waggon, and Tovya raised his eyes on high and said, Lord of the Universe, I don't know whether I did that for the sake of the commandment or for my own private pleasure; may it be Thy will that in me shall be fulfilled their blessed saying in the Talmud, "Though not for its own sake to begin with, it comes to be done for its own sake."

CHAPTER EIGHT: IN THE COMPANY OF SAGES ·
TEMPTATION They took their way from thence to the
village of Kitishetz, and from Kitishetz to Yasnishetz, and
from Yasnishetz to Sertetz, and from Sertetz to Pedbarzetz village,
and from Pedbarzetz to Ratishetz village, and from Ratishetz to
Tchestipad, all the villages lying between Pedkomin and Zalozetz.
In all those places you find innkeepers of great wealth who carry
out the commandment of hospitality and do deeds of charity.

Here they stayed overnight, and there they ate by day; here Reb
Yudel received a piece of silver, and there they gave him handfuls
of copper coins; happy the man who fills his pockets with them. Nor
did they forget Malensky village and Shishkevitz and Zaveshin village, and Batkef and Nedevey; until at last they reached the Holy
Congregation of Zalozetz hale and whole.

Zalozetz is a fine place with a river in the middle dividing the new
town from the old, and the two stand one facing the other, gazing
into the water like two women, one old and the other young, who
gaze at their beauty in a mirror; and the river gleams with the
brightness of them both. Amid marshes and pools rises an ancient
fortress with many loopholed towers and turrets from which the
warriors were wont to shoot upon the hosts of the Tartars when
these latter came warring against them, until Chmel the evildoer, may
his name be blotted out, came and destroyed it; and the duke came
and rebuilt it and turned it into a weaving factory. There is a large
park surrounding this fortress in which grow handsome limes, from
the buds whereof the townsfolk make a drink like tea or coffee.

And the city is filled with synagogues and Houses of Study, and
renownèd men are there who study Torah in dire poverty and
distress and solitude and loving-kindness; and within them the heart
always burns to fulfil the commandment, "Thou shalt surely reprove
thy fellow man." This is their heritage from the great preachers who
used to live in Zalozetz and rouse their hearts with their reprovings.
Nonetheless they held themselves dumb by reason of the verse in
Psalms which says, "I shall guard my mouth with a muzzle while
evil is before me"; as it was interpreted by the holy preacher, Rabbi
Joseph Moses, I shall guard my mouth with a muzzle and not reprove

[97]

as long as an evildoer can say to me, Take the beam out of thine own eye.

Therefore most of them are silent, with their mouths buried in their beards, and they moan much and walk bowed and think on ways and means for raising the Shechina, the Divine Presence, from her dust; and some of them do fashion poems and songs. Not like the Brod singers who turn their poems into sort of ballads to be sung in inns and cookshops, nor like the "enlightened" *maskilim* of Lemberg who write their poems to the greater glory of their choice style, but after the fashion of our age-old rabbis of blessed memory, who used to utter song and reproof in order to arouse the soul from drowsy temporalities, and strengthen the heart in His blessed love.

Nor should you wonder that these have never been published. Buczacz was likewise a place that was chock full of Torah; whatever scholar you may name can find more than his equal there; but they do not publish their wisdom in books. Sometimes a father will teach his son the art of writing by composing a poem; and to prevent him growing weary of his reproof and of his copying, he prepares him a fresh poem every day. So surely may I merit to see the Levites at their duties in the rebuilt Temple as I have known a child who began to copy the alphabet and whose father daily wrote him a new poem according to all the rules of the Hebrew poetry of the Middle Ages, containing much sound morality, and having the name of the boy as an anagram at the commencement of the lines.

Reb Yudel held Zalozetz in high esteem because of his comrade Joel who dwelt there. Although he had not seen him for twenty-two full years and they did not write letters of their weal to one another he had not forgotten him. For when they were little they had studied together, sleeping on the same bench and covering themselves with the selfsame blanket, and were as linked together as two adjoining fingers; and when they had come to man's estate Frummet's father had wished to wed Frummet to Joel; but of the Lord had she been wedded to Reb Yudel, and Joel took himself a wife of Zalozetz and followed her to Zalozetz, while his friend remained in Brod.

And so when Reb Yudel departed from Brod and came to Zalozetz he at once went in search of his friend. Said Reb Yudel, The friend of a man's youth is not to be compared with other men who are forgotten of the heart; for the friend of a man's youth is never forgotten. How hot his hands were to embrace him; yet when he saw him he could not even greet him and ask if all was well. And why? Well, it was like this. When Reb Yudel reached Joel's house a man who was standing outside dragged him in. It was a surprise to Reb Yudel, for how could Joel know that I have come to Zalozetz? And if he does know, why doesn't he come out himself to honor me? Although, said Reb Yudel, a man should keep his distance from pride, I must confess in all truth that I was annoyed at my friend for not coming out to meet me. But when I entered his house I recognized that they had not gone out in honor of Reb Yudel, but for the sake of the first Reb Jew who might happen to come along to complete the quorum of ten; for Joel's wife had died during that very week, and they were praying at the mourner's house.

Reb Yudel, entering the mourner's house, saw a lad with rent garments seated on the ground; and the hair of his beard had begun to sprout. Joel, cried Reb Yudel. Thereupon an old man turned his face toward Reb Yudel, stared at him a while, recognized him and said in a gentle voice, Yudel, are you here? Said Reb Yudel, Joel, you recognized me and I hardly recognized you; I never expected to see you, and now God has shown me your seed as well. How like you your son is; his face is the face of Joel when he left Brod.

Joel groaned and said, Yudel, so many years have passed since I saw you, and now I have to see you when I am sitting on the ground mourning for my wife. Reb Yudel groaned in turn and said, I thought I would surely rejoice with you but now I have come here my heart is sorrowful and weeps. Woe's me that I fulfill the words of Ecclesiastes, "Better to visit the house of mourning than the house of feasting."

For the entire week of mourning Reb Yudel prayed at the mourner's house, where he learned to know many of the chief men of Zalozetz, such as the rabbi, Reb Zelig, son of the preacher, Rabbi Benjamin of blessed memory, and the Hassid Reb Joseph Elkana, son of the preacher, Rabbi Joseph Moses of blessed memory, who came to comfort the mourners. These two golden vessels had the merit of making their holy fathers known by giving their writings to the printers. But whereas the rabbi, Reb Zelig, printed all that his father had written, the Hassid Reb Joseph Elkana could only print his father's commentary on the Passover Haggada; but his work upon the Five Books of the Torah and upon the Sabbath Additional

Portions read from the Prophets and on the five Scrolls, namely, Esther, Song of Songs, Ruth, Lamentations and Ecclesiastes, as well as the sermons he had been wont to preach to arouse the hearts of Israel, were still left with him in manuscript.

Come, consider the worth of his works if Reb Joseph Elkana himself had heard his father the author of blessed memory say, when I die the spirit of Rashi of blessed memory will come to meet me, because I explained his words in all correctness.

The manuscripts had lain for a long time before coming to the hands of Reb Joseph Elkana; and some were faded and some were indistinct, so that his eyes grew dim in the light they transmitted. But Reb Joseph Elkana did not let them out of his hands until he had copied them.

During the winter he would sit until midnight copying each word and taking care not even to correct as much as the grammar or style. If he lay down to sleep and then remembered that he had made an alteration he would rise and correct it. If the ink congealed he would warm it to make it flow freely and would then go on writing. And when he found that this led to delay he would not go to sleep without the inkhorn in his bed. And the sages had had nothing but praises for these manuscripts, but by reason of the costs of printing he had not had the merit of publishing them.

With Reb Zelig too did Reb Yudel rejoice in love which is the love of the Torah. The rabbi, Reb Zelig, did not dwell in Zalozetz, but would come to the city where his father of blessed memory had dwelt as comes a guest; and there he came and went in the house of Reb Joseph Elkana, with whom he drank a liquid called tea, which they made from the buds of the limes of the fortress gardens. And this is how the drink is made: the buds are picked when they blow, and are laid out in the sun and later boiled; and their essence is a specific for those who are sick in the lungs.

The rabbi, Reb Zelig, had the merit of aiding the multitude by putting through the press the writings of his father of blessed memory, which were: the Book of the Love of Lovers on the Song of Songs, the Book of the Wallet of Benjamin on Ecclesiastes, the Book of the Portion of the Lawgiver on the Passover Haggada, and the Book of Gold Rows on the Torah. How many reverses he underwent before he printed them! At the time of the great fire they had in Zalozetz he stood before his house watching it burning, and longed to clasp to him the very dust of the house in which his father's writings and manuscripts were buried. Yet The Name in His manifold mercies so wrought that no more than a small part of them were burnt.

After the fire he gathered together all the manuscripts, and the Lord making him find favor in the eyes of his kinsfolk and acquaintances, they undertook to do well with him and print the books; but by reason of their poverty they could not do so. At that time the Holy Congregation of Osovetz received him as Rabbi and Father of the Court, and provided him with an honorable living. But he was not happy in his residence there and removed to the Holy Congregation of Radvil to live with his own and his wife's kin, all of them faithful of spirit and upright.

Then he said, Here I remain, but he found no rest; for thieves came by night and took all his wealth and property. Then he recognized that this thing was of the Lord, and that he would not rest in peace until he had published his father's writings. And assuredly his first spouse, Mistress Dishel, may she rest in peace, should be remembered for good because of expending all her possessions and jewels and silver vessels on the printing of the first of the books. And his second spouse gave up still more, this being his modest spouse, Rebecca Bella, long life to her, who expended all she had and bore all the torments of time and mischance for the sole sake of printing the books of the father of blessed memory. And he wrote all these facts in the book, but nonetheless would tell of them with tears.

During the early part of his stay in Zalozetz Reb Yudel diverted his attention from all his affairs and used to go early and late to the house of mourning; and the rest of the day he spent reading the works of the holy preacher, Rabbi Benjamin of blessed memory, or the commentaries of the preacher rabbi, Rabbi Joseph, which veritably whistled with the Fear of Heaven. At the time I read them, Reb Yudel told us, I derived satisfaction for all my five senses. And how the eyes saw and the mouth read and the ear heard and the hand felt and the nose smelt the scent of the holy sheets.

But the rabbi, Reb Zelig, asked Reb Yudel when they were sitting together in the house of Reb Joseph Elkana drinking the drink they call tea, Have you attended to the matter of your daughters? Have you collected much money here? Said Reb Yudel to him, I hesitate to ask for money here. And why? said the other. Said he,

I see the city filled with students and Hassidim, so I suppose there can't be any spare pence, and how shall I ask for something they need for themselves? To which Reb Zelig replied, Have no compunction about that, for what a man gives he gives not of his own but of the property of the Holy and Blest One, and He, may He be blest, has plenty.

And Reb Joseph Elkana said, I have something to add to the words of Reb Zelig; the holy Alshech of blessed memory pointed out this difficulty. It says in the Book of Exodus, "And they shall take an heave-offering for me"; now if the whole world takes who can be the givers? But the earth is the Lord's and the fullness thereof, so what a man vows is therefore not his own but the property of the Holy and Blest One; so when a man gives charity it is as though he takes money from His blessed property and places it in his own private property (i.e. of good deeds).

Reb Zelig added, Similarly my father and teacher of blessed memory produced this interpretation of the verse in Leviticus, "If any man of you shall bring an offering unto the Lord, ye shall bring your offering." Albeit the earth is the Lord's and the fullness thereof, your offering is your own because you remove it from His blessed property to your own. Thus when a man gives charity, although he may be in need of charity himself, it is as though, since he does not give of his own but of the property of the Lord, he merely removed something from His blessed property; and I have no qualms regarding the Holy and Blest One since the Holy and Blest One has a great deal.

But Reb Yudel paid no attention to the matter of his daughters, for he was reading the holy writings of the preacher, Rabbi Benjamin of blessed memory, and of the preacher rabbi, Reb Joseph Moses of blessed memory. He used to say on the words of Ecclesiastes, "And I saw that there is nothing better for a man than he should rejoice in his actions"; these are the good deeds of his own self, "For that is his portion"; that is his veritable portion for himself, exactly as the preacher rabbi, Rabbi Benjamin of blessed memory, expounded in his book the Wallet of Benjamin, "Let no man say I shall toil for my sons and leave them much money, even though this may involve the neglect of Torah and prayer; for the son is the merit of his father and after his death will give him merit. Yet if the son is an evildoer he is left bald on either side (as the Talmud tells of the man with

THE BRIDAL CANOPY

the old wife and the young wife that the old one pulled out his black hair and the young one his white hair); after this wise he did nothing for himself, that is, he did not serve the Holy and Blest One but depended on his son, and his son turned out to be an evildoer. What do folk say of him, Woe to him, for he toiled all his life for his son, and were he to rise in his grave and see for whom he toiled he would go and perish again for shame. Happy is he who serves his Possessor and toils for himself and does not depend on his son. It is this that Ecclesiastes means when he says, "And I saw," that is, by my understanding, "that there is nothing better for a man than to rejoice in his actions," meaning good deeds of his own, and he should not neglect the service of The Name to hoard up money for his sons; for He, may He be blest, Who gave them life will give them food.

And Nuta? Where was he? Is it possible that he left Reb Yudel alone to go his own way without reminding him of the commandment of bringing the bride under the Bridal Canopy? But Nuta was busy with his own troubles. You will remember that when they found their way to Vidri village and stayed the night in the roofless inn, thieves had come and tied up the doors from without and taken out the horses; and when Nuta had sensed this he had jumped up and sprung down plump on the backs of the thieves, who had run away. Ever since then his height was bowed, his body was out of order, the brightness of his face was gone with his good cheer, and he went about groaning, Oh my back, woe's me my back.

And since he was always in good health he did not trouble to have himself put to rights, but depended on his body putting itself in order, until he came to Zalozetz and became ill.

Nuta stayed at the house of the granddaughter of Reb Yerahmeel, the teacher, whom he had met when he stayed overnight with Reb Yudel at Ushni village. As is well known, a man who has no peace at home can fix himself up anywhere; and all the more so a waggoner who is accustomed to inns. So Nuta stayed with that woman while he was recovering. When his aches and pains would let him be, he would gather together the children of the woman, sit them on his bed and tell them of the wealth of Reb Yerahmeel, their great-grandfather, and how he achieved his wealth, and how the cow Reb Yerahmeel took for himself gave such good milk the like of which couldn't be found anywhere on earth. At that time it happened that the Kaiser became sick; and folk told him, If you drank a single glass of the milk of Reb Yerahmeel's cow you'd recover at once. So they came to Reb Yerahmeel, took his cow and paid him its weight in gold.

He also told them the story of the bear and the story of the pot. Sometimes he related them as separate happenings, and sometimes he linked them together. In what way? Once he was going to Brod with a waggonload of pots when a bear came and stood in the middle of the road and said, Nuta, we're going to gobble you up. Said Nuta, Wait and give me a chance to get down from the waggon. So he got down from the waggon and took a pot and shoved it over the bear's head. But before he could climb up onto the waggon again there came a robber-at-arms, who wanted to slay him and take the waggon with the horses and the pots as his booty. But when he stretched out his hands to do so, the bear flung itself upon him and tore him to little bits.

Then the woman's children said to him, And if you're such a great hero, why are you yelling, Oh! Oh! Oh! all the time? To which he replied, Children, I brought it on myself, for once I was traveling along the way with Reb Yudel when we came to an inn where we stayed the night. But thieves came there to steal the prayer book of Reb Yudel in which he has three charms written: one to be invisible while seeing, one to make people fond of you, and one so that no hand can take hold of you; and the thieves tied up the doors of the inn from the outside; so I raised myself to my full height and burst open the roof with my head and fell down upon the thieves and squashed them under me without so much as disturbing a single hair on my chest; only that, while smashing the roof, I destroyed a bird's nest, and in the Court of Heaven I was sentenced to be punished in the World to Come for doing so. Said I, God forbid; Nuta won't let even a single hour of Paradise slip out of his hands. Said they to me, We can't let you off without any punishment, but since you're Nuta tell us what you choose; and I accepted suffering in this world.

During the whole of that time he was suffering pain in his limbs and used to yell that swarms of ants were swarming over his back; and in dream they had shown him how the ants had taken one piece of the backbone and opened a grave and vanished with it. At first Reb Yudel paid no attention to the words of Nuta, because Reb Yudel said, There is no man without pains and aches, and if pains come a man's way he must accept them with love, since pains erase transgressions and purify the body. But when he heard this dream Reb Yudel said to Nuta, Reb Nuta, give me your hand and we'll talk this thing over; it is written in Deuteronomy, "And thy camp shall be holy", and the books say that the places of mankind are called camps, and that when a man hallows himself and behaves in a holy fashion his limbs are called the Camp of the Divine Presence, of which it is written in Leviticus, "And I shall be hallowed in the midst of the Children of Israel and shall be present in their midst"; but when he uses his limbs in no holy fashion each limb attracts to it an evil demon, thereby bringing upon him all manner of bad sicknesses.

My friend, you must know that the two hundred and forty-eight members and the three hundred and sixty-five vessels and sinews are subservient to the two hundred and forty-eight active commandments and the three hundred and sixty-five negative commandments, and as a man's members, vessels and sinews are divided according to the number of the commandments, so are the domestic animals, beasts of prey and birds of the air divided into members and vessels and sinews, each of them subservient to some one of the six hundred and thirteen commandments.

For instance, the scorpion is subservient to the commandment of circumcision, and so, if a man is stung by a scorpion, they set upon him the holy covenant which has never been blemished, meaning that of a babe who has never yet harbored sinful thoughts; and the danger ceases. My friend, instead of yelling with pain, take thought as to what caused your pains; maybe you wear a garment of wool and cotton mixed, or a garment in which a transgression was committed. But in any case I advise you not to vilify your pains but to accept them with all due affection.

But the friends of Reb Yudel disagreed with Reb Yudel. One of them advised that he should go to the cemetery and say what had to be said, while the other said he should rub his body with vinegar and drink plenty of tea. Nuta, however, instead of listening to either, went to the doctor and had some blood let; and in this he is supported by the Gemara, which says that whoever has a pain paining him should go and visit the doctor.

And why have we given so long an account of Nuta's sickness? To explain how Reb Yudel came to be free to devote himself to Torah;

for as long as Nuta was sick Reb Yudel was to be found at the books of the holy preachers of blessed memory, as was explained in the beginning of this chapter under the head, "In the Company of Sages." But once Nuta's aches and pains went their way and he regained control of his limbs he began urging Reb Yudel to depart.

On that day Joel rose from his mourning. They brought brandy and different kinds of round cakes, and drank with all those who prayed for the ascent of the soul of the woman; then they departed and nobody was left with the widower excepting Reb Yudel, his boyhood friend. Joel did off the slippers he had worn during the time of mourning, did on leather shoes, bent his head and remained silent; Reb Yudel took a glass of brandy, blessed, drank and took his friend's hand saying, Long life to you, Joel, long life. Joel responded in a faint voice and sighed.

Reb Yudel pressed his friend's hand, released his own hand, pressed back his full beard toward his neck, kissed the other and said, Joel, why are you sighing so? Then Joel pointed to his wife's bed and said, Who's going to cook me a spoonful of soup now? Who's going to bake bread for me?

Said Reb Yudel, My friend, I have never grieved for such vanities. On the contrary, it seems to me that the world should weep for the excess of feeding. My friend, my friend, I am a fellow who mingles with people and knows the world; if I were to start telling you what I have learnt concerning that, the years of Methuselah wouldn't suffice.

Said Joel to Reb Yudel, Yudel, you're talking like a ninny, if you'll pardon my saying so. If so, said Reb Yudel, I'll tell you what happened to me in a village near Brod. Forty years I wasn't sick, but when once I ate to repletion I was punished with all kinds of awful pains, may you never know their like. And in case you should think it was only me that happened to, here's Nuta the waggoner who went through the same thing with me. A man eats what comes his way, and in any case man does not live by bread alone.

Said Joel, Here I am reminding you of the verse in Genesis, "It is not good for Man to be alone", and you answer me, in the words of Deuteronomy, "Man does not live by bread alone." In that case, said Reb Yudel, you are justified.

Yudel, then said his friend, you're journeying for the sake of the Bridal Canopy? Yes, Joel, that is so, said he. And you have three

daughters? asked Joel. Three daughters, long life to them, answered
Reb Yudel. And you want to marry them off? asked the other. A fine
question to ask, answered Reb Yudel; of course I want to marry
them off.

Then said Joel, Yudel, I've found a bridegroom for one of them.
I'm ashamed of you, my friend, cried Reb Yudel. You find a bridegroom for my daughter and don't even open your mouth? Where
have you been till now? The day is not yet over, quoted Joel in reply,
nor is the sacrifice useless. Yudel, this thing was of the Lord that you
married Frummet and I married somebody else, and now, when your
daughter has attained the age for marriage, my wife has died
upon me.

At this Reb Yudel sighed and said, How I longed to rejoice with
you and I have to come here to find you mourning over your wife.
Said Joel, Yudel, by your life you came at the right time. The All-
Present brought you here only for my sake. Here's you needing to
marry your daughter off and here am I requiring to marry a wife; so
I'll take one of your daughters as she is, without any dowry.

Reb Yudel was happy to make a bond with his beloved Joel, and
his beloved Joel was happy to find himself a wife. And how Zalozetz
wondered at Reb Yudel's success; for Joel was a wine merchant with
a good business, who had already married off his sons and daughters
and only required a wife to look after him and the house. But when
he repeated the details to Reb Joseph Elkana, Reb Joseph Elkana
took him by the hand and said, If I didn't know you I would say that
you have no faith in the sages; didn't the Rabbi of Apta tell you
that as much as the father of the bridegroom should undertake to
provide for his son, so much should you undertake to provide for
your daughter? Hence there must be a father to the bridegroom and
there must be a dowry; but here there is neither a father to the
bridegroom nor any dowry; so how can this be the heaven-made
match of which the Rabbi of Apta knows? And the rabbi, Reb Zelig,
nodded his head and said, This is no heaven-made match.

Thereupon Zalozetz became strait in Reb Yudel's eyes as the
mouth of a sword sheath; his friend wished to act to his advantage
but he would have to tell him, Your good deed has been taken and
cast away upon thorns. Nuta would never have done so. In payment
for the pot meal which Nuta had eaten at the innkeeper's he married his daughter, yet I refuse to give my daughter to my friend.

Yudel, Yudel, though you accompany the sages you have not yet reached the grade of the simplest and plainest man in Israel. And he had further reason to regret the matter; for he thought he had reached the end of his journeyings, whereas the way was still full long.

CHAPTER NINE: THE TERROR BY NIGHT ᴫ Reb Yudel might have made a match for his daughter, Pessele, and returned home, gone back to his House of Study, sat at Torah and prayed with the congregation, instead of wearying himself by journeys long and lone and diminishing his fat and his blood; but Reb Yudel was precise and meticulous in according with the exact words of his Rabbi, who had said, Promise your daughter as much as the bridegroom's father promises his son; and so when his friend Joel desired to marry his daughter without money or dowry he did not make a match; and thus merited at the last that the entire blessing of the saint should be fulfilled and he be found a worthy match; one worthy in knowledge of the Torah and in good deeds and in dowry, for his father provided enough gold and silver to cover him over. Yet Reb Yudel grew full weary and sore ere he found Pessele's match; he went trundling down many a road and found himself returning to many a place he had already visited, and underwent all kinds of troubles ere the engagement contract was written.

In case you should suppose that the troubles that tired Reb Yudel henceforward were any less than those he had hitherto undergone, or were like the troubles he had already undergone, let me tell you now and at once that each trouble he met from this point forward was greater than the one which preceded it. It can be compared to a human king who set his eyes on one he loved, took him by the hand, drew him to him, embraced him and pressed him to his heart until the very bones of his friend did crack; then gave him a great gift and thereafter sent him back to his home.

To be brief, Reb Yudel left Zalozetz and went to Tristinetz village, and from Tristinetz to Hikalovetz village, and from Hikalovetz to Ivtchitz village, and from Ivtchitz to Pedlevitz village, and from Pedlevitz to Zarvenitzi village, and from Zarvenitzi to a certain place called Varonkes, and from Varonkes to Yasinovitz village. From Yasinovitz they decided to betake themselves to the Holy Congregation of Zlotchov; and blest be the Lord day by day, for each day in turn they found their daily bread, as it says in the ancient book Mechilta, "He who created the day created its living." And Nuta also benefited therein; as it says in the Midrash on Lamentations, "If my master's satisfied, so am I."

THE BRIDAL CANOPY

In brief, they left Yasinovitz village and started out for the Holy Congregation of Zlotchov. But before they reached the town the snow at length began falling and the waggon dragged slowly and heavily. The sky grew dim and the earth turned white; each one of them made its way into the bounds of the other; and between one and the other, the world grew murky and dim to the inhabitants thereof. Reb Yudel cowered within his greatcoat, slipped his hands inside and recited the Section of the Incense in a mournful voice, thinking to himself, If I hadn't gone atraveling I could have been sitting in the House of Study praying with the congregation and responding Amen to the blessings. How thankful should those be who hear the reader reciting the blessings and respond with a bitten-off Amen that lacks life or joy; how the sages have wailed on this neglect of the response of Amen, and still the world doesn't know that day by day harsh distresses renew themselves, but when Israel assembles in the synagogues and responds "Amen, may His Great Name be blest", the portals of comfort are opened to them.

And the waggoner thought to himself, If I could only find an inn I'd go and sit by the stove and warm myself at it and not go toiling through the dark. Who knows whether we'll reach any inhabited place today.

And Ivory said to Peacock, Brother Peacock, do you remember the times before the roads were put in order, when travelers never journeyed by night because of the perils, but betook themselves to the inn while it was still day, and the horses could rest in the stable and put their bones to rights? But now the roads are in order we have to travel day and night without a chance to gather strength and rest our limbs, so that the horse forgets he's a horse but dashes along like a crazy beast, excuse my mentioning them both in the same breath.

Said Peacock, Shut up and don't remind me of the early days. For Peacock had known better times, being well brought up and eating and drinking and happy and glad, yet having now fallen so low as to be a yoked beast and a burdened steed. And so he was not fond of reminiscences. Like a young prince round whose neck was hung a fine jewel which he went and lost. So whenever he went out he would sink his chin on his chest so that nobody should notice the loss. And both Ivory and Peacock turned their heads and sighed for the days of their youth which had fled and could not be caught afresh.

And Ivory began mourning at heart, Days mine, days mine, where are you, days mine, days mine, whither are ye fled? We are held by the bit, but how are ye held? We are placed in a stable, but where are ye placed? If we go to the south ye flee to the north; when we go to the east ye flee 'to the west. When we come to the north we do not find you; we return to the west, there too you are vanished. Even the shadow which is not real doth ever accompany us, but ye do not treat us even as doth the shadow. Woe to the waggon that loseth a wheel, and still greater woe to the creature that loseth its days; the waggon hath another wheel set in place and proceedeth, yet who shall return us our years that are lost?

Nuta, noticing that his horses turned their heads back toward him, said to them, I know it's hard for you to tramp through the snow, so I'm spreading a cover over your backs to keep off the chill. So he got off, took two sacks, covered the horses with them and said to them, to the horses, Come along, come along, we'll be nearing some place where I'll put you to rest in the stable and give you a feed of oats, and you'll eat and drink and rest until tomorrow; and tomorrow I'll change the waggon for a winter sleigh so that you can travel easily.

Said Ivory, Pretty hopeless comforts Nuta is trying to comfort us with, as it says in the Wisdom of Sirach. I'll tell you what it's like; its like a horse to whom all the other horses came and said, Brother, give us your head and we'll hack it off, and then we'll give you a whole houseful of straw and barley. Said he to them, Fools o' the world that you are, if you're going to hack off my head who'll be eating of the straw and barley? He says he'll let us rest in a stable, but before ever we come near any stable we'll be weary and dead, and who'll need his stable then?

Meanwhile Nuta went back to his place on the waggon, prayed "Happy are they that dwell in thy house", interpreting the words for himself in their plainest possible significance, as though it referred to human habitations, saying to himself, Happy the man who sits at home and doesn't need to take the road like this.

And Reb Yudel finished reciting the Section of the Incense, and considered how many vicissitudes the Israelite must undergo whatever he takes in hand, even though it be the fulfillment of a commandment; and he sighed that these long winter nights were passing over him without Torah.

At last he gathered up his strength, put his hands out of the waggon, moistened them in the snow and prayed, while Nuta drove the horses in silence. When he reached the end of the prayer he wished to turn the waggon round, but the horses began jumping and dragged it forward. Hence Nuta recognized that they must be near some inhabited place and was glad.

Within a few minutes they had entered a village and in addition could hear the voice of Torah-study. Reb Yudel stretched out his hands in joy and said, Wisdom crieth aloud in the streets; there's nothing sweeter in the world than the voice of Torah. Reb Nuta, come and see His blessed mercies in making us lose our way and taking us through the snow and freezing the world and darkening the sky and setting the horses to revolt against us and bringing us to a place we don't know, and at the last letting us hear His voice; as a man calling to his little sons and saying, Come, my sons, come on; by your lives you'll come out of your toil to comfort and will enter a chamber brightly lit, where you'll sit before the stove and be fed on cake and study Torah. Reb Nuta, please turn your waggon toward that house. By your life, no sooner shall we reach there than the master of the house will come out and take us by the hand and say, Come in, come in, and give us to eat and drink; and he and I will sit down before the stove and learn a page of Gemara together; by your life, Nuta, there's nothing finer in the world than a page of Gemara, and all the more so during these long winter nights when the body derives double joy from the Torah.

Said Nuta, If there's no Jew where can your Torah come from? Only because your soul longs for the Torah so much you imagine that you can hear the voice of Torah. Said Reb Yudel, Reb Nuta, why must you use words that make you resemble a horse and cart? The cart hasn't started but the horse is already on the run. Before you've stopped to listen you start speaking; so listen first and then begin your speaking.

When they had gone on a little he asked, Well, what is it, Reb Nuta? Maybe, said the other, it's a traveler happened on the village and sitting and studying. Whether he's a traveler, said Reb Yudel, or whether he's no traveler, he's studying Torah. So Nuta turned the horses' heads toward the voice and they reached a peasant house half earth and half straw, with a litter of pigs nosing at the dungheap by the house; for it is the peasant custom to keep their beasts in their own houses.

And at the same time Ivory and Peacock stamped their feet and opened their nostrils and neighed and dug their heads under the snow and licked the ground; for they had been born and brought up in that village and there they had lived until they had been taken to the Ropshitz horsefair, where a thief had stolen them from their owner and sold them to a horse dealer, who had sold them to Nuta, the waggoner; since they had been reft from their home they had never yet returned thither; and so now they were back they stamped their feet with joy and took hold of the earth with their mouths lest it should vanish beneath them.

Reb Yudel descended from the waggon, entered the house with Nuta and greeted the household with joy, saying, May His Name bless your good night. There was a village woman there with a sort of gentile face who answered them in the gentile tongue. Said Nuta to the woman, My love, tell me who's sitting in your house studying our Holy Torah? That's my husband, said she.

So they looked round and saw a certain man with shaggy hair and matted beard who sat with an open Gemara before him studying to a chant. The Hassid ran to greet him, seized his hand, gazed into his face as one gazes into the face of his beloved out of great affection, and said, As grapes in the desert do I find thee, O Israelite. The other greeted him in return and sat him down before him. My dear man, said Reb Yudel to him, how do you come here? The master of the house smiled and replied, The Torah is very sweet; I converted myself a trifle, and now I sit and study the Torah in peace and plenty.

Thereupon Reb Yudel's soul all but departed from him, and had it not been for Nuta he would have passed out of the world without any confession before death. But what did Nuta do, he seized Reb Yudel and fled with him, and they delivered their souls in the waggon. Nuta started the horses off at a gallop, but they would not move; instead they stamped and kicked, and stamped and bit their reins in fury, and all but overturned the waggon. And Nuta began yelling, Woe's me, I'm done for, that convert has bewitched the horses so's they shouldn't go. And Reb Yudel, thinking that man must be a Jewish demon, the Merciful One deliver us, wailed out loud.

Yet a few moments later they were delivered from their straits and out of the village.

As a man who fled the lion, and the bear met him, and came to the house and leaned his hand on the wall and the serpent bit him, so had they fled from the cold and met the convert; now they fled the convert they entered a mighty forest without end and heard a dread and fearsome voice. Said Reb Yudel, That demon has opened the mouths of his tribe to come and swallow us, God forbid. And he repeated various tried and holy Names which may be employed at an hour of need; but we do not record them here lest unfit men who might come and employ them should destroy the world.

Ere Reb Yudel had finished Nuta howled, Wolves! And he said to his horses, Surely you'll not forsake your master Nuta at a time of trouble; they're coming to swallow us alive so that we won't even be brought to a Jewish grave, God forbid. Reb Yudel, say your death confession; wolves are coming. And thereupon they heard the call of the wolf, and his two eyes appeared burning like two torches, and his breath began mounting in their faces so that their blood froze with fear and they could not move. What is there to begin telling and finish telling? The wolf is an evil beast who rends and eats, as we have learnt in the Tractate of the Fasts where there is the tale mentioned of the wolves who ate two children; and had our heroes entered the mouth of the wolf there would have been no remnant nor fugitive left, of the foes of Israel be it said. But, since danger was close, salvation was not distant. For the horses lifted up their legs and fled.

Being done with that peril they came to yet another; the waggon entered a cemetery, which was the cemetery of the Holy Congregation of Zlotchov where the road passes between the graves; when the government began to build roads they wished to remove the holy bones, but a miracle occurred, for the graves removed from their places and the cemetery was divided into two. Now the graves in the two parts of the cemetery stood covered with snow, and the wind shook off the snow and blew it into their faces.

When they desired to pass on, a certain grave yawned open and something garbed in shrouds came forth and shook its shrouds at them. Both of them cried out in terror, Hear O Israel! If they turned back the wolves would eat them, while if they stood still they would find their graves here.

[114]

THE BRIDAL CANOPY

But The Blessed Name does not deliver His sons from one trouble in order to slay them by another. Within another moment or so they saw a light coming from the cemetery hut and heard a voice wailing, How long shall there be weeping in Zion; and further they heard, Gaze at these three things and you will not come into sinfulness. Know whence thou comest and whither thou goest and before Whom thou shalt in the future render an account.

Let us go toward the voice, said Reb Yudel to Nuta. Better to die in the cemetery among the holy graves than to be slain by wild beasts. And they took one another by the hand and went thither. There they found an old man garbed in shrouds, like a corpse standing at the entrance of the deadhouse, keening in a mournful voice, Unto the place of earth, worms and graveworms; and they stood as though the graveworm were crawling through their bodies like the thread in the eye of a needle passing through cloth.

Then Reb Yudel asked the old man, How do you come to stand in the cemetery? And he answered, You have asked a serious question; by your life I also ask how I come to be standing on the earth when so many, greater and better than I, do lie buried in it; yet such is the will of Him Who liveth evermore. Notwithstanding, I never distract my mind from this thought, but I stand here every night.

And presently the old man said to Nuta, Are you a waggoner? Said he, I'm a waggoner, and these two are my horses, Ivory and Peacock, and this is Reb Yudel Hassid, with whom I have journeyed here from Brod. All my life long, said the old man, I have never envied anybody except the waggoner; for whenever he so desires he turns his horse toward the Land of Israel and journeys thither. And he revealed to them that he was about to ascend to the Land of Israel.

Thereupon Reb Yudel saw that he himself must be beneath all contempt, because he was trundling along the roads in a waggon; and all to what purpose, in order to return to Brod. Reb Yudel told us of three things which he recognized in that hour; his heart was in the Land of Israel although his members were without the Land, and he felt prepared to leave his household to fend for themselves as long as he himself might ascend to the Land of Israel; and he was prepared to give up his portion of World to Come for the sake of the Land of Israel. So Reb Yudel took his money out of his coat and said to the old man, I pray you, take all my money. Said he, What use would this money be to me? For the costs of the journey, answered Reb Yudel. But I ascend afoot, answered the other.

But when he pressed him greatly he took from him one coin, which was the one Yudel's friend had given him when he left home. Now his friend had given him that coin to do charity therewith when he reached the haven of his desire, and had Reb Yudel drawn anywhere near his haven of desire? But Reb Yudel argued, What can be the haven of desire for any man of Israel other than the Land of Israel? Although I have not attained it my heart and soul are already there.

When the eastern sky lighted up they saw Zlotchov before them. Nuta was happy that he and his horses had reached a town, while Reb Yudel rejoiced that he had reached a place of Torah and fear, the sounds of which are heard afar like the welling up of knowledge at its source; and is it not a matter of course that every man with power to hymn aloud shall sing in phrases sweet and proud the praises of Zlotchov the sacred town?

> *Bring me now to Zlotchov town*
> *Where the soul doth know delight.*
> *Seraphim stand within the streets*
> *And walk upon earth by day and night,*
> *While from earth to heaven, I've heard,*
> *Rises a ladder, they say, on high,*
> *And human beings can clamber aloft*
> *Over the synagogue into the sky,*
> *And the goodly scent of the Fear of Heaven*
> *Can be savored in every home.*
> *Bring me now to the town of Zlotchov*
> *There to reside a while, nor roam.*

They immediately descended to the town and went to pray in the House of Study of the holy Rabbi Michele, may his saintly memory be blessed. Reb Yudel was filled with joy at having reached the place where that saint prayed, and felt in all his limbs that some vital influence was poured out upon him; according to the teaching of the Kabbala that all light leaves some trace, even though it may be departed from a place. Wherever a Jew prays with devotion on a spot where saints have prayed, and pure and holy Hassidim who purified the air with their prayers (and where, for that reason, no destructive spirit can wait to thrust his prayer aside, God forbid), the prayer will assuredly mount aloft like unto a palm.

And Reb Yudel worked into his prayers the letters of the name *Yehiel Michel,* who was the holy Rabbi Michele of saintly and blessed memory, also the letters of *Isaac,* who was the great reprover, Rabbi Isaac of blessed and saintly memory, father of the aforementioned Rabbi Michele, also the letters of *Joseph* who was the martyred Rabbi Joseph, father of Rabbi Isaac, father of Rabbi Michele, may the memory of all those saints be a blessing. And the Rabbi Joseph of blessed and saintly memory vouchsafed him a great favor after this fashion: during the prayers he showed Rabbi Yudel in the very senses how he, meaning Rabbi Joseph, had toiled and troubled in order to ascend to the Land of Israel; and in virtue thereof Reb Yudel was strengthened in his resolve not to let the thought of the Land of Israel depart from him; and in his thoughts he began wandering through the Lands of the Living, whence the Divine Presence has never departed since eternity.

And so he stood in his tallith and tefillin until Nuta came and said, Reb Yudel, put your things together and we'll be moving on. And why? Because a famous saint has come here, and all the folk are bringing that same saint their spare money and won't leave Reb Yudel as much as a bent copper.

Now to what can I compare and liken thee, Reb Yudel? To a priest standing unshod and about to bless the congregation with the Divine Presence resting upon him, who has his shoes suddenly thrown in his face. He moaned and said, Aie aie, Reb Nuta, you've diverted all my brain, so he rolled together his tefillin in the prescribed fashion and slipped them into their case, folded his tallith and prepared to depart. Not, indeed, to a different city as the waggoner urged him, but to greet that saint. Reb Yudel called on that saint and the saint gave him his blessing and sent him away in peace. But within a few moments the attendant of the saint came and said to Reb Yudel, Our Rabbi needs you. So Reb Yudel returned with him to the saint.

I wish to ask you something, said the saint to Reb Yudel, Tell me, when you entered my house I saw round your head the great light which is the light of the Land of Israel; have you been to the Land of Israel? Rabbi, Reb Yudel answered him, I have not yet merited the ascent to the Land of Israel; but only yesterday a certain old man taught me the matter of the Land of Israel, and now I cannot turn my mind from all its holiness for even a moment.

Then the rabbi took him by the hand and conversed with him of the matter of the Land of Israel which sums within itself all holinesses, and told him, A man should always beseech mercy for himself, so as to merit to ascend unto the Land of Israel. If he merit to ascend let him accept with joy all that may befall; for if, God forbid, he blemish the Land of Israel he straightway drops back into Exile even though he be in the Land of Israel.

Once I spent my Sabbath with the holy Rabbi of Apta. At the departure of the Sabbath the rabbi rose, put on his coat, took his stick and went forth. When he returned I asked him, Rabbi, why did you put on your coat and take your stick and go forth? A great saint, he replied, has passed away in the Land of Israel, and in Heaven they proclaimed that folk should accompany his body. After a while he put on his coat again, took his stick and went forth. When he returned I asked him, And why did you depart now? He sighed and said, A saint far famed has passed away in the Land of Israel, and all the greatest of the angels went to accompany him, but no more than a few human beings came; and the saint sighed and said, Had I been without the Land how many hundreds of Jews would have come to do me the last honor! Thereupon all the angels left him and I went forth to bear him company.

When Reb Yudel took his leave of the saint the saint gave him his blessing and then bent his own head before Reb Yudel, saying, Yudel my beloved, bless me too.

CHAPTER TEN: THE MESSENGERS DO HASTE ✤ Having taken his leave of the living saint, he desired to make his way once more to the graveyard and prostrate himself at the grave of Reb Michele of blessed and saintly memory; for he did not know that Reb Michele had forsaken his body at Yampole, whence he did depart this life at the third and final Sabbath feast while pacing hither and thither in his room and quoting the words of the Zohar, "With this desire did Moses, the true prophet, depart from the world"; and two full years before his death his footprints were already to be found in the Upper Eden, so that watch had had to be kept on him for fear his soul should depart with so great cleaving unto the Blessed Creator.

Now Reb Yudel had already been on the road more than four weeks; for he had started out at the beginning of Kislev, being the end of November, when potatoes were being dug up from the soil, as we found occurred the day he stayed with Paltiel, who did not delay him long because the time had come to dig up the potatoes; and now Hanukah was already past. If you reckon from the commencement of Kislev until after Hanukah you will see for yourself that more than four weeks had gone by. Yet from Brod to Zlotchov is a journey of eight hours, and ought to be even less for a man traveling with Nuta's horses whose legs cover a deal of ground at a stretch.

But because Reb Yudel delayed on the way the country expanded before him after the fashion of the Land of Israel in days to come. Indeed, that entire district is known as the Lesser Land of Israel, for it is a pleasant land with pleasant people dwelling therein, and Brod is seated in the midst thereof after the fashion of Jerusalem, with many a saint scattered throughout the surroundings; and even the nations of the world recognize this. The tale is told that when the Kaiser of Austria came to Brod and saw his Jewish subjects standing to receive his presence he said, This is my Jerusalem; for the kings of Austria seal their edicts with the title King of Jerusalem, even though Jerusalem be in the hands of Ishmael.

In brief, Reb Yudel started out for Zbarev on counsel tried and true, while Nuta flicked his whip over Peacock and Ivory too, and on the waggon trundled all down the road, as though it were swimming along with its load, and sinking to the axles now and again, you'd think for instant burial it were fain, with both of its horses and both of its men. They had not traveled far before they ran across a constable; for the government had stationed all kinds of constables to ask the wayfarers their names and callings. So the constable asked Reb Yudel, What town are you from? I'm from Brod, he answered. And what's your name, he went on. Said he, Yudel's my name. And your family name? Nathanson.

No sooner did the constable hear this than he stood at his service as a slave before his master, saying, My lord, pardon me for delaying you; and he patted the horses and took his leave and departed from him. Now why should the constable have treated Reb Yudel with so much honor? Because his name misled him into thinking he addressed the wealthy Reb Yudel Nathanson of Brod.

And Nuta, in his turn, made a mistake, for he thought Reb Yudel changed his name to that of the rich man; so Nuta, the waggoner, said, Reb Yudel did well to mislead the constable, and felt happy at his wisdom and surprised at his cunning. But was Reb Yudel a liar, God forbid? No. In all truth his family name was Nathanson, but one was wealthy and the other poor; so the former was known by his family name and the latter was not, saving when he was in the presence of a Gentile and gave his name in full.

When you find that a man who has been in trouble was delivered from it, know that his case is under consideration and has been adjourned in order to give him time to repent. If he does not repent, some greater trouble is brought upon him. From the moment Reb Yudel saw the constable he was very downcast, but put the blame for his dejection on the course of nature, since the Talmud says, "Let the awe of the government rest ever upon you"; so he did not scrutinize his actions nor trouble at heart until some other trouble befell him.

It happened like this: when they reached the Holy Congregation of Zbarev Reb Yudel descended from the waggon to betake himself to the House of Study, while Nuta went on to the inn to feed and rest his horses. As Reb Yudel entered the market place he heard a yell, Catch him, don't let him go. Turning his head back, he saw folk running after him. His soul all but departed and he turned to flee. Who could tell, maybe the government was out for his life. And the voice never stopped but kept on louder than before, Jews, Jews, take care he doesn't run away.

At this all the shopkeepers began closing their shops and chasing him, yelling, Stop thief, stop thief. The butchers dashed from their stalls, their knives in their hands and their aprons dripping blood and the dogs between their feet tripping them up, the noise of them rising to the very heavens. When Reb Yudel saw there was no escape he raised his eyes aloft, said, Into Thy hand I entrust my spirit, and stood still.

Straightway they seized him by his earlocks and beard, crying, Have a look at this here fellow dressing like a rabbi and robbing decent folks; and meanwhile they were flinging question and answer backward and forward, What's he been doing, what's he been doing? Stealing. Who'd he steal from? Why, you can see they're chasing him from Reb Ephraim's house, so that's where he must have been stealing. From Reb Ephraim's house? Don't you believe it, he's been a robbing o' the church. He's pinched their god and sold it. Just fancy. Profaning the Name like that!

But meanwhile Reb Ephraim's folk had come up, and said to Reb Yudel, We're not going to let you go until you've been with us to Reb Ephraim's house. And a crowd of boys on every side spread the noise both far and wide, and right and left did mock and bawl, This is the cock who stole.

CONCERNING THE HOSPITALITY OF REB EPHRAIM

Reb Ephraim, the hospitable, belonged to the family of the Haham Zvi Ashkenazi, the holy pedigree of which goes very far back, retaining its purity in all generations and all exiles. Rabbi Israel Baal Shem Tov, may his soul be treasured up on high, used to say that there are three families in Israel which have remained pure generation after generation all the way back to Father Abraham, may he rest in peace; and this is one of them. Instruction went forth to Israel from them which illumined the entire land with its glory. And as the fathers were a crown to the sons, so were the sons a halo to the fathers.

There were those among them who fashioned a *golem,* as is told in the Responsa of the Haham Zvi; on their account the countryside was blest so that the waters grew sweet and the fish returned to the rivers, as the Gaon Rabbi Jacob Emden of blessed memory relates in his own account of his life called *Megillath Sefer*. Rich folk and magnates offered great sums to have them wed into their families, and used to supply board and support for their sons-in-law to fulfill the Torah in plenty. But at their deaths they left little wealth to be inherited; for they were zealous on behalf of the Lord of Hosts, quarreling with evildoers, and by reason of their disputes and contentions their wealth vanished, and of their properties not even so much was left as might suffice to maintain the children or pay the widow the jointure stipulated in the marriage contract. Wealth and property they might not leave behind them, but a good name they did leave behind; to wit the name of the Torah which is dearer to a Jew than all the money in the world.

The house of the Haham Zvi desired to increase the honor of the All-Present, and so the All-Present increased their honor. Reb Ephraim's father, like all his kin, never left his son property or wealth. At his decease he took with him both Torah and good deeds, and when he passed away he begged his wife to forgive him and forego her jointure under the wedding contract. Yet The Blessed Name did not forsake the children of that righteous man, as it is said, "And I have not seen the righteous man forsaken nor his children begging their bread." When the young Master Ephraim reached the age for applying the chapter, "It is the man who marries," a wealthy man settled much money upon him, gave him his only daughter for wife, undertook to board and lodge him and in addition made him a partner in his business, which was the coral trade.

Now that is a very big business, for there's no decent woman among the folks of the world who hasn't a string of corals round her neck. And Reb Ephraim merited a good and clever wife, unlike his cousin Rabbi Jacob, the "Sweet Gaon" as men called him, of Lissa; and he merited to dwell peacefully, unlike his holy forefathers of blessed memory who had had to weary their feet traveling from place to place by reason of the home truths they had been in the habit of telling every man to his face.

Despite the fact that Reb Ephraim tended to melancholy, the Merciful One deliver us, like his uncle, the Gaon Rabbi Jacob Emden of blessed memory, he dwelt at peace with all men. The testiness which he had inherited from his forebears was not absent from him, though. It would seem that the time had not yet come for this quality to be sweetened.

THE BRIDAL CANOPY

When Reb Ephraim entered his father-in-law's house and saw all the good things outspread in the house he began pleasing his heart and concerning himself with his body and delighting him in the pleasures that vanish; for as long as he had been in his widowed mother's house he had never eaten to satisfaction. But ere long he recognized that it is not the purpose of man to eat and drink and derive pleasure from the pursuits of the body; and he began to take an opposite course. As how? He never ate broth on a weekday and drank no liquor except water; saving for the Friday night hallowing and the Saturday night *Havdalah,* also the four glasses drunk on the first two nights of the Passover; and on those occasions he drank raisin wine. Neither did he eat as soon as he was hungry, nor drink as soon as he was thirsty. He also used to fast a great deal, in order to weaken the powers of that desire which first cleaved to Adam when he ate of the Tree of Knowledge.

A rich man who deprives himself of pleasures will end by becoming cruel to the poor; for it is obvious that if he who has all the delights of the world derives no edification from the world, the poor man who has nothing must perforce do without. But Reb Ephraim, who skimped on himself, spent extravagantly on others. Men said of Reb Ephraim that his house was always open to the poor, to whom he was always supplying different dainties and before whom he used to stand as before the Shechina, the Divine Presence itself; since the Holy and Blest One stands at their right hand, as it is written, "For He shall stand at the right hand of the needy." And when he made wedding feasts for his daughters the poor and the rich were seated together at the same table—unlike other wealthy men, who always provide a separate table for the poor on such occasions.

Yet he kept Hassidim at a distance and never gave them of his bread. And why? Because the world, in former generations, had gone astray after the sect of Sabbethai Zevi, and he imagined that error to have arisen anew. So it followed that his actions were desirable before God because he fed the hungry and proffered honor to the poor, but were undesirable because he did not derive pleasure from all that the Holy and Blest One created in His world for the satisfaction of mankind; and because he made a distinction between one Jew and another.

But the commandment of hospitality wrought favorably on Reb Ephraim so that in the end all his actions became desirable. Once there came a guest to him; he did not know that the newcomer was a Hassidic rabbi, but had the table prepared and said, Master, go wash your hands to eat. The other washed his hands and said the blessing over bread; then, noticing that he was not eating, Reb Ephraim asked him, Why aren't you eating? And why isn't your honor eating, he replied. Reb Ephraim stammered and said, I'll tell you the truth, I'm not eating because I'm fasting. And is today a fast day? asked the other again. Said Reb Ephraim, It's a personal fast. On account of an evil dream? persisted his guest. No, replied Reb Ephraim. Thereupon the guest pushed his plate from him saying, When the master of the house is fasting, shall a guest dare to open his mouth to eat? Reb Ephraim, seeing how far matters were going, immediately washed his hands and sat down to food with his guest. Thenceforward, if a guest came he would interrupt his fast to eat with him; but if there were no guest he would complete his fast.

So what did his worthy wife do? If a pauper came banging at the door she would let him in, spread the table before him and come and tell her husband, There's a guest come to the house. Indeed, she even acted with guile and had guests brought from without the house. And before long the news spread abroad that at Reb Ephraim's house they gave meals to the poor; and people began coming on their own. And there was always a chair standing ready between Reb Ephraim and his family, so that the poor guest should feel at ease and eat to satisfaction. It once happened that a fellow with scabs ate at his table, who dribbled at the mouth. All those at table were sickened and turned their chairs away. And at once the master of the house took his spoon and ate from the same dish as his guest, despite his being a delicate man whose vessels none but he himself might use.

They say that this was done as a test. From that time forward the household honored the guests more than they did themselves, since but for them the master of the house would fast. Often they would hire somebody to come and eat with him. In his time no inn could be opened in the town, because his folk dragged guests to his house like one shopkeeper dragging customers from another's shop. Reb Ephraim did away with the free kitchen for the poor as well as the arrangement of tickets for sending the poor and the wayfarers to the houses of members of the community for Sabbath meals; until his time the poor man had had to grow weary chasing his food, but during his time no poor man need seek for an inn.

His wife did his will in all these things and never uttered a hasty word, fearing the anger of her husband, one of those descendants of the Haham Zvi whose anger is notorious. They said of Reb Ephraim's wife that she always emulated the deeds of the Matriarchs Sarah, Rebecca, Rachel and Leah; yet nonetheless he would grieve her. If a man has a hasty temper, can he go and say, So-and-so is an evildoer, so I'll go and be angry with him, while so-and-so is a saint so I shan't be angry with him? No; if a man has a hasty temper he vents his spleen on whoever comes to hand. He also raged at his wife for not bearing him sons, although he understood of himself that he had been punished in this because he had departed from the deeds of his forefathers and had broken the chain of the rabbinical succession in his family.

When his father-in-law died Reb Ephraim enlarged his business, so that there was never a fair in Podolia in which you would not find his agents selling their strings of corals. In those days people used to sing, "The farmer's took his cow to sell, and bought some corals for his Nell." His fathers before him strung together letters in the Torah, and he strung together coral beads and sold them; and many a poor maiden in that town sat at home stringing coral beads and putting away their pay as a dowry against marriage. And Reb Ephraim's own daughters also sat stringing coral beads until they got married; but he used to dedicate their work to charity.

Reb Ephraim's townsfolk should have been very thankful to Reb Ephraim, since were it not for him their daughters would have sat waiting for marriage until their hair turned white; but because he gave them something to do they could save up enough for a dowry; but nonetheless they used to call him the crazy rich man, since his peculiarities would sometimes hide his virtues. Half the town made its living at the hands of Reb Ephraim, and he himself used to live just like one of the townsfolk, saving that he enlarged his household through practising hospitality. I am surprised that the Gaon, who was Father of the Court at Yavrov and Horodanki, and who gives details of his pedigree and kinsfolk in his book of Responsa The Word of Moses, should not have mentioned his kinsman Reb Ephraim. Even supposing that he lack erudition and acuity, he still remained possessed of the qualities of charity, righteousness and hospitality. Many are the jewels and precious stones set in the diadem of his ancestry and kindred; yet one precious jewel has been omitted which is necessary to complete the diadem. Blest be He who has given such a son to our Father Abraham, may he rest in peace, and Blest be He who has aided us to relate his good deeds.

In short, to come back to our subject, Reb Yudel went along with Reb Ephraim's folk to a big house. There they entered a room full of silverware and copper basins and tin dishes and many books, with the picture of the Haham Zvi hanging on the Eastern wall of honor, a big table in the middle and the master of the house standing praying the Afternoon Prayers and growling in the midst of the silent prayers, *nu, nu,* meaning that they should wait for him. Upon ending his prayers he ran to greet his guest with joy, and said, Blest is he who comes, blest is he who comes. The mistress of the house entered with her face flushed for happiness and said, The wonder done here is greater than the wonder which was done to Father Abraham; for when the angels came to Abraham it is written that it was the heat of the day, while now it is a time of frost and cold.

Said Reb Yudel to the master of the house, there are two things here that I can't understand; I'll ask you, if I'm so important as all that in your sight, Why did you have to inflict such shame upon me? And then, Why are you so happy to see me? Why, you don't even know me.

Fool that you are, replied Reb Ephraim, do you think it's you, whoever you may be, that I'm so glad to see? No, it's the guest sent me at the hands of Heaven. Thereupon Reb Yudel grew still more astonished than ever. But the wife of Reb Ephraim said to him, Wait a moment and I'll explain. Ever since my husband has grown to manhood he will eat only if there is a guest with him; and now that one of the wealthy men of the town has married off his only daughter, all the paupers have gone there so that nobody is left to sit down at table with him; and two full days have now passed without his eating anything, for if there isn't a guest at table he can't eat.

At this Reb Yudel's face grew bright, and saying, Blest is He who has brought me to a son of Father Abraham, he washed his hands, sat down at table and with great fervor ate all kinds of food together with the master of the house; eggs chopped with radish and onion, grits with meat of breast and shoulder, goose-craw huge as Og, king of Bashan, different kinds of horse-radish and plums and raisins, some things sharp and others sweet. And Reb Ephraim's wife stood serving him like any servingmaid, urging him to eat and drink because this was a fest in fulfillment of a commandment, since had he not come there her husband might have had to give up his ghost with hunger, God forbid. And the master of the house sat on a wooden chair dipping his shaving of bread in salt and drinking water to stay his thirst, and wondering at his guest who enlivened the soul with his eating and physical enjoyment.

What are you doing here in town, Reb Ephraim asked Reb Yudel at length. Reb Yudel took out his letter of recommendation and said, Since my daughters have attained marriageable age and I lack the wherewithal to marry them off, the Rabbi of Apta, long life to him, amen, has given me this letter to serve as my mouthpiece before our fellow Jews with their generosity worthy of the people of the God of Abraham, to stir up their hearts to my advantage and the benefit of the commandment of the Bridal Canopy.

But before he had finished, Reb Ephraim was purple in the face and he shouted, What's your letter to do with me and what accounts have you with me anyway? Who's this come to order me about in my own house and get my money out of me! I shan't even let you have a doit. Let the Almighty help you, but I don't propose to let you have anything. And until he had cooled off again he berated the Hassid like one of the mean and worthless.

But what has this here Jew done you, Reb Ephraim's wife entreated him, that you have to go shaming him here? Did he demand any money of you? You asked him a question and he answered you, so why must you go making him turn white like that?

What accounts has he got with me, answered Reb Ephraim. I'm not even going to give him a bent copper. It's not enough that I'll have to go down to Hell on his account for having shamed him, I suppose, but I'm expected to pay him as well? Thereupon Reb Ephraim's wife said to Reb Yudel, Please don't pay any attention to the man's evil temper and shouting. You can see he's crazy.

Crazy am I, eh! cried Reb Ephraim. Certainly, if you're so fine and generous, why haven't you borne me any male sons? By your life and your head, if you had I'd ha' married them off to the daughters of this here Jew. I'm one of the grandsons of the Haham Zvi who like to tell the truth.

When at length he calmed down he took out his handkerchief,

wiped the sweat from his brow, took a pinch of snuff tobacco, offered Reb Yudel his snuff box and started again, I shan't give you anything; it's not my habit to waste my money for nothing; but I'm ready to pay you for your trouble. Let's make an account; if you had also been at the wedding of that idiot who's beguiled all the guests from my house, and I'd had to send a waggon after you, it would have run up for me to two or two-and-a-half gulden; so here's two-and-a-half gulden for you, and don't say a guest came to my house and I've robbed him of something. And now maybe you think you'll run away? By your life you don't move from here until all the guests come back.

Meanwhile the sun had set and the rim of the sky had turned to silver. The master of the house looked out of the window and said, The time has come for the Evening Prayers. Let's pray and then eat supper. Reb Yudel wished to leave the house and go to the synagogue, but Reb Ephraim said to him, Don't go, for they're a real den of thieves. You can see they are, because last Sabbath they took two guests out of my very hands.

So he took his girdle and while tying it round his loins cried, Blest be He who reminds us of that which is forgotten! And he began clapping his hands until his servant came in. Go and see, Reb Ephraim ordered him, where this Jew's horses are, and tell the innkeeper to give them oats on the account of the Holy and Blest One. Just the same, take some money with you and let him have a handsel until he presents the account; and when you find the waggoner what should you tell him, Yes, to come along here and eat with us.

The lady of the house lit the lamp, snuffed the wick and went off to the kitchen to prepare the evening meal. After all, said Reb Ephraim, we can also prepare a feast; a guest's as good as a bridegroom. And he expressed his desire for good food to be prepared, with fish and meat. Thereupon all the servant girls began scraping fish and plucking geese and baking loaves of white bread. And the lady of the house her very own self began preparing some calf brains in order to offer the guest something more than usually good. She opened the brain under salt water, removed its membranes, pounded onions, then put the brain and the onions in seething fat, sprinkled salt and pepper upon them, stirred them together, took three spoonfuls of flour, six of water and two eggs, leaving the whites in another vessel, made a soft dough which she dipped in meal, folded the dough over and put it in the oven until a crust formed; then she beat up the whites of the two eggs until they were like snow in order to beautify the cake.

And the master of the house rose and prayed the Evening Prayers with his guest; after which they sat gladdening their souls with stories of the saints until the table was spread with all manner of fine things, flesh and fish and warm loaves of white bread, according to the custom of Reb Ephraim's house where they baked white bread every day for the guests (and not merely in honor of the Sabbath), while Reb Ephraim and his household ate the stale bread.

Reb Yudel ate and drank, while Nuta also came and ate for a congregation of ten Jews and drank like a Gentile priest, pardon the allusion. And at night came the sons-in-law of Reb Ephraim, Zeida Shapiro and Frumtshi his wife, and big Menahem Aaron who was named after his grandfather, Menahem Aaron, with Rebecca his wife, and little Menahem Aaron, who was so called because he was born on the New Moon of the month of Ab, on which day Aaron, the High Priest, died, with Rachel his wife; and Kemuel Halprin with Perele his wife. With them they brought their sons and daughters, and in their father's house they drank tea flavored with Assyrian apples which we call lemons and sugar, and rejoiced with the Hassid who had veritably kept their father alive; and tried to persuade him to stay there a few days since their father's soul had verily become linked with his.

Reb Yudel would also have wished to stay there, but the commandment of the Bridal Canopy urged him to depart. Now among those present was a young man named Zechariah, the rich man's son-in-law, who was a native of Brod and wore a square skullcap on his head after the fashion of the enlightened Brod maskilim. He, upon seeing Reb Yudel, had rejoiced with him in particular as being his townsman. So Reb Zechariah said to Reb Yudel, Reb Yudel, you and I are Brod folk, so sit down and I'll tell you the story of the Brod merchant who was going to the Leipzig fair to buy goods.

THE STORY OF THE MERCHANT AND THE END TO WHICH HE WROUGHT

There was a certain merchant who used to journey to the Leipzig fair to buy wares. On one occasion an innkeeper on the road said to him, Would you care to stay with me until tomorrow, for I'm having my son circumcised? The merchant assented, stayed with him and didn't journey.

When they were seated at the feast which the innkeeper made on the day he inducted his son to the Covenant, there came the waggoner and said to the merchant, Why's your honor sitting here when we have to continue our journey? But the merchant sat eating and drinking and never budged from his place. So the waggoner began again and said, Householder, householder, it's time we went.

And why are you shouting so much? said he to him. In order, he replied, that your honor should rise and go. Go where? he asked. To the fair, he answered. And why? he asked again. To buy goods. And when I've bought the goods, said he, what will I do with 'em? Your honor will sell them, he answered.

What for? he persisted. In order, replied the waggoner, that you should earn money. And what, the merchant went on asking, will I do with that money? Why, he answered, your honor will buy food and eat. And now, said the merchant, see what a ninny you are. If I tire myself out like that merely in order to eat and drink, why should you demand that I should start journeying again at the very time I am sitting eating and drinking?

Reb Yudel drew the right conclusions from the story of the merchant and no longer urged that he must hasten his departure. Instead he remained in Reb Ephraim's house until the seven days' marriage feast at the wealthy man's home was over and done, and all the poor folk came back to the town, bringing with them full many a guest, paupers and beggars of alms in quest.

Even then Reb Ephraim would not let Reb Yudel depart from his home but continued honoring him in every way, after the fashion of noble people who do not forget when all is well the good deed done them when things went ill. When the guests saw Reb Yudel to be so important a person they in turn began esteeming him in their deeds, drinking toasts of long life with him so energetically that he had no time to raise his glass to his lips.

While one would be shaking him by the hand, someone else would be grabbing it and pumping it up and down saying, Long life to you, Reb Yudel, long life, goodness and peace; may The Name satisfy the requirements of our heart to all satisfaction as regards children, life and victuals; and may we have the merit of seeing our righteous Messiah speedily and in our days, amen.

Before ever he had finished, somebody else would shove him aside, make a grab at Reb Yudel's hand and say, Long life, Reb Yudel, and good; may it be His Blessed will to provide us and His entire House of Israel with our victuals in all honor and respect, and may we merit the table on High, amen.

With this one halfway through his toast the next would already be saying, Long life, long life; what are we making such a long song about? May His Name prolong our days and make salvation blossom for us ere long, seeing that in salvation are included all blessings, as we pray thrice daily, "For we hope for Thy salvation all day long and keep watch for salvation." And it is necessary to say the words and think the thought "and keep watch for salvation" with full devotion and intention, as was written by the Ari, Rabbi Isaac Luria of blessed memory, in order that, when they ask you at the Day of Judgment whether you kept watch for salvation, you should know what to answer; since salvation is the main thing.

In brief, long life to you, long life; may it be His will that we merit Salvation, salvation being the main thing; and may we meet every day and at all times and at each hour in all joyful places. And never let joy be a small thing in your eyes, for out of joy comes the praise of the Holy and Blest One. As how? When on the morrow the Holy and Blest One brings us together again at some other spot what will we say? Blest be the All-Present, blest be He who hath brought us together again.

By that time Reb Ephraim felt sorry for Reb Yudel's arm, which was being so tired that on the morrow he would not be able to as much as hold a spoon. He did not rebuke them because of his respect for his guests, nor could he restrain his wrath because of his pity for Reb Yudel's arm. Reb Zechariah, recognizing what was passing in his father-in-law's heart, feared he might rise and say something which would not be fitting, and thus shame his guests.

So what did Reb Zechariah do but tell the guests, Something I noticed has reminded me of a story. At once their ears opened wide as mill hoppers. He himself shifted the square skullcap on his head after the fashion of Brod folk when they have something good to tell

THE BRIDAL CANOPY

and fear they may forget part of it or somebody else may tell it before
they do. Then he began to relate

THE STORY OF THE TWO BROD MERCHANTS, ONE WISE AND THE OTHER FRIENDLY, WHO JOURNEYED TO THE LEIPZIG FAIR TO BUY WARES, WITH ALL THAT BEFELL THEM ON THE WAY; THAT ALL MANKIND MAY LEARN THE FITTING TREATMENT OF GUESTS.

Two worthy merchants, Reuben and Simeon by name let us say,
journeyed from Brod to Leipzig. Night fell along the road as they
neared a village, so they descended from their waggon, entered the
inn, washed their hands and stood to pray. But before ever they
started, the innkeeper had put out his hand to greet Reuben who,
instead of greeting him back, shouted at him, Go to the devil, fool
that you are! So the innkeeper turned toward Simeon saying, Ho, ho,
a testy Jew, a testy Jew upon my soul. Said Simeon to Reuben, You
astonish me, Reuben; here's a fellow Jew greets you, and you have
to shout at him. Do you call that politeness? Brother Simeon, replied
the other, wait a bit and then utter your reproofs.

The innkeeper now offered his hand to greet Simeon. Simeon at
once returned the greeting in polite style and friendly fashion, partly
to appease him for Reuben's behavior and partly because Simeon was
always good-natured and friendly. Blest be he who comes, said the
innkeeper to Simeon. And blest be he who is here, Simeon responded. And whereabouts may you be from? the innkeeper asked
Simeon. We're from Brod, he answered. From Brod itself? asked
the other. Sure enough, answered he.

Then the innkeeper said, That there Brod's a real big city before
God. Don't look down on me for being a villager, because all the
same I'm as familiar with Brod as a Jew with the Afternoon Prayers.
How many Jews, for instance, are there in Brod? And how many
citrons, for instance, are sold in Brod? But before I begin asking your
honor about the welfare of all Brod, 'twould be only fitting and
proper for me to ask your honor your honor's name, as it says
in Genesis, "For therefore are they come under the shadow of my
rooftree." For instance, what might be your honor's name?

I'm so-and-so, said Simeon. If that's the case, said the innkeeper, then your honor must belong to such and such a family. That's right, said he. Well, continued the innkeeper, and if your honor belongs to that family you must be related to this here family which is connected with that there family, and so it follows you're connected not only with this here family but also with that there family. Now I'm as knowledgeable about all them families as I am, you might say by way of example, with my toenails and fingernails. And don't reckon I'm just an ordinary villager, because all the same I know how to mix with folks. And so we were just saying how your honor must also be connected with that there family.

Not exactly, said Simeon. That's a wonder, said the innkeeper, and how might that be? We were connected, answered Simeon, through such and such a woman who was married to so-and-so and was divorced by him, and so once she was divorced the connection came to an end. Now why did they have to get divorced, marveled the innkeeper, because couldn't they have lived together till·a hundred-and-twenty year? And I'll ask you, if you don't mind, is there anything better, for instance, in the whole world than man and wife, like folks has the habit of saying, Man and wife is man and wife; and now why should they go and be divorced?

I don't know, said Simeon. Now that's just what I always says, said the innkeeper; townsfolk live a long way from one another, nobody knows what his neighbor's up to. But before ever I ask your honor about other folks' affairs I suppose I ought to be asking you about your own business, as it says in the Talmud, "A man's closest to himself." And so what might your honor be doing in these parts?

When we reached the village, answered the merchant, it grew dark and we came to the inn for a night's lodging. Well, and if that's the case, said the other, the question still needs to be asked, What was the point in your honor's coming to the village? We're on a journey, replied the merchant. And where might your honors be journeying, he asked. To Leipzig, he answered.

Thereupon the innkeeper clicked with his tongue, saying, To Leipzig; and what might you have to do with Leipzig? We have to buy goods, answered Simeon. And what goods, he persisted, might you be intending to buy? Fur skins, he answered. Then why must you go to Leipzig? continued the innkeeper. Because, replied the merchant, that's the proper place for such wares. And why, for instance, went on the innkeeper, shouldn't you go to Vienna, where you ought certainly to be able to find such wares?

There's not so much of it, explained the merchant, to be found in Vienna. Now that's a real wonder, exclaimed the innkeeper, that that class of goods ain't to be found where the Kaiser is. It can be found there, said Simeon, but it has to be brought there from Leipzig. And if, said the innkeeper, it's brought to Vienna, why shouldn't it be brought to Brod? Now that's what we're traveling for, agreed Simeon, in order to bring it to Brod.

Now why should you take so much trouble, went on the innkeeper? Your honor could just as well send an agent along, as it says in the Talmud, for instance, A man's agent is as good as he is. It isn't everybody, answered the merchant, that has an understanding of the quality of these goods. Now however can you say, exclaimed the innkeeper, that it ain't everybody as understands the quality of these goods? After all, goods is goods, and what difference does it make whether Judah buys it or Levi buys it?

Goods, said the merchant, need to be understood. What needs to be understood in them? he asked. Whether it's the pelt of an animal that died a natural death or whether it was killed; whether the hair falls out; whether its color comes from Heaven or is the handiwork of the dyer; whether the goods are in season and place, and whether they're worth the money paid for them. Now how can you know, he asked, whether the goods are worth the money paid or that they're in season and place, or whether the animal died itself or was killed, or whether the color is its own? Anybody knowing this class of goods, replied the merchant, will know for sure the moment he sees the stuff with his eyes and feels it with his hands.

Thereupon the innkeeper caught hold of his overcoat and began feeling it and said, You say that when a fellow sees it with his eyes and feels it with his hands he knows at once, but here am I feeling away with my hands and looking my eyes out, and yet I don't know neither the nature of the goods nor their value. Goods, said the merchant, have to be studied. And how's it studied? he asked. The fellow with eyes to see, answered Simeon, and a power of telling one thing from another and a life spent at this business—I can depend on him to know.

And if he caught a fox, pursued the other, and came to sell it—is one fox the same as another? There's one fox can be fat and in the pink of condition with a fine pelt and fine hair, and there's another which can be thin and wizened which is bad, with a bad pelt and bad hair. But as we're talking of goods I'll ask your honor something important. Do all the beasts o' the world come to Leipzig to be caught and skinned and sold there?

The trappers, explained the merchant, and those who buy them from the trappers, bring the furs there. If so, went on the other, why must they foregather only at Leipzig and nowhere else? The merchants, said Simeon, chose the place. If you'll permit me, said the innkeeper, I'll say something sensible to you. Let me hear it, said the other.

Then he said, I suppose the king of beasts dwells there in Leipzig and all the beasts gather to ask his weal and bring him gifts, and when the trappers see the beasts they betake themselves at once to their arms and kill all they can. But let's come back to what we were talking about. What might be the cost of a foxskin, for instance?

Do you know what your question is like? said the merchant. It is like the man who asked the shopkeeper, How much will a coat cost an orphan? I don't know rightly yet what sort of coat he wants, maybe jacket, maybe overcoat, maybe breeches and what kind of stuff does he want it made of, wool or flax? And how old is your orphan; is he little or big; and how much money has he to lay out on the clothes, and will he pay spot cash?

Said the innkeeper, What difference would it be whether he pays cash or not cash? If he pays cash, said the other, the price is reduced, while if he pays after some time the price must be raised. But the goods are goods, said the innkeeper. So what reason would the shopkeeper have to increase or diminish the price?

This is the general rule, replied Simeon. If the vendor receives cash he does not need to borrow money at the bank and he doesn't require to pay interest. And what's a bank? the innkeeper persisted. A treasury of money, said the other. If a man needs money he comes and takes it from there.

How fine Brod folk must be, said the other, if they make a bank for any man to come and take money. They don't give it, said the merchant, except to people who can be depended on to repay, and who they know will return it. So if you have to give it back, asked the innkeeper, why borrow?

Because, replied the merchant, meanwhile he can use the money for buying goods and selling them and making a profit; then he gives the money back.

And what happens, the innkeeper went on, if he doesn't give it back? They take him, said the merchant, and shove him into prison. Why, cried the innkeeper, this bank you're talking about is worse than Sodom, taking a Jew and shoving him into prison. It's done, explained the merchant, in order to keep the world in order and as a safeguard against swindlers. And does your honor, continued the innkeeper, also borrow from the bank?

But at this point Simeon grew furious to bursting and shouted at the innkeeper, What do you come worrying me for, you idiot? And before he had cooled down he took the waggoner's strap and lashed the innkeeper with it, crying out, Clear out of here and may all the devils take you! Have you ever seen the like of this fellow setting himself on me like a scab on the head, God forbid! And the innkeeper stared in astonishment at Simeon, the merchant, and said in wonder, At first I thought he was a friendly sort of fellow, but now I see he's as testy a Jew as the other.

And what had Reuben been doing while his companion was conversing with the innkeeper? He repeated the Evening Prayers, washed his hands, sat down and ate his supper, had a glass of something hot, stretched his bones to his satisfaction and smoked happily, smiling the while. Here's this nuisance been driving me out of my mind, complained Simeon to Reuben, and you go smiling! Didn't I tell you, replied Reuben, to wait a bit before you begin reproving me? If there's a chance that when I begin treating him in friendly fashion I'll have to finish by kicking him, it's better to kick him to begin with and then he won't trouble me any more at all. Brother Reuben, said Simeon, you're quite right. It's of you and suchlike folk that the Talmud says, "Who is wise? He who foresees what must come about."

When Reb Zechariah had completed his entire tale the faces of those sitting round all shone, and they said, He was smart, was Reb Reuben, as folk say, Who's wise, he who has money. Still that leaves a question; for his companion Reb Simeon was also a wealthy man, so why didn't he do the same as Reb Reuben? What an idiot of an innkeeper, when two wealthy men such as these come to his inn, to go bothering them with cross-questions and crooked answers. What have you to do with merchants? Clear off to the likes of you.

And the sons-in-law of Reb Ephraim said to their sister-in-law Tsippele, Reb Zechariah's wife, Tsippele, your husband's a whole granary of tales; nothing happens but he has a tale for it on the spot. And Reb Ephraim himself said, My son Zechariah's a true book of right conduct and moral tales; and he smiled and said, Well told, well told.

CHAPTER ELEVEN: IN ORDER TO RECORD THE PRAISES OF REB ISRAEL SOLOMON OF BLESSED MEMORY, A MAN IS INTRODUCED WHO BEARS HIS NAME SO THAT THE CONVERSATION MAY TURN ON HIM; ALTHOUGH THIS IS A SEPARATE MATTER IT IS REQUISITE FOR THE STORY ᴥ Between the soup and the meat there entered a man garbed as a traveler, and said to the master of the house, I have just come from the road and do not know which way to turn; so seeing a brightly lit house I came in. Please be so good as to tell me whereabouts I can find an inn here.

Reb Ephraim turned his eyes away from him and returned no answer. Then the man said, God forbid that I should come to disturb you, and if I have come it's only to ask you to show me where I can find an inn. At this, one of those present said to him, From your words it's plain that you're from some distant town, for otherwise you'd know that nobody leaves Reb Ephraim's house without eating and drinking. And Reb Zechariah added, Pour yourself out a glass of brandy. And the mistress added, Then wash your hands and sit down and eat.

Thinking to himself that he needn't wait for the invitation to be repeated, the fellow bowed, said, There's nothing to say no about, poured himself out a glassful, wished long life and drank. Said Reb Yudel, I was expecting your honor to do like everybody else and drink before saying long life, but your honor went and blessed long life before drinking. Now what was your reason? In order not to need to break off in the middle of drinking, replied the other, and so that nobody should start shaking me by the hand and spilling the glass. Further, after washing his hands he wiped them on the towel upward instead of downward, as folk do in the ordinary way; and that was because towels are usually dampish below and dry above.

After he had eaten and drunk, Reb Ephraim asked the guest, Which place are you from? I'm from Shebush, he replied. Tell me, said Reb Ephraim, what news is there of Reb Israel Solomon? To tell you that, answered the other, I'd need to hire a gentile. Thereupon Reb Ephraim said, Blessed be the Righteous Judge, and sighed from the bottom of his heart. And when, he then asked, did Reb Israel Solomon render up his soul?

THE BRIDAL CANOPY

That, said the newcomer, I don't remember, but I know my father used to be proud of me and would tell people, this is my boy, Israel Solomon, whom I named after Reb Israel Solomon. Which means to say that when I was born Reb Israel Solomon could no longer have been alive, for had he been alive they would not have named me after him; and if we reckon that I was born the year he passed away it would mean that from his death till the present thirty-two years have gone by.

Then Reb Ephraim asked, How many children did he leave, who used to care for Israel like his own children?. Children he did not have, said the newcomer; good deeds are more important than children. Would you care, then said Reb Ephraim to Israel Solomon, to tell us of some of his deeds in order that we may derive benefit from them for our souls?

The desire of the master of the house, said the other, does me honor, but I don't at all know where I should begin, for Reb Israel Solomon, may he rest in peace, was chock-full of good deeds and meritorious, and the moment I want to tell you one I remember another which is still finer. I fear, remarked Reb Zechariah, that because there are so many tales to tell we shan't hear even a single one, as happened with the teacher who knew all manner of trades yet couldn't make a living out of all of them put together. And what's the story, they asked him. Thereupon Reb Zechariah began to relate the story of

THE JACK–OF–ALL–TRADES.

There's a story told of a teacher of little children, a very poor fellow indeed, may the Merciful One preserve us from his fix, who made up his mind to sell snuff tobacco. So when he'd be sitting teaching children at the table his finger would be keeping the place for them while his foot would be pounding the leaves; yet it didn't give him what to eat. Then thinking it over he began teaching girls how to read, cypher and add up; and he'd write them charms to be attractive; and for women in the family way he wrote slips for guarding the newborn baby and keeping the not-good ones at a distance. Besides which he used to recite the Torah for pay, and blow the shofar, and take his place before the Holy Ark to pray for the congregation; and he would whisper away warts and bake the extra special matzoth for Passover. And still he didn't have what to eat.

So he decided to become a beadle. He hired himself out to the Court and became its beadle and signed as witness on bills of divorcements. And still he didn't have enough to eat.

Then he said to himself, See here, I meet the girls and I'm the beadle of the Court, and if any man divorces his wife I'm the first to know about it; let's go and become a matchmaker. So he went and began to spend his time making matches, and even then he didn't have what to eat. Well, said he, since I have to sign all fit and proper on bills of divorcement I'm becoming well versed in the art of writing; and he decided to become an engraver of inscriptions upon tombstones; but even then he didn't have what to eat.

So he stood and prayed and wept before Him, may He be blest, and he said, Lord of the Universe, so many of the kinds of crafts to be found in your world do I know, and yet must I die of starvation?

At this His Blessed Name signed to Dikarnusa, the angel appointed over sustenance, to give a living to that teacher of little children. Off went Dikarnusa. When he returned the Holy and Blest One said to him, Have you given him sustenance, Dikarnusa? All through the town I went, said Dikarnusa, without finding any teacher of little children, only there was a maker of snuff tobacco. Said the Holy and Blest One to Dikarnusa, by your life, Dikarnusa, I didn't mean anybody else except that fellow.

So Dikarnusa went off. When he came back the Holy and Blest One asked, Well, have you made him a living? All through the town I went, said the angel, without finding either a maker of snuff tobacco or a teacher of little children; but maybe you were thinking of the fellow who sits teaching the girls and writing their mothers slips for the safety of their newborn babies? By your life, said the Holy and Blest One, he's the one I have in mind.

So Dikarnusa departed. Upon his return He asked, Well, have you given him a living? By Your Great Name I swear, said the angel, that it's all through the town I've been and visited all the girls without finding him. Said the Holy and Blest One, Maybe he's standing at prayer or reciting the Torah or blowing the shofar or wishing away warts or choosing wheat for the extraspecial Passover matzoth. Go and see.

When he returned he said, it is known full well before Your Glory Seat that I've been everywhere you said without finding him. Your Holy Torah says I haven't seen him, the ears of wheat say none of us know of him, the warts say we have not heard as much as a whisper, the angels created by the blowing of the shofar say he has not brought them to being. Maybe he's been busy at the Court and delayed there, said God.

So Dikarnusa went off. Did you find him? God asked on his return. No, said the angel. Then he must be standing pairing matches, said He. Dash off to him before he has a chance of perishing of hunger. So off rushed the angel and back he flew. Dikarnusa, said the Holy and Blest One, he's still wailing about his living. Quick, be off to the graveyard where he may be hammering inscriptions.

Dikarnusa spread his wings and set off with a bar of gold, to find him in the graveyard, perished of hunger and already cold.

I'm ashamed of you, said Israel Solomon, wealthy son of wealthy folk that you are, to go comparing a chief and a leader with a poor teacher. It's not the man that's important, replied Reb Zechariah, but the tale and deeds to be told, as our sages say in the Talmud, "A man is judged only by his gestes." Well, when I came here, said Israel Solomon, you all looked to me like folk who had come together at a betrothal feast, and therefore I'll tell you a story of a pairing, and how the daughter of a certain man came to be the wife of a certain man at the hands of Reb Israel Solomon of blessed memory. And Israel Solomon began relating

FROM THE WRATH OF THE OPPRESSOR.

When Reb Israel Solomon, the warden, had completed the Morning Prayers he put on his warm cloak, being wishful to return home; but seeing the ground was slippery with ice he did not wish to go alone for fear he might slip and fall. So he went to the stove to tell the beadle to conduct him home, but did not find him; for at the time the beadle was standing outside, keeping watch and ward to make sure that nobody came to release a man he had put in the pillory. You might have supposed that Reb Israel Solomon would enjoy his revenge for the judgment executed on the evildoer, yet his anger went on mounting; seeing who was it caused Reb Israel Solomon to be hanging about in the House of Study, when he was all

but fainting for a glass of something hot, if not the shameless ones
of the town? And even were he to wipe them all out, Simeon
Nathan would be left. That commoner always pushing himself forward was still happy and serene; and what was more, the beadle
had to be kept busy on his account at the time Reb Israel Solomon
himself required him.

Seeing a lad standing warming himself at the stove, Reb Israel
Solomon stirred him with the ferrule of his stick and said, Shift
yourself and come along with me. Thereupon the lad took the
tallith and tefillin of Reb Israel Solomon in his left hand, took hold
of Reb Israel Solomon himself by his right as carefully as though he
were a fine citron on the first day of Tabernacles; and although the
ground was as slippery underfoot as ice, Reb Israel Solomon did not
feel the slightest danger in walking. He felt as though he were not
walking but sitting, like the day he had been elected warden, and
the folk had chaired him home from the House of Study.

When they reached his house he stopped and said, Here's the
place. The lad released his arm, returned him his tallith and tefillin
and prepared to go his way. Come, said Reb Israel Solomon to him,
and I'll give you a glass of brandy. Taking hold of the bag once
again, he entered the house with the master. Out came the servant,
helped his master off with his cloak, took his stick and put it away
in its proper corner, pulled his master's tallith and tefillin away
from the lad in annoyance and hung them up on the proper hook,
turning his nose up at him after the fashion of the servants of the
wealthy towards those of their poor brethren who do not serve
the wealthy as they do themselves.

Meanwhile Reb Israel Solomon took out his bunch of keys and
opened a big box filled with bottles of brandy, some sweet and
some dry; he poured the lad out a glass and said, Drink. The lad
calmly took the glass, said the blessing, drank a little, put the
glass down, bowed with raised shoulders and moved his lips after
the fashion of those modest people who thank without words. Another glass? Reb Israel Solomon asked the lad. More power to
you, he replied; your honor doesn't need to trouble yourself on my
behalf.

This made Reb Israel Solomon wonder, for is it common for a lad
to refuse a glass of brandy? Anyway, Reb Israel Solomon found
something interesting in the novelty. If that's so, said he, I'll give

you some cake. And he cut him a slice of cake and said, Say the blessing over divers kinds of food; for it was Reb Israel Solomon's way to tell people eat and to tell people drink; if he so desired, you ate, if he so desired, you drank, and if he so desired, you neither ate nor drank. So if he told you, say the blessing, it meant he was satisfied with you and would treat you in right Jewish fashion, as that though you entered his house ravening as a Yeshiva student you would leave it full as a charity warden. And what was more he would treat you well; while what was still more, the effects that might result from this cause were sometimes such as a man doesn't grasp at first glance.

Meanwhile the servant returned, prepared the table, spread a cloth over half, put bread and salt in place, brought water for washing the hands before the food, took out a clean napkin and went off to the kitchen to hurry Tsirel Treine with the food. Tell Tsirel Treine, Reb Israel Solomon called after him, to add another plate at the table, and don't stand there twisting and grimacing, man, like the devil in the shofar!

Thereupon the servant understood that the beggar would be eating with the master of the house, and that his master did not wish him to be present while they ate. So he nodded his head, said, My master's wish is my pleasure, and went out. Reb Israel Solomon washed his hands, cut the bread and signed the lad to wash his hands and eat. Tsirel Treine meanwhile had brought cabbage cooked with meat and potatoes, the fat of it still seething and bubbling in the dish and sending up a sharp, sweet, appetizing smell. Reb Israel Solomon plied spoon, knife and fork and ate to satisfaction, while the lad sat facing him, his nostrils distending over the food yet not eating out of respect for the master of the house, and meanwhile pressing his lips together to hold the smell of the food in his mouth.

While Reb Israel Solomon was eating he turned his head toward the lad, whose spoon was quivering between his fingers, and asked him after the fashion of a man whose question is its own answer, Not from these parts, are you? Whereabouts are you from? He told him the name of his town. And where are you going? he asked. If His Name so decree, he replied, I shall even stay here. And what's your trade? asked the warden.

I was, said the other, an assistant to the beadles in the Yeshiva. And what are you doing here? asked Reb Israel Solomon. Said the other, Whatsoever His Blessed Name shall command I shall do. I used to keep myself going with the fee the children paid me for hiring volumes of Gemara, but the lads of the Yeshiva came and took away my living. The poor fellows needed to eat just as much as I did, and what could they do in order to make a living?

Reb Israel Solomon banged with his spoon on the dish and said, What's-a-name, the food's growing cold. It seemed to him that he had been permitting this beggar to speak a little too much at his table. The lad stopped speaking, put his spoon into the dish, swallowed a little and waited a moment, broke bread and ate it with the food, eating respectably and courteously. Reb Israel Solomon, watching him, saw that he did not eat like a greedy glutton but like the son of a householder in Israel, who is shy and reserved. A fellow, thought Reb Israel Solomon to himself, eating his first meal at his father-in-law's house isn't better behaved than he is.

And what did the beadle say to you? Reb Israel Solomon asked him. Never a word, replied the lad. When I entered the synagogue I didn't find him, and while I stood waiting for him your honor called me. Which means, said Reb Israel Solomon, that I'm the first person to have seen you here. And while speaking he crumbled his bread in the dish and asked, Are you married?

The lad lowered his head shamefacedly after the fashion of bashful Jewish youths, and replied in the words of Scripture, He shall come alone, I still pray without any tallith. Reb Israel Solomon smiled and said, Excellently said. Are you a scholar? Where there is no flour, quoted the lad, there is no Torah. Meaning? asked Reb Israel Solomon.

The lad sighed and said he had no possessions either in Writ or Talmud; his father had never taught him and he never had a teacher, so how should he know anything? And still more, he had a sick mother whom he had had to support. With millstones round his neck, how should he busy himself with the Torah? And if so why had he left the Yeshiva? Because they had taken away his living and so he had to go? And truth to tell he would have had to go in any case. Why? Because when he saw the lads a studying he had not been able to withstand his longing for the Torah. But that which his soul desired could not be acquired.

Truth is recognized. Reb Israel Solomon recognized the nature of the lad. In verity he was unlettered and silent, but once he was brought to speech he spiced his conversation with the spice of Torah, so that you could not tell whether he was branded of the rabbis or an ignoramus; as the sages say in the Talmud, Great is the service of the Torah. Torah you never studied, said Reb Israel Solomon, but you must know the habits of those students of the Torah who sit in the House of Study and sway over an open Gemara and pretend to be studying, as well as they do themselves. I know how to sit and sway, said the lad, as well as the best of them, but I never learnt it from them. The ox has a long tongue and still he can't blow the shofar. To which Reb Israel Solomon smiled and remarked, Well said.

Reb Israel Solomon ate and said benediction. Then he took the lad into a room full of all kinds of clothes and said, Put on what fits you best and you like best; and he himself returned to the winter house. And the lad stood amid all the garments like a besmirched man come among folk and ashamed, while Reb Israel Solomon sat waiting for him, his fine bright eyes darting here and there through the room, looking for something to divert his impatience.

Suddenly he noticed the cat lying under the table, eating and licking her chops. The master of the house put out his hand and stroked her leopardlike fur, which is not the habit of a Jewish householder, threw her a bone and said in the gentile tongue, *oti Lasunka,* meaning what a glutton. Meanwhile Tsirel Treine in the kitchen was parching lentils before grinding them up for soup; and the scent of the parched lentils spread all through the house, spicing the digestion of the food. Reb Israel Solomon quoted, A smell's a real thing, and pictured to himself the dish of soup he would eat after rising from his noonday sleep. And in order to rouse his faint hopes he rose and went to the kitchen, his pipe in his hand, and entered as though for a burning coal. Seeing Tsirel Treine standing with the parching pan in hand the pleasure of the smell was transferred from body to spirit, so that his spirit felt at ease and happy. They say that all day long Reb Israel Solomon never needed to visit the pigeons he kept in the house to smell their odor; the smelling of which, as we know, is good to those suffering with their nerves and from sudden aversions.

Meanwhile the lad, who was not accustomed to fine clothes and handsome coats, waited a long while before daring to slip them over his arms and legs and make the rest of his members at home in them. After dressing he stood hesitating whether to come before the master of the house dressed in them or to take them off first, for how did he come to do on, in a plain weekday, such garments as neither his fathers nor his forefathers had done on even on Sabbaths and festivals? The very reflection he saw in the mirror on the wall was gazing at him in astonishment. But what could he do if he did not dare say, I don't want all this. He blessed Him Who is good and doeth good, as befits a poor man receiving a garment from a rich one, and returned to the winterhouse in an array worthy of a bridegroom.

Reb Israel Solomon, remembering what he intended to do with him, felt satisfied, saying to himself, This fellow's face is like the face of someone of good stock. Sure enough he was absolutely created for my purpose, prepared for it from the Six Days of Creation.

He raised his voice a trifle and said, You're a stranger here, you said? Without relative or kinsman? Excellent, excellent, and you want to study, your soul longs for the Torah? Excellent, excellent. If that's so, run along to the House of Study, for why should you waste your time here?

The lad turned about and moved toward the door, preparing to bid him farewell as he went. Here's a fine gentleman for you, said Reb Israel Solomon, he's in a hurry. What are you so anxious about? Is rain falling from the ceiling to spoil your fine new clothes? So the lad stood waiting.

Reb Israel Solomon took a huge pinch of snuff tobacco, rubbed his left eyelid, crammed his pipe with tobacco, lit it and sat gazing at the lad, all wreathed in tobacco smoke. At last Reb Israel Solomon said to him, Go along to the House of Study, choose yourself a place, take a book and don't as much as move from there. If anyone asks who you are, don't answer, and even if the study warden asks how you are, don't answer him. And if you do this you'll have your food brought you to the House of Study; and on Sabbaths and festivals I invite you to my house where you'll eat at my table together with me.

Eat what's set before you, said the lad to himself, and think whatever you like; he agreed to do whatever the master of the house told him and then set off for the House of Study. Reb Israel Solomon opened a Gemara and sat down in his easy chair beside the stove, the fire of which never ceased from the end of Tabernacles until the Lesser Passover a month after the First Passover; he drooped his head upon the cushioned back of the chair and fell asleep.

Along came Lasunka and lay herself down between Reb Israel Solomon's feet, rubbing her back against his slippers, and began rasping her claws. Suddenly Reb Israel Solomon opened his eyes a trifle. It seemed to him that a rat must have stuck its head out of a hole and the cat had begun switching with its tail. The snuff had begun dribbling between his fingers and Lasunka had quivered a little. Then she once more began rubbing her back against his slippers until it was time for dinner.

In the town of Shebush, where the Torah doth reside and all the Houses of Study are full of wisdom, the arrival of a fresh youth to join the students does not create a great impression. When he enters the House of Study they greet him, ask him, Where are you from and whither is your face turned, and with whom did you study, and what did you study; and should he be wise they accept him within their borders. Having accepted him, they do not say, that man so-and-so is wise, for Shebush swallows up all who study there.

Great is Shebush, all the sons of which are learned of the Lord. When a youth comes to Shebush, even though he be a wonder for wisdom all remark concerning him ceases as soon as he is absorbed by the townsfolk.

But the beginning of this youth was not so. He came to the House of Study, opened a tractate, found himself a place to be seated and began shaking and swaying until his earlocks danced and he made a wind. In the middle of this he would rise, go to the bookcases, take out many volumes of all shapes and sizes and begin searching through them as though he hoped to find something he had lost.

Nonetheless nobody greeted him and nobody entered into conversation with him. The men of Shebush are possessed of a virtue known as humility; when a newcomer arrives in the town they do not enter into conversation with him, so that you might suppose they have too low an opinion of themselves to trouble him; but the truth is that this is no virtue but merely the quality of laziness resulting from pride. God forbid that the men of Shebush do not greet a newcomer, but they do it in their own way.

As how? When a stranger comes to the House of Study they pay no more attention to him than if he were not there. When the new-comer sees that nobody greets him, he takes a book and begins to study. All of a sudden he finds an old man or a lad beside him who looks into his book, seizes his hand and greets him as a man might who catches somebody doing something not quite nice, and immediately disappears. Thereupon the newcomer begins to wonder what he has been doing and thinks to himself, Why should I seem different from all other people? When a man comes to any other town they greet him and make him feel at home, while here when I find somebody who greets me he vanishes away the same moment. At last he drops his eyes to his book again and concerns himself with the Torah, and thereupon back comes the other fellow casually, like the sheet they fluttered in front of the preacher during his sermon; and he asks something, swallowing his words indistinctly, twines himself round about the newcomer and eats his heart like a worm.

Meanwhile the day had passed and the Evening Prayers were said. The beadle ascended the platform, opened the box of candles, gave one candle to each young man and one to each group of lads. And our lad also received a candle without saying a word or twitching his lips. Now the beadle knew that none of the lads could escape his hand, which included this one, who ought to make himself small before him and open the conversation first. So he thought to himself, did the beadle, Dressed like a prince, my lad, are you? Well, even if you turn white and green and blue your time will come, by your life, and I'll square any accounts there may be. But that day never came.

Before the students went off home the maidservant of the beadle's house entered, loaded with many dishes, and asked, Which is the new lad here? And as soon as she recognized him she opened her bundle, spread a tablecloth and arranged a meal on the table before him, with onion and radish and liver before the meal and fried plums for dessert, and grits and half a roast goose for the main course; for roast goose was always to be found on the warden's table.

The lad washed his hands, sat down and began eating; and since he was not versed in the eating of roast goose he ate very slowly, using knife and fork as though the two instruments had been revealed on Sinai; he chewed the garlic and swallowed the congealing fat and separated the meat and gnawed the bones for the marrow, and the fat bubbled in his mouth and coated his fingers. And the beadle, who was acute and well versed in the way of the world, recognized from this meal that it did not mark the end of the acts of the warden toward the newcomer, and that he still had many a benefit to confer on the lad. Just as the smell of garlic fried in fat is a sign of the dish to follow, so was this fine feast a sign that the warden would have much more to do with this youngster.

And while the beadle stood there with his mouth watering, the maidservant said to him, Prepare him a comfortable bed while I go off and fetch him a feather cushion. When the beadle heard this he bowed and scraped toward the lad like a very worm and said, Come and lie down on my place beside the stove. And the beadle himself went and found himself a sleeping place wherever he might, and shivered with frost and cold because all that day long he had been standing in the open on Reb Israel Solomon's orders, keeping his eye on the scamp he had put into the pillory, in order to make sure that Simeon Nathan's people did not come to release him.

And so the lad sat shaking himself over the Gemara, wrinkling his brow, rolling his earlock round his index finger and slipping the end of it into his mouth and letting it go again after the fashion of those who are intent on their studies; but he did not raise his voice while studying, so that nobody should recognize him for an ignoramus. Should anybody desire to enter into conversation with him he would not reply, though the other might stand over him all day long. So silent a fellow, they said, had never before been seen in Shebush.

The other youths came against him with their claims, boiling over like Hell itself and saying, Here's an upstart for to see! The warden invites him to dine, and now he's fit to burst with pride. And they wished to have their revenge on him, but the laziness of them kept them from it. There was once a great rabbi in Shebush who used to say, Why do you suppose the Shebush folk don't throw stones at my house according to the usual custom of this land, where they throw stones at the rabbi's house and smash his windows? It's not that they have any pity for me, but just that they're too lazy to pick up a stone and throw it.

And so the lad sat silent in a fashion that was quite unnatural. Folk began asking, What's this, in all astonishment. The wide-awake ones said, And is that all you have to wonder about? There's a man in Brod who has been standing in tallith and tefillin next to the Holy Ark and has been silent more than eight years. Well, said the others, and if that's the case it's also something to wonder at. And who's a stopping of you, asked the wide awakes.

At last they went to Reb Israel Solomon and asked him, Reb Israel Solomon, what sort o' case is this? This is a fellow, replied Reb Israel Solomon, of whom all the great ones of Lithuania say that the like of this balsam has never been savored for fragrance. And why, they asked, is he silent? Silent, repeated Reb Israel Solomon. Why, with the modest is wisdom, said Solomon in his Proverbs.

And Reb Israel Solomon went on to say, He expounded a something big in the way of novellae to me this Sabbath regarding Mixtures, where the Taz, Rabbi David of Lemberg himself, had overlooked a clear statement to be found in the Tossafoth. And what clear statement was that?

And therewith Reb Israel Solomon, in the name of the lad, was launched forth on one novella after another, one piece of pilpul after another, until the eyes of the questioners glistened with the radiance of the Torah. And while speaking he stretched his arm out and said, This piece of pilpul may seem a fine bit of dialectic and casuistry to you, but it's no more than a crumb of his wisdom; and yet you go asking what sort o' case he is. And this novella he sprung on me quite casually, and still you ask what sort o' case he is.

And he rose and went to his bed, opened the box standing under the bolster and took out some manuscripts and said, These are some of his novellae on the Torah; and because I hold they are valuable I've hidden them away here. And where did the manuscripts really come from? It once happened that the leaders of the age were suspected of holding with the sect of Sabbethai Zevi, and they left their manuscripts with Reb Israel Solomon and fled.

So now these people asked Reb Israel Solomon, And why did the lad see fit to come here? To which Reb Israel Solomon replied, Ere you ask why he saw fit to come here it would be better to ask why he left his own place. In that case, said they, why did he leave his own place? Thereupon he bent his head forward and whispered to them, He fled from the wrath of the oppressor. This at once put them in mind of the words of Rabbi Sabbethai Cohen in his book, who wrote, "And I fled from the wrath of the oppressor"; and they became as excited as though Rabbi Sabbethai Cohen his own honorable self had come to the town. And they said, This lad must be something very much out of the ordinary.

THE BRIDAL CANOPY

The jealousy of him vanished at once, and they began twining him garlands of honor and praising him to the skies, as folk praise those forerunners who scorch no present man by their proximity, or as they praise those sages and geonim who live at the other end of the world and scorch no present man. And all those days they retold the tales of the slain of 1648 at the time of the Cossack incursion, and of Chmel, may his name be blotted out, the leader of the Cossacks; also of the great men in Israel who lived in that generation, some of whom were slain by all manner of unnatural deaths and some of whom fled from the wrath of the oppressor.

And on the tenth day of Teveth, early in January, when men cease studying by reason of the fast, they sat crowded together reading the book, *The Straits of the Times,* and drenched the pages with their tears. The clock dials looked in astonishment from their frames, asking, What has come over these to divert their attention from us? Isn't it a fast today when everybody keeps his eyes on us to see when it's time to refresh himself? And they began ticking louder and louder as each hour passed by; but nobody paid any attention. And what were the permanent students of the House of Study doing? Peeping at that lad with their eyes weeping till they drenched the pages.

And since he never troubled to converse with them their affection for him became permanent, since love which has nothing else in view does not disappear. Nor was it the students of the House of Study alone; every maiden of marriageable age wept bitter tears for this youth of tender years, who had been tried with sufferings so grievous. And they were all ready to provide him with a father and a mother to replace his own father and mother who had perished from the wrath of the oppressor. Thenceforward when maidens sat solitary 'twas the youth they had in mind, while when womenfolk met together 'twas of the youth they spoke. And what was it they said? If only we might find merit before Him, may He be blest. Before they could finish, their daughters would be all ablush like the apples on top of the children's flags at the Rejoicing of the Torah. And what did the modest and worthy daughters of Shebush do? Went out awalking in new gear, come Sabbaths and festivals. And whenever the lad left the House of Study the other youths found themselves sneezing at the scents of the girls' dresses. The matchmakers set forth with energy and speed; and the lad still sat silent.

Now the father of this lad had had a friend who had been great in Torah but afflicted with poverty. All his life long he lived in need and want, lacking the wherewithal to support and maintain his wife and daughters. So he rose and hired a horse and cart, took provision for the way, and applying to himself the verse in Genesis, "Get thee out from thy land and from thy birthplace and from thy father's house," went journeying with his womenfolk from town to town in the hopes of finding a post as Rabbi or Head of a Yeshiva; and he went on from one place to another; and everywhere they told him, The rabbinical office has not succeeded in burying its incumbent as yet; similarly regarding the Yeshiva they turned him away until he despaired of ever finding himself a living and desired to return home.

Then his wife and daughters said, But your money has run out, so how shall we return to so long a distance? Better go to the warden and say, I'm a preacher, and he'll give you permission to preach in public, and maybe you'll bring people back to the right way and serve us as well and earn wages from the Lord and from Israel.

He took their advice and did so. And so he journeyed from town to town and preached in public and maintained his family until his garments began to fall apart on him; and the sage Ecclesiastes has long since said, "And the wisdom of the poor man is despised"; and they would pay no attention to him, so that at last he was compelled to go from door to door like the rest of the poor folk.

At last he came to Shebush, where his wife and daughters died upon him of the cholera, the Merciful One deliver us, and he too was sick, may the Merciful One deliver us. Once the lad passed by and, recognizing him for his father's good friend, rejoiced to see him and told him the entire story. The old man saw that the warden had not taken the lad out of love of him, for those who know the world are not happy at such good acts; but his wisdom did not aid him to see what the warden had in mind.

He sorrowed that his friend's son should be an ignoramus and said to him, I knew your father, may he rest in peace, for a remarkable scholar and man of erudition, and why shouldn't you become like him, my son? As for a living, your food is given you and your clothing is provided, while as for books, in any case you find yourself among them. As the saying goes, when a man's near money, money sticks to him. I can't bring myself to believe that the warden's doing a poor lad a favor for the sake of Heaven; it's certain there's some purpose behind all this. But in any case, you can derive some benefit from it. As how, you'll come to me an hour today and an hour tomorrow, and I'll teach you a chapter today and a chapter tomorrow. And once you've learnt Torah what are you short of?

When the lad heard this his heart verily went out of him for joy and he said, Blest be He Who hath merited me to study His holy Torah in truth. And so he went to the old man and learnt Torah from his lips and prospered in his studies. And the old man, who had acquired wisdom and was erudite in all the chambers of the Torah but who, by reason of the mischances of the times, had not merited to be seated in a Yeshiva with students—now he had a fine student and worthy, he did not let him out of his hand until he had taught him Bible, Mishnah, Law and Legend.

Likewise the lad, who had the great advantage of having been blest of God with an understanding heart, a hearkening ear and a quick grasp, but who had had no opportunity of studying by reason of poverty—now the All-Present had prepared him such a master, he took every word he uttered to heart till all he heard was quite at home there, and he meditated on the connection of each thing with another; and since he had not learnt as a child he was in no way spoilt by the oversharp dialectic of the times, but put together all he heard properly. Our sages of blessed memory said in the Talmud, "Torah study is like water; as water, descending in drops, becomes streams, so with the Torah; a man studies two legal provisions today and two tomorrow until he becomes an overflowing stream."

So it was with this lad: he had sat at Torah and been bored to death; the old man saw him and recognized him as the son of his friend, so took him, sat him down next to him, and expounded for his benefit Mishnah, Gemara, Law and Legend; he had full reason indeed to rejoice. And in virtue of this rejoicing he raced from one Mishnah text to the next, and from one Tractate to the next, until he was able to study on his own without his master's aid.

Meanwhile Reb Israel Solomon still supposed everything to be going forward as he desired. Once it happened that the lad was seated at his table and Reb Israel Solomon said to him, Eat and drink, for the Torah absorbs a man's strength. And although the lad had a beautiful comment to make thereupon, he knew the value of silence and kept his comment within his bowels and ate and drank. And as a reward for this modesty he merited to be set in bridegroom's array, and, indeed, that Reb Israel Solomon should be his grooms-man.

All the matchmakers were busy in the houses of the rich folk of the town, and while there they drank a glass of brandy and ate all kinds of sweetmeats and swore by their share in the Garden of Eden that the match was all but arranged. What one matchmaker was saying in one house a second was saying in another house. The Name willing, they said, after the warden shall have risen from his noon sleep I'll drop in on him and explain that he can't find himself a better match than this one. Why, I saw him at the House of Study at Morning Prayers and he nodded his head at me and asked, Well; and if so why didn't I speak plain and clear with him? So that nobody should over-hear and spoil it all, seeing we live in Shebush where it's the habit of folk to go and do harm.

The Holy and Blest One, as we know, does not punish the match-maker for his falsehoods, and he goes on praising the brandy as being worthy of the blessing said over it, and the cake which melts away in the mouth, and the bride who is well deserving of that bridegroom. And as one does in one house, so a second does in another. It is true that matchmakers had been to Reb Israel Solomon and had treated with him concerning matches; but whatever match they proposed he thrust from him with both hands, just as though that lad were his own son and nobody in Shebush was worthy of him.

And now Reb Israel Solomon found his opportunity of settling his accounts with the Shebush folk; Reb Israel Solomon knew that they wished to make a match with that lad, whose guardian he was, and so they would bear all the shameful things he had to say without opening their lips, yes, even if he recounted all their misdeeds and re-proaches for generations back. Men say that such peaceful times were never known in Shebush as those days in which Shebush heard all its ill repute and had nothing to reply.

But if there was peace in Shebush there was none to be found in the household of Simeon Nathan. Simeon Nathan had a wife named Shprintsa Pessil, who had the gift of the gab and was quick with her hands as well; and whenever she heard a woman mentioning the name of the lad she would be at her husband, shaking him like the palm fronds at the Feast of Tabernacles and yelling, Murderer and son of a murderer that you are, why must you slay your daughter with your own hands with your going and meddling in a quarrel that has nothing to do with you, just to anger the warden? All the beggar women in Shebush will have been and gone and married off their daughters to the warden's lad, all except my daughter, as though she'd been born behind the fence, God forbid. May the whole of Shebush go up in flames with you together and all your household and your ugly mug and your swollen neck so long as my daughter marries that bridegroom there! And or ever she had calmed down she had shut him out of his own house. Shut him out, you ask? By never letting him sit in peace unless he went to intercede on behalf of the daughter that he was not worthy to be the father of.

So if he could find no rest and quiet in his own four walls, where could he go if not to the House of Study? There he observed the greatness of the lad, with books around him on this side and books around him on that side. And what were folk talking of? So-and-so had promised so much and so much as dowry, but matters were still shaky; for the fullness of the whole world wasn't enough for Reb Israel Solomon regarding the lad. And when they saw Simeon Nathan they disregarded the quarrel between him and the warden and said, Simeon Nathan can't be the old Simeon Nathan; his daughter has grown up and yet he doesn't move a finger. Meaning that he can't be in a position to.

Can't be able? Why, we always knew that Simeon Nathan's mouth is bigger than his pouch. He used to be all right. Used to be? The warden kicked him out, and his good time stopped. Kicked him out, you say? Why, he sent for him and had him given a thrashing. Simeon Nathan got sixty lashes, may The Name guard us! Can't you see his face is black as the sooty bottom of a pot? We ought to feel sorry for him, by my life; after all, he used to be a fine proper Jew.

And so they sat discussing matches for the lad, and when they came to Simeon Nathan they would dismiss him with a sigh and the past tense as though he were dead and done with, the Merciful One deliver us. Now a fellow who has no food and can't eat is not to be compared to a fellow that has food and can't eat; the former is happy not to need to eat while the latter is sad not to be able to eat. So much gold and silver he had, had Simeon Nathan, so much property; and why wasn't he marrying off his daughter to this disciple of the sages? Only because the quarrel between him and Reb Israel Solomon had not come to an end.

Henceforward he therefore avoided disputes. And what did the wags of Shebush have to say about it? They said, And now even if the warden should order the Miracles Prayer which should only be repeated during Hanukah and on Purim to be recited on the ninth day of Ab when we mourn the Temple, or if he were to order that the Haman's bag cakes should be made with four corners instead of three, you wouldn't have Simeon Nathan complaining.

It seems that this change didn't escape the eyes of Reb Israel Solomon, who in turn changed his accustomed courses and, in communal affairs, humbled himself to ask the approval of Simeon Nathan, according to the wise saw, if you can't hack your foe's hand off, kiss it. In leapt those that pursue peace, saying, The hour has come to make peace between them, while Shprintsa Pessil did not remain idle with folded arms, but did whatever had to be done until they made peace between themselves.

But when they came to Reb Israel Solomon and told him, Simeon Nathan desires to wed his daughter to that lad, he thrust them from him with his pipestem, saying, The Sabbath of Israel does not fall upon the same day as the Sabbath of the gentiles. When they came again his right hand thrust them from him while his left brought them back; and when they came again he received them in friendly fashion. Our sages of blessed memory, said Reb Israel Solomon, were wont to say, Israel was crowned with three crowns: the crown of Torah, the crown priestly and the crown royal. The crown priestly was the portion of Aaron; the crown royal was the portion of David; but the crown of Torah stands ready waiting for all Israel; whosoever desires may come to win it. Who am I to object? This way or that way, a lad must finish off by getting married; if not today then tomorrow; if not Simeon Nathan, then some other householder in Shebush. The milk of white goats and the milk of black goats is just the same; the only thing is that he must promise his daughter a large enough dowry.

Straightway Simeon Nathan went to the warden's house, taking his money pouch with him wherein were three hundred gold pieces. And Shprintsa Pessil came as well, decked and arrayed as befits a mother-in-law, and called on Esther Malka, Reb Israel Solomon's wife, speaking words of peace and affection to her, saying, Esther

Malka, my life and soul, may I merit to cut pieces of wedding cake at my daughter's wedding which will be as sweet as you are in my eyes. May the fiend take all the beggar women of Shebush who go talking scandal and spite about us. It isn't for naught that folk say it would be better for a poor man not to have been created than now he is created. And at once they forgave one another and kissed one another as is the way of women.

Before long the Engagement Contract had been prepared, and the parties had agreed to put up the Bridal Canopy quickly, so that the bridegroom should find quiet and a home. Reb Israel Solomon would also have agreed to have the canopy put up at once, in order that Simeon Nathan's downfall might not be delayed; but the Council of the Four Lands was about to meet just at that time, so he deferred the wedding until he returned; and he rejoiced at the vengeance he would wreak on his antagonist upon his return to Shebush. And when Reb Israel Solomon's time came to set out, they made him a big procession, and even those who had always fought against him followed his carriage as far as the Sabbath-day's boundary, and besought him not to defer his return too long lest the town become as a living widow.

The great ones of the country gathered together to the session of the Council of the Four Lands, which was held that year at the Holy Congregation of Boberek in order to strengthen the valuables of Heaven; for in those times the Torah was the sole ruler, obeyed by the whole people; and the chiefs of the communities and the sages and geonim of the age kept heed over the welfare of Israel and passed their ordinances and added to them or changed them according to the requirements of the time and the hour. The Council of the Four Lands used to meet whenever necessary, and the rabbis sat in session on the seats with the wardens of the communities standing behind them, each warden behind his own rabbi; and they supervised the ways of the country and imposed taxes on communities and individuals, and they mediated in disputes and decreed decrees, threatening the public with penalties to make sure they would be observed; and if the times required it, God forbid, they would fine and punish and ban and banish and excommunicate and enforce their words.

And since, by reason of our many sins, Satan is dancing in our midst and no man defers to his fellow, they occasionally fell aquarreling. But Reb Israel Solomon, may he rest in peace, was gentle to his companions on that occasion and went out of his usual habits, and amused himself thinking of the wedding of the lad with the daughter of Simeon Nathan. All those days his eyes gleamed bright, and his solid paunch, filled with Lemberg chicken crops and Kolikov bread, with which there is none in the world to compare, shook and quivered with laughter. Just come and see how much trouble Simeon Nathan had gone to in order to give his daughter to that lad—and such an ignoramus as that lad was! Taking leviathan on his hook— and it turns out to be a minnow.

Now what was the lad doing all the time Reb Israel Solomon was away at the Council? He was sitting studying without a break until he had the whole Mishnah by heart. And when the old man saw that he had filled his belly with the Six Orders of the Talmud and with the later authorities, he said to him, Go to the rabbi of the town and he'll give you your rabbinical authority with its license to instruct. I know that there's nothing in the license to instruct, for either it's unnecessary or the majority of the public don't trouble about it; but anyway how does it harm you to have a license to instruct?

So one day the lad stood at the entrance to the house of the rabbi, who was very poor and so had not gone to the Council of the Lands. In came the rabbi's wife and said to him, The warden's lad has come to visit you. Call him in, said the rabbi, and he entered. The rabbi took him and sat him down on a chair. Rabbi, said he, it's a license to instruct I want. And is there anybody, said the rabbi, worthy of being a teacher and instructor in Israel that would hide his face and not come to visit me? Rabbi, said the lad, with regard to you I ful- filled the words of Job, "The lads saw me and were concealed."

So you're the lad, said the rabbi, whose fame is heard from one end of Shebush to the other; sit down, my son, sit down; may such as you multiply in Israel. And he began investing him with problems of the law, and before long he took his quill and wrote his rabbinical diploma in the traditional terms, Assuredly let him instruct, assuredly let him give judgment. Let him who has been occupied with the Torah come and claim his reward.

Out went the lad, happy at having been found worthy of a license to instruct, while the rabbi rejoiced that he had become a groomsman to the Torah and had done something to make the warden glad. Nor was he the only one; many rabbis in the hamlets around Shebush, who had not been able to journey to the Council of the Four Lands on account of their poverty, gave him license to instruct; and since they knew that his wedding was drawing near they said, This will serve as a gift for the wedding address; and you treat it as such and do not reveal it until after the wedding. Some of the rabbis handed the document over at once, and others withheld it until their minds should be settled to write it in fitting terms, not wishing to give him an offhand authority.

So before ever Reb Israel Solomon returned from the Council the lad had been awarded his rabbinical authority. And when he sat at his books the edge of the table no longer pressed against his chest, by reason of the documents of ordination in his bosom which intervened between him and the wooden edge.

When the sessions of the Council came to an end and the ordinances had been written and sealed, Reb Israel Solomon took his leave and returned home. And all the way the face of Simeon Nathan tickled his fancy, so that he paid no attention to his driver, and if he did beat him did so only in order to carry out his duty, striking him not with his stick but with his pipestem, as intending not to thrash him but to hurry him up; indeed his driver wondered what had come over Reb Israel Solomon that he should be sitting there behind him like a stuffed kid. And so they came to Shebush in a very short time.

The men of Shebush turned out to meet Reb Israel Solomon, who climbed down from the waggon and walked to his house with them, while the driver went ahead to apprise Esther Malka of her husband's arrival. Out she too came to meet him, bedecked as a bride, and urged him to wash his hands and eat luncheon. Reb Israel Solomon, remembering that six hours had not yet elapsed since he had eaten goat cheese on the way, wished to satisfy himself for the moment with a slice of cake, and leave the meat meal for the evening. But Esther Malka regretted the stew that would spoil by standing.

Thereupon one of the bystanders counseled that Reb Israel Solomon should say the Afternoon Prayers first, and while praying the full six hours would have elapsed. Just then Lasunka scented the master of the house, came and stretched herself at his feet, caught hold of the tassels of his girdle and meowed once and again for happiness. Reb Israel Solomon looked down at her affectionately and said, I'm sure these cruel folk must have neglected you; and he asked, Did you feed her every day? Did you give her white bread and milk? You didn't forget the lad? And while speaking he gently withdrew the tassels from the cat's claws.

God forbid, they replied; just as we didn't forget Lasunka we didn't forget him; the one who gave her her food took him his, and he eats well and drinks well and studies. And what's more, all his wedding requirements are ready and waiting, and all he needs do is come under the canopy. The servant, seeing the master of the house in a good mood, began praising Lasunka and saying, Lasunka recognizes the lad and treats him just like one of the household. And the men of Shebush, seeing that it was the cat's hour, all began flattering her.

Make an end, said Reb Israel Solomon, to all these praises of Lasunka; and he diverted them to speak of the lad. Thereupon they all began praising the lad with the exception of Esther Malka, who found no place for herself in the world from the day the match had been made, all because Shprintsa Pessil bought up whatever poultry there might be. And Reb Israel Solomon likewise began praising the lad because of the impending downfall of Simeon Nathan at his hand.

Just then Simeon Nathan entered and, seeing them all standing about to pray, had his impudence aroused, though this time it was an impudence of officious humility. What's this, in-law, said Simeon Nathan, your honor's just come from the road and finds nothing better to do than pray? Better sleep a while and afterward eat and then pray; by your lives the Afternoon Prayer won't grow cold.

We also advised him to pray, the others answered him, only because we couldn't think of anything else, but now there's another course advised we all agree that he ought to sleep a while first and then eat; for sleep after travel's a pleasure. And they rose on their tiptoes and departed from the room, so that nobody was left with Reb Israel Solomon saving Simeon Nathan and the servant.

The servant removed Reb Israel Solomon's boots and went out to make sure that no waggon should clatter past the windows; Reb Israel Solomon stretched himself on his bed, took out a silver-mounted pipe he had brought from the way and filled it with tobacco, while conversing with Simeon Nathan regarding the day to be fixed for the wedding. Simeon Nathan lifted a glowing coal, bent down and held it over the pipe bowl; and the silver of Reb Israel Solomon's pipe bowl set up a gleam on Simeon Nathan's nose, red as it was with all his wine-tasting in preparation for his daughter's wedding.

Simeon Nathan ordered all the good things there are in the world for his daughter's wedding, in order that the men of Shebush and all the ages to follow might know once for all how Simeon Nathan married off his daughter, and to whom he had wedded her. He had casks of honey in his cellar, so heavy that they squashed the earth of the cellar under them; Simeon Nathan brought a dozen porters and had them shifted up into the house. And the kneading dishes in the house, which were big as baths, were full of flour; bakers and baking women stood there with jugs of oil and bags of raisins and nuts and cinnamon, which they emptied into each trough and mixed with the honey.

The elders of Shebush sneezed with the scent of the cinnamon; when the Sabbath departed, stingy folk dispensed with spices for the Havdalah service because of the scent of the cinnamon; God-fearing folk going out into the market place used to hold their nostrils closed to prevent it entering, because they did not know whether they needed to say a blessing or not, seeing that hot bread and the like should not be smelt because the authorities differ as to whether it requires a blessing or not. And Shprintsa Pessil bought up all the fat cocks and hens; were it not that she left the scrawny ones alone it's doubtful whether there would have been any left to serve Shebush for the Atonement custom on the Eve of the Day of Atonement. They say of the woman that there was never a goose or a duck or a swan or a dove in all Shebush that she didn't have slaughtered. Doves were for grilling, swans for boiling, ducks to be stuffed with apples and then roasted, while geese were both for roasting and for boiling. Besides which she had a number of beasts slaughtered, the red flesh of which was hidden by the white fat.

While the squawking of the poultry still sounded from town's end to town's end, and beasts were lowing from the slaughter house, the wheels of a waggon came creaking through the street and there appeared a waggonload of vegetables with a deer walking ahead of it, its horns decked with greens, and a crown of red peppers on its head, and the lord of the manor's cook walking behind.

What's all this here, they asked him. This deer, said he, is being sent by my master, the lord of the manor, to his Jew, Simeon Nathan, and I'm going with to show him how to cook it. And all the folk nodded with their head and said, In all truth, my love is like to a deer. And the children ran along behind, singing, Flee my love and be thou like to a deer.

And in addition the lord of the manor sent fish wonderful to see; and if they hadn't been hacked up in chunks no vessel could have contained them, so large were they. Some were prepared with onions and pepper, some with good red wine and honey cakes and sugar and raisins, some were pickled in wine-vinegar boiled with laurel leaves and onions, while some were fried. Those with onions and pepper were for after the ceremony, those with raisins for the morning feast since in the morning folk enjoy sweet things. The pickled ones were for the entire week of feasting; while as for the fried, it sometimes happens that a man doesn't want to wait until they set the dish for him, so instead he picks his portion up in his fingers and eats standing.

Meanwhile the men of Shebush were undecided whether this was a wedding made by the warden, in which case they had to bring presents worthy of the warden, or whether this was an orphan's wedding for which any present is good enough. Silly husbands, said their wives to them, can't you make it out? Do you reckon it's a plain and simple wedding when the warden goes out of his way to marry off an orphan? Now why is the warden marrying off an orphan? Because he has no children of his own; and if he had children of his own and were to marry them off, we'd be making ourselves new clothes—well, that's how it is now; the orphan can be reckoned as his son and the wedding as the wedding of his son, and so we and our daughters must have new clothes. Must we lose just because he happens to be childless? And they straightway began putting their principles into practice and ordering new clothes for themselves and their daughters, the swish of the hems of which could be heard two full Sabbath-days' journey from the town.

And Simeon Nathan invited all his kindred and friends, and sent waggons and horses to a number of towns to beseech the sages of Israel to come and light up the wedding with their honored presences. Some came bringing with them outstanding lads and desirable lads, saying, Since the bridegroom's an orphan and has no family to be present, let us go and treat the Torah with love.

When the wedding day came, the town was swarming with guests. And there was never a waggon coming to Shebush which didn't bring

crowds upon crowds of poor folk and needy, and beggars and wayfarers and tramps attracted from any number of leagues by the smell
of the honey and the roasts.

Shebush put on Sabbath garb and went to the bride and sat the
bride on a wooden seat; and the marriage jester, Reb Joel, stood
in front of her and said his say of admonition in song and tears. And
it was in this fashion he sang and chanted to her:

> *Raise thy voice on high, sweet bride,*
> *Forth as water pour thy heart.*
> *Know that at this present tide*
> *Heaven meteth thee thy part.*

And when the women standing before the bride heard the voice of
Reb Joel they began weeping and making the bride weep with him,
saying, Lift up thy voice, sweet bride, pour forth thy heart as water.
And he went on:

> *Who knows whether ease hath been*
> *Portioned thee from out the skies,*
> *Or if some grave deed of sin*
> *In thy balance heavy lies?*

And the women around wept and set the bride a weeping with
them. And he went off with the guests to the bridegroom's house,
all of them singing in the streets, the jester ahead of them. Entering
the bridegroom's house he recommenced before the bridegroom with
contrite thoughts, and sang with tears:

> *Alas bridegroom bridegroom, bridegroom so sweet,*
> *They name thee a king; thou 'rt proud as is meet.*
> *Bridegroom forbear, and hark to my voice,*
> *Forsake thy amusements, thy gauds and thy toys.*
> *Today thou art king, tomorrow who knows?*
> *Some rule with the rod and are ruled by their woes.*
> *Can this be dominion o'er matter to rule?*
> *Hold sway in God's fear, Scripture doth school.*

And so he sang, wringing their hearts till their eyes were emptied
of all their tears. Then the friends of the bride began dancing and
they lit plaited tapers and each girl took one, leading the procession
till they came to the Chief Synagogue and together with the bride

went round the bridegroom who stood under the canopy; and the gaon, Father of the Court, wedded them to one another. Thereupon the musicians began fiddling and fluting and playing all their other instruments, and they led bridegroom and bride and all those present to the feast.

They sat down to eat and did their hearts good with food and drink, wine, dainties, fish and all manner of flesh, beast and fowl. The great men of the Torah were all sitting quivering in eagerness to hear the address of the bridegroom who had maintained silence up till now, but whose time had come to let his light shine forth. They tossed and turned upon their seats, asking one another, When will he begin so that we can hear some pearls of Torah from him? And Reb Israel Solomon said to himself, It's about time he began, so that I can see the downfall of Simeon Nathan. Simeon Nathan, meanwhile, went to and fro among the guests, clapping every man on the shoulder in satisfaction; while Shprintsa Pessil thrust herself through, shouting, Jews, make room for me to listen as well.

But the bridegroom kept his mouth shut and stared at the upright horns of the hart, which stood on the table garnished with all manner of good things. The rabbi made a sign to the lad; he turned this way and that and fixed both his eyes on Reb Israel Solomon. Reb Israel Solomon, making believe, said, Open thy mouth and let thy words give light. Thereupon the bridegroom rose and gave his address on the problem in the Talmud of the woman riding the ass with a bundle upon it and two men walking in front of her, who says, These two are my slaves and the ass and bundle are mine, while each of the two men claims that he is the woman's husband and the other fellow is his slave; and he gave an exposition of the case and its solution that was sweet as honey. Then he went on to homiletics and legend, and gave an exposition of the Reward of Torah.

Then the jester rose on his chair, each one brought him his wedding present, and he proclaimed it in rhyme and rhythm:

> *The magnate renowned, sire of the bride,*
> *With his modest spouse, his crown and pride,*
> *Shprintsa Pessil and Simeon Nathan,*
> *Present to the bride and bridegroom one*
> *Pair of candlesticks silver pure,*
> *May their star shine bright and their star be sure,*

THE BRIDAL CANOPY

While I the jester, Reb Joel hight,
Sing sweet song till Messiah's in sight
To honor thee bridegroom, and thee O bride
As the sun and the moon so clear and bright,
And all who can sing will sing and cheer
Till the end of a hundred and twenty year.

And the worthy uncle of the bride,
(Her uncle on the mother's side),
Gives them a current bill and leal,
Written and stamped with the duke's big seal.
Let my love to his garden to eat his fruits
And the Lord send him the blessing he boots.

The worthy kinsman tried and true,
Presenteth a wooden mortar and trough
For matzoth, as Passover draweth near,
So sure may Redemption come to us here
When we'll eat of the offerings, the special and the plain,
And sing thanks to the Lord again and again.

The honoured Reb Elkanay, sterling as a guineay, gives as his gift—
a silver wine cup and spice box for spices to be whiffed, one for hal-
lowing the Sabbath on Friday night, and one for the ending of the
Sabbath tide; upright let him walk in the Lord God's light, being
saved from disease and blight and shielded always, to the very end of
days.

Now what is the worthy gift of the fine and wealthy aunt? A copper
laver as well as a mortar shows she regards her niece with favor just
as she oughter.

Last but not least that leader of Israel from belly and birth,
The princely Reb Israel Solomon, ruler over our synagogue hearth,
Who reared the bridegroom as though he were an only son,
And took him and set him in a resting place all his own,
Delivering his soul from hunger and cold,
Feeding him, clothing him in fine array
And giving him dainties day after day,
Now offers him the scepter of gold,

Presenting him the four-volume Turim with every comment
And margins full broad for what he holds is meant.
O bridegroom, awaken, bestir thee, awaken, arise,
Show those margins thou 'rt learned in Torah and wise;
Buckle thy learning upon thee and straight
Up and attack with thy quill; 'tis their fate.

The jester still stood on the chair looking this way and that and saying, What's the name of that fellow there, who hasn't given any present yet? And all those who had reckoned on getting away without any gifts trembled for fear of the jester's rhymes, and gave a coin which the jester would raise on high before the bride, saying in rhyme and rhythm:

This here coin, desired bride,
Has the face of the king upon one side.
Let the Face of the King before thee be
And kingly rabbis be born of thee.

Then Reb Joel, changing his voice, cried, From the bridegroom's side, from the bridegroom's side. Thereupon the rabbis rose, brought forth their documents from their pockets and handed them over to the jester. Taking out his eyeglasses, Reb Joel set them on his nose and, taking each document in turn, read thus in rhyme and tune:

Our master and rabbi, our rabbi so great, our mighty standby, our tower of fate, grinding the hills to dust with thought, famed in each gate and sage of the age, Father of the Court, in this town so sweet and rich, has given the groom his Permission to Teach.

From the holy garden of angel stock, the hammer mighty as a lightning shock, sage of the age who wrote the book The Booth of the Skin of Leviathan *saith to the son-in-law of Simeon Nathan, "In all matters that may be brought to thee, judge and decree, judge and decree."*

And so he stood reading all the other ordinations, those of the Rabbi of Monastrich and of the Rabbi of High Leshtshi, and of the Rabbi of little Pitshi and of the Rabbi of Lor nosewhere, all those places to which the lad had betaken himself to ask for his License to Instruct. The jester took document after document and handed it to the servant, who handed it to Simeon Nathan, and he set it on a silver salver in front of his son-in-law. And Reb Israel Solomon sat wondering and picked up the ordinations once and again, and read them through once and twice, and fingered them and crumpled them so that you could hear them rustling, as though he were trying to make the rustle drown the rattling of the bridegroom's knowledge of the Torah in his ears.

Who has caused this lad, Reb Israel Solomon asked himself, to achieve all this? Here was I wanting to gloat over my foe, Simeon Nathan, and now not only have I no chance of gloating over him but I've given his daughter a husband outstanding for knowledge of the Torah and for wisdom. As it says in Psalms, "He marked a pit and digged it, and fell in the trap he made." To what might Reb Israel Solomon be compared? To a man who fattened a cock all the year round to be his atonement on the Eve of the Day of Atonement; and just ere the Eve in question was reached the cock flew away.

Simeon Nathan rose with a glass of wine and came over to him. Reb Israel Solomon rose and drank to long life with him and they said the blessing, and each called the other in-law with pleasure. And he also took the bridegroom by the hand and conversed with him concerning the Torah so that both their faces shone. And the guests got up and danced and sang and danced until the old man came forth from his room and the sick from his bed, as the prophet has it.

Among those who came was the old man who had taught Torah to the bridegroom; seeing the honor of his pupil he rejoiced exceedingly, because the Lord doth not forsake forever by reason of His holy Torah. He began speaking on the glory of the Torah, and rejoiced both the All-Present and His creatures. They set him at the head and set before him old wine which pleases the aged, with flesh and fish. He drank, ate and drank, forgot his own sufferings and continued to expound the Torah till his name rang through the town. And when the judge, who aided the rabbi, went up to the Land of Israel, he was appointed righteous judge and righteous teacher in his stead.

Henceforward there was true peace between Reb Israel Solomon and Simeon Nathan's party, and Simeon Nathan's daughter bore sons and daughters, while her husband dwelt secure and merited to write a worthy study on the Tractate Kiddushin which deals with laws of marriage; thereby fulfilling the words of the prophet Isaiah who said, "Instead of copper I shall bring gold." Instead of the ignoramous bridegroom whom Reb Israel Solomon had wished to bring to Simeon Nathan's daughter, he brought her a scholar deeply versed in the Torah; and so peace upon Israel one and all.

A man may think his revenge he wreaks
And bringeth evil upon his fellow,
And yet be so tangled by the thing he seeks
That out of his action good must follow.

C HAPTER TWELVE: WHICH IS NOT AS LONG AS THE ONE BEFORE, AND IS SHORTER THAN THE ONE AFTER ♪ The party rose from their chairs, cried, Good luck, good luck, like folk at a wedding feast, filled up their glasses and drank afresh. The honor of Reb Israel Solomon, remarked Reb Zechariah, may rest where it is, but what he did to Reb Abele doesn't redound to his credit. And what was the story? It would have been better not to have been what it was.

Brother Zechariah, said Reb Kemuel, husband of Perele, Reb Zechariah's wife's sister, a good story's good to tell. Of the dead, responded Reb Zechariah, nothing should be said but praise. What's all this, Reb Zechariah, they cried, you have a story on the tip of your tongue and want to keep it from us?

Thereupon Zeida laughed—he was the husband of Frumtshi, Reb Zechariah's wife's sister—and said, Don't be worried about him remaining quiet. I know that when my brother-in-law Zechariah has a tale to tell he'll break off his prayers in the very middle in order to get it out of him.

And Reb Zechariah shifted his squarish skullcap about on his head and said, It would be better not to tell, but for two reasons I'll let you hear all about it; first of all, it is a good and pious deed to tell words of truth, and second, even so eminent a person as Reb Israel Solomon may not be flattered. And therewith he began telling of

THAT WHICH IS CONCEALED AND THAT WHICH IS REVEALED.

In Reb Israel Solomon's time there was nobody in Shebush to compare with Reb Abele. Reb Abele had a big tannery, with a district of his own for those who pursued this calling that lay east o' the town; quite a few Jewish families made a living at it. All the quarter was filled with houses and huts and great boilers and tanners' troughs; and waggons piled high with hides were always coming in or going out. Reb Abele's servants and their servants in turn were to be found all through the countryside, and never an animal was led to slaughter but they came and bought the hide. In Shebush it used to be a sort of proverb that the end of a beast is slaughter while the end of its hide is Reb Abele's tannery.

As a general run the servants and agents were to be found in all the hamlets and villages; the butchers brought any hides that they had, the tanners stood up to the waist in fat and manure and oil and pools of water, while Reb Abele sat at Torah and the service of the Lord. Excepting, of course, on the night of the departure of the Sabbath, when he would go down to his winter house and go over his accounts with the butchers and servants and agents, and give them money for the coming six days of the week; the rest of his time Reb Abele would spend studying Torah like his fathers and forefathers before him. If you never had a chance of seeing Reb Abele himself, have a look at his books which are full of emendations of his own and his forefathers.

All his life long Reb Abele fled from office and never took part in communal affairs. Though he did not take part in communal affairs, he did not withdraw himself from communal needs but together with the rest of the congregation bore the burden of taxes and levies for the needs of charity and the redemption of captives. In brief, Reb Abele concerned himself with the affairs of this world without ever forgetting that there is also another world. And can anybody say that that's not the proper way?

But what was no defect in our eyes was a grave defect in the eyes of Reb Israel Solomon, the warden. How could Reb Israel Solomon feel happy in his office when there was somebody who tried to dodge office? Had Reb Abele come and tried to replace Reb Israel Solomon, Reb Israel Solomon would have met him and mastered him; but if Reb Abele avoided office it was a sign that being warden was not good enough for him, from which it followed that he showed disrespect to the name, fame and rank of warden. There's a homely old saying that just as the hole in a ring of dough isn't a hole if the ring of dough isn't there, so office isn't office unless there are others trying to get the office. In short, Reb Abele sat at Torah and the service of the Lord, made money in a decent, law-abiding way, and went and brought up his sons and daughters to Torah and the Bridal Canopy and good deeds. And when the time came to think of settling his daughter Hannale, he had the idea of making a match with the fine families of Brod.

So he sent a special person to Brod. There his messenger found a lad of the best, everything that he ought to be and a member of one of the proudest families of the district. Then Reb Abele sent absent-minded Reb Zimele to sound the cask of the lad; and when Reb Zimele came back he reported a perfect cluster, a vessel of merit. And the proposed bridegroom's father sent someone frivolous to Shebush to view the bride; and back went he to report that she was nine full measures of beauty, a model for Queen Esther, the apple of Rabbi Akiba which dimmed the beauty of all the best stock of Brod. Reb Abele named so-and-so much as his daughter's portion, and the in-law of Brod so-and-so much; and they met at a village halfway between Shebush and Brod to write the Engagement Contract.

When poor folk marry off their children they put their trust in their Father in Heaven. The Blessed Name, they say, will aid. But when rich folk marry their children off you might suppose that there is nothing left for the Holy and Blest One to do. The representative of the bride promises to give so-and-so much, the representative of the bridegroom promises to give so-and-so much, and it would seem that there's no more needed for bride and bridegroom than to place themselves under the Bridal Canopy.

To cut a long story short the match was arranged. They didn't waste much time. Reb Abele kept as silent as usual; and the in-law, one of the puffed-up Brod aristocrats, assuredly didn't pour forth nine measures o' chatter. They arranged what they had met to arrange and went back home, one to Brod and t'other to Shebush. The bridegroom's father came and told his son that he was a bridegroom, while the bride's father came and told his daughter she was a bride. And preparations for the wedding began.

The Brod personage had wedding clothes brought from Ginsprink and Leipzig, while Reb Abele and his wife went to the Lashkevitz fair where they purchased whole rolls of wool, silk, satin, alpaca and so on for the bride's garments, all of the finest and the best, as befits a wealthy man who has made a match with a wealthy man. Apart from this they brought from foreign parts a complete set of the Talmud with all commentators and the synopsis of Alfasi, together with all his armor-bearers; and they sat tailors and seamstresses down in two rooms; and set aside a room for the bookbinder and his apprentices to bind the set of the Talmud in red parchment, as a gift for the bridegroom on the occasion of his marriage. The sewing and the binding were as nothing against the cooking and the baking, the cakemaking and the frying; for the wife of Reb Abele brought many a cook and baker and confectioner.

And there was so great a slaughter of chickens in Shebush that you couldn't get an egg with which to smear the Sabbath loaves before baking, not even for a guinea a smear; and Reb Abele made many feasts for the poor before the wedding, and prepared many gifts to give the needy on the occasion of the wedding, apart from their being summoned among all the other guests to come and rejoice with him at the wedding itself. He even arranged to bring a poor bride under the canopy on the day of the wedding of his praiseworthy daughter, Mistress Hannale; and the name of the poor bride was also Hannale. For that was the custom in those times among such of the God-fearing as merited to maintain two tables, one for themselves and another for the poor.

Yet how shall a man beware the workings of time? They made all those preparations, prepared to rejoice so full and free, had the blessings of plenty all ready for the young couple, and quiet and ease awaiting the bridegroom; but God gives the beard and men pluck it out and tear their cheeks. Immediately following the seven days of feasting the bridegroom sent a divorce to his wife; the very lips that were still repeating, Behold thou art hallowed to me, now said, Sundered from me; just as though the father-in-law of Brod had gone aloft to the Upper Assembly and heard behind the veil that his son and Reb Abele's daughter had not been divinely ordained for one another on high forty days before their birth.

Now why did the father-in-law see fit to annul the marriage? That which is concealed is for the Lord our God, while that which is revealed is for us and our children. And that which is revealed to us we shall tell.

You already know there was a barrier high as a mountain between Reb Israel Solomon and Reb Abele; and presumably Reb Israel Solomon wasn't letting any chance of crossing Reb Abele go by. Reb Israel Solomon wasn't the sort to sit and do nothing. But what could he do when Reb Abele, in turn, wasn't the sort to boil over? The more taxes and levies he put upon him, the more cheerfully he paid. If he sent the collector ahead of time Reb Abele settled his demands quietly, and what was more paid him in current coin of the realm;

which was not like Shebush folk who are tricky about charity and give worn-out coins, the accepter of which is bound to lose.

Folk who like to stir up strife used to say, Reb Abele, Reb Israel Solomon is taxing you a bit too heavily. The warden, replied Reb Abele, knows what he's doing. Oh yes, said the troublemakers, Reb Israel Solomon certainly knows what he's up to; he's doing this to annoy you, Reb Abele. And should a decent Jew, said Reb Abele, regret that he's given an opportunity of devoting his money to charity? And that would lock and seal the mouths of the trouble-makers, so that they departed ashamed. And meanwhile Reb Israel Solomon waited impatiently for his opportunity to arrive of venting his spleen on Reb Abele.

It is usually the case that you don't find a warden without any number of idlers and good-for-nothings hanging about him, these being a sort of folk who came into the world only in order to destroy souls in their bodies so that the End of Days may be brought near. And in the city of Shebush with all its other fine and exalted qualities there was naught lacking of the class of men who lived up to the ancient hymn-writer's metaphor, "And featureless creatures came forth from the fat of their eyne, expressing all evil and thinking some wicked and bitter design"; a rabble of sinful fellows who were ready to jump down into hell at the slightest sign of the warden, and bring even their own fathers back from thence, shackled in iron fetters.

And so it came about that not long before the day of the wedding Reb Israel Solomon summoned one of his chosen. And whom should he summon if not Pinye Pest? And Reb Israel Solomon did not need to do more than hint to Pinye that he was interested in the match. Pinye at once understood all that was meant. He gripped his beard in wonder, chewed the hair between his teeth and then let it fly loose. Reb Israel Solomon wiped his face, gave him his expenses and said, Here's the teacher's fees for your children and my household will keep your wife in fish and flesh for Sabbaths. And Pinye going out with a parting blessing kissed the mezuzah on the way; and the warden nodded his head and said, Well, well, go along, and the Lord prosper thy way. In brief, everything and everyone in Shebush was ready for the wedding, and in Brod they were busy inviting the guests to leave for Shebush with the bridegroom; and meanwhile Pinye started out for Brod.

Brod's a big city before God with many houses in it, each o' them bigger than Og, king of Bashan. And there isn't a house that doesn't contain double the number of people to be found in all She-bush. There you'll find bankers and merchants and peddlers and smugglers and steady students and writers of books. Some come to get an approbation on their books from the sages of the Close; some come to ask for signatures of the kind known as subscriptions; and there are wealthy pedigreed gentlewomen whom the porters carry on their shoulders of a rainy day, and charity wardenesses toddling along with red handkerchiefs in their hands. And there are any number of shops with all kinds of clothes and all kinds of good things and all kinds of liquor; you can find brandy and honey water and plum juice, and bread, honey and fruit, and stuffed fish and salt fish, and spices and balsams, and precious stones and pearls, and crowns and kerchiefs, and caps and hats, and shoes and leather, and satin and lawns and silks. Each of the shops has great windows, and every window has wooden stands in it that are covered with fine clothes, so that your heart grips you to see the habits of the men of Brod who waste their money on wooden shapes that have no feel-ing, and go and dress them and shoe them and adorn them with fine ornaments when so many scholars are walking about naked, without garments, and barefoot, for want of shoes.

And each of the shops is full of customers and agents, agents who have come with the customers and agents who have come despite the customers; and every customer that comes brings two experts with him, one to earn something and the other to exercise his judgment. If you never saw Brod you don't know what a great city and mother in Israel looks like.

And Pinye, seeing Brod in all its wealth and plenty, said to him-self, Since I've come here I'll just try my luck a bit from door to door. It would be a sin to take pity on the Brod ninnies. And so he went abegging from door to door until he reached the home of Reb Abele's in-law.

Now in the house of Reb Abele's future in-law everything was ready for the journey to Shebush; they were already packing and locking cases, and loading them on waggons and painting the coaches. One day a pauper entered; before they could even hand him an alms he had fallen to the floor in a fit. All the household gathered around him at once and rubbed his body with vinegar until he came to himself. And where are you from, the household folk asked him. From Shebush, he replied.

The magnate at once called him into his own room and gave him a glass of brandy with honey cake. Do you know Reb Abele? he asked. And to which Reb Abele, asked Pinye in return, might your honor be referring? Maybe to Charity Abele who stole from the Charity Funds and fled to Wallachia, or maybe to Abele Kindling? The magnate stared at him and said, Reb Abele, the tanner, spitting the name out in a fury. Of course I know him, said the pauper. And who should know him if not me? As sure as I'm a Jew I knew your honor must be referring to that Abele, only I says to myself, I says, Don't start off with all you know, I says. As the proverb says, You go along to a feast to feed on meat, yet you starts off wi' radishes and onions. A fine question you asked me whether I know him; why, we're neighbors. Abele the tanner fits his name and his name fits him. Seeing he once tumbled head over heels into a tanner's pit and so they all began calling him Abele tanner. Great jokers they are, the men o' Shebush.

Is all well with him and his daughter? asked the magnate. All's well with her *now,* thank God, he answered, and stressed the now. The other jumped and said, Now? Do you mean she was sick? The pauper twisted his mouth and said, Sick? We—ell, not exactly, and yet I suppose you could call it sick in a way. What do you mean? said the magnate.

Thereupon Pinye took the bottle, poured himself out a glass and said, Well, truth to tell, her sickness can't hardly be reckoned a real sort of disease, as you might say. And while speaking he stopped, stretched out his hand to the householder, raised his two eyes aloft and said, Long life, long life, long life, may the All-Merciful deliver us from that disease. Long life, responded the magnate impatiently, his ears big as mill hoppers. And the pauper poured himself out a second glass, drank, wiped his mouth and began telling his tale to the householder.

Once, he began relating, it happened as that there wench gave a come in to borrow a pot from my missus, and the two women fell a chatting. Hannale, says my missus to her, Hannale, it ain't the pancake as is important, only the stuff you puts inside; you know as how one of us poor folk, when we've been working in wealthy folk's houses where everybody has been enjoying of her cooking and baking—well, when she becomes a mistress on her own her grub don't never have no sort of taste.

Missus, says I to my missus, what for do you need to go abroad for a case? It's the daughter of our Abele you're a speaking to. Why, the warden can't even eat any grub if she don't cook it, and yet if you go and eat at Abele's you find his bread's half straw and half ashes. It's the same hands, and it's the same making, only the dough makes all the difference. Well, Hannale, says my missus to Hannale, and what ha' you got to say to that?

Hannale opens her mouth. But before ever she had a chance o' beginning to speak her face began twisting up and her eyes began bulging and she fell to the ground wi' her arms and feet thrown out and screeching fit to frighten you, the Merciful One save us, and her lips began foaming all colors. And how sorry we all felt for her that time. But her mother came along and said, Leave her alone and she'll get up by herself. And then we knew it was the falling sickness she had, may it never be told of us nor of any other Jewish man.

In a few moments she stirred and roused from her sickness and was quite all right, only her face was bruised from her fall and so was her forehead. Nor could you even recognize as she had been sick, because that's what the folk what suffers from the falling sickness take on like; today they lies all stretched out like a corpse and tomorrow they're quite all right. And you don't need to be afraid it may come back and she'll fall again some time; that won't be happening because one of these days she'll be coming under the Bridal Canopy and once she'll be in the family way her sickness will leave her.

And so Pinye sat discoursing of all manner of events that had never happened, like a man casually chatting, and while speaking he turned his eyes aloft in piety. At last the magnate remembered the sort of fellow sitting before him, took out a Rhenish gulder and gave it him. The beggar opened the door and went his way, while the other remained sitting silent.

Along came his servant and said, Master, everything is ready for the journey. The magnate stared around at all the preparations and said, What's it all for? All his family stared at one another, going red in the face, and began asking one another questions and whispering together. But it was impossible to get a word out of him. So they start out a sighing.

Let him write a divorce, said the magnate to himself, and not return the Engagement Contract to the bride, the shame being too great for a daughter of Israel. An evil eye must have overlooked my son. The Merciful One desires an atonement.

But it was not with dancing waggons and joyful throngs that they all made their way to Shebush. Instead they started out with only two waggons and a few relations, all of them sitting like mourners, the Merciful One deliver us. And that was the way that the wealthy man of Brod traveled to wed his learned son with the daughter of the famous and princely Reb Abele.

The in-laws came to Shebush. At the Sabbath boundary they found themselves awaited by a nice few dozen people, no evil eye upon them, who had come out to meet them. And Reb Israel Solomon began to fear that Pinye Pest must have toiled in vain. But pride and foolishness are the wickedness of human beings in the second degree. Even the father-in-law himself had thought for a moment that the beggar must have come to deceive him; but who can be compared with Brod folk for gullibility? It's with good reason they're known as the Brod gulls.

And so he never said to himself, I listened to all he had to say without making any inquiries, but made the mistake of thinking that these folk were the wags of whom the beggar had spoken, and they had come to deride and mock. Then their garments misled him, for the folk of Shebush are not so particular in dress as the folk of Brod. The Shebush folk deal mostly in meal, and those in the flour line take the trouble of coming to them, like a bird that smells seed and comes a flying. But the men of Brod, who deal in all manner of goods, travel to many places, and where a man is not known his clothes speak for him. And so the magnate thought that these folk had changed their clothes like the Purim players in order to make mock of the parties.

And besides, his pride prevented him recognizing the truth. Here he had come with so few people, not at all in accordance with his standing; and was it likely that everything had been properly arranged by the bride's people? No, whether he liked it or not, the bride's father must be a pauper and a rogue, and all those who had come out to meet him must be worthless folk, and he would show them how he would deal with them. And once he began along such lines he followed them. His family, who felt superior to the Shebush

[177]

folk as dwellers in large towns do feel superior over those who live in little places and have never tasted the joys of a great town, also disregarded the respect due, and spoke to the Shebush folk as a man might speak to his servants.

And what did the Shebush folk do thereat? Went back home, saying, Have a look at these stuck-up Brod ninnies. In our cemetery, thank God, we have just as great aristocrats as those, buried without even a tombstone over their graves or a fence round them; and the swine still root among their bones. And they added, It's better to sit and do nothing; and so they never went to the feast.

Now when everything is ready at the feast, who needs who? Do the guests require the feast or the feast the guests? It's clear the feast requires the guests. Indeed, let the Brod aristocrats consume the whole of the grub themselves, and may they profit of the shining of the Shechina in the near future. So in brief the cream of the congregation never went to the wedding, and the only ones there were butchers, tanners and hide dressers.

Where there is no decent man the worthless rule with a high hand. At the ceremony the scapegrace boys came with pins, and began pricking the bridegroom and his relations in their private parts, as is the custom at the weddings of the ignorant. And there was nothing to distinguish between Hannale, Reb Abele's daughter, and the wench Reb Abele was marrying off as a good and righteous deed. And what was that wedding like? Like a Purim play as far as the outer world was concerned, and a house of mourning, the Merciful One deliver us, to those concerned. As the Palestine Talmud says, that's what levity is like; it begins with pains and ends with destruction.

The townsfolk rubbed the sleep out of their eyes with the dawn, remembered that the night before Hannale had come under the Bridal Canopy, and stood wondering. Heavens, was it Reb Abele's way to marry his daughter off like that! And the Brod father-in-law, remembering that he knew Reb Israel Solomon, went to visit him.

He found him sitting in his easy chair in front of the stove, where he always sat whether it was sunny or rainy; the Tractate on Sacrifices was open before him, his pipe was in his mouth, and Lasunka lay curled up between his feet arching her back and rubbing herself against the wool of his white hose while he dipped bread in milk and set it before her. The Brod worthy entering greeted Reb Israel

Solomon, who puffed at his pipe, blew a cloud of smoke round the other, asked, And whence might your honor be? And while asking he recognized him, greeted him back and cried, Esther Malka, Esther Malka, prepare some refreshments; we have a guest from Brod.

And what, Reb Israel Solomon asked the Brod worthy, might your honor be doing here? Why, hasn't your honor heard, replied the Brod worthy, that I have just married off my son. *Mazal tov, mazal tov,* replied Reb Israel Solomon, may it be in a good and prosperous hour. And with whom did your honor make a match? Surely not with anybody of Shebush. Most assuredly, replied the other, with somebody of Shebush. Well, said Reb Israel Solomon, I'm astonished to hear there is anybody of such standing here. And with whom was your honor's match arranged?

What's the meaning of that with whom? exclaimed the other. With Reb Abele the tanner. Reb Abele, Reb Abele, the tanner, repeated Reb Israel Solomon thoughtfully. Reb Abele, the tanner, your honor says. It surprises me to hear there is such a Reb Abele here. There can't be such an Abele.

What do you mean there can't be, cried the Brod worthy. Why, I took his daughter as wife for my son. The secret of the Lord, quoted Reb Israel Solomon, is for those that fear him, and He shall inform them of His covenant. I've never had the merit of knowing such a Reb Abele.

And Reb Israel Solomon called his wife Esther Malka and asked, Esther Malka, do you know anybody here named Reb Abele, the tanner? Whom do you say? asked Esther Malka. Reb Abele, the tanner, said Reb Israel Solomon and the magnate together. Reb Abele, the tanner? asked Esther Malka. Yes, said the magnate, Reb Abele, the tanner. Then Esther Malka asked afresh, Reb Abele the tanner? And she drew the name out dubiously, adding, It's the first time I've heard that name. Our friend here, said Reb Israel Solomon, says that Reb Abele, the tanner, has a daughter who went under the Bridal Canopy yesterday.

Why, Blessed be He, exclaimed Esther Malka, who brings back to mind that which is forgotten! Oh, said Reb Israel Solomon, so you know about it; tell us. Why, didn't a lass get married yesterday, said Esther Malka, and didn't we sent her a gift through Tsirel Treine, because sometimes that lass used to help Tsirel Treine in the kitchen?

[179]

Tsirel Treine, Reb Israel Solomon explained to the other, is the servingmaid in our house.

Israel Solomon, Esther Malka continued, you know the bride as well; surely you remember the lass who bakes stuff for you. Thereupon Reb Israel Solomon began praising the bride, and was so carried away by his praises that he took out a cake and said, Your Honor must taste some; this is a cake she made with her very own hands.

Not that Reb Israel Solomon and Esther Malka were lying, God forbid; but they were not answering what was asked. The in-law was asking about Reb Abele's daughter who had been married the day before, and they replied about the orphan girl who had been married at the same time. And the magnate listened to all the praises of the bride as a man hearing bad news for which he is as yet entirely unprepared. And meanwhile the warden wound up his praises of the girl by taking hold of a single hair of his earlocks and saying, A fine question to ask whether I know her.

Thereupon the Brod worthy took his leave and departed in a fury, ordered his driver to harness the horses, took his son, the bridegroom, together with his wife and kin, and began to prepare to return to Brod. What's this, in-law? Reb Abele's people asked him in astonishment. Instead of entering into conversation he quoted the words of the Talmud, "And have I been waxed so hard and fast to you?" And he told his driver, Turn the horses and start off.

What is there more to tell than I have told? May the Lord preserve all those that love him from such a wedding. The young woman went about like a shadow, her hands on her shaven head. Reb Abele, who was never shaken by the mishaps of time, was left tottering at the blow. His wife grew sick, and all his household held their heads drooping with shame and worry. Thus passed the seven days of feasting, without comfort or hope. When the seven days of the feast were at an end, a messenger arrived from Brod and delivered a divorce to Hannale.

CHAPTER THIRTEEN: FROM ONE STORY TO ANOTHER, WITH A STORY IN THE MIDDLE; APART FROM THE STORY OF MECHEL, THE WHICH IS A STORY IN ITSELF ᴓ Israel Solomon leapt to his feet, saying, God forfend that Reb Israel Solomon ensnared anybody. Why, his very pet led to a great deliverance for Israel. How did such a thing, they asked, come about through his pet? Well, and I am astonished, he replied, that you never heard tell of it; why, the whole country rang with the story of Lasunka——

At this point the voice of the beadle was heard, summoning Israel to serve the Creator. They emptied their glasses, water was brought for them to wash their hands and they said grace in the Name of God, according to custom when there are more than ten present. Then they went forth to prepare themselves for the Morning Prayers. In came the maidservants to clear the dishes and shake the table-cloth; and the cat between their feet snatched at the bones and the scraps of meat; and they gave the crumbs to the chickens and brought the mistress of the house the cocks and hens, so that she should choose the best for slaughter. And of those slaughtered they made two meals, one for the day, it being the custom in the lands of His Majesty the Kaiser to eat meat in the daytime, and another at night to fulfill the words of Exodus, "When the Lord doth give you meat to eat in the evening."

It is one of the things that I cannot explain, Reb Yudel related. I was awake all night long, and all the same it seemed to me that I was at a party. I don't know how I got there, whether with the two merchants of Brod or by means of Ivory and Peacock; but there I was, and it's clear to me as the sun that, among those who came to see the feast, I saw my daughter Pessele, and she was weeping.

Daughter, said I to her, why are you weeping? Father, she answered, I'm not weeping. But I can see you are weeping, said I to her, so why do you tell me you're not weeping? I'm standing here, said she, to view the bride, and if my eyes are weeping what should I do to them? There and then I began sorrowing for her and said, Daughter, as sure as you're standing watching the happiness of others you'll merit to see your own rejoicing; and I promise you that all these people and many more like them will soon come to see you standing with your bridegroom under the Bridal Canopy. As is well known, Reb Yudel continued, a man's brain is divided into two parts, as is mentioned in Reb Yom Tov Lippman Heller's commentary on the Mishnah of Chastisements, so that if he's sick on one side he should feel it on the other side; but that day my head ached all over, that is, on both sides. I can't say whether it was because of the wedding music in my dream, or because I was so sorry for my daughter.

And Reb Yudel continued, Good wardens there used to be in Israel who directed their generation with wisdom, and dealt faithfully with the interests of the community, and increased the honor of the All-Present; and they departed the world with a good name, and once dead were forgotten. But Reb Israel Solomon's name still rings and echoes like a bell, and whenever his name's mentioned people grow cheerful. And this happiness of theirs about Reb Israel Solomon, may he rest in peace, was in part shared by Israel Solomon, long life to him. They showed him much honor, for folk followed him about asking him to tell them the tale of the lad for whom the Holy and Blest One had established such a warden as Reb Israel Solomon, in order that the lads might know that the Holy and Blest One does not withhold the reward of those that study Torah.

But Israel Solomon used to give them short shrift, after the fashion of Shebush folk who don't mix too freely with those below them. And what's more he mocked them, saying that Zbarev folk are donkeys for calling that fellow a lad, seeing they ought to understand for themselves that he had already grown to be a man old enough to have sons and daughters whom it was time to marry off. Still they stood crowding round him on all sides; and while those stood there their friends and their friends' friends came crushing and cramming onto his very knees and shoulders and chest.

I remember, related Reb Yudel, the day he went out into the market place. By your lives even the prophet Jonah was never in so tight a fix when the whale swallowed him; for when Jonah entered the bowels of the fish the Holy and Blest One made place for him there, so that he entered as a man walks into a large and roomy synagogue; and the two eyes of the fish were like windows for Jonah to peer up into the heights and down into the deeps. But Israel Solomon was caught and squashed among that host; so that while Jonah had been able to pray at ease in the bowels of the fish, Israel

Solomon wasn't even able to let out a single oh! in the press. When at last he did escape from his peril Reb Zechariah went forth to meet him and led him to his own room; and there they told one another stories, the one of Shebush and the other of Brod, until the rafters began hopping and dancing with the laughter.

In the course of conversation Israel Solomon told Reb Zechariah that he was an emissary of Reb Jacob Moses, Simeon Nathan's son-in-law, who had a worthy son that he wished to wed to the daughter of an outstanding person. Reb Zechariah, said Israel Solomon, when I arrived here, I saw that your father-in-law Reb Ephraim has a young daughter who ought to be thinking about marriage, and it struck me as a good idea if a match were to be made between her and Simeon Nathan's grandson.

Now don't be surprised that he began by belittling Simeon Nathan and at the last said, Give your daughter as wife to his grandson; he did it wisely, after the fashion in which Eliezer, Abraham's slave, told his master's kin, "And Sarah, my master's wife, bare a son to my master when she was old." Those last four words, "when she was old", seem to be unnecessary at first sight; what should I care whether she bare in her youth or her old age? But it was because the scandal-mongers of those days went about saying that Sarah had conceived from Abimelech, king of Gerar, and Eliezer feared that Bethuel and Laban might also have heard the tittle-tattle and could say, We do not desire Abraham's son, it not being in accordance with their honor to make a match with a man who is in any way suspect, God forbid; and he therefore got ahead and said, We know what the scandal-mongers say, and so on.

So it was with Israel Solomon. He knew that if he said to these aristocrats, Give your daughter to Simeon Nathan's grandson, they would tell him, Pack up your feet and clear off; and he therefore began by telling the tale of the youth, as much as to say, We know just who Simeon Nathan was, and yet Heaven itself did him the favor of giving his daughter to a disciple of the wise; and if Torah's there everything's there.

And so they began telling one another stories of matches, and Israel Solomon said to Reb Zechariah, Come and have a look how much trouble the Holy and Blest One goes to in order to pair off two human beings, and yet there's never a match in this country but other folk go out of their way to try and spoil it. Just at that point

Reb Zechariah's wife came in and said, Woe to the eyes that see the like—two Jews sitting and discoursing of Torah when it's almost Natal night already. So they laughed and went to pray.

Afterward folk came from town and sat down to play cards with the household, while Reb Ephraim sat at the end of the table preparing toilet paper for the whole year. The players shuffled the cards and took out their loose change from their pockets and put it beside them. Now you could hear the cards shuffling and now coins jingling, and what with one and the other the heart lusts after the small change. God forbid that they played away their days at cards, wasting their time in a place where they acquire themselves the life of the World to Come by studying Torah; but cards were prohibited in the generations before our own for the sake of public order; and because the authorities feared that folk would give way to their evil inclinations and transgress the prohibition, they provided that it did not apply to Hanukah and Natal night. But the meticulous keep their hands from cards at Hanukah.

Happy are they and happy their portion that they do not lose their money at cards and do not waste the days of Hanukah in laughter and lightheadedness, as is written in the books, "In the days of Hanukah a man should wisely give thanks and praise and lauds, by reason of the wonders and miracles which the Holy and Blest One performed for the sake of our fathers in those times"; he should not, God forbid, waste them in cards which were invented by the cardinals of evil. For when the Greek Empire strove to make His blessed Torah forgotten, they invented thirty-six cards against the thirty-six tractates in which the Torah was given. What is card-play on Hanukah like? Like a man, to whom a king has done good, going out of his way the same moment to annoy the king. And therefore he who fears the Lord carries out his duty on Natal night merely by obeying the prohibition to study matters of Torah.

At the same time the gentile women were sitting in the kitchen where straw was spread on the floor, and a sheaf of green corn lay on the bench pointing toward the likeness of their object of awe, and a cloth was spread on the table with garlic and green corn underneath it. After they had had their belly's fill of rye bread, sesame, wheat, honey, cabbage, buckwheat, dried fish and fruit, the oldest of the company took a spoonful of the food and flung it at the wall;

then she went to count how many grains remained stuck to the wall in order to know how many benefits, blessings and comforts the Holy and Blest One would be giving the master of the house in the coming year; and she set aside the pot in which she had cooked the meal, and the spoon with which she had stirred it, for the souls of their relations to come that selfsame night and eat thereof. And the young girls opened the door and stood listening to hear from which side the barking of a dog would first come, since it was from that side that their bridegrooms would be coming for them.

But Reb Ephraim and his household sat in the big room, Reb Ephraim at the head, Reb Yudel at his right hand and Israel Solomon on his left. After they had eaten and drunk, some of those present said to Israel Solomon, Reb Israel Solomon, and now tell us the tale of Lasunka. Thereupon Israel Solomon crossed his legs, stroked his beard and said, Your desire honors me.

There were a few students there who had not been present the previous night, and one of them asked another, What sort of thing is this Lasunka? Why, said the other inventing on the spur of the moment to conceal his ignorance, it's a term in a Passage in the Mishnah of Bechorot (Firstborns). Blessed be He who brings forgotten things to mind, said the first. I myself completed the Tractate of Bechorot during the first Nine days of Ab and so ate meat, which would not have been permissible otherwise; and on that same page I cleared up the grave disagreement between the Tosaffists and Rashi. Before he finished his sentence another broke in, Yes, and that explanation was given long ago by our Master Rabbi Solomon Luria. Or ever this one had finished his words somebody else had interrupted.

Blest be the All-Present, blest be He, said Reb Yudel; although He has exiled me from my home He has exiled me to a place of Torah, where the disciples of the wise sit vying one with another in erudition. And the desire for study entered into him so as verily to pain him to the heart. At the end of the table sat people who were not quite such great scholars. What's Lasunka? one of them asked a second. I'm astonished at you, said the one asked, for not knowing what Lasunka is. Being ashamed to ask again lest he be thought an ignoramus, he remained silent.

And now Reb Ephraim rapped on the table with his fingers and said, Well? Israel Solomon stroked his beard afresh, joined together his thumb and index finger in a circle, and sat relating the story of

LASUNKA
or
MAN AND BEAST.

One Thursday Tsirel Treine took the knife to cut up the meat and found that her hand wouldn't obey her. What's this, Tsirel Treine, said she to herself, all these chickens that you prepared today, and the New Moon feast you prepared for the fine folk of the town, without anything wrong with your hand, and now it has to go and trouble you? She spat behind her, stuck the knife in the poultry and carved them up into pieces, putting each piece in the pot, took the innards of the chickens and set them on the floor so that Lasunka could come and take her due.

But Lasunka never came. Tsirel Treine laughed to herself, saying Oho, Lasunka, proud you're becoming, eh? Well, we'll see who needs who? And in this Tsirel Treine erred, thinking that Lasunka required her; this was not so, for had it not been for Lasunka the meat would have been spoilt through lying about, but Lasunka's movements forced her to be spry.

Just then she heard Esther Malka calling, Tsirel Treine, have you prepared everything? Tsirel Treine lifted up her knife and called back, Mistress, mistress. Into the kitchen came Esther Malka and asked, What is it, a problem for the rabbi again? Tsirel Treine turned her eyes on Esther Malka and said, Lasunka's not here. Silly, replied Esther Malka, wait until she smells the innards and she'll be here quick enough. Then Tsirel Treine pointed with the knife in her hand to the offal on the floor and silently shook her head.

Esther Malka went red in the face trying to remember when and where she had last seen Lasunka. Why, she cried at length in grief, I haven't seen her at all today. And either of the two turned her pale startled face to t'other. And since they saw no reason for hope their sudden grief increased. If she wasn't in the house where could she be? Never had she been seen under a neighbor's rooftree. Lasunka was an aristocrat and knew her place, which was in front of the fire smoothing her fur on wintry days, and sunning herself in the open during summer. Observe, Lasunka used to seem to remark; everything there is in the house can equally well be found in the open. For your stove and mice in the house there are your sun and birds in the open. And therein Lasunka laid herself open to the charge of the heresy of dualism, for she did not know that Man is likewise the handiwork of the Holy and Blest One, so that if he did stoke the stove and warm up the house, it was all equally of His blessed light.

And now Esther Malka remembered that her husband would be returning from the House of Study and, sitting down to eat, would wish to feed pieces to Lasunka—and she would not be there. So Esther Malka stretched out her two hands and cried, Lasunka, Lasunka, where are you, Lasunka? Tsirel Treine, seeing the sorrow of Esther Malka, said to herself, Seeing that the mistress takes on so, it's a sign that I shan't be held responsible for Lasunka but she will be; it isn't from me the master will demand Lasunka but from her. And she straightway, having found herself some comfort, returned to her work.

And so Esther Malka was left standing and scratching her head, as was her habit when confronted by matters beyond her understanding. Since she saw no way out she said to herself, Lasunka won't be found so quickly, so what am I to do but see that Israel Solomon is delayed and doesn't sit down to eat at once. For Esther Malka waited on Time to do its work. It was like the case of the tollkeeper to whom the lord of the manor gave a dog to be taught to pray in the prayer book. If I refuse, thought the tollkeeper, he'll kill me out of hand, so instead I'll fix him a time; meanwhile either I'll die or he'll die or the dog 'll die.

After Tsirel Treine had scrubbed the pot and wiped the knife she went out into the street and asked the passers-by, Maybe you've seen Lasunka? And she stood asking, Have you seen Lasunka, have you seen Lasunka? And straightaway everybody knew that Lasunka had run away. Folk began joking and said, Now Reb Israel Solomon will have to feed his leavings to the mice.

But when they thought the matter over they began wondering what Lasunka could have seen to run away. Particularly on a Thursday when kitchens are full of chicken gizzards and innards. One man in the street came out, after the fashion of such, with the explanation, Why, it's plain as plain can be; this is the month of Adar, which comes out the same time as what the gentiles call March; and it's a widespread custom throughout the cat world that in the month of

THE BRIDAL CANOPY

March cats go out climbing on the roofs; rest assured Lasunka hasn't cut herself off from the rest of the cat community.

It happened that just then along came a village Jew who had been expelled from his inn, and now came to beg Reb Israel Solomon to intercede with the lord of the manor on his behalf. Said he, Stop your joking. Who knows what this vanished Lasunka was ere she was a cat, or what incarnation she might have been? And all the townsfolk cried out in wonder, An incarnation now?

The village Jew looked all round him first, and then whispered, I'll tell you. Probably Lasunka was Reb Israel Solomon's beadle in an earlier incarnation, and Reb Israel Solomon didn't treat him properly; just as he oppresses all his servants, so he oppressed that selfsame beadle. And when that beadle came to die it was decreed on high that he must return to This World, as it says in Proverbs "to punish the just is not good"; and our sages of blessed memory said in the Talmud, "Nobody on account of whom a fellow man is punished is brought within the bounds of the Holy and Blest One"; and therefore he descended and was incarnated in a cat; and now that Reb Israel Solomon has righted in Lasunka what he wronged toward the beadle, and the soul has been righted and the days of the incarnation are at an end, that selfsame soul no longer has any business to attend to in this Lower World; and therefore Lasunka has vanished, and I tell you there's no hope whatsoever of finding her.

When Reb Israel Solomon heard that Lasunka had vanished he quivered at the tidings as at a blow. Nonetheless he did not put any blame on the folk of his household; but the sorrow glistening in his eyes seemed to speak all the iniquities in the world. You might have thought that whoever did not return Lasunka to him must have smuggled her away. And on the Sabbath Eve he felt her absence even more. Reb Israel Solomon was accustomed, when he entered his house on Sabbath Eve and began repeating the "Peace be unto you, angels of peace, ministering angels", to have Lasunka jumping up toward him and catching the tassels of his girdle; the savor of the hallowing wine and the fish made her very wise, as it says in the Talmud that wine and scents make one clearheaded. He in turn would amuse himself watching her motions and jumping, and with a sweet voice would sing "Who shall find a woman of valor."

But this Sabbath Reb Israel Solomon entered his home as one might enter a house of mourning, the Merciful One prevent us and deliver us; he repeated the "Peace be unto you" in a low voice, and hallowed the wine in so dejected a tone that Tsirel Treine's eyes filled with tears and she vowed a half-pound of candles to the synagogue when Lasunka would be found. She also thought upon going to Issachar Demon so that he might tell her where Lasunka was.

Reb Israel Solomon broke bread and dipped it in salt, sat back comfortably in his chair and stretched out his legs, expecting that they would meet Lasunka's plump body; but they remained hanging stretched. And to whom might Reb Israel Solomon be then compared? To a man falling in dream from the roof into a deep pit; although he is not injured the feeling of tumbling shakes him up.

That night Reb Israel Solomon paid no attention to the guest he had brought home with him for the Sabbath. The guest, seeing that the house was full of good cheer and the household vessels bore witness that the master of the house must be wealthy, sat wondering why the faces of the household folk should be so downcast, and all the more so on the Sabbath. Seeing that the great trouble of that poor fellow was how to make a living he could not so much as imagine that there might be any other worry. But being modest and humble he did not even dare to open his mouth and ask.

Instead he remembered that in the countries of the west there is a wealthy Jew who cannot eat unless he be told something new; all the desirable things of earth are worthless to him compared with travelers' tales, and whoever brought him news of something fresh was well entreated by him. And he thought to himself, How many tales I have heard on my travels, like the story of the gluttonous preacher, and the story of the horses that went astray, and the story of the reprover who stuck his head inside the Holy Ark during his sermon and stole the holy vessels. And these tales are so well fitted to cheer downcast spirits, like those two men in the Talmud who diverted the sorrowful; and if the master of the house were to hear them he would pay me well, so that I could buy grain and send it to my wife to do business with; but what can be done when poverty puts me out of my mind, so that I can't even open my mouth before such great folk.

Directly after the Sabbath night Havdala ceremony Tsirel Treine put on her weekday clothes and went off to Issachar Demon. She found Issachar sitting on a clay bench plaiting twigs for a besom. As she came in he dropped the twigs and shaded his eyes with his hand to see who had entered. Recognizing her he rubbed his two hands together and asked, Well, Tsirel Treine, what news have you to tell? I wish there weren't any news, she replied. Haven't you heard that Lasunka's run away? Then you're the only person as doesn't know.

To which Issachar replied proudly, If I'm not told I don't know anything. And while speaking he held his ear to the oven wall as though he was told everything from thence. The oven creaked and Tsirel Treine jumped. Don't be afraid, silly, Issachar scolded her. Some dead bird fell down from the chimney. I'm no Master of the Holy Names nor do I practice witchcraft.

She took heart and told him the whole story. I see, said Issachar, that you were told before I was, so why have you troubled to come to me? And Tsirel Treine began fearing to utter a word lest she spoil everything. I don't need your chatter, added Issachar, and you don't have to tell me anything. And while speaking he bent a number of rods into all manner of peculiar shapes. Tsirel Treine stood in despair, not yet certain what she should do. A sudden thought occurred to her; she put her hand in her pocket and began jingling the coins she had there, in order to let Issachar know she didn't want him to have all his trouble for nothing; and she called him Reb Issachar in order to flatter him. Where's there a Reb Issachar? Issachar scolded her again. Who's Reb Issachar here? Do you think I'm a Master of the Names? If you annoy me I'll tell you a Master of the Names saw that Lasunka of yours and killed her so's to turn her skin into parchment for charms.

At this Tsirel Treine's legs began trembling, and she came over weak; and if she hadn't remembered that all the prospects of finding Lasunka depended upon that seance she'd have tumbled over backward. And there was an angry silence until the wind could be heard blowing amid the twigs. Issachar rose and said, Do you know what the rods are twittering? She'll be back, whisper the rods; She'll be back, whisper the rods. Tsirel Treine took out four groschen to pay him and hurried out before he'd have time to prophesy otherwise. Once she was outside she said to herself, Womenfolk are highty-flighty and forgetful. Why didn't I ask him when? She was in two minds whether to return or not; but going back is a bad sign, may it be for the foes of Israel. So she up wi' her legs and went back to her mistress' house, half hoping, half annoyed.

As long as the mice had been afraid of Lasunka you never

even heard the whisper of a mouse; but now she had vanished they could be heard all over the house. Once it even happened that Reb Israel Solomon woke thinking the beadle had knocked him up, and went to the House of Study before the stove had so much as been stoked. All that time, they say, there was no end to the turmoil and disturbance in Reb Israel Solomon's house. There was a complete set of the Babylonian Talmud there which he had inherited from his fathers, and which had never passed through the hands of the censor. The mice made a conspiracy against it and turned it into a pile of paper scraps. There were manuscripts in the house which the great ones of the age had left with him when they had been suspected of belonging to the sect of Sabbethai Zevi; the mice conspired against them and turned them as well into a pile of paper scraps. Tsirel Treine, in haste to fulfill her vow, bought half a pound of candles; but before ever she had a chance of taking them to the synagogue there was not even as much left of them as the tail of a wick. His in-law, Simeon Nathan, sent him his own cat, Shinra, which killed many of them. Thereupon the folk of Shebush, growing jealous of Simeon Nathan, wished to send their own cats as gifts to Reb Israel Solomon; but all this happened in the month of March, when the cats go up on the roofs about their lawful occasions, and you couldn't find a cat for a guinea. The scamps and loafers went up on the roofs after them, and came back with scratched faces and eyes and torn clothes and empty hands.

Meanwhile Shinra took up her residence with Reb Israel Solomon, at whose home they gave her food and drink while she did her duty by him. And she too kept Tsirel Treine lively, while Esther Malka secretly began to hope that her husband would stop grieving for Lasunka. But Reb Israel Solomon couldn't even let his eyes rest on Shinra. He knew, did Reb Israel Solomon, that Lasunka wasn't dead; a dead thing or person is sure to pass out of mind, but Lasunka still kept her place in his heart.

Now the village Jew already spoken of would often come to beseech Reb Israel Solomon to entreat with the Lord of Shebush for an inn to be leased to him, but Reb Israel Solomon wouldn't take any notice of him. Throughout those days Reb Israel Solomon disregarded all the affairs of the community, and did not even attend to wheat money for the poor. As long as the community could get on without Reb Israel Solomon it was not so hard, but as soon as it

[191]

proved impossible to go further without Reb Israel Solomon, matters became very serious indeed.

It happened that gentiles came to return the Jews the fine clothes they were wont to borrow on their Sabbaths when they go to their churches, and they reported that the chief of all their priests was coming to Shebush from the metropolis. How can we honor this great bishop, asked the Jews, when he comes to Shebush? It is a time-old custom that when a prince comes to a town the Jews go out to meet him with the Scrolls of the Torah, and the gentiles, pardon the allusion, with bread and salt. They go with theirs and we come with ours.

There were such present as protested against that selfsame custom, saying, God forbid that we should drag about the Scrolls of the Torah for the sake of an evil and vicious oppressor of Jews; and what 'll we do if his wicked mind tempts him to do to the Written Torah what his comrade, may his name be blotted out, did to the Oral Torah when he went and burnt all those sets of the Talmud? But the others repeated, A Jewish custom's the law and a custom can't be changed. But in order to prevent any quarrels we'll take out spoilt Scrolls and array them in expensive covers and holy vessels, and the bishop won't know.

And something similar was told them by a certain Sephardic Jew who came to sell raisins for Passover wine, and related how in his city it was the custom, when a pasha came to the town, to take the silver cases (in which the Sephardim keep their Scrolls of the Law) without any scrolls inside, and bring them out to greet him. But once when the pasha had to come there was a certain convert who came to the pasha and said to him, Don't imagine for a moment that those Jews give you the honor you deserve. And how do you know? he asked. Tomorrow, answered he, they will come out to meet you with their Scrolls. Tell them to open their cases and you'll see they're empty.

On the morrow the pasha came to the town and all Israel came out to meet him; and he at once ordered them to open their cases. But what had the Holy and Blest One done? He had prepared the remedy before the blow. The night before, the beadle of the synagogue had dreamt of all this, and had gone and put the books back in their places; and so when the evildoer opened the cases he found them full of Scrolls. Thereupon the pasha hewed the evildoer in little pieces, but always favored Israel thereafter.

At which Shebush said, We'll do the same. As the Talmud says, Miracles aren't to be depended on. They sent to Reb Israel Solomon but received no reply; they sent again and still received no reply. So they visited him to hear what he thought. Just then Pinye Pest passed by. Reb Israel Solomon saw him and banged on the window-pane. Enter Pinye. Pinye, said Reb Israel Solomon, Well? What are *you* doing? I swear by my beard, said Pinye, seizing it, that I shan't depart from the world until I've brought her to you. So seeing how troubled and despondent Reb Israel Solomon was they decided to hold a second meeting.

And what were the gentiles doing meanwhile? They were draining the puddles in the streets and repairing the roads and sweeping away the snow and whitewashing the outsides of their houses. Gentle-folk among them came and borrowed fine shawls and cloths of the Jews for to adorn their windows, and Shebush, the city, was bright and lively. Her houses hummed and her streets were full. Women were selling crucifixes in the streets, and all manner of sweetmeats made to look like the great bishop robed in his vestments, with little angels dancing and prancing round about him.

Those cakes were baked by the aunts of the town priest, for it is the custom of their priests, who do not marry, that they keep their aunts in their homes to look after the household. And they were busy cleaning and polishing their ikons and images, and framed them in silk and set a big box in the hands of the chief image, so that it should open the hearts of the gentiles to give much charity. And at the entry to the town they put up poles on either side, joined by planks on which they hung all kinds of flags and a silken canopy beneath it, so that the bishop might enter with fitting ceremony and honor.

But the Children of Israel remained at home in sorrow and con-cern, taking no steps to entreat the bishop with honor when he might arrive in Shebush, even though this might lead the gentiles to say, You hate your fellow men; here's our bishop come to town and you haven't lifted a finger to receive him; and the following day he would deliver venomous sermons in order to harm them. There was never a Jew in Shebush at the time but grieved that Lasunka had run away.

On that day the village Jew of whom we have told went out of town. Said he to himself, there are many gentiles will be coming to town from the hamlets, and they'll be sure to bring poultry with them for sale, so I'll go along to meet them and buy a chicken for the Sabbath. But though he stood without the town he found nothing, for all the gentiles had already gone to church. When the Lord approves the paths of a man, said the village Jew to himself, he will not forsake him. With the words yet in mind and on the tip of his tongue he saw a cat before him, and he laughed and said, That's the Shebush saying, a cat or a cock, long as there's a fowl for the Sabbath. And he made a dash for the cat.

It stood calmly as though it were awaiting him. When he reached it, it scratched his hand and his face and fled. The village Jew took some of his spittle and rubbed it into the scratch saying, Lord of the Universe, come and have a look what you've done to me. Here I came out to buy a chicken and found a cat. I didn't keep any bad thoughts in mind about Your methods but said, I'll take the cat to town and they'll pay me for my trouble and I'll make Sabbath; but when I tried to catch it, it ran away, and what's more it scratched me across the face, and how shall I go back to town now? For he had recognized that the cat must be Lasunka.

While he was standing there he suddenly saw some poor man before him. You've set some fine marks on yourself, said he. Your mother wouldn't mix you up with anybody else now. That's right, said the villager, go mocking me when I'm in pain. God forbid, said the other. But I can tell you sure enough that this here's a queer town. Shebush piles up its troubles from all the world over. You're making two mistakes, my friend, said the villager. First of all I'm not from Shebush, and, second of all, Shebush enjoys a right good laugh. Well, says the other, a man can't know more than what his eyes tell him. One Sabbath not long ago I was the guest of a rich Jew named Reb Israel Solomon, and he's the warden of this town if you don't mind; and he couldn't even taste a crumb of bread because of the grief that reigned in his house.

Why, said the villager, even my botheration only comes about because of Reb Israel Solomon's sorrow. And what have you to do with Reb Israel Solomon? asked the other. Reb Israel Solomon, explained the villager, had a cat called Lasunka which has run away. And maybe you ask what I have to do with Lasunka? I'll tell you. You see these hands? They all but caught Lasunka. Do you see this face o' mine? Lasunka did that to me. And had I been worthy in the eyes of the All-Present I'd ha' caught her and brought her to Reb Israel Solomon, who'd then pay attention to my needs; but now I haven't been found worthy I stand here empty-handed.

The poor man began comforting him and he, his bitter mood being gone, said to the other, I see you're going back to town. But I must warn you that it's bad to go there because the townsfolk are angry with the Jews for not going out to greet that bishop o' theirs. And so maybe you're wondering what we're going to eat? Here's a spring, and I have something in my bag. So let's wash our hands and sit down.

When they sat down to eat Lasunka smelt the food. Said she to herself, That smell reminds me of eggs and onions; I'll go along and give a sniff. Out she jumped and went and stuck her head in the bag. And what did they do? The poor man threw the skirts of his overcoat over her, and the villager tied her legs together with his girdle. And once they had Lasunka safe and sound in their hands they up with their feet and ran towards town, shouting, Lasunka, Lasunka.

As soon as their voices were heard, all Shebush began wailing, Woe's us for we're lost; the townsfolk are coming to take our lives. And thereupon the butchers said to one another, why are we sitting quiet, waiting for them to come and break our necks like so many calves? If he can't save our lives, we'll save the Scrolls of the Torah. So they armed themselves with their cleavers and out they went. When they were out of the Jewish Quarter they saw two Jews running and yelling, Lasunka, Lasunka, and understood that Lasunka must have been found. Thereupon they too lifted up their voices for joy and ran along with them yelling, Lasunka, Lasunka.

At the fresh outcry the porters called to one another, How long shall we sit quiet and do nothing while Jews are suffering? So they clapped their hands and out they went as well. Once they were out they heard that Lasunka had been found. And straightaway they raised their voices, began yelling Lasunka, Lasunka, and went along with the others in great joy.

When the smiths saw the porters starting out, they applied the argument to themselves, saying, If those porters can go off to see what can be done although they have nothing more than shoulders on which to carry loads, shall we sit with arms folded when we all have our hammers and sleds? Up they heaved their tools and out they too went. Once they were out they heard the meowing of Lasunka. And they too raised their voices and began shouting, Lasunka, Lasunka, and joined the procession and ran along with tremendous joy.

Thereupon the tanners said, How long are we going to let the other artizans crow over us and say, you smell too bad to be given a share in anything holy? Now we'll show what we can do. So out they all went in turn. Once they were out they heard the noise around Lasunka. And they too raised their voices, yelling, Lasunka, Lasunka, and began running happily along with the rest of the procession.

When the householders saw all the workmen and artizans going off they wailed, Woe's us for these ruffians who bring down the anger of the gentiles on us; now they'll say all the Jews are murderers. So there was weeping and wailing on the one side and joy and dancing on the other. But when a long while had passed without anybody having been hurt they said to one another, It's written in Leviticus, "Thou shalt not stand over the blood of thy fellow", and came out of their hiding places.

When they came out they saw Jews running along yelling, Lasunka, Lasunka; and they understood that Lasunka had been found. Then they too began clapping their hands and yelling, Lasunka, Lasunka, until their throats were hoarse and they were so breathless they could only gasp, La, La. When the children saw that their fathers had gone out they too went out after them, climbed up the newly erected gate of honor and there stood crying, la la la. The women-folk, hearing their children's voices, and recognizing how joyful they sounded, said to one another, It seems as though the Holy and Blest One must have wrought a miracle. And at once they put on their finest clothes and went out into the open and began clapping their hands and calling, la la la. The fiddlers and music makers peeping out saw women dressed in their best and dancing, and said to themselves, There's gladness in town. So they took their instruments and went out blowing and drumming and fiddling for all they were worth, and took up their stand near the entrance to the town.

And there was never a Jew in Shebush but went out to meet and greet Lasunka. They were following two Jews and patting the bundle those two held, and stroking Lasunka through the bundle and calling her by all manner of pet names. The butchers went ahead clashing their cleavers and fighting imaginary duels; the smiths swung their hammers until the sparks flew; the porters flung up their ropes on high, caught them as they descended and flung them up again; and the music makers were making music. And just at that time the bishop came past and saw all the Jewish population jubilating. Said he, And all these have come in honor of me; and at once he turned a bright and cheerful face upon them and began to speak in praise of them. And what was more he repented his former ways and became a lover of Israel. When the fine folk of the town saw how greatly the bishop approved of the Jews they said, And that's not all the Jews have done in your honor; the fine clothes the townsfolk are wearing in your honor today were borrowed from the Jews without any charge or fee. And they even admitted that the curtains and shawls with which they had adorned their own houses were borrowed from the Jews.

Meanwhile the poor man and the village Jew came to Reb Israel Solomon, bringing him Lasunka, who lay down on the ground and cried meow. Tsirel Treine began hugging her and loosened her bonds and cheered her up and said, What's the matter, Lasunka? Aren't you Lasunka? Aren't you my pussy? And Esther Malka came along and spoke sweetly to her, saying, Lasunka, Lasunka, her voice promising the cat all manner of good things for the future; and she bent and looked into Lasunka's eyes with her own fine weary eyes; and although there was no happiness on her face you could see that a great load was off her mind.

When the cat arrived Reb Israel Solomon was sitting in his place by the stove reading new legends and stories; for ever since Lasunka had disappeared he had not been in a condition to study as much as a page of Gemara; and his pipe was out. Esther Malka entered with the brightest of faces. What's the matter, Esther Malka? asked Reb Israel Solomon. Come into the kitchen a moment, said she. And why, asked Reb Israel Solomon, should you want me to come into the kitchen all of a sudden? I noticed your pipe is out, she answered, and thought you might care to take yourself a coal from the kitchen. He peered into her face, then cried, Lasunka? And Esther Malka turned her laughing face from him and went out.

He rose and followed. Before he reached the kitchen door he

heard a meow and recognized that it was the voice of Lasunka. He opened the door, saw Lasunka couched on the floor, stretched out his hand to stroke her back and said, *oti Lasunka,* meaning, she's a glutton. But realizing at once that he was making mock of the unfortunate, for her shape bore witness that she had long forgotten the entire lore of eating, he ordered them to bring her white bread and milk. Then he bent down to the hearth to take himself a coal.

Thereupon the poor man on the one side, and the villager on the other, leapt forward to serve him. Reb Israel Solomon raised his eyebrows and asked, Who are these? These people, said Esther Malka, are the fine fellows who brought back Lasunka. Reb Israel Solomon looked at them again and said, I believe I've already seen you both.

Thereupon the village Jew began to tell him the whole story of his inn. But Reb Israel Solomon said to him, My dear Jew, now's no time for words; and he gave them a purse full of coins to share. Then he took them into the winter house, opened the box filled with bottles of brandy, poured them out two glasses and cut them two slices of cake, gave one to each and said, Say the blessing, and invited them to eat dinner with him. After they had eaten, drunk and said benediction they entered a House of Study and divided the money between them. The poor man went to the meal sellers with his share, took some sacks of meal with which he did business, and made much profit. After a time his business began to grow. Then he sent meal to the village Jew. The village Jew entered the business, left his inn, established his dwelling with that of his family in town like all the other Jews, prayed with full congregation every day and brought up his sons to a knowledge of Torah.

To return to Tsirel Treine, with whom we began. Tsirel Treine remembered the prophecy of Issachar Demon that Lasunka would certainly return; and now that she was back, she went to buy a besom from him so that he should also derive some benefit. But Issachar mocked her, saying, And do you suppose that I can take besoms out of my beard and earlocks? Don't you know that I've sold all the besoms I made; because of the great dust that was raised on Lasunka's account all Shebush began to choke with dust, and they haven't left me as much as a single besom.

Now to return to Reb Israel Solomon. When Reb Israel Solomon saw Lasunka eating and drinking as usual he felt a great pity for her and asked cunningly, Well, Lasunka, will you forsake us again to follow the evil desires of your heart? But Lasunka never left Reb Israel Solomon again; for she recognized that all the things she had thought pleasures, and in which she had steeped herself, were not equal to a single hour of quiet with a dish of milk and slice of bread or chickens' innards or fishguts lying on the floor before her. And she already desired to forget all she had done, but penitent thoughts led her to twitch up her lips and stick out her pointed tongue; while a sort of satisfied smile hovered round her mouth by reason of the pleasures of life which she had tasted in her time.

Under the watchful eye of Tsirel Treine her strength returned and her belly grew sleek and round and full. And Lasunka then left behind all her youthful indiscretions, and no longer continued to meditate on unworthy matters, such as the heresy of dualism and the like.

And though she might have lost her speed she retained her stealth, and the dread of her remained so strong among the mice that they veritably lost their senses at her voice. And at the end of the appointed period her womb brought forth many tiny creatures the like of which she had never seen in all her life. But before long they had grown to delight the eye of everyone who saw them, with their charm and graceful movements. And she brought them up to do their duty and hunt mice and make an end of them in Shebush.

At this point the voice of the beadle was heard in the street outside, crying his summons to the early Morning Prayers, Israel the holy, awaken, rouse and rise to serve the Creator; and he beat three times upon the door. That's a new voice I'm hearing, said one of the guests. Whose voice is it? The voice of the beadle, they said. Do you suppose I don't know the voice of Mechel the beadle? he exclaimed. Why, they explained, Mechel has given up his beadledom and is just as good as any other householder. And now, added Reb Kemuel, Reb Ephraim's son-in-law, this beadle who wakes up all the householders to come to prayer knocks at Mechel's door as well; and what's more, he knocks up all the householders with three raps, but Mechel he knocks up with three times three. The night before the Eve of Passover he brings him a wax candle to search for leaven; and he brings him willows at Tabernacles, and he beats him on the Eve of

Atonement and he keeps him wise in the calendar and lets him know when the anniversaries of the deaths of his father and mother come round; and Mechel is more particular than all the other house-holders about all those duties a beadle owes to the members of the congregation. Then the same guest asked, And why should he be as particular as all that? Because, they told him, he's the husband of the rich widow, Sarah Leah. And how comes Mechel, the beadle, the guest asked those present, to Sarah Leah? That's a separate story all to itself, they told him.

And what is it? he asked. Well, they said, it happened like this. But before they began telling it was already time for the Morning Prayers. They immediately emptied the glasses, water was brought and they said benediction and went forth to prepare themselves for the Morning Prayers.

And the servantgirls came and cleared the plates and shook out the tablecloth, and Yaxina kept getting between the feet of the girls, with her head to the table and her face to the bones. And they gave the chickens the scraps and brought the mistress of the house all the cocks and hens, so that she might choose the best of them for slaughter. And they prepared two meals of them, one for the day-time, as is the custom in the lands of His Imperial Majesty, the Kaiser of Austria, and one at night to fulfill the words of Exodus, "when the Lord giveth you meat to eat in the evening."

There are many who have heard the tale of Reb Mechel, the beadle, and the wealthy Sarah Leah. At the same time there are as many who have not heard it; and for those who have not heard it, it is worth the telling. Although it is a story all to itself it is not unconnected with our main theme, for it also leads to the Bridal Canopy.

THE CELEBRANTS

This is the tale of Mechel, the beadle. When Mechel, the beadle, left the House of Study on the first night of Passover his mood was cheerful. Blest be The Name, said he to himself, that the Eve of Passover is over and done with so that I too can rejoice this night like other folk. But when he had locked the doors and found him-self proceeding homeward his good mood left him. He knew that he went to no royal feasting hall but to a tumbledown dwelling; that

he would be sitting not on a fine handsome couch but on a torn
cushion unmended of woman's hand; and that he must trouble himself a deal to warm his food.

For at the time Mechel, the beadle, was a widower; there was no
woman in his home to prepare his table, make his bed or cook his
meals. Truth to tell, many of the householders had wished to invite
him to celebrate the Passover feasts with them. Reb Mechel, they had
said, tonight the whole world is rejoicing and all Israel feast with
their households, so why should you celebrate on your own? Be
happy, Reb Mechel, that the demons have no power this night; but
even so there is a peril of sadness, which is as much prohibited on the
Passover as leaven, the Merciful One deliver us. Yet Mechel refused
all offers of hospitality, for he did not wish to burden another's table
at the festival.

The streets had emptied, and all the houses of the town shone with
Passover light. The moon was bright and gracious, and a spring
breeze blew. Mechel began to turn his mind away from himself and
enjoy the wonders of the Creation, jingling the keys of the synagogue
like a bell. But hearing the sound of the keys he grew sorrowful and
began to remind himself bitterly how he was the beadle of the House
of Study, toiling hard and doing all sorts of work; and how, when he
had completed his work and returned home, he remained cramped
and lonely between the walls, never even tasting cooked food; since
if he put food on to warm he would be asleep before it was cooked.
So he would stay his hunger with an onion roll or some bread and
radish, or the potato a woman might bring to the House of Study so
that he should pray for the souls of her near ones to rest in peace.
But what you may do all the year round, and rest satisfied, you may
not do on a festival when we are bidden to rejoice.

On the way home he noticed that one house had a window open;
looking again, he saw that it was a window in the house of Sarah Leah,
the widow. She herself was standing at the window looking out.
Mechel bowed to her with the greeting, Festivals for joy, Sarah Leah.
Holidays and appointed times for gladness, Reb Mechel, responded
Sarah Leah. Whence and whither, Reb Mechel? I am coming from
the House of Study, said Mechel, on my way home to prepare my
table and sit and celebrate. Sarah Leah nodded her head and sighed.
I see she would like to say something to me, said Mechel to himself,
and stood waiting.

[201]

Seeing Mechel standing waiting, she said, I just opened my window to see if it were time to leave, for I am celebrating at my neighbor's. I've prepared all sorts of good things, by your life, and I'm short of nothing in order to celebrate the Passover down to the last detail, and all the same I have to leave my own home and burden myself on others. It's not enough that I go burdening them every Sabbath and festival, when I suddenly appear among them for the Hallowing and the Havdala; I have to go bothering them on Passover as well.

Well, it may be a bother in your eyes, said Mechel, but others regard it as fulfilling a commandment. A commandment, d'you say, Reb Mechel, responded Sarah Leah. Do you suppose such commandments come easily to those who perform them? Here's a man who's busy all day long and never sees his wife and children; Passover comes, a time of rest; he wishes to sit quiet with his family when in jumps that widow all of a sudden and sits down among them. May it be His Will that I shouldn't sin with my words, the years grow less and the world grows wearier and weaker. In times gone by a Jew would bring any number of guests home with him and there 'd be room enough; and nowadays there's no room even for a lonely widow like me. I remember Passover at Father's, may he rest in peace, when we'd have ten Jews and more there. And was my husband, may he rest in peace, accustomed to celebrate Passover without a guest? And I have to leave my home now. And am I short of anything here? If it's wine a body wants, here's wine and enough to spare for an extra glass; and if it's matzoth, here are the extra special matzoth; if it's meat, here's a turkey cock whose wings were absolutely hidden by fat. Why, what did the neighbors say, Sarah Leah, don't tie him to the foot of your bed or he'll drag you across Sambatyon River. That's no bird, that's an aurochs. But as long as a woman's in her husband's house it's all worth while; and once he's dead even the whole of the world isn't worth while. At first I was thinking of inviting a guest, only folk would say, That old woman's a fiend from Hell, wants a man for to serve her well.

Mechel smiled, sighed and quoted the Talmud, " 'Tis better to dwell in trouble than to dwell in widowhood." And although the saying was in Aramaic, a tongue Sarah Leah did not understand, she nodded her head like a person saying, You've said it well and true. Mechel's an upright man and assuredly has some good thought in mind. And she added, There's everything here, but if there's no master in the house what is there in the house? I often ask myself, Sarah Leah, what are you doing here and whom have you here? I have reared children to their full size and they forsook me, so now I am bereft and forsaken, as a table after a feast. I thought of ascending to the Land of Israel to be near the holy places, and not be thinking all the time of my loneliness; but then I am again faced by the difficulty, how can a woman go alone to a place where she is not known? All Israel are brethren, but nevertheless my heart troubles me at the thought of ascending alone.

Mechel felt full of pity for her. He took hold of his right earlock and wished to say words of comfort to her. Yet he could get nothing out, began stammering and at last said, Woman, is my luck any greater than yours? You, God be praised, are adorned as a bride and eat fine food, while I am chidden and mourning as a widower. But no man in Israel has other to depend on than the loving kindness of the Holy and Blest One. What has any living person to grumble at? The festival should not be degraded.

And from seeking to comfort her he began to feel sorry for himself and he said, And what is a man? Something bare in the waste. Blest be He that did not make me a woman. Blest be His Name that I know how to hallow the wine and prepare for the Passover according to the law. But now go to a tumbledown dwelling and warm up half-cooked food and sit on a broken bed, and then sit on a torn cushion and think you're like a king. It was with good reason the Yalkut says, All sufferings are hard to bear, but those of poverty are hardest of all; all sufferings come, and once they are gone leave things as they were; but poverty dims the eyes of a man. I'm only saying this to balance your saying, I'm a woman. And what's more the Holy and Blest One has brought a bad cough upon me, may you never know its like, which takes away my breath and steals the life from me and will drive me out of the world. And before ever he finished speaking he had begun coughing. Reb Mechel, said Sarah Leah to him, don't stand out in the cold; winter may have gone but it's still chilly. Better come into the house and not stand about in the open.

Mechel bowed his head between his shoulders, entered and found himself in a fine dwelling with handsomely decked cushions to recline upon, and a table covered with silverware in the middle of the

[203]

room, and a bottle of wine on the table, candles burning in all the candlesticks and every corner of the room gleaming and shining with festival. His first words were in honor of the place, for he said, How fine this room is, where the hands of a woman have been employed. Sarah Leah at once rushed to show him all she had ready for the table. Matzoth and bitter herbs lay there, parsley and *haroseth,* eggs and a sheepshank and flesh and fish and a fat pudding and borsht red as wine.

And who, said Sarah Leah to Mechel, needs all this array? I'm just about to go off and bother somebody else, but it's hard for me to forget that I'm a housewife, so I prepared a Passover for myself as though my husband were still there and he and I were celebrating like all other folk.

Mechel's heart warmed within him, and he wished to say something, but a furious fit of coughing overcame him. Sarah Leah stared at him with her two eyes and said, Don't eat too much bitter herbs and don't eat sharp foods, Reb Mechel; you cough too badly. You know what you need? It's a glass of hot tea you need. But who have you at home to make something hot? Wait a few moments and I'll put the kettle on for you.

But scarce had she finished her sentence when she struck herself on the mouth, crying, What a silly head I have, to forget that we have to hallow the festival first. Maybe you'll celebrate here? And since the thought had found expression in words she repeated, Maybe you'll celebrate here? Mechel saw all the goodness of the housewife and could not move, as though his limbs were fastened to the spot where he stood. He began stammering and swallowed his indistinct answer. And Sarah Leah began preparing the feast as had been her wont when her husband was still with her.

So Mechel took the keys of the House of Study and put them away somewhere, staring meanwhile at the white cushions that Sarah Leah had prepared for reclining on during the celebration as though the Higher Light shone from them. Within a few moments he had let himself down among them, by reason of the thought that the woman would again ask him to celebrate with her. When she saw him at his ease she filled a glass with wine. With one eye on the wine and one on the household ware, he thought to himself, What a fine spot this is, where a woman's hands do the tending. While thinking, he found

THE BRIDAL CANOPY

the glass of wine at his hand, and his lips of themselves began repeating the hallowing of the wine.

Sarah Leah sighed with satisfaction; her face grew bright; her clothes were suddenly filled with her body, as happens with a rejoicing person; and she thought to herself, How fine is a Jew's voice when he utters holy words. And within a moment she had brought him a ewer of water. He washed his hands, took a leaf of greenstuff, dipped it in salt water, broke the matzoth in half, put one half in a cloth and hid it away for the dessert, lifted up the dish and began reciting, "This is the bread of affliction, the which our fathers ate in the Land of Egypt."

And Sarah Leah wondered at herself, saying, Just a little while ago I was preparing to leave my house, and now here am I sitting at home. And she watched Mechel's hands, observing how accustomed his hands were in holy things, until her face grew red and she lowered her eyes in shame. Then she filled the glasses afresh and uncovered the matzoth. Mechel made her a sign. Sarah Leah blushed like a child, dropped her eyes to the prayer book and recited the Four Questions to their close, "This night we all do recline." Thereupon Mechel set the dish back in place and repeated in a loud and joyful voice, "We were the slaves of Pharaoh in Egypt"; and he continued reciting the Relation of the Departure from Egypt as far as the feast, interpreting to her in Yiddish all that required interpretation and seasoning the entire Relation with parables and tales of wonder. His sufferings and troubles far from him, his head resting on the cushion, sweat caressing his earlocks and the cushion growing deeper beneath him, he continued. His blood beat through his limbs and his heart might have leapt forth; a single hour here was preferable to his whole life in This World.

The Order of Passover came to its appointed end. The whole town was silent; the moon spread a canopy of light over the house of Sarah Leah. Mechel tunefully sang, "May His House soon be built", and Sarah Leah responded, "Speedily, speedily, in our own day soon." From the other houses of the street came the chorus, "God rebuild, God rebuild, rebuild Thy House soon." And the fantasy that is root and branch of Man led them to imagine that here was a strip of the Land of Israel, and they were calmly and happily singing the Song of Songs.

The night passed. The morning birds rose to repeat their portions of song. In the home of Sarah Leah could be heard the voice of a man chanting the Song of Songs.

Here ends the tale of Mechel,
On whom God did bestow
The wealthy lady Mistress
Sarah Leah, the widow.

Now to return to Reb Yudel. The long and the short of it was that Reb Yudel stayed in the town a number of days with that man of renown in company wise and worthy of praise, sustaining his frame, increasing his fame and illumining all of the halls of his soul. The body diminisheth and wasteth away and withereth in the earth, but the soul's light illumineth for ever and ever. Happy is he who hath not passed away his days in futilities, and hath not extinguished the light of the soul. When Reb Yudel's time came to depart, Reb Ephraim entered his private room with him and made a just account; that is, for the amount he would have had to expend in order to hire a waggon and bring a guest for each meal; and he paid him generously. Nor did Nuta depart empty-handed, apart from all his horses ate and Reb Ephraim paid for. I trust Reb Nuta will never come up against me with an appeal if I say that he and the innkeeper had made a deal, so that whatever Ivory and Peacock left he used to fill his sack, and the innkeeper rejoiced and Nuta was happy to have no lack. The mistress of the house also did the same as her husband, and gave Reb Yudel some silver coins and provisions for the road.

CHAPTER FOURTEEN: THE USE OF TIME · WHY REB YUDEL DESIRED TO TURN BACK WHEN HALF-WAY; AND WHY HE NEVER TURNED BACK ٭ Nuta smeared the wheels, harnessed the horses, prepared the seats on the waggon, took the reins in hand and said to Reb Yudel, Take a seat, Reb Yudel, take a seat. And he himself mounted and started them off. Ivory and Peacock shook the dust of Zbarev from their hoofs and started off toward Pommoren. When they were seated comfortably Nuta said to Reb Yudel, Reb Yudel, the story of Mechel doesn't seem nice to me. And why? Because a man should rejoice in what is prepared for him from on High, and whosoever changes finds he's worse off. If you're a carter drive your hosses, and if you're a Hassid be a Hassid, and if you're a beadle summon folk to the Service of the Creator; for when a man's born his star's born with him.

But, objected Reb Yudel, it says in the Talmud that Israel has no star, Israel being above the need for a star. I don't know what the Gemara says, answered Nuta, but I know what I've seen for myself, and I tell you that what happened to my brother will happen to Mechel. And what happened to your brother? asked Reb Yudel. Before I begin telling you the story of my brother, replied Nuta, I need to tell you the story of my mother, may she rest in peace; and not only the story of my mother but also the story of my father, may he rest in peace, that is, what happened to both of them, may they both rest in peace; for leading out of the story of both of them your honor will get to the story of my brother, since a waggon can't reach a town without first passing through its outskirts.

In that case, said Reb Yudel, start off with your parents' story. That, answered Nuta, is a long story, but although it's long it comes to an end, as folk say, "Vayezatha son of Haman spelt his name with a double-sized V, yet they hung him in the end!" And now I've mentioned the name of a sinner I can't go all in the same breath and tell the story of my parents, may they rest in peace; like Father Abraham argued with the Holy and Blest One in Genesis, "Wilt thou also destroy the righteous with the wicked, that the righteous should be accounted like the wicked?"

Reb Nuta, said Reb Yudel to him, now you've mentioned the name

[207]

THE BRIDAL CANOPY

of Father Abraham, may he rest in peace, you can safely go on with the story of your parents. Well said, Reb Yudel, answered Nuta. Although I mentioned the name of Father Abraham without meaning to do so, nonetheless it's a good sign; but I don't know what I ought to begin with first, seeing if I begin with the story of the divorce you might ask why it was that Father wanted to divorce Mother; and if I begin with the marriage of my parents you could well ask what the point was in telling you, since we all know there can't be a divorce without a marriage happening before it. So first of all I'll tell you why Father was about to divorce Mother, from which you'll understand the implication that Father and Mother were wedded to one another; and what's more you'll hear the story of my brother Jacob Samson's birth. And since the name of my brother Jacob Samson came on my tongue I'll begin with him after all.

THE BIRTH OF NUTA'S BROTHER, JACOB SAMSON, AND THE END HE CAME TO

Before my brother Jacob Samson was born, my mother, may she rest in peace, was barren for many years, and used to spend her time appealing from one of the saints of the age to another to beseech mercy for her so that she should bear children; and she used to trudge her feet out from place to place, seeking all manner of charms and remedies, even of the old Tartars, excuse my mentioning them, who used to perform all kinds of witchcraft for her; nor was there a single charm or remedy she didn't use. She had even swallowed the foreskin of a weaned baby and a dried pig's stone chopped, pardon the allusion a thousand thousand times, into citron conserve. She even prepared a dish of wax and put in it what she had to, and hid it in the earth under an apple. I don't know whether the apple grew into a tree, but I do know my mother wasn't helped.

And since she was so busy all the time with all manner of charms and remedies she didn't enjoy a single day's peace with her husband. In this fashion ten years passed without any children, and they already despaired of rejoicing like other Jewish folk, but accepted the harsh judgment, saying, If it's the decree of His Name that we shouldn't see children, we accept it with love.

But all my father's family began to incite him against Mother, may

[208]

THE BRIDAL CANOPY

she rest in peace, and were glad to see her ashamed, and began to
call her all manner of rude names; and day by day they used to urge
Father to get rid of that woman and give her a divorce and take himself another wife to bear him sons and daughters. And they used to
crowd about him at his home, crying woe on him for dwelling with a
barren woman and passing his days without joy.

He wouldn't divorce her because he loved her, and he couldn't
stay at home because of his kinsfolk, so he began to go on long
journeys. But when he returned home for Sabbaths and festivals all
his kinsfolk would gather together and crowd round him on all
sides, and cry out upon him that he shouldn't move thence until he
had given her a divorce. Once they got into such a rage that they
ripped off the top of the sealed oven and threw the Sabbath hotpot
in Mother's face, may she rest in peace.

What did Father do? Went and stayed in the House of Study, and
as soon as Sabbath was over he harnessed his waggon and started
off for distant parts, seeing that all his wanderings and bumpings
and wearinesses were easier for him to bear than those quarrels and
disputations at home. Father had been accustomed to return home
on Sabbath eves, but now he only returned once in four weeks, and
now and again half a year went by without his hosses seeing the
walls of his stable, for he used to journey to the land of Wallachia
and all sorts of other distant parts.

But once he was back home his trouble started again, because his
brothers and sisters and father and mother and other kinsfolk came
at once and began mourning him, wailing, Oh, who'll say the
Mourner's Prayer after your soul; even a gentile, excuse me, wants
sons, and this poor fellow dwells with a barren woman without son
and heir.

Once he came home on the Eve of Passover and his kinsfolk never
came to bewail him; and the entire festival of Passover passed
without one of them saying a word. So Father and Mother rejoiced
the whole festival through, and offered praise and thanksgiving to
the Holy and Blest One who had permitted him quiet at home; and
he rejoiced with his wife like bridegroom and bride. When the time
came for him to start out, he found the stable crowded with his kin.
You're not going to go away from here, said they to him, until you
give her a divorce and send her away.

After living with her all this time, he answered, You tell me to

[209]

THE BRIDAL CANOPY

divorce her? I shan't go away and I shan't divorce her. And by reason of all that grief and suffering and shame he fell sick abed. They all came to visit him, and once they had come they began troubling him till he saw no way of escaping them. Then he said, did Father, to his kinsfolk, Please leave me alone first of all to get well; for if I divorce her who's going to feed me when I'm in bed? Who's going to cook me a spoonful of soup?

That set them yelling at him, Here he goes troubling about his body and taking no care for his soul; who's going to say the mourner's prayer for you, may it be after a hundred and twenty years? Who'll even light a candle to your soul? Only divorce her and marry somebody who'll give you children.

Meanwhile the month of Iyyar had begun a fortnight after the Passover, and in our town it's the custom not to prepare bills of divorcement in Iyyar. And why? Because there's a doubt whether Iyyar should be written Iyar with one Y or Iyyar with two Ys. But whether there's one Y asked about Iyyar or whether there are two, it passed at length; as people say, even when a waggon stands chock-full of Jews, Time doesn't stand still with them. And when Father saw that he could not withstand his kinsfolk he agreed to divorce his wife.

So Father took Mother and went with her to the rabbi's house. The scribe began preparing paper for the Bill of Divorce, and the rabbi's wife comforted Mother so that she shouldn't weep. And all Father's kinsfolk and his brothers and sisters and father and mother stood happy to see, offering praises and thanksgiving to The Blessed Name for opening Father's eyes and giving him sense enough to divorce his wife.

All of a sudden her face changed and she fainted, may it never befall you; and they saw that she was in the family way. Then Father said to the scribe, I'm sure your honor will forgive me; some other time I'll pay you for your trouble. And when did he pay? When her time was finished and he had him write charms for the safeguarding of the child.

And all their kinsfolk conducted them home again with songs and dances, and they rejoiced with Father and Mother all the time until she bore a son.

Up to this point it is the story of the birth of my brother, Jacob Samson. And since my brother Jacob Samson, while in Mother's

womb, had smelt the scent of Torah at the time Father, may he rest
in peace, was at the rabbi's house about to give Mother a divorce,
his soul desired to study Torah, and he toiled at the Torah until he
became far famed for his knowledge. But seeing he was a waggoner's
son, neither the rabbi nor the chief Jew of the countryside gave him
his daughter for wife.

And at this point your honor must forgive me for confusing one
issue with another. There's a man at our place named Berchi, who
used to hire horses to the travelers and had been very successful
and wished to come close to those who study Torah; and he gave
my brother his daughter Freidele to wife, provided him with a special
room and undertook to see him in food at his table all his life long.
And my brother, Jacob Samson, spent those years peacefully, and his
wife bore him sons and daughters and his eyes saw and his heart
rejoiced; there's no demon or no evil plague; and he would journey to
town and tie up his horse at the rabbi's door, and enter and discuss
and argue and quibble with him concerning Torah; and the rabbi
held him dear and used to say, Jacob Samson's good enough to make
up for my having lost the divorce fee on his account.

In brief, Jacob Samson had all he might wish, from milk of doves
to garlic cloves, set before him on a dish. Once there came a lord
whose carriage had been overturned along the road, and whose horses
and driver lay like dead corpses, and he hired other horses, and
there was nobody to drive them. Thereupon Jacob Samson said,
Father-in-law, I hear they've appointed a new rabbi in the town to
which this lord wishes to travel. I'm anxious to tap his cask, so if you
permit me I'll go with this lord and drive his horses.

Now his own mouth trapped him. He had thought of the honor of
the Torah and they that study therein, and his star proposed to set
him back at his own proper task and place and duty. Thenceforward,
when they needed a hostler, Berchi used to say to him, Jacob Samson,
harness up to the waggon; Jacob Samson, drive to so-and-so. And so
he spent half his time at Torah and half his time with the hosses.
When the time came for his wife's sister to marry, Berchi said to
him, Jacob Samson, pack your wife and children on the waggon and
make place for the young couple. So Jacob Samson set his wife and
sons and daughters on the waggon and went off in aggravation, receiving the waggon and hosses instead of dowry, and bowed himself
under the yoke of earning a living and the yoke of the hosses and

the yoke of the travelers, and came just where his fathers and forefathers had been before him.

That's why I said we have no power of departing from the customs and ways of life of our forefathers. Even when a man grows
rich and honored and studies Torah, if his father was a waggoner
he'll be sure to finish up as a waggoner; and not only he but his
children and his children's children to the end of all generations. And
that's why I say that Mechel's a fool for trying to get rid of his own
work, for no man can jump out of his place and position. So I,
Nuta, the waggoner, don't try to jump out of my place, God forbid, but stand firm at my appointed task and duty, sometimes traveling with a beast of a priest, and sometimes with a Jew like an angel
at least. May it be His Will that with this waggon and these hosses
I may merit to receive Messiah, the king, when he comes, may it be
speedily and in our days, amen.

Well said, Reb Nuta, commented Reb Yudel. Happy are you to
have reached the opinion of the Talmud, which holds that a man
should not change his calling from that of his fathers, and that he
that is born in one branch should not jump into another. King David,
may he rest in peace, likewise said in the Psalms, "Nor have I gone
along high courses or things too wonderful for me."

And he himself began meditating on his deeds in leaving his
house and cutting himself off from the Torah and not praying with
the congregation every day; and although he went to fulfill a commandment and at the order of the Rabbi of Apta, he began to
despise his travels.

He spent his blood in vain, his days went by and would never
return again. Days, my days that I might have spent in the House of
Study, how are you passed over me without Torah? Nights, my
nights, long winter nights when the body derives double pleasure
from Torah, how are ye passed over me without pleasure? Now in
a hamlet, now in a town, in either case I go my way without Torah.
Were I adwelling in my house, how many pages of Gemara I
would have studied. But woe's me that I am gone afar from my
house and find myself fulfilling the words of the Psalmist, "And unto
the wicked God saith, How dost thou come to declare My statutes?"
Yudel, Yudel, don't dismiss the matter and your responsibilities by
saying you journey for the sake of the Bridal Canopy which is a great
commandment; have you forgotten the words of the Talmud in the

Tractate on Blessings, in the chapter on standing gravely erect to pray? There we learn, "The rabbis said to Rav Hamnuna Junior at the wedding of Mar, son of Ravina, 'Sing for us, sir.' Said he to them, 'Woe to us that we must die.' Said they to him, 'As for us, what can we respond after thee? Where is the Torah and where the commandments that shall shield us?'" And on that passage Rashi of blessed memory comments in his sweet fashion, "Where is the Torah with which we concerned ourselves, and where the commandments that we fulfilled in our lives, to shield us from the verdict of hellfire?"

And if such were the case with those celestial hosts, what shall I say, being dust and ashes and not so much as a mustard seed compared with them? Woe's me and alas! What shall I do should God arise and visit me, and how shall I respond? What doth the Lord thy God demand of thee saving to fear him? And yet thou must needs follow thy supposititious and imaginary requirements, and forget the purpose of thy days and the use of thy time. For what is the purpose of days, if not indeed the nights, if not to study Torah; as was said, there is no Torah song saving by night. But how dost thou spend thy nights? Eating and drinking and sleeping and enjoying thyself and in the idle conversation of people, and in the pursuit of pelf and Mammon.

Back to Reb Yudel's mind came his house where, whether there was food or there was no food, there was always prayer with full congregation; where, whether there was or was not a bed to sleep upon, his cock, Reb Reveille, would rouse him night after night to serve the Creator; yet now he ate until his belly was fit to burst and slept in the bosom of sluggardliness, as though he had been created for no other purpose saving to eat, drink and sleep.

Why, the holy Rabbi, Reb Zisha, fasted three months on end merely in order to make no oral demands. And if you argue my wife and daughters? Well, then, Reb Nahman of Bratislav, may his merits shield us, when the thought of ascending to the Land of Israel rose in his mind, disregarded his wife and his daughters and ascended, achieving a mighty perfection. While I, Yudel, travel from place to place, dressed like a worth-while person, misleading people and stuffing my body until this supplementary belly, the cushion which has not left my body since I departed Brod, is quite unnecessary and serves me no longer.

THE BRIDAL CANOPY

And Reb Yudel began keening, Yudel, Yudel, you can no longer look down and see whither you go. Tomorrow the clothesmoth will make its home in the cushion and the worm in your body. When the moth enters the cushion, the cushion does not feel it; but when the worm enters thy flesh 'tis as a needle in the flesh of the quick. Yudel, Yudel, thy hour has come for to turn back in penitence to righteous ways. Even beast and bird are acquainted with their appointed season, yet thou doest not know thy times and moments. Hast thou in all thy days seen a cock err as to the hour for reciting Hear O Israel? I, notwithstanding, created as I am to serve my Maker, have done evil. And since his cock came back to mind Reb Yudel's eyes filled with tears, for he said to himself, Maybe Frummet could not withstand her trials and has slaughtered him.

And remembering Reb Reveille, he also remembered his family which he had left without food, clothes or shoes, while he stuffed himself like a calf and wore fine clothes and slept on feathers, and his clothes were so heavy with coins as to drag him down to earth. On the morrow thieves might come and rob him of all his money. Why should he not return to Brod and give his wife the money so that she could buy food and sheets, and have cushions and pillows made, or else hide the money under the threshold so that nobody should know that he possessed money? But it is the way of money to confuse the mind and rob a man of his understanding; so that anybody with money, though he may not be rich at all, becomes as foolish as the wealthy and has no pity, neither for his own life nor for that of others.

He began to despise his travels, and even began to despise himself. Another in his place might have drooped his head saying, My hope is gone and my prospects are at an end; but he rallied himself as a man, took out the prayer book edited by Rabbi Isaiah Hurwitz, author of the *Two Tables of the Covenant,* and began reading the chapters on penitence until his eyes ran with tears; and the Holy and Blest One sent a chill wind which froze the tears so that they glittered up at him from the pages of the prayer book like so many pearls and precious jewels. And he continued reading until he reached the words of the sage who wrote the Book of Morals, "A man who departs from This World without repenting is like unto the king with ten princes under him, whom he loved. Once they took foolish counsel together, came to the king's palace by night, digged a hole under the walls, entered the king's treasury and stole thence vessels of silver and gold, and jewels and precious stones. The king came and found all his treasures stolen and all his collections despoiled, and gave order that an investigation should be made to find the culprit who had dared commit this crime. The servants of the king told him, O lord king, the ten princes whose seats you set on high over all your lordlings are they that robbed your exchequer and stole your treasures.

"The king grieved exceedingly for these princes—far more than ever he gave consideration to the thefts—by reason of his love for them. 'Tis false, said he, they are faithful men and I do not believe you. Liege our lord, they replied, thy thefts have been found on their hands. What can I do? the king asked himself. If 'tis very truth I shall not be able to deliver them from the mob; yet how can I slay them for their transgression?

"What did he do? He took counsel with himself and said, Bring them before me and I shall see whether the thefts were found in their hands as you have stated. Now between the dwelling place of these princes and the king's palace there was a river, which had to be crossed in a boat by such as would come before the king. The king sent one of his body servants to inform them, When you cross the river to come to me, cast the theft into the river from you, lest it be found in your possession and you be slain. Nor should you feel regret for the gold and jewels; the gold and jewels are of no account in my sight by reason of the love I bear you.

"So they all cast away the theft into the river, excepting one, who did not dispose of it. Then they were brought before the king, who commanded that their clothes should be searched; but nothing was found saving in the garments of the man who did not cast his share away; when they searched him they found part of the theft. Thereupon the king grew very angry and said to him, Why didst thou not cast all this away as thy comrades have done? And he had no reply.

"And the king continued, Thy second transgression is even greater than the first, to the commission of which I believed thine evil spirit had misled thee; yet now when I have offered all of you counsel whereby ye shall be delivered from death, and thou hast seen thy comrades casting their theft from them, why didst thou not obey my counsel that would have delivered thee? Now, therefore, since thou hast held my words in small esteem and hast not repented by cause of thy evil deeds, I shall pay thee that which thou hast earned. And the king commanded him to be slain with grievous tortures; but his nine comrades he sent rejoicing and glad to their homes.

"Such is the state of Man in This World; the Holy and Blest One giveth him warning to repent, that he perish not in his iniquity, as is written in Ezekiel, 'Return from your evil courses, for wherefore should ye perish'; and it is likewise written in the words of that prophet, 'For I do not desire the death of him that dieth', and so on."

In that hour Reb Yudel took upon himself the need for absolute penitence, and resolved to forsake his courses entirely, as the prophet Isaiah said, "Let the wicked forsake his way"; and to return to Brod, home to his House of Study, to Torah and to prayer; and indeed to return straightway and without delay; and he said to his heart, Heart my heart, dost thou not know that thou art dust on earth below and must needs take heed, for thy days are decreed and told and thy life will be cut off and end in mold, and day by day dost draw near to the tomb, where thou shalt fly without wings to thy doom upon the shoulders that bear thee high, ere being cast down in the earth to lie. There dread and shame shall mark thy term, and the garb of thy frame shall be the worm; for that is the dread and awesome day that cannot ever be ransomed away, a day for long weeping and bitter rue, a day for trembling and wailing too, a day of destruction, lament and grief, when God's fury and zeal flame without a relief, and His rage flares and burns like a coal in the day of the going forth of the soul forsaking the body, like a broken bowl alone to bide, unable to turn from side to side. And thou, son of man, to whom shalt thou flee for aid or of whom shall a hidingplace be prayed? Surely thou'lt cry, Woe's me, what did I do, and why did I think the word of God to despise and eschew, taking the pride of my heart as my cue? And in that fashion Reb Yudel sat on the waggon rousing his heart to repent; and this gave him the strength to tell Nuta to turn the horses round in order to return home.

But it was not yet time for Reb Yudel to return, for the bidding of the Rabbi of Apta had to be fufilled in its entirety. Come, consider how mighty are the words of the saints: he ordered Reb Yudel to travel until he found a worthy match, and when he desired to rid himself of his errand and return home Nuta turned the heads of the horses about; yet within a little while he recognized that they were not returning to Zbarev but were still on the road to Pommoren, that is, to the place to which they had first intended to travel. How astonished Nuta was; here they had started out from Zbarev bound for Pommoren, and he had turned his horses about, so it stood to reason that they ought to be on their way back to Zbarev; and yet the end of it was that they were near Pommoren. Nuta, Nuta, said Nuta to himself, day after day I'm atelling of you not to drink no brandy along the road. After all it stands to reason that if the water you drank on the road got you into so many fixes, how much worse brandy's agoing to treat you! He clicked to his horses and they stood still.

Staring about him he saw that they were near the village of Lavrikevitz, which is on the outskirts of Pommoren; and not at Zaridi near Zbarev, nor yet at Zbarev. Why have you stopped the horses? Reb Yudel asked Nuta. Reb Yudel, said Nuta in reply, does your honor suspect I'm maybe drunk? God forbid, replied Reb Yudel. Well, said Nuta, just as your honor don't suspect me, no more I don't suspect my hosses, but how am I to account for it that after turning my hosses' heads towards Zbarev I now find myself near Pommoren?

Come, consider then, Reb Yudel comforted him, that all directions in which a man may turn are to his advantage and benefit. You turned the horses about so that we should return to Brod, and now the horses' heads have been turned about we find ourselves near Pommoren. And why? So that we should not free ourselves of the order of the Rabbi of Apta; and now since the horses have gone this way it means that we have to come to this place. The hosses, assented Nuta, lead a man the way he wants to go. If you want to go this way we'll lead you this way. But first of all we'll hear what Ivory and Peacock have to say about it.

So saying, Nuta cracked his whip over the tails of the horses, not as a waggoner who whips up his horses to move livelier, but as a man may clap his friend on the back to ask his advice. Up they raised their hoofs at once and began trotting; and the bells round their necks went jingling and singing ahead of them.

CHAPTER FIFTEEN: THE BOOTH OF PEACE ✒ The horses went along after their fashion, now leaping and now crawling, while Nuta switched his whip about their tails to remind them that no horse may shift along without a director. And why did Nuta see fit to agree with Reb Yudel? Because, said Nuta, since Reb Yudel respects my horses and goes along the path they lead him, I'll likewise show respect to Reb Yudel by accompanying him whither he desires to go. For Nuta did not realize that 'twas not of his own wish that Reb Yudel desired to go whither the horses took him, just as it was not of their own wish that the horses went on, and just as the whip does not crack on its own; but that which is high is guarded by that which is higher, while there are yet higher to keep watch and ward over these in turn.

At length they came to Pommoren. Why tell long, long stories? Pommoren is a tiny place, and when a horse arrives there its head sticks out at one end and its tail at the other; nonetheless Reb Yudel did not depart empty-handed. One gave him a small coin and another the half of it, and coin added to coin made a whole fistful of money.

From Pommoren they went to Rezvadef, and from Rezvadef to Pelichef, and from Pelichef to Ermin, and from Ermin to Dretchetz, and from Dretchetz to Henevitz; and He who created the day created the sustenance thereof and therein. And thus they journeyed on until they reached Brazan, which is eight-hours journey from Brod and is a city and mother in Israel, full of the sage and the wealthy.

In brief, Reb Yudel reached the Holy Congregation of Brazan and stayed with Reb Moshe Goldsmith who had wedded Esther Gittel, the daughter of Mistress Deborah, the hospitable, of Benif village. Pleased was Reb Yudel to fall in with the children of his benefactors, and pleased were they to hear from him how their parents fared; and pleased are we to tell of such worthy folk.

Reb Yudel remained sitting in the house of his benefactors and watched Reb Moshe at his work, weighing gold and melting it and working it into a vessel, and setting jewels and precious stones in place, being absolutely precise regarding each grain, and keeping a gold weight in his mouth in order to prevent himself uttering any idle words; and all his movements were weighed and measured. Had it not been for Nuta, Reb Yudel could well have sat there the rest of his days, for it was as much as though he were studying Torah concerning the conduct of daily life.

But what did Nuta do? He came and took hold of Reb Yudel and led him forth, saying, to your work, Reb Yudel. So Reb Yudel departed from the house of his well-wishers and went to call on the sage Reb Leibush Nathanson; and why he went to Reb Leibush Nathanson first of all was that Reb Leibush was of the Nathanson family which is likewise to be found in Brod aplenty, for instance, Reb Judel Nathanson, the courtly, and his brother; so Reb Yudel considered himself, as you might say, a townsman of Reb Leibush, and feared the latter might be annoyed were he not to visit him first of all.

But it happened that Reb Leibush was occupied at the time, though I do not know whether it was in the writing of his learned work, *Bethel,* on the more difficult problems of the Talmud, or in his mundane affairs, for Reb Leibush used to make roads for the government; and he disposed of Reb Yudel at the hands of his attendant. Thereupon Reb Yudel's heart grew soft as wax, and he wished to return to his lodgingplace. But Nuta said to him, Are there no beasts in the forests apart from the lion? (And he said this in raillery; for in the Yiddish-Teutsch tongue Leibush is the same as Lionel or little lion.) No, in Brazen there are many beasts such as Reb Dov Bear Heilprin and Reb Gershon Dov Bear, son of Reb Baruch, and Reb Zev Wolf, son of Reb Nisan, and Reb Zvi Hart Shtolzbarg and Reb Jonah Dove and Reb Fishel. Or maybe your honor would like to see the flag the Poles won from the Turks? And all this was said in raillery, after the fashion of Buczacz folk when they say that people are staring at the fine statues and figures of the Town Hall. But all Nuta's urging was of no avail. You can only urge those who can be urged.

Now if all Reb Yudel's journeys and travels were for the purpose of bringing the bride under the Bridal Canopy, why do we delay so long in Brazan, when he achieved nothing here at all relative to that commandment? But do you suppose we are merely telling tales for the simple sake of telling? Consider how many people Reb Yudel met on the road, and how many of those were given a lift by Nuta in the waggon; and have we even as much as hinted that they were met? But we deal with Brazan at length because, when Reb Yudel was ultimately to marry his daughter off, and the bridegroom was actually standing under the Canopy, he would suddenly remember that he never prepared any wedding ring, and Reb Moshe Goldsmith was to give him a ring; and in case you were to ask, Who's he, we relate in advance that Reb Yudel was in Brazan and stayed in the house of a certain goldsmith. And now, having mentioned the incident at this place we shall not return to it at its proper point, in order not to tell the same things twice over.

From Brazan they turned southwest, that is, toward Lemberg; for the places between Brazan and Lemberg are more copiously wealthy than any others; and they reached a certain village called Kozshan. It was Thursday, and Reb Yudel desired to celebrate the Sabbath there, for in all his travels it was his custom to stay in one place from Thursday until Sunday morning. But since he found no place there in which he could immerse in honor of Sabbath, he started out to find some other spot. Somebody else in Reb Yudel's place might have said, Where there's no special ritual bath for the Sabbath immersion I can't immerse; but not so Reb Yudel. Instead he remarked, It's worth a man's while to travel a few miles on Sabbath Eve for a special ritual bath. Why, there's a story of a certain saint on his travels who found himself in a place where there was no ritual bath, and he went and sold his share in the Garden of Eden to somebody, and gave the money to have a ritual bath made.

In short, they left Kozshan and bowled along toward the Holy Congregation of Rohatin. On the road they noticed an old man on the hillslopes. Let's approach him, said Reb Yudel. Maybe he wishes to go to town and will travel along with us. When they reached him they found him digging clay. Prithee, grandsire, said Reb Yudel to him, what is it you do here? I dig clay, replied the elder. And wherefore? asked he. In order, he replied, to smear the floor of the house in honor of Sabbath.

It would seem, said Nuta, that you're not short of houses. What leads you to think so? asked the old man. Said Nuta, Because your sack is so big. I bring this clay, said he, to town, and Jewish women use it to smear the floors of their homes; and as payment for my trouble they give me raisin wine, candles and loaves.

Then load your sack on the waggon, said Nuta, and come along to town with us. God forbid, said the elder. Why? asked the other. When I have this opportunity of fulfilling a commandment, explained he, shall I hand it over to your horses? Thereupon Reb Yudel recognized that the old man was one of the perfect and entire servers of The Name, and that from him might be learnt the ways of simple and full service; and his soul desired to converse with him. Who are you, asked he, to go digging clay with such fine thoughts at your disposal? Wait till I return, replied the other, and you will both receive the Sabbath with me. And the old man heaved up his sack on his shoulder and went off, leaving Reb Yudel joyfully awaiting him.

To be sure, said the waggoner to the Hassid, we shan't perish of starvation this Sabbath, because I have a little provender for the way with me. But if we have to share it as well with that old man, who has the face of a corpse, I doubt whether we'll be able to feast in honor of the departure of the Sabbath as is fit and proper. Fie on you, Reb Nuta, said Reb Yudel; if you had found a store of silver and gold and jewels and pearls, would you trouble so greatly regarding your victuals? No; you would haste and gather together those imaginary treasures; and now I have found such a treasure of God-fearing ways as this ancient, shall I let him go because of food? That stopped all the arguments of Nuta, who began to roll with laughter inside the waggon so much that it started the waggon moving on its own, while Nuta gasped, Jews, Jews, I haven't the strength to laugh any more.

But in a little while the old man returned from town with his sack as full as it had been; not with daub and clay, however, but with all manner of food and candles; and he said, Dear Jews, come, we'll go to our lodging. And his words should be noted with great precision, in that he said to our lodging and not to our house; for can the lodging wherein a man passes his days and years in this World of Falsehood really be considered his house and home?

And while speaking he took the horses by the bit and they sped not like horses running along the ground but like birds flying; and they came deep in the wild wood and stopped. Here we are, said the old man, descending from the waggon.

How astonished were Reb Yudel and Nuta to hear him saying, Here we are, when there was not even any sign of human habitation. But the old man raised his head aloft, gazed and said, In the Upper Assembly they are already preparing to receive the Sabbath; come, let us purify ourselves in honor of the Queen. Reb Yudel followed the old man and descended after him into a creek, where the old man immersed himself full nine hundred and thirty times according to the years of father Adam's life, garbed himself in Sabbath array, and when he stood erect was a head taller than before. And then they noticed a kind of booth beneath a tree. Well, let me tell you, there was a table with a cloth spread on it and many candles burning there, and an old woman standing bowed with her hands over her eyes blessing the lights. When she lowered her hands and saw them she greeted them in most friendly fashion, saying, Blest be the newcomers. And while she spoke she kept on clapping her hands together lest they stumble and fall, God forbid, into evil thought by reason of a woman's voice, which the sages classed as a source of sin; for her voice was exceedingly sweet. And we find that this was the case with Miriam, the prophetess, of whom it is written, "and Miriam took the timbrel in hand" at the time that she sang.

The old man took a big vellum prayer book written in a fine hand, and he received the Sabbath with sweet song and chanted the hallowing tunefully over raisin wine; while it was still day he hallowed and the sun came to gaze at his glass. They likewise hallowed over the wine and broke two separate loaves; and the old woman also broke bread with her own loaf. The table was well spread with all manner of fruit, beans, greenstuffs and good pies, plum water tasting like wine, but of flesh and of fish there was never a sign. In the Talmud the sages said, "Even the emptiest among you are full of commandments as is a pomegranate of seeds." To whom might that refer if not to the waggoner, who had complained that the old man would be diminishing the delight of his Sabbath? But the old man soothed him with his words, saying, Why was it held that the essential part, in fact the commandment, of the Sabbath feast was found only in consuming flesh and fish, if not for the reason that most people derive their pleasure in food only from flesh and fish? Yet in truth it is in no way obligatory to eat flesh and fish, as has already been observed by Reb Zalman in his edition of the *Table Prepared,* that work for those that would feast with joy on the laws found in the Torah. He and she, meaning the old man and the old woman, had never tasted flesh since growing to maturity.

And at this point I shall reveal as much as a hand's breadth while keeping two hands' breadths and more concealed. That old man was one of the Thirty-six Hidden Saints upon whom the whole world of Man rests, and can therefore be presumed to have known what was acceptable to Him, may He be blest; and understand the rest for yourselves.

After the feast the old man made the guests a place beside the oven and he and she sat at the table; she read the Portion of the Week in the Yiddish-Pentateuch for women known as the "Go forth and See", and he devoted himself to the Sabbath prayers of redintegration all night long; for on Sabbath nights he never slept at all. Consider; a man who had been made king for a day might very well not sleep all night long; and were his courtiers to say, Lord king, why do you not rest and sleep, he would be entitled to answer, I have been appointed king for but a single day, and I do not wish to sleep away even the least portion of my time of kinghood.

Which makes the behavior of the old man clear. Sabbath is the ensample of kinghood, wherewith the Holy and Blest One crowns the Israelite for one single day in the week.

And he had an outstanding custom, had this elder, of speaking nothing but the Holy Tongue on the Sabbath; for the Sabbath partakes of the nature of the future Redemption, when it will not be meet or seemly to speak any tongue other than the Holy Tongue.

When day dawned he went and immersed himself and chanted his prayers with passing sweetness, being particularly joyous in reciting the prayer, "The breath of all that lives shall bless Thy Name, O Lord our God, and the spirit of all flesh shall ever glorify and exalt the mention of Thee our King." Brethren mine and friends, progeny of the holy and beloved of my soul, it is assuredly fitting that a Jew should be exceedingly joyful when repeating such a mighty lauding as, "There is no king for us but Thee", since we have merited to be subject to Him, may He be blest. And now imagine for yourself that the old man stood in the like joy throughout the prayer. Brethren mine and friends, were we to begin describing the charm and delight of that Sabbath, all the ram skins of the herds of the desert would not suffice for us; and it was all verily as a grain of dust compared with the Third Sabbath feast, when the elder sat with his head between his arms and answered Amen to the Holy Prayer of the Masters recited by Zerubabel, son of Shealtiel, in the Upper Assembly, following the homily of Moses our Master, may he rest in peace, on the Portion of the Week.

The holy Sabbath passed and the six days of labor returned. Much did Reb Yudel learn from that old man, and much more might he have learnt. Yet what could he do when his days and deeds were not subject to him himself? So when Sunday morning arrived he prepared himself for the way. Nuta likewise wasted no time but swathed himself in his prayer shawl, bound his tefillin to his brow and left arm, and began reciting the Morning Prayers while harnessing the horses.

But the sages have already said that there is no blessing in impetuousness. Ere Nuta had completed his prayers the fringes of his prayer shawl were caught in the wheel and were torn off. Thereupon he took the old man's prayer shawl and stood erect to pray. But straightaway his whole body and all his limbs began shaking and quivering, and his clothes began dropping off him, coat and shirt and smallclothes and hosen, and they all flew off through the air like so many ravens. And while the garments were still sailing through the air the fringes of the old man's prayer shawl touched his jack boots, which peeled off his legs and feet and began crawling away like so much vermin. Only the person who has undergone the like can know what went on in Nuta's heart. Finding himself naked and barefoot, he tried to cover his nakedness by pulling the old man's prayer shawl tight around him. But the fringes began slapping him across the face and roared, "They shall not wear a hairy mantle to deceive", in the words of the prophet Zechariah.

Thereupon Nuta began wailing, I'm the dregs of Israel, the very dregs of Israel. For Nuta had been wont to buy his clothes cheaply from craftsmen who had taken themselves "remnants." How much outcry the books have raised against those tailors who take part of the cloth for themselves and call it remnants, and spoil the garments they make and transgress against the Eighth Commandment. Yet they treat the prohibition as though it were a permission, and do not know how grave will be their punishment. For just as the householder must take care to pay the worker at his proper time, so the worker must take care to take nothing from the garment; and should a little cloth be left over he should return it to his employers. Happy the craftsman who hath not filled his hands therewith; he shall not be ashamed either in This World or the World to Come, as is told in the story of the tailor mentioned in the book *The Upright and Proper Line,* whose words so terse we have put into verse and song, to strengthen the pure and offer the true a tongue.

[224]

A tailor of Brisk, about to die,
Found strength enough to sit up high,
And, after confessing before the All-able,
Ordered as coffin his cutting table,
And his measure for measuring length and girth
To be set in his hand when they brought him to earth.

Wherefore, good brother, men asked, wouldst thou
Have as a coffin thy table now
And grip thy measure within thy hand?
Brethren, said he to them, understand,
To measure and table I ever appeal
As witness: at my work I did not steal.

And so Nuta wailed and wept till he was covered in tears as in a sack, and caught up the fringes and kissed them with all his might, and repented of his deeds and took it upon himself to repent. And indeed it did not take long before he repented fully and freely, and the Court appointed him inspector of weights and measures. And he used to reprove the honest workmen not to treat others' property as though it were their own.

When they had prayed, the old woman prepared the table for them and brought them their morning meal, so that they should not go directly forth from rest and pleasure to suffering and tumult. After they had eaten and drunk she brought two candlesticks of clay like those made by poor folk in our parts, and said to Reb Yudel, Here are these two candlesticks, which I have made for your daughter, long life to her, so that she can kindle the Sabbath lights in them on the approaching day, when she shall be mistress in her own house. And Reb Yudel sighed and said, When cometh the Sabbath day that Pessele shall kindle the lights for herself like any other Jewish housewife? The Sabbath light, replied the old woman, is exceeding precious, and therein my lads and my lasses shall be led in rejoicing.

And by reason of the exceeding sweetness of her voice she kept on clapping her hands together while speaking, so that they might not, God forbid, be led to evil thoughts through the voice of a woman; and the like was done by Miriam the prophetess, may she rest in peace, of whom it is said, "And Miriam the prophetess took timbrel in hand."

CHAPTER SIXTEEN: DOMESTIC BLISS ✒ Meanwhile, at the home of Reb Yudel, the Hassid, his wife Frummet and his three daughters sat on the reed mat plucking feathers for the daughters of the rich who lie on beds of ivory in palaces of pleasure. Frummet spent those days in the house of certain wealthy women and prepared many chickens for wedding feasts, receiving the feet, the crops and so on for her trouble; and in the cellar they kindled fire and boiled the meat and prepared a great feast, not forgetting Reb Reveille, the cock, either. When they had finished eating and drinking the girls sat them and sang:

> Father's gone far, far away
> And taken with some cash,
> Gone to a place where lads learn Torah
> For to find his girl her match.
>
> Master rabbi, head of the school,
> Money, thank God, I do not lack.
> I've come here for to fetch my daughter
> A scholar bridegroom back.
>
> Answers the head o' the school and says,
> There are three such as you desire,
> One a prodigy, one ever studying—
> The third is a flame of fire,
>
> You'll find none better in any school
> Or any town and land.
> Happy the man who'll choose one for
> To take his daughter's hand.
>
> Father answers and says to him,
> Three maids, Master, have I, have I.
> Answers the head o' the school and says,
> Then seize ere others do try
>
> These sprigs o' the Torah lush with knowledge,
> Lads better far than the best.
> Father's gone far, far away,
> To bring us scholar bridegrooms blest.

While their song was on their tongue, and they found hope their sorrow among, that soon or late they would come to joys, they suddenly heard their mother's voice, Lazy lasses, enough the while to sing your songs in such a style and waste your time on ringing rhyme. Come labor with speed for 'tis needed indeed, and the feathers must all of them quickly be plucked, or out of the house you'll find yourself chucked. Sadly the maidens bowed their heads, plucking the feathers dispirited, and sorrow did each of them betide as though she were an orphan bride whose heart's desire as a dream had fled and left them wounded in the void.

Then came a song that was sobbed with a choke, and the oldest daughter it was who spoke:

> *And though my love shall come,*
> *I, forlorn and numb,*
> *Shall never see thy face.*
> *Bleak my heavens and drear*
> *And all day long through tears I peer—*
> *What delays thy pace?*

The cock summoned to the service of the Creator, rousing those that slumbered in the bosom of laziness. Yet, alas and alack, the maidens shall still sit grieving, not permitting sleep to reach their eyes, for there is much to be done and the housewife urges them ever on; and they pluck the feathers and fill every sack, while Reb Yudel Hassid wanders afar without coming back.

CHAPTER SEVENTEEN: REB YUDEL DECIDES TO PROVIDE FOR HIS OWN NEEDS, AND PARTS COMPANY WITH NUTA THE WAGGONER · TEARS OF JOY ◆ It was the first Adar month on the day Reb Yudel parted from the old man. Snow had already ceased falling, and only a little was left on the hilltops. The sun stood high toward the zenith, the surface of the earth began to crease and fold over, while the wind blowing from the hilltops brought the scent of snow from afar without a body feeling its chill. In that spring hour Reb Yudel felt that nothing he desired had been withheld from him, and it was fitting that he should be under no obligations, as the pious Rabbi Behaya wrote in his work, *The Duties of the Heart,* "Let him offer praise and thanksgiving to His Blessed Name, and consider that the reason therefor is in the Holy and Blest One in Whom he did set his trust; for all things derive from the Higher Grace."

And Reb Yudel said, Here am I engaged in the great and important injunction of bringing the bride under the Bridal Canopy; and two beasts carry me about, and when I come to an inhabited spot a table is spread before me and a bed made on my behalf and I am given money; and I become acquainted with the worthy qualities of my fellows and perceive that the Blessed Creator directs His world with loving-kindness.

Lord of the Universe, continued Reb Yudel, if I have forgotten even one of the good deeds Thou hast done unto me, do not consider me, God forbid, as ungrateful; and if I have harbored any suspicion of Thy qualities for taking me forth from the four ells of the Torah, so that I desired to turn back halfway, was it because I desired to dwell quiet that I wished to return? Nay, 'twas by reason of my absence from Torah. Yet Thou in Thy manifold mercies didst instruct me otherwise, namely, that even when a man fares along the way and cannot study or pray with the community he need not grieve; for Rabbi Israel Baal Shem Tov of blessed memory was wont to explain in his own way the passage in the Pentateuch, "These are the journeys of the Children of Israel", and so on, "at the word of the Lord." Now why did the Torah have to record all the journeys of Israel? In order to inform us that these journeys of Israel, though they might divert the Children of Israel from Torah and prayer, were all nonetheless at the word of the Lord; for had I returned halfway I would never have merited to spend the Sabbath in the home of that old man who was of the water drinkers.

Said his soul, After all your probing and prying so deep into the ways of motion you have not yet reached even the smallest portion of intelligent understanding. Here you go saying, Had I returned while on the road I would never have merited that which I did merit. Now was it at all in your power to return or not to return? Why, you only stand and exist by the decree of the Blessed Creator.

Responded Reb Yudel, And was it for my own sake that I wished to return? It was for the sake of Torah and prayer with the community. As King David, may he rest in peace, said in the Psalms, "I have thought on my way and shall retrace my steps unto thy testimony."

Quoth soul, David also and previously said in an earlier Psalm, "Be ye not as the horse, as the mule lacking understanding", which do not consider the truth of their affairs but err in their animal opinion to think they proceed of their own volition, not considering in their minds that the rider or the driver doth hold sway over them, and that at his will they cease to go and at his will they proceed and go forward. Therefore, my brother, take modesty and loneliness to be thy portion, forsake pride and keep thy distance from haughtiness; and from the fulfillment and completion of the matter thou shalt know that which is known, to wit, that all thy stratagems are as nought and null, that thou art a stranger upon earth, and that it is the nature of the stranger and foreigner to know what he is, and that in virtue of nothing but the grace of the lords of the kingdom, who do pity and aid him, can he exist and maintain himself. Wake and consider that which the pious Rabbi Behaya did write in the Section, "The Soul's Accounting", and thou shalt tell thy heart, regarding the changes in thy affairs, that they are not come about at thy hands. Therefore, O my brother, accept for thyself the conditions of strangerhood and foreignness in This World; for a stranger and a foreigner art thou in the world. And the proof of thy strangerhood and loneliness in the world is that when thou didst go forth to the fence and bound of being, and wert formed and fashioned in thy mother's womb, not all those in the Universe could have hastened or hindered the appointed term of thy fashioning by so much as a single second; nor could they have made the matter easier or harder for thee.

And Reb Yudel related, Blest be The Name that I did not require all the admonitions of the soul and proceeded in the sweet knowledge that all actions are done by the decree of the Creator; so I dismissed all cares from my heart and was just like a newborn babe which is frail in its senses saving the senses of touch and taste, for whom the Exalted Creator provides food at its mother's breast; neither too much the burden whereof might weary the mother nor too little that the sucking thereof from the nipple may not weary the babe; and He fashioned the aperture of the nipple the size of a pin point, not greater lest the babe choke while sucking, nor narrower, lest the drawing forth of the fluid entail great toil. The milk is the faith wherewith I trusted Him, may He be blest, and the burden thereof was not too great, nor did I toil greatly to find it, nor was I choked thereby in having to depend upon miracles; but I felt in my pocket to see how much money I might have. Now what has faith to do with coins? But it was by reason of the words of the holy Rabbi of Apta who wrote in his letter, "lad and lass wed not unless cash be paid." Once my hand had entered my pocket it occurred to me to count my cash, which I did and found I had two hundred gulden; and had I not counted I would have entered the town and taken charity at a time I never required it. And so Reb Yudel said, Thus far have Thy mercies aided me. And he went on, Reb Nuta, when we reach town take me to an inn.

And where do I always take you, said he, if not to an inn where they give you bed, board and a trifle? I shall explain my meaning, said Reb Yudel. When we come to a town you always let me down near a House of Study and go to feed your horses. But now what I want of you is to take me to a place where I can stay, to a real inn.

And why should this town be different from all others, wondered Nuta, that your honor should want to go to an inn here? Why, the innkeepers have an eye only for money, and if you don't pay them what they ask for bed and board they take what's acoming to them from your goods and chattels and sling you out into the mud. Please, Reb Nuta, Reb Yudel besought him, do me a favor and don't press me to tell you what I have in mind. You know that I'm weak willed by nature, and if anybody asks anything of me I can't refuse him;

THE BRIDAL CANOPY

what am I to do when I have it in mind to provide for myself and eat my own bread? I have two hundred gulden and it's forbidden me by law to take charity. And so, instead of sitting arguing with me, bring me to an inn and don't ask so many questions.

God in Heaven, cried Nuta, gripping himself by the hair of his head, has Reb Yudel become possessed? Anybody and everybody goes out of his way to provide for Reb Yudel, and that selfsame Reb Yudel goes out of his way to fling his cash about and throw it away. And how about his wife and daughters? But what's the use of my arguing the toss with him? In any case he always does the exact opposite of what he has in mind.

When they reached Rohatin Reb Yudel repeated, Reb Nuta, please drive me to an inn. Hearing this he said to himself, did Nuta, Well, Nuta, let's do what he's asking of us and let's see what the finish of the business will be. So he took him to a big inn where all the best folk of the countryside used to stay.

When Ivory and Peacock saw that they were drawing up before the sort of inn to which they had been accustomed when they used to draw lords and gentlefolk, they began drumming their hoofs. At which the innkeeper came out bowing and scraping so that his head brushed against his belt, and he bent his knees and leapt and cut capers just like a frog, at which Ivory and Peacock found good reason to laugh.

And the innkeeper ran and led Reb Yudel to a handsome chamber and went off to prepare a fine meal, and said, I'm bringing you water and a towel at once, after the fashion of innkeepers who promise at once what they do not fulfill in the course of a whole hour. Meanwhile Reb Yudel said to Nuta, Sit down, Reb Nuta, sit you down. And he told him that the time had come for them both to part company; and he took out his purse, made an exact account with him and as recompense for his trouble gave him a skullcap full of coins, and likewise the bottle which Paltiel had bound about his belly; for as long as they had been on their travels they had been lodged by good folk who had given them food and drink, so that they had not needed to drink anything of their own, and the bottle had remained as full as on the day it was given them.

Thereafter he took Nuta's hand between his own for a while and began to converse in friendly and affectionate wise with him, saying, No man knows how he may have annoyed his fellow; in case it happened that I annoyed you or treated you in any unfair fashion please forgive me, Reb Nuta. And when you return to Brod and see Frummet, tell her that the Almighty did not deprive me of His regard, but has performed great acts of love to me at every step and pace; and that just as He has treated me with great loving-kindness up to the present, so may the Lord aid me and perform acts of grace toward me at all times, by reason of the injunction of the Bridal Canopy.

Listen to him saying, When you'll see Frummet, said Nuta. And is Nuta such a fool that he'll go to Frummet and tell her, If you don't mind, Frummet, please come and note that I've returned home safe and sound and hale and hearty. Why, if Frummet sees I'm back without your honor she'll burn me up sure with her breath. And she'll be quite right, for she's waiting for you from day to day, and you haven't come home yet. What do you want me to go and tell her? Shall I tell her as how you've pinched the knife of the Angel of Death and entered the Garden of Eden in the flesh, or shall I say you've gone off in search of the Sons of Moses and the Red Jews who live by the River Sambatyon beyond the Mountains of Darkness? And for all that your honor has decided to stay here, I tell you plain and simple that it's your duty to come straight back with me at once; for if you don't come back home with me you'll finish up by coming back home like Napoleon when he ran away from Russia; only Napoleon came home with his stock in his hand while you'll come back home without so much as nothing. Gee-up, Ivory and Peacock, Reb Yudel's about to start off with us.

But Reb Yudel paid no attention to Nuta's words. Instead, he remained firm in his determination to do what had first come into his mind; that being to remain at the inn and serve His Blessed Name by the study of Torah, and not to permit himself to be diverted from his purpose by any business or consideration whatsoever as long as he had any money left in his pocket; that there should be no fulfillment on him, God forbid, of those bitter words of the curses in Deuteronomy, "Because thou didst not serve the Lord thy God with joy and with gladness of heart in the abundance of all things, thou shalt serve thine enemies", God forbid, and so on.

Reb Yudel knew that when a man wishes to perform some good action he is immediately beset from all sides and not left leisure to proceed; therefore he must be obstinate at such a time in orde-

that the counsel of the evil inclination might not, God forbid, prevail in its desire to weaken the power of holiness.

Nuta reminded him of his three daughters seated at home and suffering every fashion of grief and poverty while waiting for their father to return, bringing money with him wherewith to purchase them garments so that they could go forth like all the other maidens; and maybe the matchmaker would come to discuss matters of import.

On my daughters' account, responded Reb Yudel. Tomorrow they stand beneath the Bridal Canopy, and thereafter they'll bear sons and daughters whom they will bring up and marry in turn, while they dwell with their husbands; and as for a pair on their own, what do they require? Eh, Reb Nuta? But the study of the Torah, of which it is said in the book of Joshua, "Thou shalt meditate therein day and night"—am I likely to let it go and steep myself in other affairs?

God in Heaven, cried Nuta in despair, here's this fellow's daughters growing rusty where they sit, and he wants to go on learning Torah. The Torah's not a widow, by your life, and there's enough left to take her part. All the Houses of Study there are in the world, and all the students in each House of Study, may each one get a gold hanging lamp as big as all its students put together. There's a House of Study in our town where study doesn't stop even for a single moment, because while one's studying another can go and sleep and the other way round; but I doubt whether Pessele and Blume and Gittele pass even as much as a single hour without troubles and evil dreams.

But when Nuta saw that Reb Yudel remained firm, he seized himself by the beard and cried, Frummet, I swear to you that Reb Yudel won't bring you as much as a bad pennypiece, and or ever you'll cover your daughters' heads with the bridal veil you'll cover your own face for shame. But Reb Yudel might as well have been dumb and blind; for the eyes of his understanding were now wide open so that he saw that the chief stronghold of evil inclination is in the confusion of qualities. As soon as you find the quality of holiness you are shown some other quality of similar degree to your confusion, for you hesitate and no longer know how to distinguish good from evil, what should be welcomed and what rejected; and at the last you grow negligent and remiss in your duties.

[233]

Nuta, making his last attempt, took his whip, cracked it in the air and watched Reb Yudel's feet; for whenever Nuta had been wont to swish his whip Reb Yudel's legs had made themselves ready for the journey. But when Nuta saw that Reb Yudel's legs remained motionless, he knew that all his attempts were useless, and at once despaired of inducing him to return together with him.

It was hard for Nuta to part from Reb Yudel, particularly as the parting was so sudden. For five months they had not moved away from one another; they ate and drank together, slept, as you might say, over the same page, and suffered the tribulations of the road in one; and now they were to separate. Just then Ivory and Peacock began whinnying. Nuta clicked to them in return and, speaking from the window, said, I'll be with you right away, my beauties, and we'll be on our way back to Brod; but that's not the most important thing, but that Reb Yudel's not going back with us. And I'm just as astonished about it as ever you are, only what's to be done when Reb Yudel won't be persuaded?

All this while the idea of journeying without Reb Yudel seemed very difficult to him; but once he had told his horses about it he felt easier. Said he to himself, There's no evil without good; I'll go back home and rest my limbs and see how my wife's getting on. For although there was no true peace between them he bore her in mind.

Now consider: what happened to Nuta's father happened to Nuta; only where Nuta's father kept his distance from the home for the sake of peace, Nuta kept his distance because he didn't want rows. Nuta's father used to journey far and wide because his kinsfolk were always at him to get rid of his wife and give her a divorce, while Nuta used to go off to the ends of the earth because he did not live peacefully with his wife.

Now Reb Yudel saw everything in advance and prepared a remedy for the trouble; and when they parted one from the other he gave him a tried and tested spell to produce peace between man and wife. Go, Reb Yudel told Nuta, to the market, buy a new knife from the shopkeeper, pay him what he asks and cut your fingernails and toenails therewith; then cut an apple in two and give her half to eat, and if you do this she'll come to love you at last. God forbid that Reb Yudel made a practice of using charms and spells; but the love of Israel was firmly rooted in Reb Yudel's heart, and by reason of the

[234]

THE BRIDAL CANOPY

injunction to love thy neighbor as thyself he told him of this charm.
And Nuta stormed at the Hassid for giving him so simple a charm,
as happened with Naaman that grew furious with Elisha, who made
light of the rivers of Damascus and told him to go and bathe in
Jordan. Why, Nuta used to carry a wolf's eye about in his clothes,
and all the same his wife didn't love him.

Nonetheless he did not neglect the words of Reb Yudel but went
out to the market, bought himself a new knife without arguing the
price and bought himself an apple as well; then he pared his nails
with the knife and cut the apple in two, and when he came to his
wife he gave her half; and since he brought her a gift she smiled at
him and asked, Why should today be different from any other times
that you must bring me a gift? For from the time of their marriage
he had not brought her anything. I don't know, said Nuta, hanging
his head. But she took her part of the apple and ate it, and the love
of him entered into her heart, and thereafter she did not quarrel with
him.

Yet Nuta had never known that he ought to make peace with his
wife; so how was it that he came to say, I'll go home and see how
my wife is, and so on? But you see, from the time he had prayed in
the prayer shawl of that elder of the water drinkers he could no
longer live happily with his horses, which had grown accustomed
to eating out of the cribs of others. I'll take the harness off them, said
Nuta to himself, and sell them. And he turned his thought into a
deed, sold his horses and repented fully and entirely.

Not in one day, of course, nor in two, nor in a single week nor yet
in a single month, but gradually. He had been wont to wear a straw
rope round his loins after the fashion of waggoners, but now made
himself a belt like a girdle. He had been wont to let his coat flop
round his waist, but began to let it down to his heels. His boots had
been wrapped in straw and rags up to well over the knees, but he
now took off the wrappings and smeared them with oil, and when
the iron hobnails on his soles wore out he did not have fresh put in.
Where his hat had been pulled down over his ears, he now raised
it so that it stood well back on his forehead. He always wore a sheep-
skin under his coat, and now took care that nothing should be seen
of it from the outside. And his inner self grew like to his outer appearance, and he came to that which he merited; for the Court
appointed him inspector of weights and measures. And we have

heard say that he took care that nothing wrong should be done in weight and measure; and even the gentile women who sold grits and barley, when they heard the tramp of Nuta's feet approaching through the market place, used to hide their weights until he had gone by. But that was all in the future.

Meanwhile Reb Yudel dwelt in a fine inn with a chamber all to himself, and ordered food to be prepared for him and paid with his own money, and sat all day long, not to mention the night, at Torah; and since he had fulfilled the Torah in poverty he merited to fulfill it in plenty.

And what did Reb Yudel do with the letter of the holy Rabbi of Apta? He set it over his heart and bore it as a charm. Though I were to be offered, Reb Yudel used to say later on, all the fullness of the Universe for this letter I would not accept. And it really happened that in exchange for this letter he was offered a little sweat scraped off the tefillin of the Seer of Lublin; yet he would not make the exchange. And it is still safeguarded by Reb Yudel's progeny, who keep watch and ward over it and say, We are deeply grateful to our forebear, Reb Yudel, for receiving this letter from the Rabbi of Apta. Where is there a scribe? Where is there a weighman? Find us a weighman who can weigh the worth of this letter in gold. Find us a scribe who shall know how to write such characters. We have heard that the Hassidic saints of Poland hold his holy signature in great esteem and say that its holiness gleams and shines from the very letters.

But now to return to Reb Yudel at the inn. In brief, Reb Yudel dwelt at the inn and studied Torah with devotion and application; and he saw to it that his hours and moments should not pass away unused, but crowned the hours of the day with the study of Gemara, while at night his heart did not rest but he went over what he had studied by day and added more thereto; for at night the head is clearer.

If you have never seen the clock in the Kaiser's palace, with its flowers and twining branches and its sweet chime, you should have sat beside Reb Yudel when he fashioned blossoms and branches for the Torah and studied tunefully. Frequently he would shed tears of joy for meriting to sit and study and no longer wander wide through the world. Nor should you wonder at the eye weeping when the heart rejoices; for I can show you the like in any woman whose husband has gone to foreign parts. When he returns in due time his wife rejoices so greatly that for very joy she begins to weep.

> *This my very own eyes saw*
> *With a man who went away.*
> *When he returned his wife rejoiced*
> *By weeping without let or stay.*

CHAPTER EIGHTEEN: THE DEEDS OF MEN AND THEIR STRATAGEMS ✦ And so, in short, it came about that Reb Yudel remained at the inn studying Torah, and indeed bought himself a mezuzah to gaze thereon at all times and fulfill the verse, "I have esteemed that the Lord is before me always." For each injunction hath its own claim on the Holy and Blest One, in the words of God to Job, "Who hath gone before me that I should repay him?" Hath he made himself a mezuzah for his lintel ere I gave him the aperture of a door; hath he made himself a fence ere I gave him an habitation, and so forth; and Nuta found himself other wayfarers in place of Reb Yudel.

What kind of man is this? the innkeeper asked Nuta. Nuta, thought Nuta to himself, how can it harm you if this innkeeper gives Reb Yudel a fine room and food free of charge? And he answered the innkeeper, If you knew who this fellow is, you'd go sprawling before him on your very paunch. The innkeeper wished to ask further questions, but feared to do so lest Nuta should suddenly turn on him and demand commission for having brought him so fine a person, by reason of which he would lose money, so he went off with half his curiosity unsatisfied. How his very bowels hummed to learn who the guest was that stayed with him; so he said to himself, did he, Stand at the door and put your eye to the keyhole and gaze within and study what he's doing, and then open the door and enter all of a sudden. And he went and did so.

All day long he stood bowed at the keyhole so that he seemed to have grown smaller and you might have thought a sort of hump stuck out of his back; and then he would open the door all of a sudden and walk in. And what did Reb Yudel do? Hid the place at which he was studying. But in vain does any man try to keep anything secret and hidden, particularly in an inn.

A most remarkable thing, said the innkeeper to his wife, here's a man comes and stays at an inn and pays up like one of the truly wealthy, and doesn't even leave his room to ask about business or commerce. Instead of being surprised at him, retorted his wife, go and be surprised at yourself that he's staying here and you don't know yet where he's from and what he's come here for. Well, said he, then

I ll go and put the brokers and agents on to him, and they can even get fish to come ashore with their promises.

So the innkeeper went out into the market place and found the agents standing about in knots and groups, telling one another such tales as the one of a lord of a manor somewhere who had gambled away a brandy distillery at cards. And you're the fellows, said the innkeeper to them, who claim to be wide awake and to know all that's adoing. Why, you're no more than infant teachers. There's a man staying at my place—— But before he had finished his sentence they were all in Reb Yudel's room. Or ever Reb Yudel was aware of them they were in his room, whether by way of Nature or otherwise; and never an agent came in but another was there ahead of him. And they all greeted him with overwhelming joy and said, Greeting to you, good lord and sir, is your honor a moneylender? Or maybe you deal or buy and sell? For of many a deal we have to tell,

AGENT THE FIRST:

Horses, for instance, and oxen as well,

AGENT THE SECOND:

Fells of rams vermeil in hue,

AGENT THE THIRD:

Musk and cinnamon, allspice too,

WHEREUNTO HIS COMRADE ADDED:

And you can profit, dear my lord,

AND HIS COMPANION FINISHED:

Till Messiah comes, at the cost of a word.

Reb Yudel took out his handkerchief in order to cover the volume's open leaf, and quietly said, to calm their tempest and hastihead, The Lord be with you, men honest and true, with commerce I've nothing whatever to do; indeed I regret that you have erred, for plenty of trouble you must have incurred.

THEREUPON THEY REPEATED ONE AND ALL:

Yet sir, if you will there is a brandy still which a lord lost at play and of which men say that it's worth untold thousands any day.

TO WHICH REB YUDEL RESPONDED:

That's all very well, but I don't buy or sell.

[239]

THE BRIDAL CANOPY

SAYS AGENT THE FIRST:

Maybe your honor would have a fine pile, for to reside with us a while.

AGENT THE SECOND:

Habitations of peace and rest, with trees and gardens of the best,

WHERETO HIS COMPANION ADDED:

Possessing a fence and balcony, and facing the synagogue as you may see.

BUT REB YUDEL REPLIED:

Brethren and friends, for me these will never do, since vanities I do not pursue; I am a stranger in the land, to whom such things are contraband.

AGENT THE FIRST:

But take the house for the balcony, whose windows face the synagogue as you can see,

AGENT THE SECOND:

'Tis such a fine house afacing the south; too great are its praises to come in my mouth,

AGENT THE THIRD:

If you went to the doorway, sir, you see, you'd hear them pray and respond Blest be He,

WHERETO HIS COMPANION ADDED:

And bow to the word blessèd, from your very bed,

AND ALL OF THEM ADDED TOGETHER:

Alas for the fool that neglecteth his soul.

BUT REB YUDEL ANSWERED THE AGENTS:

As for your words regarding a house being important, is not the house of which the sages spake far more so? And he straightway continued studying regarding the sale of a house, according to the Talmud, "Rabbi Akiba holds, if he sells he sells willingly, but the sages hold that if he sells he sells unwillingly."

Thereupon the agents stood staring at one another as though they were daft, and bowed their heads in shame. Here they were striving excitedly for deals, business, sales, purchases, livelihood, money, gold, houses, vanities and troubles, and at the end of it all there came a

[240]

man and as good as told them, You are all fools. Like the tale of the man from the world of void and chaos who was dashing about at the Lashkowitz fair buying and selling, until Reb Leib Sarah's came and lifted the skirt of his coat, and he was seen to be wrapped in cerements, the Merciful One deliver us.

It would certainly have been well for the agents to forsake their supposed affairs and remember their ends; but as the pious Rabbi Behaya said well so long ago in his work on the *Duties of the Heart,* Man is composed of soul and body, which bringeth him to devote himself to sensual satisfactions and to drown in lusts and to break the bonds wherein the intelligence holdeth him; and so they never hearkened to the counsel of understanding to remove themselves from vanities, but went about their concerns and attempted to drag after them Reb Yudel who, by the grace of the Lord which rested upon him, directed his course along the mediate path through the faithful Torah, which removeth a man from his lusts and longings in This World and preserveth his reward in the World to Come.

And indeed, they all leapt at him as though they would have swallowed him alive, and said, Have you ever seen the like of this here fellow sitting at ease in an inn and gorging himself like Behemoth and troubling folk all for nothing? Does he think he'll come and live here and fool all the town? And without giving themselves time to calm down they abused him to the best of their powers, Here we go expending our souls on him, said one, and he remains dumb as a stone. Can't you see, exclaimed a second, that his wits aren't in order? A golem, said a third, in form of a brute beast. May all my evil dreams, exclaimed a fourth, whether I dreamt them about myself or about others, or whether others dreamt them about me, or that I may dream yet or that others may dream about me—may they light upon his head one and all. Amen, replied all the others.

There was one agent there, a silent sort of fellow by nature, who always kept the end of his beard in his mouth, which habit helped him in many ways; for when he should have said something and had nothing to say, folk used to believe that the beard prevented him and went on speaking, which gave him time. When all of the others had talked their hearts out trying to persuade, he would take the beard out of his mouth and finish the transaction to his advantage. And so it was now. When his companions were all weary with having their say, this fellow let the end of his beard out of his mouth

[241]

and said, By your lives, it's not worth our while wasting a moment on him. When they heard this they went out.

As they filed out they turned back toward Reb Yudel and said, Why must you be obstinate? Tell us what you wish and will, and we shall hasten to fulfill your desire and bring it straight. And they departed with faces melancholy and knees that shook, while Reb Yudel himself betook to the labor holy.

When they had all gone the innkeeper went to his wife and said, Harkee, wife, I'm beginning to wonder about this fellow; he sits here like a man of means but doesn't betake himself to any sort of business whatsoever. Do you suppose I didn't send agents to him? Do you suppose they didn't offer him all manner of transactions? My heart went out o' me just listening how much was to be made, yet he paid no attention at all to them. I'm well on in years, I am, yet I've never seen the like of that fellow.

I suppose you've come to tell me something I didn't know, said his wife. I'm just as puzzled as you are. But seeing he is here we really ought to know what he's doing here. All of a sudden she gave a yell and said, Hush. What are you yelling about? asked he. I'll tell you, said she. He has a girl at home, and he wants to marry her off. And they decided to send him a matchmaker.

Now what told the woman that Reb Yudel was seeking a bridegroom for his daughter? The fact that Reb Yudel had the face of a man with many daughters; for the faces of such folk offer testimony as to the nature of their trouble. In brief, they settled the matter between themselves and informed the matchmaker. And Heaven concurred with them, in order that the promise of the Rabbi of Apta might be fulfilled, namely, his promise to Reb Yudel that His Blessed Name would provide him with a suitable match.

CHAPTER NINETEEN: DISCOURSETH OF WEIGHTY MATTERS ✌ The matchmaker arrived, entered Reb Yudel's room, coughed with seemly gravity and said, The Name aid you. Reb Yudel, raising his eyes from the volume before him, replied, Be aided of The Name. Blest be the one present, said the matchmaker. Blest be the newcomer, responded Reb Yudel. And thus each greeted the other.

After which the matchmaker took a chair, sat down facing him, brought out a snuffbox, tapped it, opened it, took out a huge pinch, sniffed at it and remarked as though in passing, Since I do happen to have dropped in here I'll just ask your honor before I forget, who was it gave your honor the trouble of coming here?

No man, returned Reb Yudel in the words of the Talmud, moves as much as a finger below without it being decreed of him on High; so if I am here it can be presumed to be His Blessed Will. Since He that is in all places, responded the matchmaker, has caused us to meet in the same place, it is to be considered within the bounds of possibility that some advantage may accrue to both of us from this meeting. In which way? asked Reb Yudel. The matchmaker began running all five fingers of his right hand through his hair and said, And supposing I were to propose a match to your honor—eh?

Blest be He Who brings forgotten things to mind, exclaimed Reb Yudel. Why, I only took the road for the sake of my daughter whose time has come to wed. And whom may your honor be desirous for? asked the matchmaker.

That's a grave question you've asked, replied Reb Yudel. King Solomon, may he rest in peace, was wiser than all other men and reigned over the Worlds Above and Below, yet after he had seen all deeds and tried all things he summed up all his words by saying in Ecclesiastes, "The end of the matter is, when all hath been heard, fear God and keep His commandments, for that is the whole of Man"; the end of everything is the fear of His Name, and if the Holy and Blest One shall provide me with a God-fearing youth who knows how to study a page of Gemara I'll give him my daughter.

And what might your name be? the matchmaker asked Reb Yudel. Yudel, he replied. And from whence may you be? he asked. From

Brod, he replied. And what might be your family name? My family name? That's Nathanson.

Now this was the reason Reb Yudel called himself Nathanson: he said to himself, If I call myself Yudel student everybody will know me at once and will call me the Hassid; but if I call myself by my family name, who's likely to recognize me? But as soon as the matchmaker heard the name Yudel Nathanson he grew very excited, for Reb Yudel Nathanson was a very wealthy man, whose good name spread its savor throughout the land like any balsam. There were many wealthy men in Brod, like that true scholar and Gaon, Reb Zalman Margolius, and his brothers, the rich Reb Getzel and Reb Jacob, likewise Reb Simeon Diza and Reb Zisskind Kaler, but Reb Yudel Nathanson was wealthier than them all and his fame had even spread beyond Brod; for he distributed much alms and performed deeds of charity, and with his own money built a large hospital for the sick poor, whom he provided with bed and treatment so that they might not perish in the streets. Great is wealth which giveth honor to its possessors, particularly wealth allied with wisdom; that is, when the wealthy man is wise enough to do much charity with his money.

I'll go to Vovi Shor, said the matchmaker to himself, and tell him that Reb Yudel Nathanson has come to town in search of a bridegroom for his daughter. He excused himself to Reb Yudel, went to Reb Vovi Shor and said to him, Why should I make a long story of it when I can cut it short? In brief, Reb Vovi, I can tell you in two or three words that a great man has come to town, but really and truly great, that is, great in wealth and great in the possession of a good name; and if I don't err it's within the bounds of possibility that something to your mutual advantage may come out of it. And if you ask the nature of the mutual advantage, I'll tell you. Young Master Sheftel, your son, has reached the age when he'd do well to be studying the chapter, "A Man Weds", while this man's daughter has reached the time for the chapter, "A Virgin Is Wedded"; and if my memory doesn't fail me the tractates on weddings and on marriage contracts aren't far from one another.

Lippe, said Reb Vovi to him, by your life I don't know whom you're talking about. Who's arrived here of whom you say that he's wealthy and his daughter needs a husband?

I'm astonished at myself, said the matchmaker, to find that I didn't tell you his name the moment I came in. By your life, Reb Vovi, his name echoes throughout the world like a golden bell. Why should I make a long story of it? You've heard of a city called Brod. If I don't err there's nobody who hasn't heard of Brod. In short, Brod is where he's from. Now I only need to tell you his family name. In short, Nathanson's his family name. Not Reb Leibush Nathanson, for Reb Leibush Nathanson lives in Brazan, and this fellow lives in Brod; but his name's Yudel Nathanson. Why make a long story of it? Reb Yudel's his name and Nathanson's his family name and Brod's his town; now put all the names together and you get Reb Yudel Nathanson of Brod. If I don't err there's nothing to add, except to say I give my son so much, and you can leave the rest of the matter to me, and upon my head be it.

When Reb Vovi heard this he said, I give my son twelve thousand gold pieces. Thereupon the matchmaker picked up his feet, went to Reb Yudel and said, The Name aid you. Be aided of the Name, said Reb Yudel, raising his eyes from the page. The soles of my feet have still left a mark on the floor before you, said the matchmaker, and I don't need to remind you who I am. In brief, why make a long story when I can cut it short, as we have learnt in the Tractate on Blessings regarding prayers, "At a passage where the reader is required to prolong, he has no right to cut short; and where it is required to cut short he has no right to prolong"; and particularly when a man's sitting and studying, how much more is it imperative not to distract him from his studies, lest he be consumed, God forbid, in embers of broom wood.

I am particularly careful in this regard ever since I heard the tale of the Rabbi of Pozen, who used to complete the entire Six Orders of the Talmud in a single year instead of the seven it usually takes. Whenever a man came to visit him the rabbi would say, Blest be the newcomer, calling him by the name of that particular sage of the Mishnah or Gemara whose words he was then studying; and he would return to his studies. If he wished to stay there the rabbi would say, Sit down, Rabbi whoever's words he was studying, and would return to his book. Once he was seated the rabbi would ask, What do you require, Rabbi whoever-he-might-then-be-studying; and back he would go to his studies. When the man would see this he would fear to interrupt his studies and would depart. On the way out the rabbi would say, Excuse me, your honor Rabbi whatever sage of the Talmud he was then studying, and would return to his studies.

Now I only told you all that to show how careful we should be not to interrupt a man at study. In brief I've come from the house of Reb Vovi Shor who's of the Shor family, and what's more he's a truly wealthy man, and what's more he has a son who's by way of being a great scholar. In brief, why make a long story of it, this great scholar, Master Sheftel, that is, the son of Reb Vovi, has reached the time to apply the chapter, "A Man Weds" while your honor's daughter has reached the time for studying the chapter, "A Virgin Is Wedded"; and if I don't err the tractates on marriages and marriage contracts don't stand far away from one another. In brief, I only came here to ask how much money your honor proposes to give your daughter. Whatever the bridegroom's father, said Reb Yudel, gives his son I shall give my daughter. The bridegroom's father, said the matchmaker, proposes to give his son twelve thousand in pure red gold. And I'll do the same, said Reb Yudel.

It follows that Reb Yudel undertook to give his daughter twelve thousand pieces of red gold and employed the name of the courtly Reb Yudel Nathanson of Brod. Did he then permit any false statement to leave his mouth? God forbid that Reb Yudel should utter anything false; for he really was from Brod and his name was Yudel and he was of Nathanson stock.

You can see for yourself that this was so; for when the constable met him along the road and asked him as to his family name, what answer did Reb Yudel make him save, Nathanson is my family name. So in all truth his name was Yudel Nathanson, which was the same name as that of the Brod philanthropist; only the rich man was rich and the poor man poor.

And indeed this is one of the matters concerning which moralist sages have given full warning, since falsehood and truth are so intertwined that great wisdom is necessary to be delivered from falsehood, evil inclinations lying ever in ambush for to make a man trip and fall into their snare. But in this present case the falsehood was exercised in the interests of the good, after the fashion in which the sages permit a bride to be praised in the presence of her bridegroom, so that folk should say she is sweet and charming even though she may not be so.

And if you persist in inquiring how he came to promise twelve thousand gold pieces when he didn't even have twelve thousand kreuzers, the reason is that Reb Yudel thought, Whatever I have done I have done in accordance with the instructions of the Rabbi of Apta, and he told me to promise for my daughter just as much as the bridegroom's father promises for his son; and since Reb Vovi has undertaken to give his son twelve thousand gold pieces it's my duty to promise as much on behalf of my daughter.

In brief no more than a very short time passed ere the matchmaker returned to Reb Yudel, bringing with him a fine upstanding youth, fully skilled in upright ways, a worthy lad with an honest gaze, and versed full well in our Torah of truth. Reb Yudel tapped his cask of knowledge, found it full of old wine well matured, and straightway felt a great affection toward him, after the fashion of the faithful believers of Israel who love the Torah and esteem those who study it. With growing affection he called him, My son, and with affection still greater he found him well fitted for his daughter.

Thereupon the matchmaker went to Reb Vovi and told him, No prophet am I nor yet a prophet's son, but nonetheless I know, Reb Vovi, that your honor will tell me, Well done, Lippe; may your strength increase, Lippe; may you be blest, Lippe. Why should I make a long story of it if I can make it short? In brief, after I went away from you I went in to see him and told him what I had to tell him. This is what I told him, I know you're Reb Yudel, but we mustn't forget that Reb Vovi's Reb Vovi. Each is a personage in his own place, and there's no need to make a long story of it on account of the story of the Rabbi of Posen; but before telling the story of the Rabbi of Posen I'll go and wish the mother-in-law-to-be *mazal tov* and good luck and say, Mother-in-law-to-be, you see this kerchief round my throat? I swear to you it won't leave my throat until I've danced with the bride. And don't argue against me, Reb Vovi, in the words of the learned work, *The Law of Life,* that it is forbidden to go dancing with the bride, even without actually touching her hand, saving with the length of a kerchief between them, as is the custom in these times, adducing as proof that in the Talmud it is written, "How do they dance before the bride", not "with the bride"; and all the more so in our own age when you won't find anybody who can say that women seem like so many white geese to him.

Lippe, said Reb Vovi to him, by your life I can't understand a word of all you're saying. Tell me what Reb Yudel had to say to you, only don't be quite so long about it. And didn't I say, asked Lippe, what's the use of making a long story out of it if I can cut it short, as we've learnt in the Talmud. The words of the Talmud are one thing, said Reb Vovi, and the words of everyday human beings are something else. If you can tell a thing direct and straightforwardly, tell me; but if not, you can save your breath.

That's what I want to do, said the matchmaker, only your honor keeps on interrupting me in the middle. Why, it's like a man eating an apple who has his mouth gagged in the middle of eating, or like somebody dancing on a tightrope who has the tightrope cut from under him; would you be entitled to ask him why he'd stopped dancing?

But what, asked Reb Vovi, has a tightrope to do with this business? Now don't dismiss the comparison so lightly, said Lippe, for we learn of a certain saint, who never even raised his eyelids save in His Blessed service, that once a man came whom they call an acrobat, and said he would walk across the river on a rope; and they set up a beam on either bank joined by a rope. All the town gathered to watch, and that saint also came and watched, and the whole town wondered to see him there. I've learnt something great from this man, said the saint to them. What he's doing he does for the sake of money, but all the same, when he is actually on the rope, he doesn't trouble about his business but thinks how not to fall into the river. Now why should I be telling you all this? In connection with my call on Reb Yudel. Although my real purpose was to earn my commission on the match, when I was with him I devoted myself to the match itself and arranged what I had to arrange, which is what I was saying when I said I saw Reb Yudel and he agreed to the match, in brief.

In short, before Lippe had ended his tale Reb Vovi was already dressed in his finest clothes and was on his way to discuss the details of the match with Reb Yudel. Reb Vovi promised twelve thousand and Reb Yudel the same, apart from gifts and betrothal gifts according to ancient custom; that is, the bridegroom would send the bride veils and gowns and a silver-embroidered stomacher, while the bride would send the bridegroom a tallith with a silver neck-edging, and a shroud worked with silver; and the bridegroom sat silent, as is the way of the world, until the two fathers-in-law-to-be rose and said *mazal tov,* good luck, bridegroom.

Immediately after the Evening Prayer the relations and kinsfolk of Reb Vovi gathered together, and the women lit many candles and laid the table with all manner of dainties, while Reb Yudel tested the lad in matters of the law. Although he had already tested him and found him full to overflowing in Torah, he nonetheless continued to test him, as we find was done by the Holy and Blest One, who tried Father Abraham, may he rest in peace, with ten trials; and when he passed safely through them all he merited a God-fearing wife.

In brief, or ever the constellations and planets appeared the Engagement Contract had been prepared, and pots and plates broken, and the heart was rejoiced by food and drink and by song and praise. And wine and beer as water were poured, while up to the heavens the blessings soared, either seized hold of the other's hand and lifting his glass to his mouth did stand, wishing his comrade blessings full sweet, and the other made answer as was indeed meet, May this hour prosper and bring all good, and His Name give happiness just as He should, long life Reb Yudel, may Thy Name ne'er withhold blessings from thy house an hundredfold.

To which Reb Yudel made reply, Your honor has spoken my words, say I, and so, Reb Vovi, long life to you, long life to the bridegroom and kinsfolk too, who rejoice with us in throng and crowd; and bless the groom's mother so happy and proud. The singers burst into song and praise, and the house was full of cooks those days, racing around to fetch indeed Sabbath loaves strewn with poppy seed, and the waiters hastened the goblets to fill, and brought all manner of fish with a will, and broths and meat and sweetmeats fine, on which a body desires to dine; and the guests sat silent and ate of all, whatever happened their way to fall, while the groom expounded both grave and gay regarding the Contract and the day, in honor of Torah which is a bride, bride holy and pure and beatified. In vain, O ye agents who deals do seek, to disturb with proposals Reb Yudel, the meek; come hither all ye who do seek for ware, with the glorious Torah what else can compare? Ye who shamed Reb Yudel on every side, as he sat in the inn his book beside, walk where ye will through alley and road, while Reb Yudel enjoyeth whatever is good. Joy increaseth around the board, the singer sings his praises again, and wine and beer as water are poured, and honeymead like to the blessed rain, and blessings do fly like the bounteous rain, and glasses are empty but hearts full again, everyone blesses the fathers twain, and the bridegroom who is so fit to admire and his mother in all her festal attire. The matchmaker tells of the Rabbi of Posen, but none doth hearken and none doth listen, one eats and one drinks and one pours out the wine, one opens his vest and thinks further to dine. Come hither, Reb Vovi's friends, for to rejoice, and at this festival raise every voice; for he has made a match for his son, and what is more has matched him with the daughter of the lofty magnate, Reb Yudel Nathanson of Brod, whose name and fame are known even beyond the bounds of Brod.

And Reb Yudel sat examining and studying himself to try and discover what changes and transformations had befallen him. Were it not that Reb Yudel, said Reb Yudel to himself, whether in joke or earnest I do not know, whom I met at Polikrif village and who was ginger, I might have thought that one Yudel has been mistaken for another. Reb Yudel did not see things properly, but his guardian planet saw; and that too not in a clear and lucid vision but as in a glass darkly; for Reb Yudel had indeed been confused, not with that Reb Yudel who was not Reb Yudel and who pretended to be Reb Yudel, but with Reb Yudel Nathanson who was known to all, and whose name was current throughout the countryside. But Reb Yudel did not go deep into the matter; as long as the heart is glad the desire to investigate has no great power. Instead he diverted himself with the groom, of whom he grew very fond, calling him son and purchasing him a watch and chain for much money. In Brod, to be sure, it could have been bought for less, also in Rohatin were one to bargain; but Reb Yudel was not particular about money; more money, less money, that did not matter as long as he diverted his future son-in-law.

Now I'll tell you something fine, said Reb Yudel to Sheftel, his son-in-law-to-be, just think, although the watch can be classified among silent and lifeless creatures, it nonetheless achieves the work of the Holy and Blest One by taking away all reason for erring as to the hour of prayer. As for myself, I don't require any such contraptions, both because I have a cock at home that wakes me up to time, and because my limbs and members tell me how time passes; but you, who have not yet subjugated your limbs and members in such a degree to the service of the Holy and Blest One, require an instrument for yourself; for by means thereof you can use your hours purposefully and keep ward over every separate moment so that it should not be wasted, God forbid.

But there is no joy without sorrow. Reb Vovi's wife had a kinsman of Brod whose name was Meshel, and who used to vaunt himself to his kinsfolk, telling how important the wealthy folk of Brod thought him, particularly Reb Yudel Nathanson; and on the day the Engagement Contract was written this Meshel had returned to Rohatin. Now he's so proud, said Reb Vovi, about being a close friend of Reb Yudel's, so let him come and we'll see who's closer friends with Reb Yudel. He sent for him, ordering that he should not be told why he was wanted.

Why should I make a long story of what happened? Were I to tell you that Reb Vovi was keeping his eye on the door all the time, saying, Here he is, here he comes, he'll be seeing Reb Yudel in a second and opening his mouth, and his eyes will come bulging out and he'll stand stock-still in astonishment—if I tell you all this it won't mean anything more than you know. And if I tell you that the servant who went had drunk so much that he was thoroughly fuddled and tumbled into a pit and lay there all night long and so didn't invite Meshel, thus giving time to Reb Yudel Hassid in order that his reproach of not being Reb Yudel Nathanson need not be revealed so fast—if I tell you all this it will not be the truth.

For the servant actually went to Meshel, said, Greetings, Reb Meshel, Blest be the All-Present for bringing you back to town, I've come in the name of Reb Vovi; and if you ask why Reb Vovi should be sending for you all of a sudden, I can tell you that Reb Vovi's writing an Engagement Contract for his son with the daughter of the wealthy and exalted Reb Yudel Nathanson of Brod, and he requests your honor to come and rejoice in their company.

Now it stands to reason that Meshel ought to have sped to his kinsfolk; but, unhappily for him, on that day when he had returned to Rohatin, he had been attacked by highwaymen, and they had beaten him too; and when the servant came he found Meshel standing with his face covered by his overcoat, weeping and wailing in the gentile tongue, Hasn't one God created us, aren't we all the sons of the same Father, why do you wish to take my life? And Meshel's wife gazed through her tears and told him the whole story. The servant returned to Reb Vovi and told him all he had seen and heard. Reb Vovi at once rose to visit him and speak with him, and in conversation he told him how he had made a match between his son and the daughter of Reb Yudel Nathanson.

But Meshel stared at him and quoted the Talmud, saying, "A

camel can do a clog dance in Media." Whom are you talking non-sense to? Do you suppose I don't know Reb Yudel Nathanson, and do you suppose I don't know that Reb Yudel Nathanson has no children, the Merciful One deliver us? At this Reb Vovi rose and gestured with both his hands like a man saying, I despair of him; and he advised a double watch to be set on him, as is done with clear madmen.

But Reb Vovi still expected that if Meshel saw Reb Yudel and remembered how he had respected him, he would feel ashamed of his madness and grow sane. So he went and brought Reb Yudel back with him to Meshel's place. They found him in bed with a kerchief round his head, telling everybody that robbers had attacked him along the road and had made a hole in his head and stuck their hands inside the hole and took out all his money, leaving him nothing more than his sense; only sense without money isn't worth anything at all, and now he had nothing with which to do business and maintain his wife and children.

When Meshel finished he began weeping, and his wife and children did their best to help him, so that the very walls of the room wept at their voice. There is no reason for you to expect that a wonder befell him at Reb Yudel's hands and his understanding recovered; the opposite happened, insofar as a great miracle befell Reb Yudel, in that Meshel's mind was not in order; for had Meshel been of sound mind, Reb Yudel would have been obliged to be up with his feet and fleeing, since it would have become known that Reb Yudel was not the Reb Yudel they thought, and the match was made in error.

Reb Vovi still expected that when Meshel saw Reb Yudel he would remember how well he thought of him and would feel ashamed; and he spoke in such a fashion that at last Meshel understood that this was the Reb Yudel who was Reb Vovi's prospective in-law. To which Reb Vovi nodded and said, Yes. Thereupon Meshel greeted him and stared at him, never shifting his gaze, now staring at his boots and now at his long coat, now at his hat and now at his beard.

Meshel was a person who loved truth for its own sake, though it might not be in place and time, even if his mind might be disturbed, the Merciful One deliver us. *Mazal tov* and good luck, Reb Yudel, said Meshel, *mazal tov* and good luck, may it be His Will that the match turn out well and that the son-in-law should not be barren as is his father-in-law, nor that the bride be childless as is her mother, for fear they produce an androgyne. And what have you to say to that, eh, Reb Yudel? Why don't you say Amen to the blessing?

But Reb Yudel paid no attention to the words of Meshel, not knowing that they had something to them and were going to cause him much trouble in the future; namely, at the time Reb Vovi would learn that Reb Yudel Nathanson, that is, the Reb Yudel with whom he thought he was making the match, was childless and had no daughter to marry off; whereupon he would vituperate against Reb Yudel in every fashion possible, and as none had ever yet abused him.

But meanwhile Reb Yudel stayed at the inn, eating and drinking and studying and having blood let on the proper days which, being found in the yearly calendar, are not mentioned here. And on Sabbath Eves he went to the bathhouse. And so he stayed at the inn until he found his pocket emptying and his money diminishing, and decided to return to Brod; for he had already made up his mind not to accept alms, although he might well do so as a gift, since that may be done by a householder going from place to place whose money gives out and who is permitted to accept alms without being required to repay them when he returns home, since he was poor and in need at the time in question. Nonetheless, since he had undertaken not to accept alms he would not accept; and when his purse was all but empty, he made up his mind to return.

End of Book One in the name of One Who doth precede
any other one;
We commence Book Two in the name of the One there is
no second unto.

Book Two

CHAPTER ONE: KEENING AND LAMENT · HE SHALL FEAR NO EVIL RUMORS · THE RIGHTEOUS IS DELIVERED FROM EVIL, AND ANOTHER EVIL COMETH ﹏ "To everything there is a season, and a time for every purpose", said the Preacher. And so it came about that Reb Yudel communed with himself and said, Although I enjoy my stay in Rohatin more than all the mischances of my wayfaring, my time is come to return to Brod and inform my daughter Pessele that I have found her her mate, seeing that I have not let her know anything. For it was not Reb Yudel's custom to write letters, since it was his view that the action of a man leaves its own mark, and he who needs to know is informed from On High.

Had Reb Yudel known the grief of his wife and daughters because of their neighbors who cried out upon them, Serpents that you are to have driven the Hassid out of house and home, he would have taken himself to his feet and departed at once; but he was occupied with mindly matters and had no time for the vain imaginings of earth. Nonetheless the sages held that when one soul is sensitive to its fellow soul and devotes its imaginings thereto and desireth its fellow, its longings do bring it to all manner of imagings until the power of imaging taketh possession of it; so that when its fellow soul is in distress it suffereth likewise from an evil humor, and seeth its fellow's straits as they were its own. So it was with Reb Yudel; as soon as he remembered his household an evil humor troubled him and began beating and chiming in his ears:

From Torah thou art fled away,
And in synagogue dost not pray.
Thine own crust thou didst not eat,
Woe's thee for thy stumbling feet.
Now thy money's at an end,
And thy toil in vain, my friend.
For there is no help or aid
To the evil and unstaid.
When thou comest home weary and worn
Thou shalt see a bier borne.
Who is perished, tell me now?

Mother and daughter, we avow,
And behind the bier walketh Gittele,
Red-eyed and side and foot all bare.
Where is Pessele, tell me, Gittele,
Where is Blume and mother where?
Mother passed away at dawn
While Pessele perished yestermorn,
And there's nothing at home, upon my faith,
Excepting Blume and the Angel of Death.
Alas that thou didst not mend thy gait,
For now thou 'rt late, Father mine, too late.
Forth to the graveyard come, alack,
And set up a canopy of black,
To my sister, who died betimes a bride
And her soul is gone to the other side.
Then on the morrow to bury deign
Blume and Gittele, thy daughters twain,
Just as their mother thou hast brought to earth
And Pessele, thy daughter of sterling worth.

In Reb Yudel's place any other person might have gone about wailing, Woe's me; but Reb Yudel accepted his sufferings with love, and acted in accordance with the words of Writ, "He shall fear no evil rumor; his heart is prepared to trust in the Lord." He was not like those who attribute all that befalls them to Chance, but like those who know how the eyes of the Lord keep watch, and His Blessed Providence doth not depart, God forbid, for so long as a single hour. And he said, All this matter has come as a trial; I have faith that my deeds have made their mark where necessary, and that my wife and daughters know what is requisite for them to know; for instance, Nuta must have returned from the road and told them all that happened.

And so Reb Yudel stayed at Rohatin, eating and drinking and studying and testing the dialectics and knowledge of Torah of Sheftel, his son-in-law-to-be. But when he saw that his funds were diminishing he took it into his mind to return. So he went to the innkeeper, paid him his score, took his leave of Reb Vovi and of Sheftel and all the others who held him in esteem, and departed from Rohatin.

THE BRIDAL CANOPY

Never was such gladness seen between in-laws-to-be as was shown by these two when they took leave of each other. Reb Yudel was glad to be returning to Brod, and Reb Vovi was glad that Reb Yudel was leaving Rohatin. Now what reason did Reb Vovi have to be glad? Had Reb Yudel troubled him so much? Why, Reb Yudel had stayed at an inn all the time, eating and drinking at his own expense. But there was a good and sufficient reason.

All the time that Reb Yudel remained in Rohatin Reb Vovi feared that unsuitable reports might reach his ears regarding his, Reb Vovi's, forefathers, who were said to have been followers of the sect of Sabbethai Zevi, the false Messiah, may his name be blotted out. It was told of Reb Vovi's grandsire that on the Ninth of Ab, when we fast for the destruction of the Temple and may not eat as much as the measure of an olive, he used to hide himself in the cellar and eat half a cherry. For he used to say, If Sabbethai Zevi, who ordained that the fast of the Ninth of Ab should no longer be observed, really was Messiah, I satisfy his requirement of feasting thereby; while if he isn't Messiah it's as good as not eating anything, seeing it's less than an olive-size that I ate.

This matter of half-a-cherry was the destruction of many a fine family, and Satan still danced; for it was hard for Reb Vovi to marry off his children because his foes used to defame him, saying, Have a look at this Sabbatian whose forefathers used to eat cherries on the Ninth of Ab; and therefore Reb Vovi had feared that some person might come along and disclose his reproach to Reb Yudel. For he did not know that the thing was of the Lord, and even if all the jealous people in the world had come and tried to interfere they could not annul the match. Had Reb Vovi known who Reb Yudel his prospective in-law, was, he would have torn up the Engagement Contract to his face; but He, may He be blest, closed his fleshly eyes for the while so that he might live to see his son's rejoicing at a later date.

And so Reb Yudel took his leave of Reb Vovi, his daughter's prospective father-in-law, and of Sheftel, his own prospective son-in-law, and their kith and clan and his own good friends, and he began to wend his way, his daughter's repinings at rest to lay, for that the Lord did entreat her well, with a lad to his heart who was sound as a bell. Happy Pessele hath found her mate, a God-fearing scholar early and late; O Lord our God, make heard with speed in the cities of Judah and Salem's fair street, a sound of rejoicing and happy tide, the

THE BRIDAL CANOPY

voice of the bridegroom and of the bride; for the Lord shall have pity upon the poor and release the needy evermore.

Now since Reb Yudel had expended all his money on gifts and board and lodging, he had no money with which to hire a waggon but had to return afoot. In Reb Yudel's place another person might have felt aggrieved at needing to travel afoot; but Reb Yudel rejoiced over every step, saying, "The paces of a man are of the Lord." And what did Reb Yudel most resemble as he strode along with his stick in his hand, his goods on his shoulder and his whole body bent? Why, a large letter Aleph with which the Hebrew alphabet begins. His stick was like the left stroke of the Aleph, his body like the somewhat crooked middle stroke of the letter, and his knapsack was like the humpy little bit coming out of the body of the letter on the right-hand side. How much trouble, consider, did the early Hassidim go to in order to make their bodies resemble the letters of the Torah, as, for instance, when they raised their two hands on a level with their heads during prayer so that they resembled the three projecting prongs of SHin, which is the first letter of the Awesome Name SHaddai, meaning the Almighty; yet that which they could achieve only while responding, Amen, may His Great Name be blest forever and unto all eternity, was done by Reb Yudel all the time.

All the way back he did not take a farthing from anybody; for once he had found his daughter a bridegroom he was no longer an emissary sent to fulfill an injunction. Formerly, said Reb Yudel, it was my duty to accept money; but now it would be stealing for me to do so. When he found a waggon along the road to give him a lift, he rode; if there was no waggon he walked. In addition he did off the fine clothes and did on his own. "A man's garb," quoted he from the Talmud, "doeth him honor." In the past you honored me, and now I'll honor you. In what way did he do this? By shaking them and spreading them out in the wind to drive out the smell of sweat, and folding them and covering them over with a sort of sheet and keeping them under his arm to safeguard them for their owners. Happy the man who doeth that which is right toward his garments, and happy the poor man who returns his covering whole to their owner.

When two people take the road together, grow to love one another and then have to part, they rejoice exceedingly should they meet after a while. And so, when Reb Yudel left Rohatin and met Nuta driving along the road he rejoiced exceedingly and thought, in the

[260]

words of the Talmud, "Peak doth not meet peak, but man meeteth man."

When he came up to the waggon he said, Be greeted with peace, Reb Nuta; bless God and thank Him for bringing us together again. But the waggoner replied, I knew your honor would be calling me Nuta; but though I'm not Nuta, I am Nuta's brother and he's my brother, so that you can say, in a manner of speaking, that the only difference between Nuta and myself is that he's Nuta and I'm Jacob Samson.

Reb Yudel, looking closely at him, saw that this was indeed not Nuta but somebody different, for he had the three signs by which the Talmud tells us you can distinguish one person from another, these being voice, appearance and mood. For this fellow was expansive by nature and had a thick tip to his nose and a long two-pointed beard, one point of which turned downward while the other tilted up toward his mouth. But as for Nuta, he had a round nose and a tousled beard and a thick voice and a snappy nature. The one who had studied Torah and fingered his beard in thought now had his beard grown into two long points, while the one who had not studied Torah had a shaggy short beard. From this Reb Yudel concluded that the person before him was indeed that brother of Nuta who had studied Torah and had finally become a waggoner, while the waggoner understood that this must be Reb Yudel, the Hassid, with whom his brother Nuta had gone from place to place to fulfill the injunction of bringing the bride under the canopy.

Come, said Jacob Samson to his horses, we shall treat him with respect and friendship and give him a lift. And Reb Yudel took his goods and chattels, heaved them up, climbed up himself and put the clothes between his knees so that they might not crumple or soil.

Did you find a dowry? asked Jacob Samson. Blest be The Name, replied Reb Yudel. Did you find a bridegroom? Blest be The Name. A scholar? May the Name's Name be blest, a scholar and of good stock. If he's of good stock, said the waggoner, his Torah will stay with him. Then he wished him *mazal tov* and good luck and sighed.

And why are you sighing? Reb Yudel asked him. I've just remembered, said he, the jar of brandy which Paltiel tied around you, and I sighed. It's a pity you let the liquor go, for if you hadn't given it to Nuta I would drink your health and that of the young pair.

When they had journeyed a while Reb Yudel said to Jacob Samson,

Reb Jacob Samson, I know that you regret having to give up the Torah on account of your brother-in-law, to whom your father-in-law handed over your quarters. Please do me a favor and tell me why your father-in-law saw fit to uproot you from the Torah and set the yoke of making a living upon you; after all, if he wanted a waggoner there were any number to be found hanging about, so why did he have to marry his daughter to a scholar and turn the scholar into a waggoner? Couldn't he have married her straightaway to a waggoner? What was he after to begin with, and what did he have in mind at the finish?

The books, responded Jacob Samson, have already considered the problem in question. It is the course of nature that the spiritual and the material do not mingle despite the fact that there is no part of the body that is not the seat of the soul; but the soul is seated upon the body after the fashion in which a waggoner sits upon his waggon; when they reach their city the waggoner turns home and the horses turn to the stable. And so it is with the ordinary man. He loves the Torah and holds those who study therein in high esteem; but his love of the Torah is not an essential part of his form and frame. As long as you have not made the spiritual elements of yourself as inseparable a part as are the wheels of the waggon, all your spiritual elements are worth no more than a bad penny. My father-in-law will doubtless forgive me when I state that he certainly loves Torah and desires to cleave to those that study therein; but love of the Torah is not an inseparable part of him, and so when he came to require my room he did what he did.

What sort of person, asked Reb Yudel, is your brother-in-law? Better not to ask, responded he. But since you have asked I shall tell you. However, before doing so I must add a short introduction so that you can understand the character of my father-in-law; as Nuta in his wisdom says, A cart can't enter a town without passing through the outskirts. And therewith Jacob Samson began to relate

THE STORY OF THE CANTOR

or

THE WINGS OF SONG.

My father-in-law will, I hope, pardon me for describing him as a very gross person, if you will excuse my saying so; but nevertheless his heart yearns toward the Torah like a horse for its stall. If a new preacher comes to deliver a sermon my father-in-law goes off to town. Every Sabbath Eve he used to do what was requisite, seeing that he lived beyond an ordinary Sabbath day's journey, in order that if a sage came to town he could go and visit him. You cannot imagine what an attentive pair of ears look like if you have not seen him standing listening to the sage's sermon. His mouth was open, his two ears were pricked up, his face bright and his heart was glad. Not that he could understand the greater part of the sermon, for he had never studied Bible or Talmud, and ever since he had come to man's estate had had to do with nothing but horses and carts. When he was young what was he but a waggoner, and when he grew old what did he do but let horses for hire. Nevertheless, half of the sermon he would manage to make out, even if he did make it out all topsy-turvy.

But there is one thing that even the most perfect and entire ignoramus can understand, and that is cantorship. My father-in-law's voice, he will doubtless forgive my saying, is like the creaking of a wheel that has not been greased for years on end; but his sense of hearing is very good, and his pair of ears are always open to songs and singing. If you ever saw a cantor and his choir you could be sure that he was hanging around them; and he would bring them home and give them food and drink and give them a curricle and not ask for pay. Why, for a good tune he would have been prepared to pawn his very soul, so highly did he esteem it. But the thing for which he would have been prepared to give up his soul finally brought him to grief. And it happened like this.

Once a fine handsome young man with a pair of flashing eyes came along and asked, Have you a cart here that is leaving for such and such a place? And if there's no cart, said my father-in-law to him, wouldn't you be able to trudge the road afoot? Because if you can't, what use are your legs to a young fellow-me-lad like you? But I'm in a hurry, he answered, because I've made a contract with the cantor there. Are you a choir boy? he asks. And the young fellow answers, Yes, I'm a choir boy. Well, and if that's the case, said my father-in-law, why didn't you say so until now? D'you think you'll have a chance of getting away from us without doing the honors of your throat? Before I begin doing the honors of my throat, said he, first go and do my throat the honors. I can see that you're no fool, approved the old man, and ordered food and drink to be set before him at once.

And the young man ate and drank for a dozen cantors—and they're no bad trenchermen, as you know. My father-in-law watching him said, I can be certain that this young fellow will one day be a cantor in Israel; as the saying goes, As their eating is their service. And when at last he had finished he said to the young man, Now you've eaten and drunk, let's see what else you can do with your mouth.

Thereupon he began singing the special festival and penitential prayers. The whole air at once filled with song, as though it were a June night with the nightingale giving of its best. How can I speak about it or describe it to you? Our feet remained in my father-in-law's house, while our souls went wandering wide through the Halls of Music. And my father-in-law might well be compared to a hunter who has caught the wings of song. He there and then began praising himself and saying, You see, didn't I tell you he was the very wings of song themselves? From the cut of his face I saw that he was the very wings of song.

Listen, my lad, said the old man to him, do you want to go along? Most certainly, said he. And I tell you that you won't leave this place, said my father-in-law. And why not? he asked. Now what is it you want to go along for, said my father-in-law, other than to be a cantor's assistant? By your life I'll turn you into a cantor yourself. Isn't it more worth while, I ask you, to be a cantor yourself than a cantor's assistant?

Now he was unwedded, and therefore couldn't rightly be a cantor; only my father-in-law had a daughter named Teibele, and it had just struck him that he could marry them to one another. And meanwhile the young man agreed to stay with them, and my mother-in-law used to see him in food and drink. And my wife and her sister used to bring him all manner of dainties in their aprons. And no more than a few days went by until the Engagement Contract was written between the praiseworthy virgin, Mistress Teibele, long life to her, daughter of the worthy Dov Ber known as Bertshi, may his Rock and Redeemer guard him, and between the bridegroom youth, his honor Master Ephraim, long life to him; the virgin Mistress Teibele, long life to her, desireth the bridegroom youth, his honor Master Ephraim, long life to him; and the father-in-law-to-be, Reb Bertshi, undertakes to maintain the bridegroom youth, his honor

THE BRIDAL CANOPY

Master Ephraim, long life to him, in all matters appertaining to victuals, likewise to clothe him and shoe him as is seemly and fitting. The worthy Dov Ber, known as Bertshi, likewise promises to call upon the wardens, may their Rock safeguard them, to appoint him, namely and to wit, the bridegroom youth, his honor Master Ephraim, long life to him, as First Cantor of the Congregation in the Large Synagogue after his marriage; and should the bridegroom youth, his honor Master Ephraim, desire to accept a group, for service as choir, of those known as singers, he has the right to do so, and it is incumbent upon the aforesaid Reb Bertshi, the father-in-law-to-be, to assist and aid him to this end. This has been agreed upon by the two parties, namely and to wit, the honorable Dov Ber known as Bertshi on behalf of the betrothed Mistress Teibele, and the betrothed youth, his honor Master Ephraim, on behalf of himself. In witness whereof cometh the sign manual of so-and-so, a witness, and of somebody else, another witness.

And thus Ephraim came to live in my father-in-law's house and ate for his life. We soon had opportunities of learning from his habits that he was not particularly God fearing, and, indeed, if you wish to say so, interpreted the law very leniently for his own requirements; but we winked the eye at his transgressions. If he was caught doing something wrong we held him blameless. Great is the esteem and affection in which a man is held, for it makes even the beam in his eye seem no more than a mote; and such is particularly the case with a bridegroom in the house of his betrothed, when his parents-in-law-to-be are fond of him and he is good-looking and has a fine voice.

Within a little while we heard that he had done this and that wrong action in such and such a place at such and such a time. Now what sort of answer did Bertshi have for the man who told him that he had seen his future son-in-law, Ephraim, doing this and that wrong thing in such a place on such a day? My father-in-law screeched at him, Mister whoever-you-are and whatever your father's name may have been, let me advise you to gouge out your eyes and stuff them into your mouth and don't go looking at things you don't deserve to see, and don't come atelling me of things I don't want to hear about. And before ever he finished he would have slapped the other man round the jaw.

All the while my father-in-law was journeying to town and back, spending his time on all kinds of wardens. At last he succeeded, by actual cash bribery, to have his prospective son-in-law, Ephraim, appointed as Cantor of the Congregation in the Large Synagogue on condition that he first married a wife. If that's the only objection, said Bertshi to the wardens, it needn't bother you at all, for he has a wife all ready waiting to wed him. And at once they began preparing for the wedding. Before the last month of the year was out they had come under the Bridal Canopy. It was then that my father-in-law said to me, Jacob Samson, pack up your traps and empty your quarters so as the young folk can come in.

But that's a chapter all to itself. Meanwhile, Ephraim married, and on the first night of the Penitential Prayers before the New Year he arrayed himself as Cantor of the Congregation and took his place before the Holy Ark in the Large Synagogue in town. Well, what is there to tell you? If I tell you that his voice was fine I've already said as much; and all the same, I can tell you that when he sang, "For Thine is the body and Thy work is the soul, therefore have pity upon Thy toil", it seemed to me that my soul was bound and united with the Creator of the Universe, and the Creator must assuredly do all He could to deliver His portion. Unless you saw my father-in-law in all his glory and pride when he watched his son-in-law before the Ark in the Large Synagogue with a silver edging to his tallith, you cannot imagine the joy that is possible to a father-in-law. For even though my father-in-law was reckoned a wealthy man he did not wear a silver crown to his tallith for fear the fine folk of the town would rebuke him.

So then my father-in-law began coddling him even more. He himself would go off to the chickens and fetch him all the newly laid eggs to soothe his throat, since a newly laid egg swallowed raw is good for the voice. I ask of you, Reb Yudel, please not to be annoyed with me for taking so long a time in telling these details, for they should be explained in Bertshi's defense when telling how he came to put me out of doors in order to make room for that wastrel. In the end you will see how our Holy Torah took her revenge of him for thrusting me out of hearth and home and keeping me at arm's length from study.

But for the present let us return to our first concern. And so Ephraim stood before the Holy Ark on the first night of the Penitential Prayers. Those who were in the synagogue held very highly of him, while those who had not been in the synagogue dismissed him for a song. But when the New Year came round, on which occasion almost all the town goes to pray in the Large Synagogue, there was nobody left to whistle him down. When he went down before the Holy Ark and began the Reader's Prayer, "Behold I, that am poor in deeds and quaking and terrified by the fear of Him Who dwelleth amid the praises of Israel, do come to stand before Thee and entreat for Thy people Israel who have sent me", a tremor of penitence passed through all hearts. I myself forgot all that had befallen me on his account, and I emptied my heart of all its secular thoughts and determined to repent my ways; and so I went on from strength to strength all through the prayer.

Of old the ancient ones complained, and indeed it is mentioned in the Holy Zohar, that on the New Year and the Day of Atonement, when we ought to consider the shaming of the Holy and Blest One and His Name which is profaned amid the gentiles, everybody bays like a dog, Give us children, give us grub, give us life, give us forgiveness and atonement. And not a man thinks to meditate on the shaming of the Holy and Blest One and upon His Name which is profaned amid the gentiles. But when Ephraim took his place and began, every man disregarded his own needs and requirements; and during his prayer everybody cleaved to Him, may He be blest. It was plain to be seen that Ephraim's prayers made their impression upon the hearts of all except Ephraim. For while he was praying one young man pulled aside the edge of Ephraim's tallith which covered his head, thinking to find him swimming in tears; and Ephraim poked out his tongue at him. Mind you, I don't say that it really was so, but I tell you what I heard.

During the Ten Days of Penitence between New Year and Atonement everybody in town was humming, "My dear son Ephraim," or else "Behold I that am poor," to the tune sung by Ephraim. And folk came crowding round the house to try and catch a note of his. But Ephraim remained silent. He was too busy eating and drinking to his satisfaction, pleasing his body and not depriving his soul even on the Fast of Gedaliah, when he did not fast because of a weak heart. On the Eve of Atonement he ate a great deal as is enjoined, and drank far more than is enjoined. The plum harvest had been plentiful that year and plums were very cheap; so my father-in-law had made a liqueur like they do in Hungary, and Ephraim dived and drank without a stop. No matter how much I warned him to stop, he would persist in drinking. I'm not afraid, said he to us. It is a tradition I have received from my rabbi, may he rest in peace, who received it in turn from his rabbi, may he rest in peace, and his rabbi again from his rabbi, may he rest in peace, all the way back to the Holy Baal Shem Tov, may his merits protect us, to whom evildoers gave wine a hundred years old which was too strong to be drunk; what you have to do in such a case is to eat an apple and your drunkenness will depart; and this the Baal Shem did and did not grow drunk. And Bertshi, may he pardon me, sat there nodding his head in approval at every glass, and making nothing of me in his heart.

Atonement Eve came to an end and we rose from the table. I took off my boots and went across to my father-in-law to entreat his forgiveness and give him an opportunity of entreating mine. Think of all he had done toward me and all he ought to have asked my pardon about. But I was in no way cruelly inclined at that hour, and was entirely prepared to forgive him. He, however, paid no attention to me; he was too busy with Ephraim. We are but creatures of earth and dust, and I certainly regretted that my father-in-law disregarded me on account of that wastrel; nor was I free of jealousy at the time. But when we entered the synagogue and I saw how many people had come to hear Ephraim at prayer, my grief went, my pain vanished, and what was more, I began to feel proud of myself because Ephraim was my brother-in-law.

In brief the sun began to sink and the Large Synagogue was full. As soon as Ephraim took up his stand and opened his mouth everybody burst out crying. I feel certain that even if a person had been present that had transgressed against the entire Torah, but heard Ephraim praying that night, he would assuredly have repented. I wonder whether Satan himself could have avoided repentance.

After the prayer we left the prayer shawl and shroud in the synagogue and went out in order to rest a while. I spent that night in the same room as Ephraim. During the night I woke up and saw him standing beside the water barrel. I thought to myself that he wished to smell the water in order to reduce his thirst, turned myself over in bed and fell asleep again. When we woke up in the morning and prepared to go off to pray in the synagogue we could find no signs of Ephraim. So we thought he had gone on ahead of us; after all he was the Cantor of the Congregation and doubtless prepared his

heart to find favor before Him, may He be blest. When we entered
the synagogue we saw his clothes spread by the reader's desk just as
he had left them the night before; but he himself was not there.

The initial reader began reciting, "Lord of the world Who 'gan to
reign ere the first being was created"; the reader of the Morning
Service began "O King seated upon a lofty and exalted throne"; but
Ephraim had not yet arrived. All the congregation devoted their
hearts to our Father in Heaven, while Bertshi and I kept watch at the
door. When the time came for the Additional Service they began
growing excited and fuming and storming and yelling, Where's the
Cantor? Whereabouts is the Additional Prayer sayer? Some of the
congregation began joking, saying that he had gone to immerse himself before the Additional Prayers. Others began shouting that they
should take another cantor and pray the Additional Service before
midnight. From the women's gallery they called down that the
cantor's wife had fainted. By the time they had roused her, her
mother had fainted in turn.

Meanwhile I didn't know whether to go to the women's section to
help my mother-in-law and sister-in-law out, or stay and look after
Bertshi for fear he should fall down in a fit. For his face had turned
black as a pot and his knees were shaking and his eyes had begun
to run, and his whole body had shrunk to less than half, while his
lips quivered, oh, the evil eye must have gained sway over us.

When midday came, the noise and shouting grew still greater.
Some of the congregation stood banging on their seats and yelling,
It's time to pray the Additional Prayers; and others shouted back at
them, No, now we have to say the Afternoon Prayers first. And one
cried to another, Where is the Cantor? Where is Ephraim? one
answered the other. Either the angels had grown jealous of his
prayers or else the demons had snatched him away, the Merciful One
guard us. And it was right of the former Cantor, whom the wardens
had displaced for the sake of Ephraim, to go rebuking them, You
thankless lot that you are, it serves you right for forgetting the
Prayer-sayer who offered up prayer for you and your households year
after year till the reader's desk began to rot with his weeping, and
for replacing him by this worthless youngster whom you didn't know
in the beginning and whose end nobody ought to try and guess.

In brief, Ephraim did not take his stand at the reader's desk, but
somebody else had to replace him. After the Day of Atonement was

at an end, Bertshi summoned all his men and sent them everywhere in search of my brother-in-law. Reb Yudel, by your life I would have preferred to make a happy ending of it, but The Blessed Name desired to finish matters otherwise. The following day we heard that in a neighboring town they had found a Jew drunk and snoring in a waggon on the very Day of Atonement. Although nobody mentioned his name we knew that that sinner could be nobody but Ephraim.

And what was the story? Well, it was like this. On the Eve of Atonement he felt exceedingly thirsty; so he rose and drank water, but that didn't slake his thirst. So he went to a gentile woman who gave him wine to drink; and he drank and became so drunk that he could not tell the difference between the Day of Atonement and Purim, the Day of Enjoyment. When he left her place he saw a waggon standing and mounted upon it. He didn't notice the waggon moving and the waggon driver didn't notice him. In the morning they came to the other town, and Ephraim lay there on the floor of the waggon snoring like a swine; and just then the whole congregation was on its way to prayers.

When they saw a Jew lying drunk on Atonement Day they all were startled and cried out and woke him up; he began rubbing his eyes and said, Good morrow, Jews, for he still couldn't distinguish between his right hand and his left. Off came the slippers they were all wearing to clout him over the face; nor did they leave a whole bone in his body. And when they had done with him they hauled him to the synagogue and haled him before the rabbi.

And where may you have been last night? The rabbi asked Ephraim. And just then he became possessed by a spirit of foolishness which chattered out of his mouth for to anger the Creator and His creatures. I was, he gravely responded, at the house of such and such a gentile woman. Worthless lout that you are, cried the rabbi, what were you doing on so holy a night at the house of a gentile woman! Well, Rabbi, said Ephraim, it was like this. I was very thirsty and I wanted to drink, and I had too much decency to go into a Jew's house in order to ask for a drink of wine on Atonement Eve; so instead I went to a gentile woman.

Well, what more is there for me to tell you; we thought he was easygoing and found he was an evildoer. When a butcher offers forbidden meat for sale the All-Merciful preserve us, we break the utenßils in which the meat was cooked; but what's to be done with a cantor who goes wrong? Can we take it out of the prayer books and Orders of Festival Prayers?

And what did Bertshi do? Seized himself by the hair of his head and tugged out his beard in handfuls and wailed, Woe's me for having given my daughter to such a transgressor in Israel. And this was what he said to Ephraim, Listen here, you scoundrel and evil-doer and cause of misery to Jewry, I said I was going to do you the honor of giving you my daughter, Teibele, to wife, and I prepared a fine room for you, and on your account I turned out-o'-doors my son-in-law, Jacob Samson, whose shoes you don't deserve to lick; and I kept you on the best that was to be had and bought you a prayer shawl with a silver edging and made a cantor of you in the Large Synagogue. I don't have to tell you that it wasn't for your sake or because of your drunken forefathers that the wardens agreed to let you take a stand before the reader's desk on the Days of Awe, but because of the thirty-two good gulden I wasted for your sake in straight cash bribery. And then you have to pay it all back by putting this shame upon me. Now let me swear to you as I'm a Jew that I shan't rest until I see myself revenged and you going from to door to beg a piece of bread—and nobody will have pity on you and give it. Then maybe you'll feel remorse for your sins and you'll wail, Woe's me, what have I been up to, and you'll beat your breast in penitence so that your right hand will stick to your ribs. And if you think you'll have a chance of going back to your wife and getting out of it that way, let me tell you that if you try it, by your life I won't leave a whole bone in your body. You don't know what I'm like in a real rage; you'd better go and bury yourself alive before you come to me and get me into a rage! Listen to my warning and re-member what I've told you, and now clear off!

Thereupon Ephraim found himself a place in the inns and gin palaces along with all the other outcasts; and he would drink brandy and beer with them and sing them our sacred songs; and it would happen that the gentiles would come there with their womenfolk and dance to the music of his prayer and song. And gradually he sank to the very bottom. But my father-in-law, may he pardon me, never waited until all his words had been fulfilled; instead he brought him back into his home, for he was afraid he would run away to Wallachia and leave his wife, Teibele, a deserted wife. He tried to persuade the scapegrace to give his wife a divorce, but what was his answer? I love my wife, and I shan't give her a divorce. And in that matter she too stood firm; he was light-minded and the mind of women is proverbially flighty; and so he suits her and she suits him. And so he still remains dwelling in my father-in-law's house, eating and drinking and lacking for nothing except penitence and good deeds. What is more, I have already heard the womenfolk whispering that we may soon hope to enjoy the celebration of the Covenant of Circumcision. Well, to which nothing can be added except the hope that the fruit may be better than the tree.

When Reb Yudel had heard the tale to its end he sighed and said, Ah, Reb Jacob Samson, you have indeed saddened me. A Jew drunk on the Day of Atonement! "The precepts of the Lord," quoted Jacob Samson in answer, "are upright, making the heart to rejoice." Come, let us concern ourselves with Torah and forget our troubles. You have just told me, Reb Yudel, that your son-in-law-to-be is a scholar. That being so, please tell me some of the new issues he has raised in the course of his studies.

Thereupon Reb Yudel told him some. The waggoner began raising difficulties and Reb Yudel accounted for them; Reb Yudel accounted for the first difficulties and the waggoner raised others; the horses listening pricked up their ears and began walking quietly and gently in order not to mingle the sound of their hoofs with words of Torah, as in former days when Jacob Samson had dwelt in his father-in-law's house and would ride to town on horseback and enter the House of Study and pilpulize in the Torah. And how Reb Yudel rejoiced to be sitting in the waggon like a man standing studying at a lectern!

Nonetheless, when they reached Pikef village he descended in order to visit the old man with whom he had had the merit of spending the Sabbath. Wisdom, says the Book of Proverbs, remarked Reb Yudel, crieth out in the street; and it also says there, "I shall find knowledge and sagacity"; as long as a man's heart desires to study Torah he will find Torah to study, but good qualities and the fear of God are not to be found in all places and at all times; and so, since I have come hither, ought I not to enter? So he took his things and went to that saint, his heart delighting him in advance.

When the old woman saw Reb Yudel she raised her voice and cried, Mazal tov, good luck. Then she told him that her good man was not at home but had gone to some distant place. And since her voice was exceedingly sweet she kept on clapping her hands so that none should be caused to stumble on her account, after the fashion of Miriam, the Prophetess, who took timbrel in hand when she uttered song.

Reb Yudel kissed the mezuzah on the door and departed vexed; for he did not know that the ancient had gone forth for his sake. And whither had he gone? To Brod, of course, where the greater part of the Thirty-six Hidden Saints dwell. And to what purpose? In order to take steps and abolish the decree which the government was thinking of decreeing against Israel, namely, that no man should take himself a wife while he was still a minor. Had they not found ways and means of preventing that decree from being enacted, Pessele would have had to wait, seeing that her betrothed was still young, a veritable fledgling. But this did not come to pass, since the Lord hath planted six and thirty saints in His world, and when troubles come to the world the saints overcome them.

And so, in brief, Reb Yudel went his way. As he went along he found a waggon coming toward him with many men following it, so he joined them. There were ten men in the company, who had spent more than three days over a seven-hours journey, the reason being that when the waggoner passed an inn he went inside and drank himself soused, and then left his horses to find the road; and the horses used to overturn the waggon, so that the travelers had come to the conclusion that it would be better for them to get out and push the waggon along. The road is never so bad as at the season of the melting of the snows, particularly when the waggon has to be shoved along. Nevertheless they would have been able to reach their destination had it not been for the horses harnessed to the waggon. As soon as the horses felt that the waggon was being pushed they suddenly began spreading wings like to the eagles, and flew off leaving the company behind losing their balance and tumbling forward with outstretched hands and feet, and banging their noses on the ground. When a man bangs his nose on the ground it begins bleeding and he has to hold it with one hand, leaving only a single hand for pushing with; and it's a matter of common knowledge that one hand is not so useful for pushing and shoving as two are.

Seeing how things were, Reb Yudel began to accompany them and lend a hand in order to comply with the injunction in Deuteronomy to aid your neighbor. As soon as the waggoner noticed him he

[273]

demanded payment of the fare from him. By your life, my dear man, said Reb Yudel, I haven't got it. Thereupon he wished to rob him of his clothes. But as soon as he touched them he tumbled and fell, drunk as Lot. And Reb Yudel took to his feet and fled.

One trouble calls another. As he ran he found himself in the middle of a procession pacing with banners and images of their god and singing hymns, three priests being ahead of them; they were conducting a dead man to the grave. When a man starting on the road meets a corpse it is a bad sign; when a man starting on the road meets a priest it is also a bad sign; when a man hears the songs of priests the Gates of Prayer on high are locked before him and his orisons for forty days—some have it, for eighty days. And so you can make the calculation for yourselves. Reb Yudel had met with a corpse and three priests at one and the same time, when they were chanting priestly songs. Had he turned aside he would have been delivered from his straits and would not have had to hear their songs; nor would he have come to grief regarding the prohibition of bareheadedness; but when trouble befalls a man his wisdom departs, which was what Isaiah meant when he said, "He turneth wise men backward."

For they hit Reb Yudel over the head and knocked his hat to earth together with his skullcap. Thereupon Reb Yudel put his hands on his head and cried, Aie! He must not stand without a hat because of the prohibition of bareheadedness; he could not lift up his hat because if he did it would look as though he were bowing down before the images of their god; he could not properly cover his head with his hands because he had stuck his fingers in his earholes in order not to hear their singing. So what was he to do?

But time will do what sense and understanding fail to do. At last the gentiles went their way. Then Reb Yudel took his fingers out of his ears, bent down and lifted up his skullcap and hat, and covered his head once more. Giving praise and thanksgiving to The Blessed Name Who had delivered him from the hands of the gentiles, he began to follow his feet. He went where they took him and reached the tollgate. But his chapter of misfortunes was not yet at an end.

When he reached the tollgate he found it closed and blocking the road, and long lines of waggons stood on either side of it together with wayfarers. And why was the tollgate closed? Because the toll-keeper was mourning, may the Merciful One deliver us, and he had to say the Mourner's Prayer; so he had closed the road until ten men should foregather and make up a quorum.

Come, consider, said Reb Yudel to himself, how all things that befall a man are to his advantage. Had I not run away from the waggoner and run into the funeral procession, I would not have reached this spot in time to make up the quorum of ten and pray with full congregation.

But before they had completed their prayers a gentleman entered and took a strap and thrashed the leader and all those that prayed, and kept on beating until they opened the gate for his carriage. All ye who follow the road, may ye never know such a praying; for the travelers all mounted their waggons and fled. So Reb Yudel had to finish his prayers on his own and then went his way. Turning hither and thither, he found that there was neither house nor human being; but in the distance rose a smoke, now visible and now hidden; and many, many trees stood silent, with a stream of water passing between them.

Thereupon Reb Yudel raised his eyes on high and said, And for all things may Thy Name be blest, O Lord our God. Behold I stand before Thee; do with me that which Thou desirest. And he thought to himself, What a silly you were, Yudel, to wish to flee from your trouble. When you ran away from the waggoner what happened to you? You fell into the clutches of gentiles. They had no pity upon you while he would have had pity upon you.

And Reb Yudel was very weak and weary with his running and troubles; so he set down his bundle and walked over to the stream and filled his cupped hands with water and drank. After he had restored his soul he undid his girdle, removed the cushion which he still kept on his belly out of habit, put it down on a stone and sat to rest, staring down into the water till his hunger began to trouble him. Up to the time Reb Yudel had left Brod he had a healthy frame because he never overate; but now that people had gone preparing feasts in his honor the disposition of his body had altered.

Our sages of blessed memory, said Reb Yudel, have already taught us that a man should eat when he hungers and drink when he thirsts, and not permit the wish for nourishment to depart unsatisfied lest it cause a diminution of the natural strength. So what did he do? He brought forth a slice of Sabbath bread which he bore with him from one final Sabbath meal to the next final Sabbath meal, and washed his hands and ate. Eating brought the light back to Reb Yudel's eyes, and he began meditating upon all the good deeds vouchsafed him by the Holy and Blest One, who had delivered him from the waggoner, saving him his garments, and delivered him from the gentiles and brought him hither to this spot where a stream of water flowed, and had given him the understanding to hide away a slice of Sabbath loaf; and at length his heart was roused to sing joyfully, "The Lord is my shepherd, I shall not want."

And he sang joyfully and thankfully, as though a table had been spread before him laden with all manner of dainties. When David was in the wilderness, said Reb Yudel, and did not have what to eat and drink, so that his soul was all but departing from him, the Holy and Blest One suddenly had him enjoy a whit of the taste of World to Come, and thereupon he wrote that Psalm. And now I, Yudel, sing the song which he, David, did sing before the Holy and Blest One; and what is more I sing it at the time of feasting. Is that not a foretaste of World to Come?

CHAPTER TWO: CONTINUING THE LAST CHAPTER ·
A WOMAN CONVERSES WITH HER HUSBAND ﺨ
The day gradually faded. The east turned silver and a rising
mist chilled the ground. Since darkness would soon be around him,
Reb Yudel rose, took his bundle, stuffed his cushion into it instead of
replacing it on his belly, tied his girdle round his loins and went toward
the smoke he saw rising. On the way he was met by a Jew named
Kalman Tailor, who was returning from the house of the lord of the
manor where he had been mending the clothes of the retainers. His
lower jaw stuck out in front of the upper, he was gray all over, his
face was pale and deeply wrinkled and seamed, and his eyes were
full of humility.

Where are you going, said Kalman to him, and where are you
from? I'm a wayfarer from Brod, answered Reb Yudel, and I'm on
my way home to Brod now. If you care to come along with me, said
the other, I'll give you a place to stay in under a rooftree. Do you
pray with a quorum of ten in the village, Reb Yudel asked the tailor,
and is the lord of the manor friendly toward Israel?

We round up a quorum, replied Kalman, with difficulty; as for the
lord of the manor, he's neither friendly nor unfriendly toward Israel,
but is just mad, plain and simple. He's not like his grandfather, who
used to shed blood out of sheer evil nature, nor is he like his grandmother, who used to shed Jewish blood as a joke. I'll tell you as we
go along what his grandfather did to my father. Once he returned
from the hunt without having shot anything, and he said to Father,
Climb up to the top of yonder tree. When he had climbed up he
took a shot at him so that he tumbled down dead. And then the lord
of the manor began clapping his hands with joy as though he had
shot a fine piece of game in the field. And what's the story of his
grandmother? Once she went walking alongside the river, and seeing Jews in a boat she said to her attendants, Push them under
water; and they did so. But the Holy and Blest One had his revenge
of her. A few days later she took a boat out herself on the river. All of
a sudden she began yelling and screeching. Save me, she screamed.
The drowned Jews are drowning me as well. And sure enough she
fell overboard and was drowned in the stream.

So the tailor rambled on, shortening the road with his tales until

[277]

they reached a village and entered a hut which was sunk halfway in the ground. There was a fire burning on the hearth and a sorrowful woman sitting in a corner of the room, her elbows resting on her knees and her head resting on her hands. As he entered, Kalman rested his hand on her head and said, Good evening, Reitze, bless you. Don't be so sad. I tell you that all that is done is for the best. And now it would be nice of you to rise in honor of the guest I brought with me, for he wants to eat.

Upon this Reitze rose and said, Put away your things and say the Evening Prayer while I get the supper ready. So each one stood praying in his own corner while Reitze spread a sort of dirty cloth on a barrel in which cabbage was pickling; then she set out half a big round loaf of black bread, made of rye mixed with bran and straw, and a spoonful of coarse salt, and said, Wash your hands and eat a little bread, and meanwhile I'll prepare something warm. So Reb Yudel sat with the master of the house and dipped his bread in salt; not that he was actually hungry, but he ate in honor of the injunction of hospitality.

While eating Reb Yudel asked the tailor whether he had any sons or daughters. Kalman raised his eyes aloft, saying, May the name of the Lord be praised, enough for my own prayer quorum. At this Reitze sighed so deep and forlorn that Reb Yudel's mouthful of bread stopped halfway down his throat. Why is the woman moaning like that? he asked her husband. Because, said he, it's the way of a woman to sigh and moan. Does she lack for anything here? Why, she sits in her own house like a bride under her canopy. Isn't that so, Reitze?

But Reitze answered by turning to Reb Yudel and saying, Say yourself, my dear Jew, isn't it a punishment at the hands of Heaven? I've borne ten children and yet not one of them dwells at home with me. And she went on to tell him the troubles that had befallen her with her sons and daughters. One had been taken for the king's service and had grown sick and died; another had gone to Hungary to bring back plums and had never returned; one had gone off to Brod and had attracted all her sisters after her as though there were no salt in their parents' bread.

But before she had properly begun pouring forth her bitter heart her husband broke in, saying, Reitze, don't torment the Jew and grieve him. Maybe there's a drop of brandy? None left? It doesn't matter. If there's nothing left he isn't lucky, that's all. And meanwhile Reitze wiped her eyes and brought them millet in milk; and since there had not been enough for two she added water in the pot, so that you could not find the millet and could not see the color of milk any longer. Eat, Reb Yudel, eat, said the master of the house. Hot food is good for sleeping on; even if there isn't enough to sustain the body here, there's the wherewithal to warm the inside.

After they had eaten and said benediction, Reb Yudel took out his prayer book and recited a number of passages before going to sleep, so that no destroying angels, God forbid, might harm his soul on high, and so that his body might be well guarded below and be prepared for him to rise to the service of the Creator. The cabbage in the barrel creaked, and Kalman and Reitze sat astonished; for never in their lives had they seen so large a prayer book. After Reb Yudel had ended his passages he kissed the book and closed it, and began to prepare himself for sleep. The tailor lifted up the book to gauge its weight. Then he said, If you please, Reb Yudel, tell me whether you've already prayed out the whole of this book? God be praised, nodded Reb Yudel. Such a meager body, said the tailor, whistling, how could so many prayers as all that get into it? We expect, said Reb Yudel with a smile, the prayers of Israel to ascend and mount up to Heaven; and in Heaven there's plenty of room.

The tailor now brought a hide and spread it out for Reb Yudel. Reb Yudel asked him to spread a little straw for him; then he took his cushion out of his bundle, placed it under his head, repeated the Hear O Israel, and fell asleep.

Close to midnight he found himself in Pedhoretz village, and hastened to the synagogue in order to be one of the first ten. When he arrived there he found that there was a complete quorum, each resembling all the others as closely as though they were brothers; and all of them prayed out of Reb Koppel's prayer book; but the prayer book was tremendously large, and all the same in spite of its size it trailed away like the yarn with which a needle is threaded. At this Reb Yudel stood trembling and terrified.

But he saw a man before him holding something in his hand; it was like a bottle of brandy but was not a bottle of brandy; and the man said, Mouth to mouth shall I speak with you. Seeing that through the multitude of our afflictions and prolongation of our Exile understanding grows short and hearts are sealed, therefore I desired to open you an aperture, tho' small as the eye of a needle it be. It is written in Psalms, "Rouse the harp and the psaltery; let me awake the dawn"; the purpose of which is to teach you that no man should rely upon his own sense, saying, Of course I shall awake ere dawn; but let him have something wherewith to be roused from sleep. This was the case, as the Talmud informs us, with King David, who had a harp hanging over his bed; when midnight came a gentle breeze blew and stirred the harpstrings; and David would rise at once to serve the Creator. And we know of many sages who fashioned them utensils and made them stratagems and inventions whereby they might be aroused from their sleep; yet the best preparation is the possession of a cock which knows the hour of midnight.

It was just then that the cock crew and Frummet began moaning. Frummet, Reb Yudel asked her, why are you sighing and moaning? Yudel, said Frummet his wife, and how can I do other than moan when our daughters are weeping themselves away and their hair is turning white, and all the time you don't as much as lift a finger to lend them a hand? Frummet, Frummet, said Reb Yudel, you always have to come complaining against me. Haven't I done all I can? For whose sakes have I uprooted myself from the Torah? For whose sakes have I done without my responses in the prayers? Wasn't it only for the sake of our daughters? And The Name has prospered my way so that I've already matched our daughter Pessele with a scholarly, God-fearing lad, and I've promised her a portion of twelve thousand gulden; and so you see, Frummet, that everything has turned out well; and you know it all yourself, so why must you keep on coming along and chopping me up into little bits? Yudel, said Frummet, if you have God at heart come straight back home.

Reb Yudel woke up in great confusion. The Talmud remarks that a woman converses with her husband in the third watch of the night, so it must be after midnight and I am too late for the Midnight Prayers. And he did not know that they had conversed only in dream. He at once stretched his limbs, rose from his couch, washed his hands and cleaned his body, sat down on the straw and began rousing his tears for the destruction of Jerusalem. Thereupon the housefolk also rose about their affairs. The tailor began mending some garment in order to return it to the owner ere he departed for the fields; and the tailor's wife went to the miller's wife in order to borrow a little flour for breakfast. The tailor sat cross-legged threading his needle time and again; the woman kneaded dough; and Reb Yudel put the night to rights with song and weeping until the hour for the Morning Prayers arrived. When they had said the Morning Prayers Reitze brought dabs of dough with pease. Reb Yudel ate the dough but left the pease alone; for pease are a sign of mourning, as the books record of old, among the Jews of Austria, and that was not a day on which some sign of mourning is required.

Thereafter Reb Yudel took his leave of the tailor and went his way; and when he left the house Reitze gave him some bread so that he should have the wherewithal to sustain himself if he felt hungry on the road; and Reb Yudel in turn blessed them with all the blessings that are to be found in the Torah. On the road Reb Yudel rendered himself account of all that had befallen him the previous day and of all he had dreamt by night; and he realized that Reb Koppel must be annoyed with him for having changed his prayer book, but was not really angry; for had he been really angry he would not have spoken to him at such length. Therein he was not like Frummet, Reb Yudel's good wife, who was always angry and was never satisfied whatever he might do. But meanwhile he himself decided, without taking any oath, to redeem the prayer book of Reb Koppel from disuse and dust, and to hasten home.

Were it not that the anniversary of the decease of his father and mother occurred in that very week, he would have turned and made straight for Brod and kept on walking until he came home, covering a league today and another league tomorrow; and what with one day and the next he would have reached there soon enough. But now he remembered the anniversary of his parents' death he decided to make direct for the nearest town, so that he should not need to undergo the fate that befell the tollkeeper, who prayed in the village and got a beating for his pains.

When Reb Yudel came to the crossroads he stood there staring about him, not knowing which way to turn. Along came a sort of carriage in which sat a great merchant from Western lands. This merchant had brought raisins for making Passover wine, and rumor had had it that flour was dusted over them. People therefore refrained from buying them for uncertified flour is leaven and may not be eaten in any form on the Passover; and so the merchant had to go to all the sages of the generation and make it clear to them that the white dust they could see on the raisins, which looked like flour, was nothing more than sun motes which had fallen on the raisins during drying; so that in reality they were permissible even to the most pious of the pious.

When this merchant saw Reb Yudel standing at the crossroads, Climb in, said he to him, and in Reb Yudel climbed. Reb Yudel never asked the merchant where he was off to, and the merchant never asked Reb Yudel where he wanted to go; and so at length he found himself in the Holy Congregation of Glena, where the householders purchase grain from the peasants and make a decent living. There he prayed in the Large Synagogue, which was built of stone and had no dome; and birds make their nests there under the roof; and on sunny days they spread a curtain there over the bema while the Torah is read; also they pray according to the German usage in that place, not according to the Spanish usage of the holy Ari, which Hassidim follow.

After his prayers he went to the graveyard and lit a candle at the grave of Reb Petahiah, who had been one of the Thirty-six Hidden Saints and had lived all his life in an attic, never venturing out of doors; he had had a ritually suitable bath at his home and never even prayed elsewhere than at his house, except on New Year's Day when he used to go to synagogue to hear the shofar blown; he used to wear a ragged garment like those of the gentiles; and at his death he left manuscripts behind him.

On the morrow Reb Yudel went elsewhere, since the anniversary of his mother's death had come, and it is not nice for a wayfarer to pray twice running in the same place. And where did he go? To Bisk. Nor is there reason for surprise if he did not go to Premislein; for that was the time when Reb Meirel of Premislein had gone to Mikeleiov, so that Premislein was no more than an empty husk. When Reb Yudel reached Bisk he saw he had come to Nuta's town, quarter in, district out, and the whole town nothing more than one quarter after another. Whenever you think you have really reached the town proper you find that you are outside it already.

Reb Yudel entered a small House of Study, for the large synagogue was not yet finished by reason of the habit the townsfolk had of coming and taking stones whenever they had to build themselves a stove. After having said his prayers and a chapter of the Mishnah

THE BRIDAL CANOPY

he went off in search of his lodgingplace and began wandering from
one quarter to the next, thinking all the time that he had reached
his destination when he was somewhere else; at last his strength
failed and he went in to the first place he saw.

The house he entered happened to be that of a gentile who was of
Jewish stock, for the forefathers of the householder had been of the
followers of Jacob Frank, may his name and fame be blotted out, and
had converted together with him. The whole building had a moldy
smell and there were two holes in the wall for windows, which were
stuffed up with straw and rags; the ground there was boggy, so that
sometimes Reb Yudel slipped and sometimes he began sinking; and
there was a heap of rotting straw spread there, on which lay two
sisters, their eyes glittering with hunger madness. The sisters smelt
the bread in his pocket; one of them got up and snatched it out with
her mouth. The second at once fell upon her, put her mouth to the
other's, and began biting away at the same piece so that mouth met
mouth and teeth met teeth. How Reb Yudel grieved that on the
anniversary of his mother's death he had to find his way into a gentile
house where he could not even continue studying the Mishnah. There
are, said Reb Yudel, three hundred and sixty-five nights in the
year, yet I had to find this night to stay with a gentile.

Then he remembered how his mother had told him that when she
had been in the family way with him she had been seized with a
longing for some gentile bread she smelt, and they had given her of
it. And thereupon he understood that he had come here purely by
reason of that piece of bread she had eaten. If a man knew, said
Reb Yudel, how to correlate all that happens, he would see that all
things are for the best. But it was not clear for whose best they were
until Reb Yudel explained, For the Holy and Blest One's best, for
had the Holy and Blest One not so desired, the thing would never
have come about; and so the First Cause is His greater glory, as you
might say. Meanwhile, at the house, he rose while it was still night,
took his bundle and went off to the House of Study in order to reach
it ere the sun grew bright. And when he left the gentile house he left
his cushion behind him.

The black bridges stood stretched across the river, and the water
seemed to rise and gulp at them as it approached. In every courtyard stood waggons, some loaded with boards, some with flax and
some with earthenware. The moon began to set and the sun to rise.

By the time Reb Yudel came to the House of Study he found he had to pray with the second quorum. All day long he feared that he would only lose himself again and not find the synagogue for the Afternoon Prayers; so he stayed in the House of Study all day long; and since it was the anniversary of his mother's death he studied the Mishnah; and since he had not closed his eyes all night long, they now kept on closing of themselves; and when he put his finger on the place in order to look in the marginal commentary and see what Rabbi Yom Tov Lippmann Heller had to say about the matter, he would drop off and see great lines of waggons laden with merchandise like those he had seen before dawn, all of them going to Brod. If I had mounted one of them, said Reb Yudel, I could have said the Afternoon Prayers in Brod. How astonished Brod would have been to see me all of a sudden in the House of Study, and how startled Frummet would be.

It was at this point that Zissel, his mother, came from the World of Souls and found her son slumbering over the volume of the Mishnah. Yudel, my son, said Zissel to him, I know you didn't sleep all night long and so you want to rest now. Please tell me, where is the cushion? I remember how I used to sit plucking feathers by night and wetting them with my tearful prayer to His Blessed Self that you might rest well on your cushion, never needing, God forbid, to pawn it or sell it; and yet you never had the merit of lying quiet upon it; instead you wander the road far and wide, restlessly, like a bird driven out of its nest. Geese, geese, come and be my witness; were you not slaughtered according to the Torah's requirements? Were not the two blessings on the Slaughter and on the Covering of the Blood repeated for you? Why has my son not had the merit of resting his head quietly upon you? But go on sleeping, go on, my son.

But his father at once scolded her, saying, If everything went the way you wish, he would sleep all his days away and forget that there is Torah in the world. King Solomon, may he rest in peace, was bound to the pillar by his mother so that he should be lively and fully informed of the Torah, and when he grew up he thanked his mother; yet you have to go spoiling your son and telling him, Sleep on, sleep on, my son. Maybe you'll cover him with a bedspread adorned with stars and planets, and spread it above his bed so that he can sleep the whole day through. His friends and companions are already being married; Joel's marrying Frummet, the cantor's daughter; yet your son Yudel's tied to your apron strings yet, and she has to go on telling him, Sleep a while yet, my son. And his father began shouting at him, Come on, heave up your feet and clear off to the House of Study. But his mother followed him as he went off to the House of Study, and gave him a cake saying, Take this and eat, my son, and don't say that you want to fast on the anniversary of my death. I know you have never done so all these years, and that it's only because you do not want to hold out your hand for an alms that you fast now.

Reb Yudel raised his head and found a cake before him. It was not his mother, however, who had brought him food from a place where there is neither eating nor drinking, but some poor woman who used to visit the Houses of Study and give of her own to poor students and scholars. What was more, she gave him some money too. Reb Yudel said a blessing, ate and made up his mind to give the money to some other poor man as an alms in memory of his mother, may she rest in peace, who had put him on his feet and who kept her eyes on him even from the World of Rest.

And Reb Yudel's heart was roused to pray, May it be Thy will, O Lord our God and God of our forefathers, that the merit of this study of mine, for the soul of my mother, may she rest in peace, shall mount aloft to Thee; that her soul may be joined in the bundle of life, and her place be among those saintly and pious women who stand before Thee deriving sustenance from the shining light of Thy Countenance, and mayst Thou provide her with her position among those that stand before Thee; and mayst Thou forgive and pardon and atone and erase and pass over all that she may have sinned or transgressed or done wrong before Thee, or that she may have done which was not according to Thy will; and mayst Thou not hold against her anysoever sin, transgression, iniquity and trespass; but whatsoever commandments she hath fulfilled mayst Thou remember for good; and may her spirit rest in the Garden of Eden and her soul delight in that good which is hidden away for saintly women; and may she rest in honor and peace to arise to her fate at the end of days. Amen.

He ended by completing the rest of his chapter of Mishnah and then saying the Scholar's Memorial Prayer and reciting the Afternoon Prayers, and before he prayed he gave alms to the poor. The other poor man who was the recipient was astonished indeed to see someone as poor as he was, and maybe poorer, who gave him an alms. And he himself put that alms away for some other poor man. The coins in question are round and can roll from hand to hand; happy is he to whom the chance of fulfilling a commandment cometh through them.

CHAPTER THREE: THE WORLD AND THE FULLNESS THEREOF · QUEER CREATURES · OLD–TIME TALES · BROD ‌‌ The following day he went his way and stayed where he stayed and ate where he ate; and day by day he continued to see new faces. For some people the soul was the important thing and the qualities of the body unessential; for others the body was all-important and the qualities of the soul of no great value. Now he found himself staying with one who prolonged the feast and curtailed the benedictions, and now with another who concerned himself with spiritual matters yet did not even have enough to sustain his body. One day he spent with a man who went off in search of wayfarers as guests, and the next he would find himself staying with a person who did not give as much as a doit to a pauper. O Earth, Earth, Earth, how greatly art thou declined to have become the abiding place of the mean and ungenerous.

And so, in brief, Reb Yudel's legs traversed many a place, and he saw all manner of men and was enabled to see how widely the ways of one differed from those of another. Ere he had left Brod all folk had appeared one and the same to him, as though there were no difference between one man and his fellow; but once he left Brod it seemed to him as though each individual man had many others resident within him. And since he had gone off at an angle he found that he came to places he recognized and to places he did not recognize; and there was no spot where he did not discover something new.

In Reb Yudel's place somebody else might have foundered among the vanities of the world; but Reb Yudel never lost sight of his aim, namely, to return home to his labor, which was the study of the Torah and prayer with the congregation. But since he did not wish to accept charity and alms he did not have the wherewithal to hire a waggon but followed his feet; whithersoever they led him he was prepared to go. Then do you suppose that Reb Yudel never went by waggon? Why, we have just been told of cases when he did get a lift by waggon or carriage.

But the expression, "following his feet", means that he did not arrange his travels in any set direction. It is the general custom that when a man has to journey to any place he seats himself in a waggon and is driven straight there; but Reb Yudel was not so particular in

[287]

THE BRIDAL CANOPY

this respect. If he was going north and met a waggon coming south he would ride south as well for company's sake; if he met a west-bound waggon while he was going east he would take a lift as well.

Throughout that time he never gave over repeating the verse in Proverbs, "The eyes of the Lord do watch in every place"; and he went on with a further verse from that book, "For the ways of a man are before the eyes of the Lord." For the affairs of this world have nothing steadfast in them; we do not know which of them are de-sirable. If a man does a deed it must assuredly be for good, seeing that otherwise he would not be aided in the doing; if he does not do it, that is also to the good, for were it so desired of Him, may He be blest, He would find ways and means of bringing him to do it. From the circuits and traversings of Reb Yudel he had the merit of seeing deep into the way of the world. At first sight this world does not appear worthy of close examination; but insofar as he clarified his thought and fined the acts of men in proper fashion, the world of vanity be-came clear to him as a world of true activity.

The countryside through which Reb Yudel passed is blessed with all that is good. In it you find all manner of corn and pulses, fruit, flocks, oxen, horses, fowl, bees, fish fat to a wonder and beasts slain for their skins, and lime and pitch and clay and colored earths, and sea coal and sulphur and naphtha and metals and salt and rock salt, with fine springs from its hills for the pleasure of man; and there are many factories there in which linen is woven and wool is spun and paper made, as well as glass and sugar and saltash and gunpowder and snuff tobacco and flaxen wares and brandy and beer and other kinds of liquor.

A man who had studied as much Bible and Talmud as Reb Yudel, and had been as mighty in the Torah as he, was not the person to let anything pass, whether it were great or small, without deriving some moral benefit thereof, sometimes directly from what he saw and sometimes by inference. When a man passes a tannery he holds his nose and hurries on; but Reb Yudel dawdled to look at the hides and say to himself, It would be well if I could flay myself and use the skin for great scrolls, so that I could do what is said in the worthy book, *The Rod of Reproof,* Chapter fifty-two, where it is written, "And I wrote down all the manifold sins I had so greatly sinned before Him Who had showered his acts of loving-kindness like largesse upon me."

[288]

Where he saw men twisting ropes he would say to himself, It would be well for me could I fashion cables from my tripes, as is written in Chapter fifty-two of that admirable work, *The Rod of Reproof*, "And I bound myself with them so that I might be submissive in my service of the Creator."

He likewise opened his eyes regarding the dwellers in the land, and saw that they too worshiped God after their own fashion; for he observed that the images of their gods were adorned while the worshipers went bare. Not, God forbid, that the Hassid raised his eyes to them or diverted his attention from His Blessed Unity to gaze at the images; but that countryside is disfigured by many statues and graven images, and there is no spot without some god or saint. He also observed the young being led away to the king's army while the older folk were left at home. Terrestrial majesty, mused Reb Yudel, resembles heavenly, majesty in many things saving in this. The King of the Universe waits till a man has completed his work in This World ere taking him to the hosts of the King Who is King of Kings, the Holy and Blest One; but a flesh-and-blood king takes the young, so when will their work be done? For the Kingdom of Heaven a man's soul is first taken and only afterward is he borne aloft; but the kingdom of earth takes him away alive and robs him of his soul only afterward.

And that, said Reb Yudel, is a difficult thing to grasp. What satisfaction do the kings derive in sending the folk of this countryside to another land and the folk of another land to this countryside? What difference does it make to the Angel of Death whether he has to come here or go there?

Ere he had taken the road Reb Yudel had had no time for anything but Torah and prayer; but once he did take the road he began to pay attention even to everyday matters. Whithersoever he came he desired to hear the troubles that had befallen, since there was never a town in which there had not been some troubles; but the troubles of the one town were always different from the troubles of the other, the only common factor being that they all came to oppress Israel. Here they had been smitten at the hand of Ishmael, the Turk, and there by the hand of Chmelnitski, the Cossack, as the lamentations tell. With arrows and bows and the tools of war they gathered together in troop and band; the Tartars came after the Cossacks before, to slay the Jews upon every hand; saints that were

[289]

holy and pious, men say, as angels and seraphs perished that day; wealthy magnates and men of renown in their thousands for hunger and thirst dropped down; before the father was ravaged the daughter, and sons at their mothers' bosoms found slaughter; in sight of the husbands were raped the wives and pregnant women ripped open with knives. And the lords of the manors oppressed Israel most of all. And the Holy and Blest One dips His royal purple cloak in the blood of every slain soul in Israel; its color has long been blood.

It has already been told of Reb Yudel that the day he left Brod he made the air fragrant with holy utterance for the sake of those souls that hang homeless in the trees or float upon the face of the water, in order that they might swathe themselves in the holy words. And now on his return to Brod he understood which souls those were that hung on the trees or floated on the water. These were the souls of Israel who had given up their souls on being hung from trees or flung into the water to drown; and these remained there until such time as the Holy and Blest One would require their blood, as the prophet Joel said, "And I shall cleanse their blood which I have not cleansed." Formerly, said Reb Yudel, I used to hold that this land was called Galicia because it had something to do with gales and sea and dry land; but once I heard on my travels that when the malevolent Titus, pounded be his bones, exiled Israel, some Israelites came hither and established this country, I understood that the Yiddish name, Galizien, was the right one and must come from galley slaves of Zion.

We would have held the same view as Reb Yudel were it not that the stones of the place prove that Israel came to Galicia many years earlier. For we find that many of the descendants of the prophet Jonah are buried in the Lemberg cemetery and have a fish carved on their gravestones in memory of the fish that swallowed Jonah. On some of these gravestones it is written in so many words that they are of the descendants of Jonah; some of them are named Kiknis, and the sages have supposed that the name is formed from the Hebrew word *kikyon,* which was the gourd of Jonah. This matter has already been commented on by that true sage and *gaon,* Rabbi Joseph Saul Nathanson of blessed memory, in the following words, "Who would believe our report that here in this city, distant from the place of the prophet, his progeny and offspring find their place in the land of the quick." And by reason of all the troubles and oppressions and wars and spoliations the whole countryside is filled with buried treasure; for wealthy folk used to bury their gold and silver in the ground so that they might escape the hands of the foe. Reb Yudel used to make fun of those in search of treasure who spent their lives digging in the ground and making themselves filthy with muck and mire. Treasure-trove, Reb Yudel used to say, is a find, and a find is one of the three things that come by chance and casually, as is written in the Talmud. So why must you undertake to go in search of something that can at best be found only by chance? And Reb Yudel continued, You are wise fools to go to so much trouble; why, it says in the Midrash on Psalms that all the treasures of the world will in the future be revealed by Messiah the King; so, instead of going and searching for treasures, go and pray for mercy so that Messiah may come speedily, amen, and you will not need to trouble because everything will come to hand without toil and effort.

Wayfarers make their way in groups, some afoot and some on horseback. If he met a gentile who greeted him, he responded, Amen. If he met a butcher leading a cow from the village he walked along with him. He would accompany peddlers wandering from place to place. Reb Yudel loved his fellows, and if the All-Present provided him with a companion he would companion him. The book, *Light of Wisdom,* mentions that it is a snake's nature to proceed alone because there is no peace within it; but the opposite was true of Reb Yudel, who loved peace and was satisfied with all men.

And whom did Reb Yudel resemble? The two-eyed saint whom he had once praised in a tale; on seeing a Jew, he hastened to greet him; when a man greeted him he saw with one eye his own lowliness and with the other His Blessed greatness. Albeit I am Yudel, he would muse, I am a very small and worthless creature, and yet the All-Present has to lead a son of Abraham His beloved to apportion me so much honor. If the other fed him and gave him to drink, he saw therein the greatness of the Holy and Blest One, with all His worlds and all His saints, Who nevertheless gives thought to sustain him. Often enough he would weep with very wonder. Those tears made him blear-eyed, which is the meaning of the statement in Writ: "And Leah had tender eyes"; the Aramaic version there is "and Leah's eyes were bleary with weeping." If anybody met Reb Yudel on the road he would say to himself, I wonder whether he can be anybody but one of the Thirty-six Hidden Saints. Had Reb Yudel

known what folk were saying of him he would have laughed; for
he had really met one of those saints. Reb Yudel was too humble to
desire the name of saint. It is enough, he used to say, if I am alive
and can carry out the commandments and perform good deeds. For
so long as I live what am I? In the book called *The Weaver's Work*,
it is written concerning Ezekiel's Chariot, "The Holy and Blest One
has two angels accompanying each of His creatures (as is written in
Exodus, 'Behold I send an angel before thee', and as is further written
there, 'For my angel shall go before thee'; whence we infer that
there are two angels). These fly hither and thither through the world
and cannot utter their songs of praise until they have immersed themselves in the River of Fire full three hundred and sixty-five times;
and thereafter they have to be tried and tested seven times in white
fire in order that they should be deprived of the man smell they
bring to the Heavens from below. And even then they can be summoned only when the other angels call them forth to sing their
hymns of praise." And on this it is remarked in the work, *Culled
Roses*, "and now, O brother, meditate very fully indeed upon this
passage and comprehend thine own importance. How canst thou
come to grossness and haughtiness of spirit when thou dost realize
the stench that is within thee; for after all their immersions and puri-
fications it is impossible for the angels that have accompanied thee
to utter their praises until they are summoned thereto by other
angels and thereby are hallowed themselves." In brief, Reb Yudel
fulfilled the commandments and rejoiced in the bounties of The Name
and subjected himself to sevenfold trials that he might not fall
victim to pride and self-esteem; and he had a friendly thought for his
fellow creatures and gave his mind to the affairs of the world. So because he found a moral and purpose in all things he did not belittle
or decry anything whatsoever.

The last snows were melting into water, which was bubbling and
vanishing away. The wells brimmed with water and the moist earth
gave off a good smell. The loving-kindness of the Lord filled the whole
world and the Holy and Blest One sustained the entire Universe
with His bounty. From hour to hour Reb Yudel's heart grew fuller.
Often he stretched out his arms and said, Were I to meet a Jew I
would rest my hand on his head and bless him. You can't know what
it feels like to be a wayfarer, whose heart is full to overflowing and
who has nobody with whom to converse. Somebody else in Reb

Yudel's place might have grown bored, but Reb Yudel was always rejoicing, and what was more, the road grew shorter before him. And why? Because he thought of many things all at the same time. If a man settles himself firmly round about any one single thing he grows tired of it; but when he darts from matter to matter his heart remains joyous. There is no need to say that Reb Yudel never meditated for a prolonged period on any one thing but hovered over it in thought, touching without touching; and so it was natural that his thought could race from one end of the world to the other in an hour.

Before he left Brod he had never paid any attention to the affairs of the town. But now it seemed to him as though all Brod were accompanying him, and what was more he understood one thing from another. For instance, he had heard of the incident of Rabbi Zev Frankel, the son-in-law of Reb David Nathanson, who was brother to Reb Yudel Nathanson. This Rabbi Zev had given his wife a divorce by reason of a quarrel that had fallen out between them. At the time he had paid no attention to the tale, but now when he was walking alone along the road he perceived that this must be the case which Reb Zechariah had referred to in his tale of the inquisitive innkeeper and the two merchants of Brod, where the relationship had come to an end following a divorce. This must have been Rabbi Zev Frankel, who had been connected with the Nathanson family but whose connection had ended with the divorce of his wife. Now when this Rabbi Zev left Brod he was met by the Rabbi of Josefoff, and it had happened after this fashion: When the Rabbi of Josefoff came near to Brod, his waggoner went off to eat and drink at an inn, as is the custom of folk before entering a town, and the rabbi remained seated on the waggon. While he sat waiting a fine carriage came from town with a respectable, worthy body seated within it. Who is that? asked the rabbi. And he was told, That is Rabbi Zev Frankel. And where's he going? asked the Josefoff rabbi. Why, he was told, he gave his wife a divorce today, and now he is on his way back to his own town, Risha. Thereupon the Josefoff Rabbi understood that all things are for the best, for his own rabbi, Reb Yuspe, had sent a letter at his hand to that Gaon Reb Zev; and if the waggoner had not drawn up he would have been unable to deliver it. So he at once delivered his letter. Reb Zev at once descended from his carriage, they entered the inn together and commenced a discussion which lasted from morning to evening.

[293]

When they took their leave of each other, Rabbi Zev began weeping and said, I regret having to depart from Brod; and he wrote a letter to Reb Zalman Margolius recommending that the bearer be appointed Father of the Court, since the former rabbi, Reb Leib, who had been father of the Court in Brod, had departed this life. In brief, why make a long story of it? Reb Zalman Margolius chatted with him and was astonished at his wisdom. He took him to Reb Yudel Nathanson and they appointed him Chief of the Court, and so on.

What did Reb Yudel not remember? It was as though the Holy and Blest One had opened the whole Journal of the Brod Community for him to read.

Meanwhile, what were Frummet and her daughters doing? May such doings as theirs be the lot of all the foes of Zion. Frummet and her daughters were without food and garments and fuel. Many were the days when nothing was cooked and no fire was kindled in the stove, as though it were covered with salamander blood, while the cock climbed up on it and crowed. Had Reb Yudel sent them something instead of wasting all his money on presents and board and lodging he would have saved them from hunger and cold; but his money was all gone without his having sent them anything, and they were in dire distress. One of them groans and another moans, Let the earth cover my blood and my bones. And like them their sister did weep and did wail, Why keep alive when all hope doth fail? Lord of the World what am I waiting for when Thou dost despise me and dost rage and roar? And Frummet said nought, but whisper I ought, she felt bitter indeed and sat in her need, and she thought and she thought what her goodman still sought. My flesh it is sick and my heart it doth fear, so bring me quickly some counsel here. A cock without strength lay chanticleer, wherefore, choice fowl, are thine eyes all blear? Why does thy comb not rise on high, why do thy wings never flutter and fly? Cock wise and good, rise, summon thy God, mayhap He will hear and hither return the man of whose deeds we nothing do learn. The cock arose for to utter his call, but no man came in answer at all. And all the while Frummet sat by herself and asked and asked, Where can Yudel have gone? Where can he be? For it is the usual state of affairs that when a wife knows that her husband is in such and such a place her thoughts accompany him there, but when she does not know, her heart wanders in search of him from place to place. When a woman knows that her husband will return on such and such a day she can comfort her daughters and say, Wait, daughters, wait, because Father will be back at such and such a time; but when she doesn't know she feels ashamed for herself and for her daughters.

Now she would look at Pessele, now at Blume and now at Gittele. Pessele had a clear skin and hair full and fine as gold, and big greenish eyes; at first I thought she was asleep but now I see she has just drooped her eyelids waiting for her father to come and tell her *mazal tov*. Below her sits Gittele with her curls falling on her shoulders and her lashes overshadowing her eyes so that you can hardly see their blue, and her nose is tilted aloft; at first I thought there was something prideful, God forbid, about her, but she is only raising her eyes for salvation. Between them sits Blume, tucking herself in like a swallow on a rainy day, so that you can't see what she looks like for her grief.

And at such times Frummet would commune with herself of her heart's desire, saying before the Holy and Blest One, Lord of the Universe, didst Thou create anything in vain? Hast Thou not created these daughters of mine for the purpose of marriage?

CHAPTER FOUR: MOTHER AND DAUGHTERS 🙠 Nuta returned to Brod just about then. Frummet did on her kerchief and went to visit him in order to gain a crumb of news about her husband. She found him sitting at the stove, with his wife Sarah Gittel leaning over him putting mustard on his right side; and he was crying, Oh! The moment he saw Frummet he raised his head toward her and said, Blest be your coming, Reb Yudel's wife. Transgressor in Israel that you are, cried Frummet, where have you left Yudel? I wish, replied Nuta, I had left you in as good a place as I left him. If I only told you he's at Rohatin you might say, Today he has something to eat and tomorrow who knows? And if I told you he's staying at an inn you could ask, What sort of inn is it that my husband can spend his time at? It must be the sort of place that has no roof to it, so that when the snow falls it catches on the Hassid's beard like thorns in the fleeces at the sheepshearing; and so I have to tell you that I left him at a great inn where all the fine folk stay. He has a room all to himself where he stays like a bridegroom under his canopy, and the whole place is at his beck and call.

When she heard this she began moaning and sighing. Nuta thought she must be sighing because she and her daughters were left in such distress while Reb Yudel was so well off, and wished to comfort her. But those who know Frummet well know that it was not so. Frummet knew how hard it was for her husband to change his habits; why, even the changing of his shirt was a trouble; and yet he had gone and established himself in a big inn, all for the sake of her daughters. Where, O Frummet, is the mouth with which you were wont to say that he did not even lift a finger for his daughters and wife; and even in dreams you have to turn your anger loose on him. Now she weeps and grieves for every crooked word which had fallen from her mouth against him. And so Frummet sat all alone weeping, not by reason of matters of food and drink, seeing that trouble sates a man so that he has no wish to eat; but she wept with remorse and sorrow for her husband, who went trundling about in distant places without anybody knowing when he would return.

And Gittele stretched out her two warm hands to stroke her sister, Pessele, and say, Please, Pessele, don't weep; for when Father comes bringing the Engagement Contract all the neighbors and their husbands will be in to congratulate you and wish you *mazel tov;* and if they see tears in the eyes of the bride what *will* they say? Reb Yudel's found a lame man or a blind one or an old man, God forbid, for his daughter. Isn't that right, Mother?

Frummet nodded her head and said, Quite right, Gittele, quite right. Mother, Gittele went on, you tell her as well so that she'll listen and dry her tears. Frummet nodded her head and said, Quite right, Pessele, quite right. But she too began weeping so that she could not say what she wanted to. And Pessele remained grieving and refused to be comforted, having already quite forgotten her own heart and being troubled for her father, who had been made to go to distant parts on her account and did not return home. So she rested her hands on her knees and sadly sang:

> *Sabbath joy is at an end,*
> *We can sing no Sabbath lay*
> *(We who made a happy home)*
> *Since our father went away.*
>
> *Now Thy hand is set on us,*
> *Thorns and thistles rise;*
> *(Father is away from home)*
> *Can we dry our eyes?*
>
> *And another household hears*
> *His Sabbath hallowings.*
> *And the whole seven days are filled*
> *With the song he sings.*
>
> *Hark! The crowing of the cock*
> *Is a sign of light.*
> *Hush! For Father rises*
> *To prayer at midnight.*
>
> *Alas! No man arises*
> *When the cock he crows.*
> *Dark remains the cellar;*
> *Like the grave it grows.*

THE BRIDAL CANOPY

Mother turns and tosses
On this mat at home.
Dear heart, fall asleep again—
Father has not come.

Gittele raised one of her hands from Pessele's hair and rested it on Blume's head, stroking her brown hair, and said, Father has found a bridegroom not only for Pessele but for Blume as well. Blume, I'm surprised that you should be dropping your head so; don't you know that your help comes from on High? Who's your match? A remarkable and God-fearing scholar. I can't draw him in the darkness, but when he comes you'll see him, with his long and curly earlocks which he twists with one hand while the other rests on the open pages of the Talmud and his voice sounding from one end of the Close to the other, and all your friends standing listening. Isn't that right, Mother?

Frummet nodded her head and said, Quite right, Gittele, quite right. Well then, Mother, repeated Gittele, you tell Blume, so that she should pay attention and lift her head up. Frummet nodded her head, saying, Quite right, Gittele, quite right, there's a bridegroom all ready for Blume, and not merely for Blume but for Gittele as well. The tears in her throat hampered Frummet's voice, like a thorn bush catching at a man's clothes; free yourself on the one side and they catch again on the other. And meanwhile Gittele began singing:

If God doth allot me
Long years to live,
My light in the Close
Will burn and will give

Light when the Close lamp
Flickers away,
Where my chosen learns Torah
By night and by day.

From the day of Nuta's return he dropped all his affairs. The horses stood idle, the waggon had no passengers, while he spent his time visiting the fine folk of the town so that he should be appointed inspector of weights and measures; for ever since he had prayed in the tallith of that old man who belonged to the water drinkers, and had had his clothes flying off him, he despised his craft and desired to exchange it for another. What of the mouth, Nuta, with which you used to say that a man should not change his craft?

And since he was not working he used to spend much time at his father-in-law's inn, and the rhymesters known as the Brod singers used to enjoy his words, and particularly his account of the vicissitudes that befell him on his travels with the Hassid; so much did they enjoy them that they set them all to rhyme in preparation for Purim, on which day all men rejoice. And this was what they then did: two men dressed themselves up, one like Reb Yudel and one like Nuta; and one of them told the account of their adventures on the way while the other put his hand to his ear and sang it all to set rhyme. Even before Purim the songs were known all through Brod; there was not a child which did not sing the ballad of Reb Yudel and Frummet, his wife, and his three chaste daughters, and all that befell Nuta and his horses twain on the road. There were even folk to be found in Brod who preferred the ballad of Reb Yudel to the Ahasuerus Play of Purim.

Why, matters went so far that at Purim one pauper asked another, How much did you get from Reb Yudel Nathanson, from his brother, Reb David, from Reb Zalman Margolius, from Reb Simeon Diza, from so-and-so, from such-and-such, from Tom, Dick or Harry? And the other would answer, D'you suppose anybody is paying any attention to the poor? Here's a Hassid goes out to the countryside, and all the folk in Brod have nothing better to do than sing songs about him and what he did and what was done to him. It's a fine thing it is, and did you ever see the like? Here's a Jew, who has to worry about his daughters, goes off to see what help he can get to bring 'em under the Bridal Canopy, and folk have nothing else to do but tell one another about him!

All the songs on the subject were not the work of the Brod singers; there were some which were strung together by folk who called themselves Brod singers to vaunt their wares. Such is the song, "There once was a Jew."

There once was a Jew,
Reb Judah by name,
Without home or food,
So poor—'twas a shame,

THE BRIDAL CANOPY

With many a daughter,
How many who knows?
One fair as a lily,
One red as a rose,

One bright as the heavens
On a fine summer day;
Yet alone and forsaken
And downcast were they,

For no man will wed
Without dowry, be sure,
Tho' the heart of a maiden
Be tender and pure.

But God up in Heaven
On the maidens had pity
And did the great wonder
Told in this ditty,

For He found him a bridegroom,
An upstanding lad,
And promised him cash more
Than ever he had.

And now come and give us
Some money as pay,
For the time is apassing
And we must away.

But while Brod was whistling and humming the song of Reb Yudel, Reb Yudel himself was far away from Brod. Now and again a poor man would arrive and ask of Reb Yudel's neighbors, Where does Reb Yudel's wife live? What do you want of Reb Yudel's wife? they would ask; and he would answer, I happened to meet Reb Yudel somewhere, and he said to me, When you reach Brod go and see my folk and tell them I'm alive, thank God. On such occasions Frummet would say, What satisfaction do I have if others see Yudel and I don't; but thank you anyway, gossip, and may your strength increase for going out of your way to bring me a crumb of greetings. Didn't he tell you when he's thinking of coming home?

Jacob Samson, Nuta's brother, who came to buy Nuta's horses but did not buy them after all, brought a crumb of greeting and news from Reb Yudel; it was he who told the Brod singers how Reb Yudel had found his daughter a bridegroom; for Nuta had taken his leave of Reb Yudel as soon as they had come to Rohatin, and long or ever the matchmakers had come to call on Reb Yudel. Unless you saw the two brothers together you do not know what a thing and its opposite look like in company; Jacob Samson, who was a disciple of the wise, was clad like a waggoner, while Nuta, whose whole bearing gave him away as a waggoner, disported himself like a disciple of the wise.

But to return to Reb Yudel. In brief, Reb Yudel went wandering and wayfaring from place to place, his whole purpose being to return to Brod; but he was still far away from Brod and in the neighborhood of Zbarev, the same Zbarev in which he had spent so many days at the beginning.

CHAPTER FIVE: MATES AND MATINGS ✒ Now although Reb Yudel had already been in Zbarev he did not recognize the town, for he had spent the whole of his first stay hidden away like a treasure in the home of Reb Ephraim, who would not let him out. So Reb Yudel stood in the street without knowing where he could rest his bones that night. He could not go to Reb Ephraim's because he did not know the way; nor could he go to the House of Study because he did not know where that was either. Sighing, he said, When I came traveling in a waggon the first time, they chased me to provide me with all my needs; but now I'm going afoot I haven't even a place where to stay.

He really deserved to stay in the open all that night, did Reb Yudel, for speaking as though the commandment of hospitality had been fulfilled only because of his waggon and horses; but by cause of the sigh he sighed, the All-Present lit up a House of Study before him and he entered. He found two or three men sitting near the stove reading, and one man pacing hither and thither with a long pipe sticking out of his mouth. Reb Yudel put down his bundle, washed his hands and said the Evening Prayers. In Reb Yudel's place another man might have been angry because nobody went to the trouble of greeting him, particularly after having been carried shoulder-high, you might almost say, on his first visit. Reb Yudel, however, was not only not annoyed but disregarded himself and thought of other people. I remember, said he to himself, that while I was staying with Reb Ephraim he was visited by a man whose name, I believe, was Israel Solomon and who came in connection with arranging a match. I wonder whether the Holy and Blest One brought the right party his way.

After finishing his prayers he took a book from the case, sat down at the table and heard two men chatting together. What's the news in these parts? one asked the other. I've heard, said the second, that Sarah Leah has taken a divorce from her husband. And why? asked the other. The woman, explained the former, was wedded to Mechel in order that he might ascend with her to the Land of Israel; but since he didn't want to ascend she went and demanded her divorce. And why didn't he want to ascend all of a sudden? asked the

[302]

former. Well, explained his companion, the Second day of the Festivals, which is observed only in the lands of Exile, appeared to him in dream with a shamed and blackened face; and he realized that it was hard for him to change the holiness of the Second day of Festivals for the sanctity of the Land of Israel, where that second day is not observed.

From their words Reb Yudel understood that they were discussing the same beadle of whom he had heard at Reb Ephraim's, that had wedded the wealthy Sarah Leah, the widow, but had at the last been betrayed by his good fortune. How true, said Reb Yudel to himself, were the words of Nuta, who said that no man should depart from his appointed sphere. And afterward when relating this he found occasion to say, did Reb Yudel, The only person I envied in my life was a certain woman who went up to the Land of Israel; nor did I ever despise anybody except Mechel, the beadle, who might have ascended and did not ascend. If only, said Reb Yudel, I might ascend to the Land of Israel; the Second day of Festivals might well forgive the insult done it.

A little later one of the men raised his head and at once whispered to his companion, Why, that's the poor man from Brod whom Reb Ephraim kept wrapped up like a citron; and he signed his friend to pay no attention to him, so that Reb Yudel should have no excuse for asking them the way to Reb Ephraim's house. They at once began studying at the tops of their voices. And Reb Yudel sat reading until the lids of his eyes joined in sleep.

But on the morrow Reb Yudel did reach Reb Ephraim's house; and what was more he arrived at the very time they were writing the Engagement Contract for Reb Ephraim's daughter. There he found Reb Ephraim and his wife, and Reb Zechariah and his wife, and all the other daughters and sons-in-law of Reb Ephraim, and Simeon Nathan from Shebush with Reb Jacob Moses, his son-in-law, and Israel Solomon, son of Reb Jacob Moses, this Israel Solomon being the bridegroom, together with Israel Solomon who had arranged the match and all the fine folk of the town. The cantor of the town stood singing for them, and Mechel, the beadle, stood serving them, since the wealthy Sarah Leah had demanded a divorce from him. Happy the eye that observed Reb Yudel sitting with the in-laws, as though he were a wealthy man with gold coins to his name. In honor of that occasion Reb Yudel put on his fine clothes.

When all those assembled sat down to the engagement feast they all began speaking in praise of the match.

Reb Zechariah, Reb Ephraim's son-in-law, began telling stories of matches, and told how the men of the Holy Congregation of Ostro built a new synagogue and gave the father of Our Master, Rabbi Samuel Eidels of blessed memory, the honor of laying the foundation stone. In recompense for the honor he donated gold to the same weight as the stone he laid. Yet afterward he lost all his possessions and property, but had the merit of Our Master, Rabbi Samuel Eidels, who is known as the Maharsho of blessed memory, being born of him. And the Maharsho of blessed memory was born in the house of a baker because the baker's wife had pity on the Maharsho's mother at the time of her delivery; and the two women gave one another their hands that when they grew this son should wed the bakewife's daughter. And when he grew up he kept the promise his mother had made, and what was more he added his mother-in-law's name to his own, Maharsho being the initial letters of Master and Honored Rabbi Samuel Eidel's; Eidele having been his mother-in-law's name.

And Reb Zechariah went on to tell of those who are matched and paired from Heaven itself prior to birth, and told the tale of Rabbi Sabbethai Cohen, known as the Shach, and his sister. In the days of Chmelnitzky, may his name and fame be blotted out, their father, Reb Meir, was slain. The son fled in the one direction, the daughter in another, joining a troop of homeless and hopeless beggars who wandered from house to house and from city to city and from land to land to go begging at the doors, until at last she found her brother and recognized him by the chant to which he studied, this being the chant of their martyred father in study; and he recognized her and made a match between her and his father-in-law who had then been widowed; and the Shach of blessed memory was grooms-man and as wedding gift promised them that she would bear a son who would light up the world with his Torah; and it was so, for the son grew to be the scholar, Reb Meir, who wrote the work *Ponim Meiros,* meaning, in the English tongue, the radiant visage.

Israel Solomon in turn began to tell of matches made in Heaven, and related the tale of the widow of Cracow whose husband had left her two kilns outside the town, one for pitch and one for lime. At the time the Pope wished to build a new palace and sent two priests from city to city for to collect money in plenty. In due course they came to Cracow; when they reached the town it was not yet day and the gates of the city were still closed so that they could not enter; and they had no house in which to stay. But they saw the fire of the lime and pitch kilns and entered there. Beloved, they said to the aforementioned widow, we hunger and thirst; prithee give us bread and wine. After eating and drinking they went forth for to bathe in the river and spoke so highly one to the other in praise of the woman's beauty that they began quarreling one with the other, the one saying, She shall be mine, and the other saying, Never indeed, for she shall be mine. As they were standing in the river one of them seized the other to drown him. When he saw this, he seized his attacker and pulled him under with himself; and so they both were drowned.

An hour or two later the woman's workers arrived and told how they had seen clothes lying on the river bank, but no person was near by. And the woman understood that these must be the clothes of the two priests who had come to her house while yet it was night. So she went and took the clothes and put them away in the cellar until the return of the owners. And there they stayed until they rotted away. When they rotted a lot of money fell out of them. She took the money, hid it away and decided to stay her toil. Just at that time a wealthy man was widowed; he was a father in Torah though tender of years. So the widow summoned a matchmaker and said to him, Here are a hundred pieces of gold; go and tell him that such and such a young widow has given you a hundred pieces of gold to go and propose that you should take her to wife, tho' all your silver and gold and wealth are no more than a drop in the ocean compared to her wealth. When the man heard this he said, The matter must be of the Lord. Thereupon she did on her Sabbath garb and went to his house. He, seeing how gracious and modest she was, hallowed her to himself according to faith and law. And she left her house and kilns and came to dwell with him; and they saw a life of wealth and honor and she bore him sons and daughters and did many a good deed and charitable.

And Israel Solomon began again regarding matches and said, Why should we go abroad to learn, when we can study at home? Reb Israel Solomon, may he rest in peace, and Reb Simeon Nathan, may he be parted from the aforesaid by a long life, were foemen one to the other. But since the daughter of Reb Simeon Nathan was intended for Reb Jacob Moses, his opponent himself had a hand in the matter.

At this point Reb Ephraim beat on the table and said, My masters, 'tis time for the Morning Prayers. They said benediction in the name of God and prepared themselves for prayer. Thereupon the servant girls came and removed the dishes and shook the cloth, with Lasunka standing between their feet. Lasunka was the cat which had been called Yaxina, but now her name had been changed to that of the pussy belonging to Reb Israel Solomon, may he rest in peace, as was told by Israel Solomon in the tale regarding Man and Beast.

The day passed very quickly. Reb Zechariah told tales from the Community Book, and Israel Solomon told tales of the warden. The tales of each differed from those of the other. The tales of Israel Solomon might be compared to qualities and virtues which had assumed the shape of Man, while Reb Zechariah told moral tales; whatever you heard told by Reb Zechariah informed you how the Holy and Blest One treateth his righteous saints with love and rewardeth the wicked according to their deserts. Nor was it without good reason that Reb Ephraim said, My son Zechariah is a real book of morals, but he knows how to clothe his words in parables and metaphors; for Reb Zechariah was careful never to open his mouth save to words of wisdom and virtue.

When all the taletellers had told their tales Reb Ephraim began to tell of his good stock all the way back to his forebear, Haham Zvi Ashkenazi of blessed memory, and still further to the Gaon who composed the work known as *The Gate of Ephraim* of blessed memory, and who set up his tent, as they put it, in the Holy Land. And Reb Ephraim went on to speak of his fine kinsfolk, and pointed out the prayer book edited by Rabbi Jacob Emden, son of the Haham Zvi.

Simeon Nathan sat at the head of the table; and since his wife had not come with him by reason of old age, you might have thought that the whole world belonged to him. After all, he had had all that he desired. When he married his daughter to Jacob Moses he had been wedded to the Torah, yet he still lacked good family; now that he was matched with Reb Ephraim he had become connected with a noble family which had even had a hand in the preparation of

the prayer book. Although he himself habitually used the Dueren-
furth prayer book, the moment he heard how one of Reb Ephraim's
kin had edited a prayer book it seemed to him that but for that
family Israel could never pray to God in His Heaven. From time to
time he would rise and sit down at Israel Solomon's right hand;
and as soon as anybody fresh entered, he would change place and
sit down again at the head of the table, so that they should know
he was the bridegroom's grandfather. Beside him sat his son-in-law,
Reb Jacob Moses, bowed as though leaning on a stick although he
held no stick, and nodding his head to everything that was said. And
all the while he kept on repeating the verse from Psalms, "I remembered Thy Name by night, O Lord, and shall guard Thy Torah";
at night during a time of trouble and gloom I remembered to study
Torah; "This I had because I observed Thy orders", that is, as reward for observing Thy orders.

Reb Yudel took his leave of the in-laws and went his way, and
wherever he came he was given his bread; in the words of the
Midrash, "A Jew's a lodger, and wherever he goes God is with him."
Where he stayed overnight he was given his night and morning
food; where he stayed for Sabbath he ate the three Sabbath meals.
Reb Yudel saw any number of towns while on the road, and met
any number of fine lads. Had he had the matter in mind he could
have chosen bridegrooms among them for Blume and Gittele; but
they were intended for better, and so he disregarded them. Nor
should you be surprised that he disregarded them; it was Reb Yudel's
way not to hasten the right hour, but for every sign of loving-kindness
afforded him from Heaven he would offer lauds and thanksgiving
and say, Were it His will that I should receive more He would have
sent me more.

He was not like those who, when they receive a drop of well-being
and benefit, think that it is nothing and keep their hands outstretched
crying, Give, give, give us more, give us more, until at last that
drop evaporates and evanisheth, and they find they have lost what
they had; for he was of those who know that His Blessed Self affords
every man all that he requires, and therefore if His Blessed Name
were to see that he needed more he would give him more, and who,
because they bless on the lack as on the gift, do always profit. Why,
he had found a match for Pessele, yet had not until then sufficiently
related the praises of the All-Present. Blest be the All-Present, blest

THE BRIDAL CANOPY

be He; although the matching of human beings is difficult as the dividing of the Red Sea, He is seated mating people; therefore if not today then tomorrow, and if not tomorrow the day after. If a man is in a hurry to marry off his nubile daughter he lacks the wherewithal for to do so; if he does not bear the matter in mind, a bridegroom will be brought into the very house.

Thus you find that when Reb Yudel went about the business of the Bridal Canopy and everybody knew that he needed to wed his daughters, no bridegroom came his way. When he was at the dairyman's and saw three lads like oaks, none of them were fitting for his daughters; when he visited his friend in Zalozetz he found him a widower but nonetheless unsuited to his daughters; he came to Reb Ephraim, and Reb Ephraim swore by his wife's life that if she had borne him male sons he would have wed them to Reb Yudel's daughters, but Reb Ephraim's wife had borne only daughters and so he did not find his daughter a bridegroom; he visited any number of Jewish villages dressed as a worthy person with an important letter written by the hand of the holy Rabbi of Apta and had said, I'm Yudel with three daughters whom I have to marry; yet no match had come his way. But as soon as he made himself comfortable in an inn and forgot about his daughters he was brought a bridegroom for his daughter.

In brief, Reb Yudel went from Zbarev to Kodovenetz, and from Kodovenetz to Oliov, and from Oliov to Tristenetz, and from Tristenetz to Zalozetz. In none of those places did he do more than stay long enough to snatch his prayers, excepting Zalozetz whither he went to see the weal of his well-wishers. He did not find the town as it had been before; the rabbi, Reb Zelig, had gone elsewhere; Reb Joseph Elkana was lying in bed with a bandage over his eyes, which had grown dim with the brightness of his father's writings; and there he lay and moaned for his forced abstention from Torah.

When Reb Yudel entered, Reb Joseph Elkana recognized him by his voice and wished him *mazal tov* and good luck. Reb Yudel, said Reb Joseph Elkana to him, it isn't because I'm a prophet that I've congratulated you, but because of my faith in the sages; and since I believe that the words of our holy Rabbi of Apta cannot go to waste, there is no doubt whatsoever in my heart but that you have found your daughter her mate. And he went on, Rashi of blessed memory writes that Abraham's servant, Eliezer, had a daughter whom he desired to wed to Isaac; but Abraham said to him, My son is blest but thou art accurst, and the accurst cannot join the blest; now it is written of Eliezer in the Torah, "Come, thou blest of the Lord"; yet there is no difficulty in squaring the two passages and views; in the former place it was ere the Lord had prospered his way, and in the other, after The Name had prospered his way; for when The Blessed Name maketh the way of a man to prosper he comes under the general rule of the blest, to whom blessings come of their own.

After taking his leave of Reb Joseph Elkana he went to visit Joel, who behaved at first like a man with a grievance at heart against him. Reb Yudel, however, paid no attention to that, but made the house ring to his voice till Joel's heart warmed within him; and within a little while they were sitting wishing one another well like two old friends should; Reb Yudel congratulated Joel on marrying a second time, and Joel congratulated Reb Yudel on having found his daughter a mate. And Reb Yudel asked Joel, What have you found? Joel sighed and answered in the words of the Talmud, "A man does not find satisfaction saving with his first wife." Just then Joel's new wife entered and turned an angry face on them. Reb Yudel would have departed at once, but at that moment the words of the sages of blessed memory came to mind and mouth, namely, the passage in the Talmud, "The reception of guests is greater than the reception of the Divine Presence", together with the other passage, "If a man and his wife suit one another the Divine Presence is found with them"; from which it might be inferred that for the sake of a peaceful home a man may give up hospitality. It is in order to prove that view a misapprehension that we are told elsewhere in the Talmud how the reception of guests is more than the reception of the Divine Presence.

From Zalozetz he went to Petbarzi, and from Petbarzi to Ketetch, and from Ketetch to Polikrif where he stayed with Tobiah, the leaseholder. There he found Tobiah and his wife and sons and daughters, and Reb Hayyim Kora of Buczacz, and Reb Nisan of Yazlovetz, and Reb Yeshurun Danzig, and Leibush Coppersmith and Lippe Potseller.

During the meal the old man told what had happened to him with a certain German, and how the unearthly creatures came dancing through the snow, all as related in the account of Reb Yudel's earlier travels. And Reb Hayyim Kora of Buczacz remarked, Although

Maimonides of blessed memory denies the existence of demons one should beware of them, since on occasion a man may be harmed exceedingly by denying their existence; in our town it once happened that in the tanner's quarter all kinds of strange whistlings were heard at night, and trees and stones were torn up by their roots, and everybody fled because of the harmful sprites. There was a certain sage there named Rabbi Judah, and he said, I must show in honor of His Blessed Name and of our pure faith that there are neither demons nor mischievous sprites there. So he went and hid himself in a big copper boiler in which hides are cleaned; and from there he looked out. When midnight came a huge stone was thrown which struck the boiler, and that Rabbi Judah became deaf in both his ears. Afterward it was found out that a crazy but handsome wench lived there who had a number of followers; and they used to throw stones so that she should come out to them. But I don't know whether Reb Judah still denies the existence of demons, because he has grown deaf and doesn't hear what people are asking him. From which we learn that it's harder to disprove the existence of demons than it is to believe in them.

And from this they went on to tell one another tales of demons, visitations, incubi and the like, such as the tale of the Woodcutter and the tale of the Rabbi and the Guest. But as these have no bearing on the matter of the Bridal Canopy they are not included here but may, God and the readers willing, be told elsewhere on another occasion. Then there were other tales they told at the home of Tobiah of Polikrif, but as they are well known we are not repeating them. Blest be He Who vouchsafeth wisdom to Man that we should not do what others can do just as well, but limit ourselves to the things others cannot do. Reb Yudel also had much to tell, as the story of Nuta and the witch, and the story of the wolf; but since he was not used to lay discourse he remained silent; nevertheless from these legends and tales he derived the necessary morals, recognizing that we come into this world only in order to be tried and tested, the methods of testing and proof being many and various. Sometimes the testing evil will inclines us by means of holy things only, such as prayer with the congregation, in order to hinder a man from doing that good deed which he should be about doing. And at this point Satan came to tempt Reb Yudel; and in what way? By a suspicion of pride. Why go elsewhere, he asked, to find an instance; take yourself. Didn't you yourself undergo that very temptation? And why if not for the sake of the commandment of bringing the bride under the Bridal Canopy?

But Reb Yudel at once understood what Satan was about, and that he wished to introduce pride into his heart. And did I really go, he answered Satan, for the sake of fulfilling the commandment and injunction? Most certainly not. Our Rabbi of Apta told me to go, so off I went, and that's all. What, said Satan, and you speak as though you're not commanded to hearken to the voice of the wise! To which Reb Yudel responded, Well, since I must, I'll confess the whole truth; if the rabbi alone had sent me I wouldn't have budged, but it was really my wife who sent me off, and that's why I went. Why, said Satan, that's also a commandment to be found in the Five Books of the Torah, for we find that the Holy and Blest One said to Abraham, "Whatever Sarah telleth thee, hearken to her voice." Well, answered Reb Yudel, and was I in any way interested in fulfilling that commandment? No. I was afraid of her shouting and noise, and ran away plain and simple.

And after he had refreshed himself with food he took his prayer shawl and tefillin in one hand, his other belongings in the other, kissed the mezuzah on the doorpost and departed.

CHAPTER SIX: BREAD TO EAT AND CLOTHES TO WEAR ✍ So Reb Yudel left Polikrif village for Pedkomin, where he entered the House of Study without being recognized; for he had left them in fine clothes and now came among them garbed as a beggar. I'm Yudel of Brod, said he to them. Woe's us, they said, grieving for him, he must have been robbed on the road. And they set food and drink before him in order to restore his spirits. But one rose, took the Book of Genesis and turned the pages till he came to the passage, "And Rebeccah took the fine garments of Esau and arrayed her son Jacob, etc., and she gave him the savory meat and the bread that she had made"; said he, I want to ask you the point of that passage. What was it our Holy Torah desired us to infer here? Does it make any difference whether she clothed him first and then gave him the savories and bread, or gave him the savories and bread first and then arrayed him?

Well, then, said they, let's hear your point. Said he, The Torah is written in those terms only in order to teach us proper behavior; for it is our duty to fit him out in decent clothes first of all, so that his spirit should be eased and he should eat to repletion. To what case, they countered, did the words you quote apply? To the occasion when Jacob went to take savories to his father; but nowhere in the whole of Writ do we find that he did on other clothes when he sat down to eat. And what was more he actually set food before clothing, as we find written, "If the Lord be with me and so on, and giveth me bread to eat and a garment to wear."

Blest indeed be the All-and-Ever-Present, cried Reb Yudel, when the acts of a man are not complete and independent in themselves but explain the essence of many Biblical verses; and he opened his bundle to show his clothes, saying, His Name knows and can be witness that it was not in order to preen myself before Him, God forbid, that I did on fine clothes, but in order that Israel might turn a charitable eye upon me for the sake of the injunction of the Bridal Canopy; for when a man is well dressed they give with a pleasant eye and free hand. So now the garments have done their duty I have no right to make use of them, but have to return them to their owners.

Not even among a thousand men of integrity, they then exclaimed,

will you find his like! Who led him to tell us anything about his
clothes? Why, if he had just remained silent he'd have received
money and clothes! May your mind be at rest, they then said to him,
for having set our minds at rest; but since you went out in order to
bring your daughter under the Bridal Canopy and now tell us that
the garments have done their duty, it implies that you have found
a bridegroom. Thereupon he related the whole incident, and they
congratulated him and wished him *mazal tov,* sat him down at the
head of them all and ate and drank.

The one among them who was a wag said, Reb Yudel, do you remember the day you fared so ill with Reb Misery? And he tried to
persuade Reb Yudel to go and visit Reb Misery again so that Reb
Misery the miserly should have the misery of having to share his fare.
But Reb Yudel said, It isn't seemly to go and make mock of a Jew;
and he didn't go and visit Reb Misery. Nor did he visit Heshel,
since the company of the Godless sappeth and destroyeth faith. But
he remained with wholehearted God-fearers who are generous and
openhearted. Many a tale did he hear and forget on that occasion,
but from them all he derived moral profit, as Solomon says in his
Proverbs, "The wise do secrete knowledge."

We already know how, during Reb Yudel's first visit, he was a
guest at the home of a certain Hassid named Joshua Eleazar, from
whom he learnt the correct explanation of what constituted a meal
that did not satisfy the eaters thereof. On his return the same Hassid
found him and took him to his home, which was a tumbledown
dwelling with vermin crawling up and down the walls, and rain
seeping in from the roof, and gutter water dribbling through from
the street. The householder entered, kindled a light, took a pot full
of potatoes, set them on the table, removed the cover and said to
Reb Yudel, Bless and eat. But seeing how he hesitated he said, Why
aren't you eating? Said Reb Yudel to him, because I've heard that
the holy Rabbi of Ropshitz says over them the blessing, "At Whose
word everything came into being", while everybody else says, "Who
created the fruit of the earth"; and I don't feel inclined to stick my
head into any such dispute. I'm prepared, replied Reb Joshua
Eleazar, to let all other foods go and to cook myself nothing but
potatoes, for they may be eaten at all seasons. This is not the case
with other victuals; pease are not eaten save on days of mourning
and semifasts; nuts are not eaten on the New Year because they

increase the phlegm and hawking of a man, and so interfere with his prayers; and water is not to be drunk at the four turns of the year. But that is not the case with potatoes; a man can eat them at all times, whether baked or boiled, in oil or in butter, both during the Passover and all the rest of the year. And what is more, said the householder, I can tell you that potatoes were revealed only. in order to be a sign of the Redemption.

And how, you ask? Consider for yourself: When Israel was in the wilderness the Holy and Blest One gave them the manna, in which they could taste the flavor of bread, of meat, of fish, of locusts, of everything that is to be found in the world—with the exception of onions and garlic, for fear women in the family way might smell and be harmed; but we do not learn that it was with the exception of potatoes. From which it follows that the flavor of potatoes was included. But by reason of our manifold sins and iniquities the tastes and flavors have, alas, been scattered far and wide. If you eat bread you taste bread; if you eat meat you taste meat; you can't achieve the taste of different flavors without tasting different foods. And this is a characteristic scattering, as one might say; for you must eat many foods to enjoy many flavors. Now the world still lacked the flavor of potatoes until they were revealed afresh; so that all tastes and flavors should make up the full tally when we merit to be fully redeemed.

As soon as Reb Yudel heard this he grabbed and ate. I do not remember, related Reb Yudel, the fashion in which I blessed over them; but I do remember that their taste was better than anything in the whole world. And ere he took his leave he heard from him a fine exposition of the verse in Psalms, "Troubles have broadened my heart." I laugh, said David, at those who dwell in large houses and eat roast duck and drink old wine and travel in dancing curricles and say that all those things make them heart-free; but I rejoice when I receive from Thee, my God, a great trouble, for thereby Thou dost enlarge my heart in order that I may see Thy providential eye keeping watch and ward over me without concealment, and can believe that all is for the best. And therefore David said, Troubles have enlarged my heart; for through troubles I become heart-free.

I, too, said Reb Yudel, desire to receive sufferings with love and affection, but through them I come to abstention from Torah and prayer. But go to the end of the same verse, said Reb Joshua Eleazar

to him. What is written there? "Bring me forth from my straits."
Lord of the Universe, said David, in case You say, I sustain you with
things that make you heart-free, why then must you wail and weep
because of your hard times? I reply to you, Just as it is the way of
the wealthy who spend their days in pleasure and the pursuit thereof
to come on occasion into distress, as when he expends more than he
receives, so it is with me; my troubles are grown so many that on their
account I may, God forbid, be compelled to abstain from Torah and
prayer; so therefore, "Bring me forth from my straits."

Reb Yudel took his leave, and just before departing asked after
his host's wife, in accordance with the advice of the Torah. And
why had he not asked earlier? Because the woman was sick and
spent all her time alone at home and therefore spoke a great deal
to herself like a cricket chirruping within the wall, and would raise
her voice in a chant; and Reb Yudel feared to be led astray by the
voice of a woman.

It was then the season of the melting of snows, so that the roads
were too muddy to be followed, and Reb Yudel was compelled to
stay in Pedkomin a number of days; and as a result he grew very
friendly with Reb Joshua Eleazar. Without having seen those two
in one another's company it is impossible to know how Hassidim
spend their time together. Sweet were the words they uttered; great
were the thoughts each one expressed to the other in words. For
just as a man, when born, is born tiny but complete with all his
members which grow together with the man, so all words which
attract to themselves His blessed greatness can be called great.

On the Sabbath day the wealthy folk shared his meals among
themselves; on Sabbath Eve he ate with one, Sabbath morning with
another, and the third meal prior to the Departure of the Queen he
ate with the rabbi, whose custom it was, as already related, to fast
from Sabbath to Sabbath and to consume during the Sabbath more
than an ordinary man eats in a whole week. It was at this third meal
that Reb Yudel merited to hear the interpretation of their blessed
remark in the Talmud, "There is no rejoicing save in flesh"; namely,
the Lord has no joy saving in the deeds of flesh and blood. It may
well be revealed to you, Nuta, may that interpretation; for you were
staying with the secret saint and were annoyed because his table
lacked meat on the Sabbath. Why, the saying, "There is no rejoicing
save in flesh", means not what you in your grossness supposed, but

that the All-Present finds joy only in the deeds of flesh and blood.

When the roads improved Reb Yudel hastened his departure to Brod in order to inform Nuta of the real meaning of the saying, "there is no rejoicing save in flesh"; and also to tell his wife and daughters that he had found Pessele a bridegroom. So he took his leave of all his friends and went his way, now afoot and now alift, passing through places he knew and places he did not know, and meeting folk he did not recognize and folk he did recognize; and never a man but he learnt something from him after his own fashion.

Thus it happened that he stayed with a person who had been a tailor to begin with and had found a treasure and given up the needle; so now folk called him the rich tailor. Even though a tailor, thought Reb Yudel, has stopped using his tools he is still called a tailor; but a Jew who, God forbid, lays aside the Torah can't even be included within the category Jew. He saw and profited much along the road; for instance, he learnt what it was that Rashi of blessed memory had meant when, in commenting on the verse in Psalms, "my rock in whom I shelter", he remarks that the rocks are a cover and shield for wayfarers against the wind and the driving rain.

Were we to relate all that befell Reb Yudel on his return to Brod we would never end, for there was never a single pace of his in which he did not see something miraculous; and if folk asked him wherein the miracle consisted he would reply, And isn't it a miracle that the All-Present doesn't need to change the whole order of Nature on my account? Nor did he put anything down to blind chance, nor did he hear wonders that set him awondering; but everyday things were always a matter for surprise to him.

When he came to Pedhoretz he met Nehemiah, the dairyman, who said, Reb Yudel, come and see my joy, because my daughter Zipporah dwells at peace with her husband and will be giving birth in due season. Aie, Aie, said Reb Yudel. Now why was he astonished? Because that young woman had formerly been in the clutches of Those that are Without, and it had been a hard thing for Reb Yudel to bear that Those that are Without should have power over her; why, wasn't she a daughter of Israel, and didn't she cry Hear O Israel? And were the ears of Those that were Without suddenly grown deaf that they did not hear and flee?

In Reb Yudel's place somebody else might have said that she was born through a reflection; for sometimes a woman sets her eyes on somebody and bears him in mind so that at last, when she grows pregnant, she grows pregnant from him too by means of the power of the imagination; and such a child is, in the nature of things, in the power of Those. But Reb Yudel could never harbor any suspicion of anybody. 'Tis better for a man, said Reb Yudel, to have his mind bristling with the difficulties he sees around him, and not to suspect other people.

But disregarding all these signs, wonders and astonishments, let us return to our main theme. In brief Reb Yudel reached Pedhoretz and came to the dairyman's place; and when the dairyman's wife saw Reb Yudel she rejoiced with him exceedingly and offered him every kind of dainty out of hospitality, and made a meat feast in his honor; for no man esteems what he possesses, and so she had no high regard for milk foods as in the tale of the slaughterer and the dairyman which we have already related. Reb Yudel remained for the meal, and ate radish and onions fried in oil, and a grits soup and a portion of meat, and then said benediction and rose to go; for he feared that the village folk would trouble him with matters of charms and cures. When Nehemiah saw that he could not delay him, he rose and harnessed the waggon in order to conduct him to Pinkevitz village which is not far from Brod where on occasion a waggon can be found which is going to Brod. So Reb Yudel took his leave, and before departing promised them that if their daughter bore a male son he would come and be present at the Covenant of Circumcision.

Reb Yudel was just about to seat himself on the waggon when the fury of a gentile woman burst o'er him; it was the gentile woman who had dealt with Nuta by means of her witchcraft and to whom Nuta had promised a bottle of brandy; but when he found that there was nothing in her witcheries he gave her nothing. Now she saw Reb Yudel, who had been Nuta's companion, she cried out, Give me, give me, give me the brandy your companion promised me. And she went on to curse him.

Her curses startled Reb Yudel very much. And why? Did he fear that she would try to put a spell on him? Why, we know that he denied that there was any power in her witcheries. But it was because of a statement made in the name of Rabbi Phineas of Koretz of blessed memory; that the numerical value of the word "male" in Hebrew equates with that of the word "blessing", whereas the word for "female" is from a root which means to curse (being, as one

might say in the English tongue, "good man" against "woeman"),
it follows that when a male, who comes from the classification of
"blessing" curses a woman it does not mean anything, but when it's
the other way round God preserve us!

Finally he gathered courage enough to say, You have said your
say, after the fashion of Rabbi Ishmael in the Midrash. This Rabbi
Ishmael was met by an idolator who blessed him; he responded, You
have said your say; then he met another who cursed him; to him too
he responded, You have said your say. Rabbi, said his disciples to
him, you have responded to them both in the same way. So it is
written, he replied, in the Torah, "They that curse thee are accurst,
and they that bless thee are blest."

And so, in brief, Reb Yudel departed from Pedhoretz and from
the troublous gentilesse and betook himself to Pinkevitz, where he
had lodged on the day he had left Brod. As soon as Paltiel saw Reb
Yudel he sprang forward to greet him crying, Blest be He who
bringeth the dead to life; and he greeted him and wished him
mazal tov and good luck, and was very happy to see him again; and
the air rang with his laughter all the while. And why did he laugh?
Because of the Song of Reb Yudel which the Brod songsters had
made up about the Hassid and his three daughters, and his travels
on the way, and how he came to Pinkevitz village where he was
received with brandy and pancakes, and how the pancakes came
into his belly and began croaking like frogs, as was told loud and
clear in the song they sang in Brod:

> *The innkeeper broke in*
> *With what he had handy*
> *And said, better drink*
> *A mouthful of brandy.*
>
> *Thereto he brought brandy*
> *The best in the land*
> *The which he'd prepared as*
> *He did well understand.*
>
> *The Hassid did hasten*
> *To do what he willed,*
> *And sat there and drank*
> *Till his tummy was filled.*

THE BRIDAL CANOPY

While the housewife she cooked
Them pancakes—none nicer—
Which are made so well
In the lands of the Kaiser—

And hours passed away
In the jolliest style,
And brandy they drank
And ate pancakes the while.

The Hassid sits cozy
With both of his pals,
When his tripes get the gripes
Of a sudden. He squeals,

Paltiel and Sarah!
He howls and he wails,
Alas and alack
For the ache that I feels.

So Sarah 'gan heating
An eathenware pottle
And bound to his belly
A hot-water bottle.

Likewise for Nuta
Who the waggoner was,
The Lord God brought many
Throes, aches, pains and woes.

So Paltiel began clapping his hands and calling to his wife, Sarah, Sarah, we've got a fine guest, Reb Yudel Hassid of Brod. Come and greet him and wish him *mazal tov*. But Sarah was not happy to see him, and what was more turned an angry face toward him; for she was annoyed because it was on his account that folk sang the Song of Reb Yudel in which she was brought into disrepute, as though the Hassid's bowels had been put out of order by her pancakes.

But Paltiel led Reb Yudel into his house saying, Do you remember how I told you you'd be rid of your daughters? Now my prophecy has been fulfilled it's only proper we should drink to life and health. Reb Yudel agreeing with him, they entered the inn. But when he poured him out a glass the wife came and took the glass out of his hand. And why? Because she remembered that when he had stayed with them the former time the liquor had turned on him in his bowels, and she had had to bind a hot-water bottle to his paunch. So she would not permit him to drink anything, but cooked him a milk broth such as is given to those with bowel troubles. Had he not eaten meat at the dairyman's, or had six hours already passed since he had eaten meat, he would have eaten the food she prepared; but as it was he didn't quite know what to do until he decided that he had better fast without eating anything, so that when he reached home where there was neither flesh nor milk food he would be able to revert to his former abstinence from excessive fleshliness.

Meanwhile Paltiel began conversing with him of current affairs, asking, What's new in the world? Plenty of things new, replied Reb Yudel, in the world. Let's hear some, responded the other. What's there I can tell you, exclaimed Reb Yudel, that you don't already know? Didn't you recite the Morning Prayers today, where it is written, "Who always and every day reneweth in His goodness the Work of Creation." Here Sarah interrupted and said to her husband, This fellow's wife sits as desolate as though she were deserted, and her soul and the souls of her daughters go out for very sorrow, and you delay him with all sorts of rubbish and nonsense; hurry up and harness the horses to the cart and whip 'em up and take the man back to his wife and the father to his daughters.

Well said, responded Paltiel, I have to go to Brod anyway. Don't you know they've brought me a letter from the government? A letter, cried Sarah, all but fainting away. I suppose, he soothed her, that Father must have appeared to the Kaiser in a dream, so that the Kaiser has given orders to investigate what happened. Twenty years, said Sarah, have gone by since my father-in-law was murdered and they never reminded themselves to demand his blood; and now that the murderers are dead and finding their punishment in Hell, the government suddenly remembers to bring them to trial. Why, don't you know, answered Paltiel, that we have a just government which doesn't leave any case untried? And I'll go bail that the death of your father will also be brought up before it soon. And so Paltiel harnessed the waggon, sat Reb Yudel in it and brought him to Brod. Which ends the account of Reb Yudel's travels, both from Brod for the sake of the Bridal Canopy and back home to Brod. Blessed be He Who giveth the weary strength.

When Reb Yudel saw that he was approaching his own town, his heart rejoiced that he should be coming to the end of all his journeyings; and at the same time his travels began to seem pleasant to him, for he forgot all his mishaps along the road. He began to meditate on all the advantages that fall to the lot of the man who goes forth to deal with his temporal and temporary requirements; wherever he goes his table is spread and his bed prepared, and the hand of every man is open for to advantage him with cash; but I and my heart do know that such is not the end and purpose of Man in This World. 'Tis like two men, one wise and t'other a fool, who went through the forest and were attacked by thieves who took out a knife for to slaughter them; so what did the foolish one say? Why, they're going to kill a chicken for me and prepare me fine food; and he remained drawn toward his appetites even when the knife was at the throat; and meanwhile the wise man stood confessing his sins and departed the world in penitence. The forest is the world, the thieves are the body of a man, the knife is the desire for food, drink and sleep.

It is unnecessary to add that Reb Yudel did not act like the fool of his fable, but felt remorse for his appetites and desires, and took it upon himself not to be led astray toward temporal vanities; since the soul is entered into the body merely in order to acquire Torah, comply with the commandments and perform good deeds. And in his imagination he already saw himself seated in the House of Study bedecking his soul with eternal adornments, which are Torah and prayer. When he reached the neighborhood of the Sabbath boundary from the town his heart began knocking and leaping up and down. Woe's me, said Reb Yudel, if I return home and do not serve my Maker. And he sorrowed for fear his desire for food and drink had uprooted his study so that he had forgotten all he had learnt, as in the tale of Rabbi Eleazar, son of Arach, in the Talmud who, being desirous of wine and bathing, came to forget his studies and misread the Portion of the Weak in public before the entire congregation.

Within a few more minutes Reb Yudel reached home. All his neighbors crowded round him and greeted him, finding double reason for rejoicing: first that he had done what he had to do and second that he had returned safe and sound; and they took him by the hand and helped him off the waggon, since wayfaring steals the strength of a man so that it would doubtless be hard for him to descend alone. Reb Yudel greeted everybody in return, entered his house, kissed the mezuzah, nodded to his wife and daughters and put down his things, that is, the clothes he had borrowed from the fine folk of the town.

CHAPTER SEVEN: MAZAL TOV· THE WORLD WAGS
ON ☙ And so Reb Yudel returned to Brod and informed
his wife and daughters that His Blessed Name had found a
fitting match. The wise man's eyes are in his head, so he doubtless
did not inform them how he came to the Holy Congregation of
Rohatin and stayed at the inn and studied Torah in wealth until
the matchmaker came and asked him, Where are you from and
what's your name? Or how, when the matchmaker heard he was
from Brod and Yudel Nathanson was his name, he went to one of
the wealthiest men of the town and so on and so forth; for Reb
Yudel approved of the words of the sage who said, Reveal neither
thy secret nor that of thy friend, and assuredly not to thy wife who is
flighty and unsettled. And the sage also said, Empty chatter is harmful anywhere, and silence is always better, as King Solomon said,
"The faithful of spirit covereth the matter."

As soon as Frummet heard that Pessele had found herself a bridegroom she grew very happy, broke all the earthen pots and pans and
cried *mazal tov, mazal tov,* caught hold of all three of her daughters
and began dancing with them for joy because the Holy and Blest
One had heard their cry and sent the bridegroom them to satisfy.
And they danced until they turned giddy and their legs slipped upon
the floor and they lay where they fell like so many corpses.

And how much, Frummet asked Reb Yudel when she had scram-
bled to her feet, did you promise for Pessele? Four times three
thousand gold pieces, he answered. When she heard this she seized
herself by the hair of her head and cried out, Heavens above, how can
you go and promise twelve thousand gold pieces when you haven't
even twelve thousand farthings? Why, he replied, I only did what
you said and what you were told by the holy Rabbi of Apta. That's
just what the holy Rabbi of Apta said, Promise for your daughter
just as much as the bridegroom's father promises for his son; and
since he promised twelve thousand I did as much and also promised
twelve thousand.

What did the woman do thereupon? Why, took the Engagement
Contract and brought it to the holy Rabbi of Apta. The rabbi read
two or three lines, then smoothed the Contract with his holy hand
and blessed her by saying *mazal tov;* then he said, Wife of Yudel,

don't grieve; for the Lord God there's no difference between twelve farthings and twelve thousand gold pieces. He who gives the one will give the other.

Thereupon Frummet returned home, told her daughters about it and asked her husband, What does the bridegroom look like? Said he, He can learn a fine page of Gemara with all the commentaries. Thereupon each one of the womenfolk imagined for herself the appearance of the bridegroom, how he was dressed in a dressing gown with a silken kerchief round about his neck and his earlocks curling down by his cheeks and a dimple in the right cheek or the left, and he must be coughing because he studies aloud; not that he's sick, God forbid, but it's because someone put an evil eye on him that he coughs; and of course he must have a mole on his neck. And the two sisters of the bride caught hold of their sister Pessele and kissed her, and sang and danced and sang her songs sweeter than honey.

> *Bride so gentle, sweet and fair,*
> *Sigh no more, be done with care!*
> *Come and dance with us among,*
> *And let us sing a happy song.*

When Frummet took Reb Yudel's bundle and took out the fine clothes, she saw how creased they were and cried out, What will the folk say from whom I borrowed them? But the wise man said long since that time can accomplish what wisdom can't; since they were in her room, which was a damp one, all the creases vanished and the clothes became smooth as though they had just come from the tailor's. Then she picked them up and returned them to their owners, and told them all of the fine bridegroom His Blessed Name had appointed for her daughter. They all wished her *mazal tov* and said, Well, anyway, the clothes deserve to be paid matchmoney. To which she replied, Please God that on Pessele's wedding day I'll give you all cake and tarts.

And the Hassid returned to his House of Study and sat there all day long, to say nothing of half the night, at Torah and the toil of the Lord just as he had been wont to do or ever he had been sent about the business of the Bridal Canopy; and as his strength then, so his strength now. When he returned home and found his wife and daughters asleep, he would grope with his hand on the hearth. If

he found some victuals he would take a bite so as to keep his body
hale for His blessed Torah; if he found nothing he would revile
himself in all imaginable ways after the following fashion: Yudel,
Yudel, glutton of gluttons that you are, and even supposing that you
found yourself face to face with a table groaning under all the dainties
you can think of, would that be a proper end and aim for you in the
world?

And he would sustain his intelligent soul with matters appertaining to the intelligence, making up the full daily tale of a hundred
blessings over a glass of water and the like, and would tap with
thumb and index finger and chant all kinds of fine and sweet things
in a whisper; as for instance, the saying of the holy Rabbi, Isaiah
Hurwitz, who wrote the work, *The Two Tables of the Covenant,* and
who is known as the Holy Sheloh, "In the place of gross feeding
and gormandizing, there is Lilith found", until at last his lids would
join together in slumber, and he would recite the Hear O Israel and
lie down to sleep in his clothes, so that he should not need to waste
time dressing; and he would sleep until the cock crowed.

In Reb Yudel's place somebody else would have kicked out against
the sufferings, and would have gone to the fine folk of the town
in order once again to borrow the fine clothes; then he would have
gone and hired himself a waggon covered over with a sort of hood
and would have gone wandering for the sake of the injunction of
the Bridal Canopy or for the fulfillment of some other commandment, wandering through one town and village after another and
eating and drinking and filling his pockets with money. But Reb
Yudel did not kick out against the sufferings, nor did he go to the
fine folk of the town, nor did he borrow himself fine raiment, nor
did he hire himself a carriage, nor did he travel from one place to
another, nor did he depend upon the tables of others, nor did he
fill his pockets with gold. Instead he filled his soul with Torah and
prayer and sat at the table of His Name and passed on in his studies
from leaf to leaf, converting his soul into a chariot for the Divine
Presence, arraying his soul with good deeds and never even feeling
that there was suffering in the world. Often he would remember the
interpretation of the verse, "Troubles broaden the heart", as explained by Reb Joshua Eleazar of Pedkomin. But he no longer found
satisfaction in his interpretation, since Reb Yudel now denied the
existence of troubles altogether. Between whiles he would rest his

head on his hands and recollect the stages of his journey. Sometimes he would remember them in order and sometimes chop and change. Sometimes he would remember the essence of them, namely, the moral lessons which he had drawn from them; for the paces of Reb Yudel did teach him understanding. There was nothing Reb Yudel liked better than thinking them over in the order they came about, since the order of their development showed him that there is nothing happens in vain. God forbid that Reb Yudel denied the existence of Cause and Effect; but Reb Yudel enjoyed realizing this afresh for each separate detail.

It is not, said Reb Yudel, merely by sitting in the House of Study that a man becomes wise; even if he takes to the road he can achieve perfection. And Reb Yudel was already wishful of reaching this quality, but then changed his mind. Though there be many a benefit, said Reb Yudel, in remembering my journeys, I shall devote myself only to the Torah, which is given to All Israel. And thenceforward he told the journeys, Get ye hence, for they led to abstention from the Torah; and he devoted himself to the Torah like an ass to a burden. This was no longer the Yudel who had worn fine garments and had had a fine paunch and had been so important in the eyes of the wealthy; now his garments were torn and dirty, he had no paunch whatsoever, and his face was black as the face of ten men a-fasting. If Reb Vovi were to come next day and see him like that, it was doubtful whether he would recognize him.

What shall we do with our daughters? Frummet asked Reb Yudel. Why, he answered, and haven't I found Pessele a bridegroom, and didn't I fetch her her Engagement Contract? If you keep on annoying me, said Frummet, I'll tell you to go and use it for burning all the crumbs of leaven on Passover Eve. Frummet, Frummet, said Reb Yudel, don't open your mouth to Satan.

And off he went to the House of Study and devoted himself to Torah and forgot his home troubles. King David, may he rest in peace, said Reb Yudel to himself, said, "One thing I ask of the Lord and I seek it, that I dwell in the House of the Lord all the days of my life"; And was it, asked Reb Yudel, such a little thing that he asked so that he had to say, But one thing I ask? But this is what it means. David requested, Lord of the Universe, what have I to ask of Thee? That I should not sit in Thy house by reason of poverty or any other reason than of the Lord, Of Thy Blessed Self and for Thy Blessed Name's sake; not as those that sit in the House of Study in order to flee from their wives, nor as those that study Torah in order to forget their mundane worries. Reb Joshua Eleazar of Pedkomin, said Reb Yudel to himself, has a wife who is sick with all manner of diseases, and when she speaks to him he's as happy as though she were aiding him in every fashion in the world. Kalman, the tailor, has a wife who is broken of spirit all her life long, and he sits comforting her in her sorrow; yet you, Yudel, have to run away from Frummet.

And then, in order to avoid thinking of a married woman, he would begin thinking again of his travels; not in the things that befell, since that implied a something of pride, but of the things that had befallen in the places he visited; such as the tale of the sweet and lovely and pleasant, when the lord of the manor robbed away the bride from under the canopy and slew her bridegroom; or the tale of the Jews of Osonovki, whom the lord of the manor drowned in the river when they came to pray in town, and the lord of the manor saw them and told his servants to drown them and they drowned them; or the tale of the grandfather of Kalman, the tailor, whose blood was shed by the lord of the manor like any beast or bird, or the tale of Paltiel's father who was slain in the forest, or of Peretz, his father-in-law, on whom they overturned a cauldron of boiling tar.

And very often Reb Yudel would study a chapter of the Mishnah and say the Mourner's Prayer for the ascent of those souls that came to an end unjustly. Of such Reb Yudel would say, So-and-so appeared to me; so-and-so has beseeched me to do him a favor.

And did Reb Yudel intend to right and correct souls? No. But there was no dead person came to his mind for whom he did not say a chapter of Mishnah and the Mourner's Prayer. As we already know, when he left Brod he said holy words for the sake of the souls that had no opportunity of repenting and are therefore withheld from their rest. Now that he was in a holy place where there were books and Jews, was it possible for him to forget them? It is like a man drawing a design of a mansion on paper; the king sees it and says, Fetch him to court and give him workers and stones so that he can build a mansion for my son who had to depart from my quarters but is now returning. In the same way Reb Yudel had gone about through wood and meadow uttering holy words, and therefore the

All-Present brought him back to the House of Study and gave him the Six Orders of the Mishnah and provided him with a quorum of ten Jews; and he fashioned a mansion for those children of the Holy and Blest One who are exiled from His quarters, whither He shall in the future return them.

CHAPTER EIGHT: PURIM GIFTS ✒ When the season of Purim arrived, the bridegroom's father in Rohatin sent the father of the bride at Brod gold earrings and a pair of bracelets of pure gold as befits the wealthy, together with a honeycake plaited like a Sabbath loaf, all of them as gifts for the bride. As generally happens when there are two of the same name in a town and valuable gifts are sent to one, to whom should they be delivered if not to the wealthier of them. And so when these gifts were brought to Brod for Reb Yudel Nathanson, to whom should they be delivered? Surely to the famous and wealthy Reb Yudel.

And Reb Yudel Nathanson was astonished at these gifts, coming from he knew not whom and intended for he knew not whom; for there was no point in sending bridal jewelry to Reb Yudel Nathanson who was childless, the Merciful One deliver us. He even began to reckon that somebody who had borrowed money from him and never repaid his debt had now repented but, being ashamed of himself, had put his money in jewelry and repaid him to the value of his debt. But his wife pointed out, When a man sends a gift to another, he will send him something that will be of use; there's no sense in sending a bald man a comb or gloves to a man without hands. Which, he said, leaves the problem where it was. Well, said she, they are probably for Miriam and were sent in her name, Miriam being the daughter of Reb David Nathanson, Reb Yudel's brother, who had previously been married to the great Gaon Reb Zev Frankel, who had been the rabbi of the Tailors' Synagogue at Brod but had been divorced following a quarrel; and Reb Yudel's wife thought that meantime she had been engaged to another man who had sent her these gifts for Purim.

So Reb Yudel sent to ask his brother, Has Miriam become engaged? No, his brother sent a message back. And is a match being arranged? he went on to ask again. No, came the answer. Then whose are these jewels and ornaments? Reb Yudel sent to ask him. Why, yours, came the reply. But I haven't any daughter, Reb Yudel sent to remind his brother. But it stands to reason, his brother sent to remind him; Your name's written on the packet and they don't belong to you; then how much less are they mine, whose name isn't written on the packet.

In that case, said Reb Yudel Nathanson at last, it would appear that there must be two Reb Yudel Nathansons in Brod, but I'm well known and the other one isn't. Well, tomorrow's Purim when a large number of people come to visit me; I'll ask them if they know of the other Yudel Nathanson, and send the things on to him.

And on the morrow Reb Yudel Nathanson sat at the head of his table with a cloth spread, and the table covered with all manner of dainties; and there were two big dishes before him, one full of silver coins and one of copper; and he was wearing his festival clothes and smoking his pipe and studying the tractate on Purim, while people came in and went out; wardens of charity and householders who had come down in the world, may the Merciful One deliver us, and the poor and needy and tramps and loafers and Purim players and people wearing masks, with musical instruments and weird faces and foolishness. And they all danced and made merry in honor of Purim, while he poured each one out a glass of wine and treated them to the cakes known as Haman's ears; and when they were about to leave he would give each one something in accordance with his standing and ask him, Do you know the wealthy Reb Yudel Nathanson? And they would all answer, Is there anybody in Brod who doesn't know the wealthy Reb Yudel Nathanson, long life to him, and would point at him with their fingers. No, he would answer, I'm not speaking of myself but of somebody else with the same name, very wealthy, with a lot of money. No, they would respond, we've neither seen nor heard of such. For who would remind himself of the Hassid when the talk was of wealthy folk, and particularly as Reb Yudel, the Hassid, was not called by his family name but was known as Yudel Student.

What did the wealthy Reb Yudel do thereupon? Began cross-questioning newcomers and trying to confuse them, asking, How much did you get this morning from the wealthy Reb Yudel Nathanson? No, not from me, but from the other fellow of the same name. And he asked again, Which of you will take Purim gifts to that wealthy Reb Yudel Nathanson? No, not to me but to the other one in town. And folk smiled, thinking he must be tipsy and no longer able to tell the difference betwen Curst be Haman and Blest be Mordecai; which is a fit and proper state to be in on Purim. So seeing that the line he was following did not accord with his self-respect, Reb Yudel desisted. Time will tell, said he to himself.

THE BRIDAL CANOPY

In brief, those went and others came, some for themselves and some for others while others were going about for them, since more is received when you go round for others than when you come in poor and ashamed on your own behalf and have not the courage to make demands. Some wore gentile garb, and some gentiles there wore Jewish clothes. And not a single one of all these callers had reason for complaint against the generosity of Reb Yudel Nathanson.

Reb Yudel Hassid also went forth to collect charity for the poor, since there were poorer folk even than he; and he wished to make himself a pair of boots so that he should not suffer the fate of the barefoot saint who revealed himself after his demise wearing fine raiment and precious, but barefoot and unshod. Rabbi, his pupils asked him, how is it that your whole body is covered with such fine clothes while your feet are bare? My sons, said he, my body which carried out the commandments and performed good deeds has been garbed in fine array; but my feet which never ran to solicit alms for the poor have been left barefoot.

On the way Reb Yudel turned in at the house of Reb Yudel Nathanson, where he met Nuta who had come to rejoice the wealthy man's heart on the festival. And so it came about that Reb Yudel stood in the presence of Reb Yudel without the one knowing that the man he sought for was in his presence, and without the other knowing that the man in whose presence he was sought him; in order that greater things and yet more wonderful might come about.

And Reb Yudel asked Reb Yudel, Do you perhaps know Reb Yudel Nathanson; I'm not speaking of myself but of some other very wealthy Reb Yudel with a lot of money. Reb Yudel remembered the incident of the Reb Yudel he had met at the house of Tobiah of Polikrif and said to himself, Here you are, even so wealthy a man as this isn't alone but has others of the same name as wealthy as he. And he rejoiced at heart that the All-Present had made rich and poor equal in this, and that just as there are poor men of identical name and identical needs, so there are wealthy men of identical name and identical wealth. But he did not have the means of giving Reb Yudel the information, for he did not know any other Reb Yudel who was as wealthy as this Reb Yudel; so he answered, Would that all the Lord's people were well-to-do. Meanwhile Nuta remembered that when he had been traveling the roads with Reb Yudel, the Hassid, and the king's constable had asked Reb Yudel his name, he had answered,

Nathanson's my name; and he was already wishful of pointing to Reb Yudel. But such is the way of those in whose heart the quality of truth has no fixed and permanent place; even when the truth lights up in their heart it is hard for them to utter it at the mouth. For Nuta considered to himself, What it's good to tell a gentile it's no good telling Reb Yudel Nathanson. And so he remained silent.

And in Brod there were many jokers known as Brod singers who used to relate all the troubles of the time in rhyme, and made up mocking songs. In the ordinary way they are held of small esteem by decent Brod folk, but at Purim they mount in the general regard, for their songs are approved by reason of the joyfulness required for Purim. Now these singers came to Reb Yudel Nathanson; one was dressed as a Hassid and one as a waggoner; the latter told the tale of all that had befallen them on the way and the former, putting his hand to his ear, sang in tune and rhyme

THE BALLAD OF REB YUDEL.

INTRODUCTION

Quoth the narrator: Come and listen to the story of the Hassid; so far you don't know who that Hassid is, but as soon as you hear the Introduction you'll all know at once whom we're a telling of.

And thereupon his companion began to a fine tune:

In the name of God Almighty, That loves us whoe'er we be,
We'll tell the tale of the Hassid and of his daughters three.

There was a certain Hassid, and a student deep was he,
The which did serve his Maker with love and piety,

And he had three fair daughters, gentle and well grown,
Whose time had come to marry; and yet they sat alone

In dire straits for they had no dowry to their name,
And so his good wife Frummet was at him with a claim

That he turned his eyes away, and would not see their tears
And did not move a finger to match them in all those years.

Then sorely he did sigh, and all his faith he set
In the Great and Blessed Name Who nothing doth forget.

THE BRIDAL CANOPY

So what did Frummet do? She went and she did cry
To our far-famed and saintly Master, the Apta rabbi,

And to him she wept her heart out, with many a bitter tear,
And told him all her troubles, and all that she had to bear.

To her the rabbi said, Come, goodwife, do not weep,
For sure His Blessed Name, His faith with you will keep.

Your husband is Reb Yudel, a Hassid of renown,
And I would give him counsel to go from town to town,

With silken clothes upon him, you never will find better,
And I'll sit down and write my true believers a fine letter

To aid him bring his daughters under the Bridal Canopy;
And may his path be prosperous and pleasant for to see.

So to carry out instructions the Hassid set forth and he
Went and hired him Nuta, and Peacock and Ivory,

Two fine upstanding hosses that can travel on their own,
They scarcely need a driver, their master himself will own.

They started along the road, and the Hassid he had on
His silk and satin garments and his silver buckled shoon

And so they went a journeying in a covered cart, you see,
For to bring the Hassid's daughter under the Bridal Canopy.

On the Way at an Inn

Quoth the narrator: Now that you know who the Hassid was and
why he took to the road it's only fit and proper that you should
know what happened to him at the beginning of his travels. This is
what happened to him at the beginning of his travels.

At which the singer began:

> *The narrator's tale is a bit too long,*
> *So the poet betakes himself to song.*

At Pinkevitz they were welcomed so much that they were lief
To do off once for all the garments of their grief.

THE BRIDAL CANOPY

The landlord thought the Hassid a first-class sort of fellow
And filled him up with victuals and drink till he was mellow

And treated him with brandy, the like he'd never tasted,
While as for the landlord's wife, in his honor she too hasted

To prepare a feast for him with the best that she could get,
And she made him pancakes filled with onions and with meat.

Each pancake was as big as a baby of a day,
He'd never seen the like in his dreams, as I dare say.

And so they went on chatting, and so the hours went by,
While the landlord went on telling tales of wonder and mystery.

They wished that he might prosper wherever he did go,
And find for all his daughters their bridegrooms, I do trow.

And so they sat together in comfort as at first
Drinking the landlord's liquor and his words with equal thirst,

Until the stars had moved around which are up in the sky
And the time for bed had passed away and the hour of dawn was
    nigh.

Then up rose the landlord's wife, and shouted out aloud,
Come look! Your very eyelids are a resting on the ground.

So up they got and stretched themselves and then lay down and slept,
Until the sun was in the sky, and they woke and up they leapt,

And washed and prayed and ate a meal in the morning tide,
And the landlord did his part towards a dowry for the bride.

> *A solitary man in a village inn*
> *Who doeth right and knoweth no sin*
> *And whose house is a place for guests to stay—*
> *His charity's bright as the light of day.*

THE PLEASURES AND DELIGHTS OF MAN

Quoth the narrator: Now you have heard of all the hospitality shown
to the Hassid and the way he was given victuals for to eat and liquor

for to drink and all the dainties in the world, you ought to hear what happened after he had eaten and drunk and enjoyed his food.

At which the singer began:

The narrator's tale is a bit too long
So the poet betakes himself to song.

They parted from the landlord, and started on their way.
Reb Yudel sat in comfort and ease as you might say.

All of a sudden his belly began to trouble him
For everything he'd eaten filled him up to the very brim,

His bowels did begin to croak and to complain,
And seethed with noxious vapors, which mounted to his brain,

And Nuta too did suffer from bellyache and pain,
The fine grub he had eaten to him did prove a bane.

Dry bread is surely better for any famished soul
Than a spirit pining because of a belly overfull.

They that do feed on dainties in misery do lie,
For folk who've overeaten do swell up by and by.

The horses also added to the trouble on that day,
For they wandered here and wandered there, and then they went astray.

THE RIGHTEOUS ARE DELIVERED FROM THEIR STRAITS

Now you have heard all the troubles that began to come his way, you might suppose that they went on coming his way. Not so; he was delivered from them and what was more came to a place where he prospered exceedingly. And how did he prosper?

At which the singer began:

The narrator's tale is a bit too long,
So the poet betakes himself to song.

They gathered strength and came to the village of Pedhoretz
And made the round of the hamlets on the highway to Zehoretz.

THE BRIDAL CANOPY

Reb Yudel made his stay with a worthy dairyman,
Where many strange adventures to come his way began.

For there he found a female, a beast in human shape,
Captured by the fairies; he helped her to escape,

And brought about full many a wonder and a sign,
And in those parts they honored him and brought him lots of coin.

His name began to sound abroad just like a golden bell,
He never suffered hunger, and his pockets were full as well.

> *Tho' a man wander sighing*
> *With clouds o'er him lying—*
> *If the Lord doth send aid,*
> *Song and joy come instead.*

The World and the Fullness Thereof

Now you have heard all the circuits the Hassid made, let's accompany him to a certain place where he spent several days and saw a large number of things. Yet although he spent a while there and saw many things, we shall not delay there long.

His companion began:

> *The narrator's tale is a bit too long,*
> *So the poet betakes himself to song.*

O'er hill and dale they traveled, as never a man can doubt,
And took the chance of seeing all the places round about

Like Koltov and like Benif, Sasov and Belkomin,
And everywhere they went they were invited to come in,

Put money in the pocket and take a drop to drink,
And give the horses fodder, and have a chat, I think.

On a mountain stands a lofty rock, and below is Pedkomin,
Where all the folk obey God's words and only one is mean.

There they received the Hassid with love and high esteem,
And one did share his meal with him and one his cash, 'twould seem.

[336]

THE BRIDAL CANOPY

One opened wide before him the portals of his home,
And slipped a coin into his hand when as he went therefrom.

The whole of Pedkomin came round and louted them full low
Because of the Apta rabbi's letter, the which he did them show.

In his place another person might well have spent his days
With singing and with dancing in a dozen different ways,

But not so our Reb Yudel, who always bore in mind
The Blessed Name and the daughters that he had left behind.

The Tabernacles of the Righteous

Had this Hassid of ours come to any ordinary village we would never
have let it pass unremarked, so now that he reaches a village where
a man famed for his hospitality resides, something worthy of the
occasion must obviously be remarked. Many things befell Reb Yudel
in that village, where he met another Reb Yudel who was no Reb
Yudel but made himself out to be Reb Yudel. Though everything
cannot be told, we shall relate their essence. His companion began.

The narrator's tale is a bit too long,
So the poet betakes himself to song.

From Pedkomin they started out, and Nuta to be brief,
Brought Reb Yudel all the way to the village of Polikrif

Where they found a gray old man, the leaser of the village,
Who had a fine big house, and granaries and tillage.

But in all his wealth and money he never took no pride
And he gave alms and charity and feared the Lord beside.

And open house he keeps to all men on the road,
And beggars, tramps and paupers, are at home in his abode.

And there Reb Yudel found prepared a table, bed and light
And ears that were wide to hearken to words of Torah bright.

Happy the upright person whose tongue doth not deceive,
Who dwells in loving-kindness and the needy doth relieve.

[337]

THE BRIDAL CANOPY

A FRIEND STICKING CLOSER THAN A BROTHER

Now when they departed from that village they went wheresoever
the horses took them, and they reached a town where the Hassid all
but found a match for his daughter. And why didn't he make the
match for her? My companion will tell you. And the other began:

> *The narrator's tale is a bit too long,*
> *So the poet betakes himself to song.*

They took their leave of Polikrif and journey to Kitishtz,
And made their way to Sertitz and from thence to Ratishtz.

And so they journeyed on till they came to Tshestipad,
And wherever they came they found there was some food or a coin
    to be had.

And so they sat and journeyed behind Peacock and Ivory
And climbed right up the mountain and down into the valley.

Beshrew me if I've memory the hamlets to recall
Or if I've toes and fingers enough to count them all,

But at the last they came out safe from all the hamlets there,
And pulled up in Zalozetz, a city fine and fair,

Most beauteous of cities, a really lovely place,
Within which Torah and wisdom were like the two cheeks of a face.

And there Reb Yudel met with two vessels of pure gold,
And the bonds of love and friendship did the three of them enfold,

And he met the both of them at the home o' his boyhood friend
At a time his friend was suffering from sorrow and torment.

For in the very week he came his good friend's wife had died;
But when he rose from mourning and his laces he had tied,

He spoke thus to Reb Yudel, and said, Friend of my youth,
See this is the thing that has come into my mind in truth,

To take one of your daughters to my bosom for a wife,
And though there be no dowry, I don't care, by my life.

THE BRIDAL CANOPY

But still Reb Yudel never gave his daughter for a bride,
For he had faith in his rabbi, whatever might betide,

And indeed at the last Reb Yudel the satisfaction had
Of finding as a bridegroom, a fine and learned lad.

Be happy, O Reb Yudel, thou Hassid most sincere,
To follow the counsel of the wise, and never at them jeer.

FROM THE STRAITS

And what befell him after he left the town? He found himself in
the middle of trouble and only got out of trouble to find himself in
greater trouble, and from that he tumbled into a still worse scrape;
why, he went astray the greater part of the night and wished and
watched for rest for his body; and when he reckoned he had come
to a place where human beings lived he found himself in the house of
an apostate; and when he fled from the apostate he was attacked by
a wolf; and when he fled from the wolf he blundered into a cemetery
where the dead flapped at him with their cerements and shrouds.
And the singer began:

The narrator's tale is a bit too long,
So the poet betakes himself to song.

They left behind Zalozetz and other towns went to sight,
When the sky came over black, and the land came over white.

The roads could not be followed, there was no life to see,
While the horses seemed to have undergone some kind of witchery.

The whip was of no use, the shout of no avail;
They will not budge an inch, tho' Nuta whack and rail,

The snow fell all around, and the hungry wolves were out,
And they almost fell a prey to the wolves, there is no doubt.

Then once they were delivered from all their troubles there,
They found themselves on a sudden in a graveyard bleak and bare.

And there the horses stopped, and the waggon out of hand,
And high above the graves each gravestone it did stand.

[339]

THE BRIDAL CANOPY

What's that! A dead man walking 'mid the graves just over there!
They had the creeps all over and like mountains rose their hair.

And their souls were all but ready (God forbid) to fly away,
But blest be He Who giveth the weary strength enough to stay.

Tales That Were Told

Having come forth from the deeps of these distresses he came to a
worthy place and stayed with a worthy and hospitable man; and
there the Hassid ate and drank and derived pleasure and joy from
the words of the wise, and heard tales linked one with the other and
close one to another, each tale of which was a novelty remarkable for
the fear of the Lord it inculcated. And the singer began:

> *The narrator's tale is a bit too long,*
> *..So the poet betakes himself to song.*

And so Reb Yudel came to famous Zbarev town
And there he lodged with a man of great renown

Who strengthened him his body and his wisdom did increase
And kept his spirit rejoicing, and his soul did also please.

The body pines and wastes and withers in the ground,
But in a wise soul wisdom illumines all around.

Praise him for never wasting his days in vanity,
And we should also mention that Nuta praised must be

Because he never urged him from that place to hurry on,
And so they heard the tales of Rabbi Israel Solomon,

Like the tale of Simeon Nathan and the tale of the wandering cat—
Read what you will and I'll warrant you never read a tale like that!

Knowledge and Understanding

And now you've heard all the circuits and circumnavigations which
the Hassid made on his travels, and how he ate, drank and lived a
fine life, you might suppose him to be drowned deep in temporal and
secular delights. Not so; he roused himself exceedingly and came to

be of the opinion that his days were running to waste, and he set
his mind on returning to his home; but the time had not yet come;
for the blessings of the saint who promised him that he would find
a bridegroom for his daughter were not yet fulfilled. And the singer
began:

> *The narrator's tale is a bit too long,*
> *So the poet betakes himself to song.*

The time came when the Hassid remembered his daughters three
And his travels seemed disgusting wherever he might be,

And he came to hold the view that his days did run to waste,
And his spirit it was startled, and his spirit was abased;

And would that he might return to his daughters and his wife,
And study Torah day and night for the whole of his natural life.

But this did not accord with the wish of The Great and Blessed Name,
So Reb Yudel Hassid never returned the way by which he came.

And so he went his proper way, for nary another had he,
And with him Nuta, the waggoner, and Peacock and Ivory,

Those two far-famed horses which swift as eagles were,
And all thro' the woods and villages their legs the dust would stir.

And so they went on journeying from Zbarev to Brazan
By way of Pommoren which is near by Kozshan.

And along the road they met on the mountain slope, I own,
A great and hidden saint of the Thirty-six Unknown

Who took them and who brought them to a huge and awesome
    wood,
Where a bright booth suddenly grew from the ground, I'd have it
    understood.

And bowed and bent an ancient and gentle woman stood,
And up to the very eyebrows she was covered in her hood.

The candles they were burning more brightly than the moon;
It was the Lord's own Sabbath, and there they did commune

And stayed there, did the Hassid and the waggoner as well,
Till the Sabbath had departed, as I have heard them tell.

Come slaughter me seven oxen and then their hides go flay
And let me write upon them how the righteous go their way.

In vain do you build houses and mansions great and fine,
In lowly habitations seek the Countenance Divine.

TOIL AND TROUBLE

Now to return to the wife of the Hassid, who had brought him out of
the House of Study and caused him to wander wide without Torah;
let us see what befell her and her three daughters while her husband
went walking the world. And the singer changed his tune:

> *Here the narrator takes a rest*
> *And instead the poet will do his best.*

Meanwhile gentle Frummet sat and waited at the house,
With eyes that had grown weary a watching for her spouse.

All day long and all night her heart was trembling and afraid;
Why, Yudel, what can ail you for to be so long delayed?

See there is nothing here at all and the very house doth sorrow,
And what can I give the maidens when they hunger on the morrow.

Then up and crowed the cock, to comfort them, thought he,
Why, Father will bring a bridegroom back, as you will surely see.

Come, gather up your pinions and wait a little while,
For soon enough he'll be in Brod, after many a weary mile.

But the blessings of the Lord they were unto Reb Yudel known,
And he always uttered praises to the Living God alone;

And out he brought his poke, his earnings to assess,
For he did devise to make an end of travel in idleness.

And thereupon Reb Yudel an oath to himself did swear
To go to an inn and dwell there in a fine room, I declare.

My song be glad and happy that the words of the wise are true;
Who keepeth the Torah in poverty will keep it in riches too.

THE BRIDAL CANOPY

The Fruit of the Righteous

So when the appointed time came for the daughter to be found her match, the Holy and Blest One put it into her father's mind to go to a certain town and lodge in a fine inn and eat and drink at his own expense and study Torah. All of a sudden a matchmaker came to him, bringing with a bridegroom.

But before the narrator could tell the whole of the tale the singer broke in and began:

And now we find Reb Yudel in a certain well-known city,
Where he dwelt at an inn like any prince, as I tell in my ditty.

And so what did Reb Yudel do while he was at the inn?
Be sure he never went astray, nor was up to any sin.

And straightaway there pounced upon him dealers in a drove,
Who scraped and pranced before him, and meanwhile they all strove

To make him do some business in a multitude of things,
Like horses, ramfells, oxen, and cabbages and kings,

But our beloved Hassid did wonders on that day,
For with a leaf of Talmud he drove them all away.

Thereafter came a matchmaker with nine full ells of chatter,
And he never toiled in vain but got a payment for his clatter,

Because he brought along with him a fine and worthy youth,
And Reb Yudel found his knowledge was a blessing in all truth.

So let us tell it early and let us tell it late,
Reb Yudel found that this here lad must be his daughter's fate.

They set the tables, lit the lights and summoned all the folk,
And wrote the Engagement Contract; and the crockery they broke,

And brandy, wine and liquor as water forth were poured,
And the joy went up to the heavens from the midst of the festive board.

This is the tale of the Hassid and all that him befell,
When he put his life in peril, as you have heard me tell,

For the sake of wife and daughters in the land of Austria,
And now our song is at an end and we bid you all good day.

Never has such laughter been seen as that of Reb Yudel Nathanson when he heard the ballad of Reb Yudel Hassid; the very walls of the house laughed with him. After he had regained control of himself he dug both his hands into the dish and took out much money and said, Reb Yudel, I also wish to take part in that great injunction of bringing the bride under the canopy.

Reb Yudel Hassid thought that the householder could only be speaking to him, and held out his hand. But somebody else was ahead of him, and that was the other Reb Yudel who had put on the clothes like Reb Yudel's. Reb Yudel stood staring at this person and could see no difference between the other and himself, neither in face nor in garb nor in movements. And to whom could Reb Yudel be compared at that moment? To the two-headed man whose father died. Said the two-headed man, I'm a first-born and so entitled to a double share, and my second head is another person and also entitled to a share of the inheritance. Not so, said his brothers, you're only entitled to two portions, one for yourself and one for your birthright. So they came to King Solomon for a decision. And what did he do? Poured boiling water over the one head, and the other began yelling; and that showed at once that they could be counted as a single head and there was only one portion between them. But the two-headed man at least received a double portion, for himself and his birthright, but Reb Yudel got nothing at all. So Reb Yudel said to Reb Yudel, Reb Yudel has taken Yudel's share and Yudel hasn't had anything from Reb Yudel, and put his hand out once again to Reb Yudel. Thereupon Reb Yudel Nathanson put his finger to his nose and said, After I've given you all that you have to come and ask for more? For Reb Yudel Nathanson could not distinguish between Reb Yudel and the one who had disguised himself as Reb Yudel. Even if you and I had been there we couldn't have distinguished either between Reb Yudel Hassid and Reb Yudel, the Brod singer; and that was even more the case with Reb Yudel Nathanson who knew nothing about Reb Yudel or the Reb Yudel who was not Reb Yudel, but was dressed in clothes like those of Reb Yudel. And so Reb Yudel could not go and ask again. Never in my life, said Reb Yudel, have I seen rich men equal one to another, but poor men are always the same and equal, sometimes even to their very faces.

Once Purim was over the poor folk returned home and arranged to expend their money on their Passover requirements, and the people with masks took them off and went back to work, and the wardens went out to collect wheat money for the poor. Blest be the All-Present, blest be He for not forsaking His children without mercy, and for providing them with good wardens, and for setting loving-kindness in the hearts of Israel so that he who doth not need to take doth give. Two charity wardens came to Reb Yudel Nathanson, and he began to converse with them at length in the hope that from their words he would learn something about another Reb Yudel Nathanson. Had the wardens come to him last of all after passing through the city from end to end, they would not have had the wherewithal to answer his questions; and still more was it the case when he was the first in the town that they came to. So he gave them his contribution, wondering all that while that there should be another Reb Yudel Nathanson in town whom nobody knew; for whoever he might ask pointed to him and said, The only Reb Yudel Nathanson we know is the one in front of us.

So then Reb Yudel said to his wife, Well, it's customary that when one man receives a gift from another he returns something in its stead; whom do we have to return something to? For since he had been through the town and had not found his namesake he was sure that the gifts must be for him. Not that he had any daughter, but he thought that the other man who sent the gifts must be a wag of some kind.

Since he has sent us, said he, bridal array, we must send a bridegroom's trappings in return. Well said, Yudel, said his wife; after all, these gifts are worth quite a little money; whether he's fooling us to the value of a little money or we're fooling him to the value of a little money, the presents at least are very nice. Had the gifts come to the house of Reb Yudel Hassid, Pessele would have put on the earrings and the bracelets, and her face would have been bright as the summer sun and her heart would have been happy; and father and mother seeing would have known their salvation was close to hand; but since they had come into the hands of Reb Yudel Nathanson they only served to remind him of his wife's sorrow and his own that they had no children and no hope of seeing any child of theirs a bride.

So Reb Yudel and his wife considered the gift they should send. What shall I send him? he asked. A watch and chain? Why, he must have one of his own and what use is mine to him? Is he a little boy beginning to study the Pentateuch that has to be dressed up with such toys? Should I send him an amber pipe? And supposing he doesn't smoke, the nice present will induce him to smoke, and what's more he may come to think that my gift gives him authority even to take snuff on the First Day of the Festivals; and so he'd be led into error through me. But I'll send the four volumes of the Turim. The sort of person, said Reb Yudel, who wants to try and joke with me must certainly lack such staid and serious and authoritative compendia of the Torah as the four Turim.

So he took a set of the Turim printed at Meziboz and Polna, for the printing of which he had donated money and had been sent two sets bound in wooden boards with red vellum covers and copper locks and his name and the name of the part in gold lettering on each volume, and a gold edging to the leaves and a ewer embossed on the cover, Reb Yudel Nathanson being a Levite and the printers making the necessary symbol in his honor since the Levite pours water over the hands of the priest at the time of the benediction. For himself, however, he kept the edition of Venice, since the Venice type is pleasant to read; and shortly before Passover he sent the set of Turim to the Holy Congregation of Rohatin and wrote a letter to the bridegroom in good style, and with the book wished all that was best/ from the bride rejoicing and blest/ whose heart was ever true/ to the lad she hoped to view/ a youth so fine and such a gem/ whoever saw them both would know they were of blessed stock and stem. And Reb Yudel's wife also took a turkey cock, tied its legs together and sent it as a gift to the groom's mother.

The gifts came to Rohatin. The bridegroom took the four volumes, said the blessing of gratitude for living to see the day so worth-while a thing happened to him, and uttered blessings and praise/ to God's wonderful ways/ in choosing him rather than another lad/ and giving him these four Turim, the best to be had/ be with me still, O Lord, as Thou hast been hitherto/ and in Thy Torah day by day I'll show what I can do. And he at once began studying the Laws of Passover, refreshing himself between chapters with the stomach of the turkey cock and its stuffed neck and its liver. And meanwhile Reb Yudel Nathanson put the entire matter out of mind so that he forgot all about it.

CHAPTER NINE: THE FIG TREE PUTTETH FORTH ITS FIGS · RICH AND POOR DO MEET ⌁ So the bridegroom dwelt in a home full of all manner of fine things, where he studied Torah in prosperity, while the bride stayed in her narrow gloomy dwelling almost giving up the ghost for hunger. Fordone she did remain in her maidenhood, ashamed to be seen out of doors. Purim had passed, Passover was at an end, yet she had not been come for. So she sat bewailing her calamity. Hadn't Father found her a bridegroom? Hadn't everybody wished her *mazal tov?* Then how was it that she never got a whit of greeting from him? She dwelt in the gloomy vault together with her sisters and raised a keen and a lament for her unlucky star, she being forgotten as a dead one might be and never hearing the voice of her bridegroom. They might well ask their father where the bridegroom was, when they grew wearied with grief and poured forth their souls on their mother's bosom. And Thou, O God, didst bring it about that even the letter wherein the bridegroom's father did ask for the date of the wedding to be fixed should come to Reb Yudel Nathanson.

When Reb Yudel Nathanson read the letter he said to his wife, Well, all I can say is that I was in a position to send Purim gifts, but how can I supply them with a wedding ceremony when there isn't a bride?

The Lord hath set more wisdom in the heart of a woman than in the heart of a man. Reb Yudel's wife was wise and goodhearted, and did much charity at all times and used to marry off orphans and make them a wedding, with drums and dances and as much joy as though they were her own daughters. And all her life long it was her great sorrow that she and her husband had no children.

So when her husband read her out this letter she said, Blest be He Who has brought this commandment our way. And how much longer, asked he, must you go piling these jobs on me? I haven't the least idea what to do. Yudel, she replied, be careful what you are about, for two Jewish souls depend upon your actions; if you dodge the issue you will be destroying a match. So sure may it come to me, said Reb Yudel, as there's anything for me to do here. Once I've come into it by error you want me to go on going wrong? Yudel, said she, we've gone wrong often enough and we'll go wrong often enough; but in the end the mistakes will be cleared up one and all.

There must certainly be a person here named Yudel Nathanson, and maybe richer even than you; but people don't know him. After all, aren't we in Brod where a man doesn't even know his next-door neighbor? But when the groomsmen come to Brod the bride's father will hear about it and will do his share. So surely may the Lord help us, said he, as you have spoken well, but all the same I don't know what to do. Then for the time being, said she, take your pen and write to the bridegroom's father that you are prepared to make the wedding at the fit and proper time. If we haven't been found worthy of seeing the rejoicing of our own children, let's at least see the joy of others.

So Reb Yudel wrote to the other party that I do invite/ manifold greetings from the uttermost height/ upon my prospective kinsman's head/ who is that scholar keen and well read/ possessed of a two-edged sword/ and standing proud as any lord, and so on. And this to Judah and he said/ to answer thee I now am led/ thy missive sweet I did receive/ and this in turn I shall achieve/ to arrange the wedding so that there never was a better/ on the date that has been mentioned in your letter, and so forth.

When Reb Vovi received Reb Yudel's letter he prepared everything necessary for the wedding and sent this invitation to his friends:

With the aid of the Blessed Name

The voice of the bridegroom	The voice of the bride
banisheth gloom	and joy doth abide.

Under a good sign and a good star we have the honor to invite you to come and take part in the joy of our children the nurselings
of our vineyard
being the deeply versed and worthy bridegroom
the youth his honor Master Shefatyah may his light shine
and the modest and praiseworthy bride
the virgin Mistress Pessele long life to her
daughter of the exalted philanthropist our Master Rabbi Judah
Nathanson

May the grapes of the vine	as the rose be fine
And flowers be gay	till the uttermost day

THE BRIDAL CANOPY

The wedding will take place in a good and prospering hour on such
and such a day of such and such a Weekly Portion
in the Holy Congregation of and so on.
And God willing we shall do the like by you at your children's joy.
Zev Wolf known as Vovi of the Shor family and his spouse.

And meanwhile the bridegroom prepared a fine and sharp address to
be delivered at his wedding, and already knew it by heart, and so
would have no reason to be ashamed of himself at the wedding.

So all the in-laws set out from Rohatin in carriages and curricles, in
coaches and on horseback, in fine array, taking with them clothes of
satin and of silk, each one according to his own standards, particularly the women. And waggons loaded with food and drink went
along with them. And from all the towns and villages lying between
Rohatin and Brod they were joined by their kinsfolk and the kin of
their kin, who all came at the rumor that Reb Vovi had arranged an
outstanding match. The sun did its duty and the trees were a green-
ing, and the birds twittered on every roof and fence and tree and
from every bush and there was a fine scent rising from the fields.
The wedding jester rhymed his rhymes and the musicians played.
When they made a halt the groom's mother brought out honeycake
and wine, and they ate and drank. At each halt there was a feast and
at each feast there was joy. Eat fat and drink sweet and rejoice in
your hearts, for it's an occasion of great joy for Reb Vovi who might
not have succeeded in finding his son a wife on account of the half-
cherry his grandsire had eaten on the Ninth of Ab; and all the same
he's now going to the wedding of his son.

And being so joyful Reb Vovi took silver money and threw it to
the musicians, saying, Here you are, lads, here's what you deserve.
Then he took some paper money, tore it and gave half to the jester;
for if it's torn it can always be pasted together again and is current
money; and if a man has received one half he can be sure of getting
the rest. And when would he get it? When Sheftel would actually
be standing under the Bridal Canopy. Gather together and come
hither all ye who word sweetly and speechify in dulcet wise, bringing
with you the words needed to relate the joy of a man going to the
wedding of his first-born son. And even then, can words tell of that
joy and song and gladness?

When they were close to Brod Reb Vovi sent to Reb Yudel Nathanson to come with his kin and greet the groom. It's a silly message, said Reb Yudel. How can I go out for a bridegroom when I haven't a bride for him?

When the day went by and nobody came, they began to be afeared lest some cause for mourning might have occurred, the Merciful One deliver us. And Reb Vovi's folk stood watching along the road which was silent all day long; and nobody came to greet them; and their concern and worry grew and grew.

Unless you have heard the tale of the bridegroom who went to the Bridal Canopy and perished along the road, so that when people came to meet him his father said, Let the music be and bring a coffin and a shroud—unless you have at least heard that tale you cannot even imagine the anguish of Reb Vovi. The musical instruments all went out of order and the rhymes ceased in the mouth of the marriage jester, and the relatives slipped stealthily away one by one, for they said to themselves, Reb Yudel has already been told the tale of the half-cherry and has broken off the match, so why should we admit our connection with such a family?

So Reb Vovi waited a couple of days, with shameful but expectant gaze, yet none drew near to ask what cheer. At length he took Reb Yudel's letters, went to Brod and asked for the house of Reb Yudel Nathanson, which he was shown at once. He entered and found him putting on his overcoat, since he was just about to go and recite the Afternoon Prayers. He greeted Reb Yudel and Reb Yudel greeted him in return, and then asked, What might your business be? Thereupon Reb Vovi began brimming over with fury and shouted, Why did you have to go and shame me in such a way? Here we've been standing waiting for you for two whole days and you don't turn up? And why, asked Reb Yudel, do you have to go shouting at me when I don't even know who you are?

At this Reb Vovi for the first time raised his eyes and used them, and said in astonishment, It's quite true, I've never seen you, sir, before today. And he brought out his letters. Yes, said Reb Yudel, those letters are mine and I wrote them. So you've been making a mock and laughingstock of me, exclaimed Reb Vovi.

God forbid, replied Reb Yudel, but what happened was this: I received gifts on Purim without knowing who sent them; and I asked whether there might be another person of my name in town, but no such person is known. Well, said I, for the present I'll send gifts in return and write the necessary letters until the gift sender comes and demands his own.

And why did you see fit to do so? asked him Reb Vovi. I saw, he replied, that your prospective in-law is not known in town, and I feared that as a result nothing would come of the match. But I am not your prospective in-law, and even if I wished to be I couldn't, because I have no children.

And so it's time to unchain you, Meshel, with your insistence that Reb Yudel Nathanson was childless, and Reb Vovi was convinced that you were crazy. Why, Reb Yudel Nathanson himself says the same, that I'm not the father of your son's bride because I have no children. And Reb Vovi caught his head between his hands and stood in shame and bemused. Anyway, said Reb Yudel to him, it's time for the Afternoon Prayers; let's go to the House of Study and maybe we'll find the man you're looking for there.

They entered the House of Study, went up to the honorable East wall but didn't find the in-law for whom he sought. They looked all around but could not discover him. At last Reb Vovi spied, behind the oven, a man sitting reading a book; his clothes were torn and his hat was torn and his belly caved in and he had a face like ten men at a fast. That's him, wailed Reb Vovi. Gently, gently, said Reb Yudel Nathanson to him. At this point the Hassid raised his head and saw his in-law-to-be, Reb Vovi; and he at once rose to greet him and was very happy to see him, and all in the same breath asked how he was and what news there was of the bridegroom.

Woe to you, you beggar, cried Reb Vovi in a fury, that haven't even a coat to your back and yet you go and promise your daughter twelve thousand. I can trust the Holy and Blest One, responded Reb Yudel, to fulfill my promise. The impudence of you, cried the other, to be standing without anything and still be impudent. By your life, in-law, said Reb Yudel to him, wait while I go and tell my folk to prepare a feast for you.

Meanwhile Reb Yudel Nathanson had been gazing at him and said to himself, I seem to know this in-law. So surely may I live to see the Comforting as he came to me on Purim and when I gave him an alms he came and asked again. And he was doubly astonished; first that he should bear the thing in mind and second that such a feckless bench presser should be so cunning.

And meanwhile Reb Yudel Hassid ran home to tell his wife and daughters that the bridegroom's father had come to town. And great was their joy on hearing it. Bride, said Frummet to Pessele, do you hear what Father's telling you; by your life he has only come to arrange the date of the wedding. Thereupon the bride dropped her eyes in confusion. And her sisters at once began anointing her and bedecking her and plaiting her hair; and they all took needle and thread and mended their clothes before meeting the groom's father. And the bride also inserted a patch in the neighborhood of her bosom, for she had sprouted and grown, no evil eye upon her; and was ready to receive her kinsman-to-be.

But no joy without sorrow. As soon as Reb Yudel told them that Reb Vovi was to come and eat supper with them, Frummet began crying, how do you dare to invite him home when the whole house is bare of food and drink! And even if I should make him a meal, is there a table to sit at? are there plates to put the food in? is there as much as a spoon to eat with? Is there anything in the house for the man to rest his eyes on with pleasure? He had to go searching till he found a maybe father-in-law, and now give him our tears for bread.

And what was the Hassid's answer? He walked up and down snapping his thin fingers and hummed softly but with joyful visage, for his trust was in The Holy Name.

Seeing this, what was Frummet to do? She put on her kerchief and went to the saintly Rabbi of Apta, and told him the whole matter. You have a cock, said the Rabbi. Take it and go prepare a meal for the bride's father-in-law-to-be.

So she went and took the cock that used to arouse her husband to serve the Creator and said to the bride, Take the cock and have it killed and I'll prepare him a meal.

And the bride, a pleasant maiden light on her feet, ran with the bird to the slaughterhouse along the street.

C HAPTER TEN: WHO GIVETH THE ROOSTER WIS-
DOM · TO THE COCK WHOSE WAY IS HIDDEN ᴣᴂ
So Pessele tripped along cuddling the cock to her bosom and
stroking his comb and chanting him all manner of things such as he
had never heard in all his days. Sweetheart, says she to him, do you
know where we're off to? It's the slaughterhouse we're off to. And
do you know what for? To have you killed. And for why? So as to
prepare a fine meal for my father-in-law-to-be. And what will we
make him that fine meal of? Of meat. And how will we prepare it?
With beans and with fenugreek and parsley which we'll add to make
the soup look nice.

Or maybe you prefer vermicelli? I'll prepare vermicelli finer and
longer even than my father-in-law's beard, so's it 'll hang down from
his whiskers and catch in his fringes under his waistcoat. Or maybe
you'd prefer to be roasted? Then I'll go and fetch a long iron spit
and pass it down through your throat and roast you and stick all
kinds of peppers inside you and sift meal over you; and I'll make
two kinds of horseradish, both white and red, and I'll fill your throat
with rice and currants and bits of fat the like of which your father's
fathers never dreamt of coming to; and I'll go and put you down
before my father-in-law-to-be and say to him, Come and sit down
and eat.

And he'll sit and eat and feel fine and say, Bless you, Pessele, my
dear, and he'll finish up everything and say, Go and fetch me water
to wash my hands and say benediction. Then I'll answer, Just try
this stuffed neck I prepared for you. And I'll bring him boiled plums
and boiled figs and ask him, Which dessert do you prefer, plums or
figs? Then he'll rest his hands on his paunch and say, Daughter,
haven't I eaten till I'm full up? Now you sit down and eat together
with all the family.

But then I'll answer, We're also full up, and have left plenty over;
and if you don't eat we'll have to throw the stuffed neck out into the
street. And then he'll wonder how clever I am and say, Folk are silly
when they talk of Brod ninnies. And he'll take a big fork and dig in
his teeth and eat. And while eating he'll go and smack his lips and
say, She's a fine girl, the one I chose to be my son's wife, and happy

[353]

he'll be with such a wonderful creature. When I go home tomorrow I'll tell my wife all I've eaten and all I've seen.

Then I'll cast down my head and hide my eyes and think to myself, Well, her turn will come to see all the clever things I know how to do, and how I can make a cock's wing into a sort of brush, to sweep crumbs off the table so that the Prince of Poverty shouldn't ever come and catch us unawares; and with its comb I can smoke the house out so that the evil eye shouldn't have dominion over us, God forbid.

And at the very thought Pesselle opens her arms wide in the air and rebukes the evil spirits and says:

> *Plague and ague   fly away,*
> *Flee and fly   and do not stay.*
>   *Begone to you*
>   *Or you shall rue.*
> *Begone to some far desert place*
> *And in the woods of eld*
> *Where dragons have themselves revealed,*
> *Hide your face   forever and aye.*
> *And He who giveth the rooster sense*
>   *Gave sense to our Reb Reveille,*
> *Because Reb Reveille started thence*
>   *And opened his wings and flew away.*

For in brief, when Pessele opened her hands to scold the evil spirits, Reb Reveille dropped from her arms and fled. And what was the reason that the cock should flee and not be slaughtered? Her own forgetfulness for not having tied his feet together as she should have done. Had she done so he would not have run away; but since she had not tied him, the fact remained that he had run away. And once he got out of her hands he fled, and being fled he ran away behind the fence. And Pessele beat her hands and wailed:

> *Alas, he has fled, and my luck is dead,*
> *Evil is come and I am struck dumb,*
> *May the Lord come and aid me, my mother will flay me.*
> *The groom's father will see how I'm shamed*
> *And bring the engagement to an end,*
> *Lord God Almighty, and can I be blamed,*

THE BRIDAL CANOPY

You do good even to those who offend,
Hearken and do not mock,
Kill me right away,
Or give me back my cock
And I'll praise you forever and a day.

And so Pessele goes on beating her hands and tearing her hair and wailing and weeping until all her limbs weep with her. If ever you have brought up a fine fat cock of which you hope to make a meal, and had the cock slip out of your hands and run away, you know what poor Pessele was going through. But in a few minutes she began chasing the cock to try and catch it again. Her dress caught on the splinters of the fence and tore, and then she was ashamed to move from her place because she was standing all but naked. So she fell to the ground and wept and cried through her tears:

O Mother, Mother, what have I done,
No, there is no excuse, not one,
Come whack me black and whack me blue,
And whack and whack till you kill me too.

When Frummet saw that Pessele was taking her time she sent her sister Blume after her. Blume ran to the slaughterhouse and found her sister lying on the ground and wailing and crying out and weeping. She grew frightened and cried out herself, What's the matter, sister bride, why are you wailing and weeping and where's the cock you took to slaughter? Pessele wanted to tell her all that had happened. She opened her mouth but was choked with grief. Then Blume took her in her arms and soothed her until at last she managed to say:

Lord God overhead, the cock has fled,
I wish I would die, for my bridegroom's gone by.
Let me be and I'll go to the mountains of snow
And weep by night and weep by day
Because unmarried I must stay.

Blume at once understood all that had happened, and dropped her own head and wept in sympathy. When Frummet, their mother, saw that Blume was also taking her time she sent young Gittele after

[355]

them. And Gittele came and found them both sitting in the field with their arms round one another, and she held her hands toward her heart and shouted at them:

The pot it boils and the fire's aflare
And here they sit to take the air,
You've rested enough, I do declare,
Come along quick, to the house go run
So that the meal should soon be done.

Alas and woe, where did my cock go?
Where has he gone, where has he turned,
That selfsame cock which always earned
The love of our heart.
The bear will come and tear him apart
Alas and alack for my lost cock,
Where has he gone and where has he turned,
And when and where was he last discerned?

Her sisters told her what had happened; and she too fell upon their necks and wept with them.

Well, and that was the way in which Frummet sent along all three of her daughters. Pessele she sent to slaughter the cock, Blume to speed up Pessele and Gittele to bring them both back home. And there stood Frummet at the hearth, and all her daughters were gone forth, and the pot did boil and fume like Hell, hurry and fetch me the cockerel. Her troubled heart did surge and knock, Whatever has happened to the cock? Her heart it seethed and her spirit sighed, and she looked around on every side, the water's boiling, the fire's gone out, beshrew me if I know what has come about. The father-in-law will soon be here, Lordy, Lordy, I'm full of fear. In vain I toil and in vain I wait, daughters, daughters, why are you late? Heavens, I suddenly feel in a quake, where is the chicken they did take? Your mother is left forlorn, she cried, return, O daughters, come, O bride.

Her heart was already beginning to prophesy all manner of evil. Maybe they had gone astray or maybe they had come to a ruin, God forbid and been reft by some demon like the woman who was going to the bathhouse and came to the ruin; and she walks o' nights embracing her son who is human from the navel up and demon from the navel down. And at this thought Frummet left the fire and the pot and went out to seek her daughters three.

She ran with all her might, crying, Daughters, daughters, where are you? At last she reached the field by the slaughterhouse and found them sitting huddled together. Thereupon she fell upon them in a fury and yelled at them, May all the evil plagues and sendings of Egypt befall you. It isn't Sabbath nor yet the Thirty-third day of the Omer, and what are you doing sitting in the field? Mother, Mother, wept her daughters, don't beat us, please, God has done quite enough, because the cock we wanted to make the meal out of has gone and run away.

At this Frummet dug her nails into her very flesh and cried, Where has he run away to, that cock o' mine? Where were you when there was no talk of a supper for the father-in-law? All my hopes are at an end. Let's dig ourselves a grave and bury ourselves there in our shame. Why do you stand there in your shame and reproach without answering a single word! They've hidden their tongues away in their mouths and can't utter a whisper.

At this her daughters all began weeping aloud. O Mother, we were born to sorrow, and the hand of the Lord is upon us. Clods of earth are pleasant things, and the grave's a fine holding sweet as honey.

Then Frummet began again, How dare you open your mouths or lift your eyes up to me when you're like the night wolves eating my flesh; may your tongues rot in your mouths and your eyes go foul in their sockets. Where has that cock run away to? Come on, get up and go round the field and we'll find the cock. A fine creature you are to run away and fly off. Did we ever hold back food from you? Didn't we feed you on Sabbath loaf and never had you slaughtered as our Atonement on the Eve of Atonement? Quick, girls, quick, let's look for it. There he is!

The moment they tried to catch it, it took to its wings and began flying ahead of them through the air. When they jumped up it dropped low; when they bent down it fluttered aloft; when they tried again it fluttered this way and that until it hid itself in a cave. When they came there they saw that there seemed to be a sort of fire alight within. Pessele began crying, Oh, the cock must have flown straight into the fire and been burnt. Brod is about to be put on fire, cried Blume, and we remain quiet. If we do nothing it will be our fault. Come, let's cry out that Brod's on fire.

But Mother, said Gittele, I've never seen a fire that doesn't give off any smoke. At this they looked closer, and saw that the fire was not fire but a treasure of gold and jewels and precious stones sparkling there. And they all stood in astonishment for fear this might be witchcraft, and began to cry out, Hear O Israel. When they saw that the gold did not disappear and the jewels did not fade away and flow like water, they knew that this was no witchcraft, but that it was all from His Blessed Hand. And they filled their aprons with the gold and jewels, and ran home.

And so consider: that for which others spent their lives without ever achieving anything came to Reb Yudel unawares. You will remember that when he was wandering the world he saw people digging and toiling to find treasures and laughed at them, saying, Doesn't the Talmud tell us plain and clear in so many words that finds come unawares; and he did not know that a treasure was lying in wait all prepared for him.

And how did there come to be gold and jewels in that cave? When the Kaiser had made war against his foes, the great folk of the country had had to go with him and first had hidden their treasures in the ground. When the troubles of that woman came before the Holy and Blest One, He revealed all those treasures to her. Blest be the All-Present; blest be He Who never turns his eyes away from Israel, and whatsoever thing He intendeth to do in the future, He doeth a whit thereof at the present time. For the nobles used to despoil Israel and rob them of their money; therefore the Holy and Blest One came and destroyed them and gave the money to whom He thought fit. The body that had coveted the wealth of others found its grave in foreign parts, and its gold and silver found their grave in the land of his birth. None had profit of their bodies save wild beasts and unclean fowl, but their silver and gold did advantage a worthy man and a Hassid. Take a lesson therefrom, all ye who pursue profit and pelf; for the Lord entreateth the poor, but the end of the wicked is to be cut off.

CHAPTER ELEVEN: A VIRGIN IS WED ❧ What did Frummet do then? Filled her apron with gold, went to the inn where Reb Vovi was staying, flung some cash down before the innkeeper and said, Take whatever there is here and prepare the best you have in food and liquor for my kinsfolk. Brethren mine and friends, sweet indeed is the talk of gold when it jingles and rolls in such profusion; brightly and mellow doth it gleam. The innkeeper bowed down before her with his hand on his heart, said, With the greatest of pleasure, and then kneeled and began picking up each coin. All the servants in the building seemed to grow shorter by an ell, and they bowed the knee to Frummet so that their faces verily scraped the floor and grew flat as the boards. Idiots that you are standing about like logs of wood, cried the landlord to his servants, can't you see that the noble lady has muddied her shoes. Off they dashed to bring brushes and polish and polish up Frummet's shoes. Have you ever seen the like for clumsy louts, said the landlady. They come to clean her shoes and mess her dress up. And off she went and brought back all manner of garments, took Frummet by the hand and said, Come, Frummet, come, in-law-to-be; and they entered another room where she garbed her in silks and satins.

Then Frummet dashed off to the house of the holy Rabbi of Apta and told him all that had befallen; and he in his great humility heard her out and said, Eh, eh, and shook his head from side to side like a man who hears a great wonder. At the last the saint ordered that the two parties should leave the marriage portions with him. And in a little while the two fathers came, both Reb Yudel and Reb Vovi, and entrusted in his holy hand all that marriage portion of twenty-four thousand, each one counting out his own share. And the saint took the whole lot, mixed it all together and set his holy hand upon it.

And how the gold gleamed and shone under the holy hand; but all the treasures of the world shall pass, yet the word of the Lord shall remain forever. Then the rabbi said to Reb Vovi, Father-in-law, for the present return home with the bridegroom and all your kin, and return here when, God willing, the bride's garments will be ready. So they took their leave of Reb Yudel and returned home. And it was a great relief for Meshel, for they all knew his words were correct and they released him from his bonds.

THE BRIDAL CANOPY

Leaving Reb Vovi in Rohatin, let us return to Brod. In brief, within a few moments it was known from one end of the town to the other that The Name had had pity on Reb Yudel and had made him wealthy; and all the townsfolk came at once, old man, young man, scholar and dunce, from every corner and every street, people great and people small, worthy and honest, rogue and cheat, burghers stout and burghers tall, mean and poor, upstart and boor, noble and lout and beggars a rout, men of the mode and knights of the road, folk who had turned a pretty penny and worthy folk who had never seen any; and one and all they shook his hand, and said to him in voices bland, So you can see, beloved friend, how at the last your luck doth mend, would that the like did us attend; and good luck, good luck, everyone said, and the whole of the street was off its head. The worthy Frummet went out to meet them, to hear their words and then to greet them, and right away a feast she made, and a tablecloth for them she spread, and treated them to cake and buns, and all manner of good things at once, and even coffee to wash it down, after the fashion of folk of renown in those very days in Brod the town. And the neighbors came and bedecked the dwelling of the Hassid and beautified it in every manner of way and hung up flowers and blossoms, so that the cellar seemed fit for a king, and candelabra they brought in a wink, and lights of pure olive oil they lit, and with all love prepared the wicks and plaited together tapers of wax. The cellar glowed and the cellar grew bright; in the words of Scripture, the Jews saw light.

And all the tailors of Brod began to get busy sewing garments, garments for the bride, garments for her sisters, and garments for mother and father. And as they worked their mouths were filled with songs and praises to the All-Present, such as, "Who raiseth the poor from the ground, the needy from the muckheap", and like, "The Lord maketh poor and wealthy, bringeth down to Hell and raiseth up." How easy it is for the Holy and Blest One to take a poor man out of his poverty and give him property and wealth—just like a man who takes one thread out of a needle and puts another in its place. And since they were working up to their necks and higher in silks, they raised their voices so that the Holy and Blest One might hear and bear them in mind as well. Nor did the shoemakers sit idle; they waxed their threads and hammered their leather and sewed all shapes and sizes of shoes. For Reb Yudel they made shoes softer than silk, so that he might not disturb others when praying; for in his prayers he used to leap up and down and stamp his feet on the ground. For Frummet they made high shoes of deerskin with fringes on either side; for when Brod women put on shoes they make them look like birds flying through the air. For the bride and her sisters they made lacquer shoes which were as bright as a clear mirror. Brethren mine and friends, may you and I come to dance at our daughters' weddings in such shoes, amen.

And surely the artizans are worthy of favorable mention for turning nights into days and finishing their work in time, so that the Bridal Canopy might be erected in due and proper season; and since they did not stint their labor they were paid a fine price and could clothe and shoe themselves from their labors. For which reason Brod does not know the saying, Tailors go naked and shoemakers barefoot. And in providing the utensils of the body they did not forget the body but baked all kinds of bread and cooked flesh and fish aplenty.

Aye, Simeon Nathan was a wealthy man, and when he married off his daughter, the honey for the cakes had to be carried on no one knows how many shoulders. But what was all the wealth of Simeon Nathan, who depended upon flesh and blood, as compared with the wealth of that Hassid who received it direct from the Holy and Blest One? Yes, Shprintsa Pessel was a brisk woman. They say that when she wedded her daughter there was never a fowl in Shebush that she left unslaughtered. But Reb Yudel's wife expended more than all Shprintsa Pessel's outlay on fowls merely to buy eggs wherewith to give the loaves a gloss. Fine feasts she made as well, of bread with saffron, and salmon, and carp in order not to put shame upon those folk who could not afford expensive fish. Blest be He Who did not leave His Universe short of the wherewithal of satisfying human folk. They were not even short of Paltiel's brandy, which Paltiel brought when he and his wife came to participate in the rejoicing of Reb Yudel; and a little cart was hitched on after their own cart; and on it sat the dairyman, come to inform Reb Yudel that his daughter had borne a son.

Before the horses had been unharnessed along came Reb Ephraim, the hospitable, who never ate without having some poor person to table with him. Now that all the poor folk had gone to Brod and there was nobody left to eat with him, his wife feared that he might perish of hunger, God forbid, and brought him to Brod, bringing

an ovenful of bread and a waggon full of fowls and a string of corals
for the bride that had been made by their daughter Zevia. As soon
as he came they set wine and confects before him to restore his soul.
He broke off a crumb of cake and sipped a mouthful of wine, and
went red in the face for shame. If you did not see him when they set
something to eat and drink before him, you never saw gratitude in
your life. He that had given food and drink to half the world, as
you might say, now blushed like a child who has received a present.
Come hither, O ye shameless and froward beggars and mendicants,
and observe how a worthy man, wealthy, aristocratic and generous,
thinks that his companion has given him more than he deserves when
he gets the veriest trifle. It is unnecessary to mention that Reb
Zechariah came with him; for Brod folk esteem Brod, and never a
waggon comes to Brod without a Brod man in it.

But before Reb Zechariah had time to tell even one story who should
arrive but Heshel the enlightened maskil, naked as a German and
hungry as the end of a fast, his pockets empty, and his very face
relating how every manner of poverty held sway over him. And
what of your wisdom now, Heshel, when you used to declare that it
was a man's duty to learn external wisdoms, and made mock of
Reb Yudel and his companions who had no more than Torah, and yet
lived to see the truth of the saying in the Talmud that whosoever
mocks has his property diminishing. Not upon you, all ye wayfarers,
may there fall such an arrival. In no carriage he came, nor yet in a
tumble-down cart, but afoot, and sighing for shame that the Lord's
salvation from him did depart, and to every side he turned about, in
the hope that someone would give him food. And he observed the
honor of those that serve The Name, and tasted a whit of World to
Come where the righteous sit with their crowns on their heads and
are sustained by the brightness of God's Presence.

And before Reb Yudel could ask how he was other guests came.
And who were they but Tobiah and his wife of Polikrif village
with whom Reb Yudel had stayed on the Sabbath following Hanuka,
and whose house was full of rooms in each of which there was a bed, a
seat and a lamp for guests; and heaps of manure lay piled before
their windows to manure the fields and always remind them not to
be proud of their wealth. They had now taken a different course; for
they were going to ascend to the Land of Israel and plant them a
tree there after the fashion of Father Abraham; on the road they had

heard that Reb Yudel was raising the Bridal Canopy for his daughter, and so they came to rejoice with him.

Ere Reb Yudel could ask them how they were, fresh guests arrived. And they were Joshua Eleazar of Pedkomin, from whom Reb Yudel had learnt two things. A legacy had fallen to Joshua Eleazar, so now he was taking his wife to Lemberg, to Doctor Port at whose right hand stands the angel Raphael, so that he might cure her.

Said Reb Yudel, Though every man has two hundred and forty-eight members, and three hundred and sixty-five veins and sinews, I have never seen every member, vein and sinew striving to achieve itself an absolute perfection save in this man. But scarcely had Reb Yudel asked after his well-being than other guests arrived. And who might they be if not the old man of the water drinkers and his gentle spouse. That old man must indeed receive favorable mention, since but for him the wedding would have had to be deferred; for the government had passed a decree that Jews might not marry while they were minors; and he had gone and gathered together the thirty-six saints and had brought about the abrogation of the decree.

When his righteous wife saw the bride she raised her sweet voice and wished her a right good *mazal tov*. And drums were verily drumming at the time, as in the hour when Miriam, the prophetess, had uttered song. She and her husband, and Reb Yudel Nathanson, the supposed father of the bride, and his wife, acted as groomsmen for the bride and bridegroom respectively.

There is no reason to make a long tale of it; many indeed came to rejoice with the Hassid. Many of these had entreated him with loving-kindness when he was engaged on the injunction of the Bridal Canopy; other were friends whom he had met once or twice. That is, all except the miser whose bottle had broken and whose pockets had torn so that they could not hold the dribltets of oil and grains of rice from the shops of his debtors; and so he had died of starvation.

Besides which the rabbi who used to fast from Sabbath to Sabbath, but who used to consume more on the Sabbath than any ordinary man during the whole of the week, and from whose lips Reb Yudel had heard the meaning of the saying of olden time that there is no joy save in meat, had also departed this life, being summoned to the Upper Assembly because the angels were jealous of his fastings and men of his feastings.

When Reb Yudel saw how many of those who had aided him in

fulfilling the commandment of bringing the bride under the Bridal Canopy had arrived, he began to expect that Reb Yom Tov of Ushni village would come, and the old man he had met in the graveyard, also Kalman, the tailor, and those two gold vessels whom he had met in Zalozetz. What might bring them? Well, they might come to seek approbations from the sages of the Close on their fathers' works, or else they might be seeking subscribers in advance. But he had to give up hope of those who did not come, and was happy with those who did come.

And at the same time a woman dashed in in great excitement, and hastened to the bride whom she began embracing and kissing, saying, Pessele, listen and I'll tell you what our aunt Pessel after whom we're both named did; yesterday she appeared to me in dream and said, Go to Pessele and wish her *mazal tov;* and she even dug her nails into me so that I should listen to her and go; and I'm so overwrought that I forgot to bring you a present.

In short, she had fulfilled the desire of the dead; and we, similarly, may fulfill the words of the Living God in the Talmud where it is written that the dead must be set aside to make way for the bride, and therefore leave Pessel alone to rest in peace while we rejoice at the rejoicing of the bride. In brief everything was ready for the Bridal Canopy, all except one thing, namely, the bridegroom.

And in a little while a man came to state in due and proper style that the bridegroom was at the town gate. Behold with his family he did await east of the city the hour of his fate. Thereupon Frummet did on her fine gown, and went forth to lead him into the town. And Reb Yudel also went to lead him in, after due hospitality shown to his kin. With them went many on the part of the bride, who on foot did walk or in carriages ride. And they joyfully marched the bridegroom around with dances and many a musical sound. At home none were left for to do anything, and they cried, Hurrah, bridegroom, who art like a king. The jesters of Brod dressed up for to clown, and upon the bridegroom and his folk they came down, all dressed in garments of many a kind, like servants in front and like lordlings behind, some like to soldiers upon a parade, and hurrah for Sir Shefatyah, the bridegroom, they said, and in joust and in tourney they showed all their might, and the bridegroom, Sir Shefatyah, was pleased at the sight.

When Nuta saw how the whole town was rejoicing he regretted

not having gone forth to meet the groom. So he doubled over the
ends of his long coat under the girdle, got out his waggon and
cleaned it and polished it as it had been when he set out with Reb
Yudel about the injunction of the Bridal Canopy, went and hung a
bell on the neck of each horse and asked them, do you want to see
Pessele's bridegroom? At which they raised their forelegs to their
heads. So he harnessed them and off they went.

When he reached the bridegroom folk wished to thrust him out
of the road; but Reb Yudel said, Let him be, for he toiled with me
and was wearied for the sake of the commandment. So they at once
made room for him in the procession, and he got off the waggon
and gave his hand to the bridegroom in greeting. But before the
bridegroom could offer him his hand in return, Nuta had him up in
his arms and sitting on the waggon. Such a little foal as that, says
Nuta, if I don't put him on the waggon he'll be crushed by the people.
And Ivory and Peacock at once started lifting their legs and racing like eagles till they came back to town.

In town they took the groom to a fine house, namely, that of the
wealthy Reb Yudel Nathanson who had appointed a special room on
his behalf; and they sat him on a great chair and stood and sang
him song and praises; and the cantor sang him all manner of songs.
And fine bright youths came to greet him and sat down to try him
out and see his sharpness and knowledge of Torah and his wisdom,
till at the last their lips were worn to tatters. Whereupon they were
brought wine and confects and all kinds of fruit fried in honey; and
they drank, ate and drank again so that it did your heart good to see.
The marriage jester came with all the musicians, and they doubled
the joy with violins and cymbals and song and rhyme until the fine
folk of the town came to lead the groom to the Canopy.

When they entered, the marriage jester rose and said to Reb Yudel
Hassid, Reb Judah known as Reb Yudel, is it your desire to give
your daughter Pessele to this bridegroom, his honor Master Shefatyah
known as Sheftel? Reb Judah known as Reb Yudel, is it your desire
to give your daughter Pessele to this bridegroom, his honor Master
Shefatyah known as Sheftel? But Reb Yudel made no answer. Thereupon the marriage jester asked a third time, Reb Judah known as
Reb Yudel, I ask you for a third time, is it your desire to give your
daughter to this here bridegroom? Thereupon Reb Yudel answered,
And didn't our rabbis of blessed memory say in the Talmud that forty

days ere the fashioning of the child it is decreed in Heaven that the daughter of so-and-so shall wed with so-and-so, and who am I to say I don't desire, God forbid. At which the marriage jester at once began singing:

Hurrah hurrah, let us all be glad
Now that the bridegroom has come to Brod.

Up wi' you players, and take your tools,
Fiddle and don't stand there like fools.

Start up a tune and bang the drum
Now that the bridegroom to town has come.

Shout out aloud, burst into song,
And the whole town will come and dance in the throng.

And you my brethren without a care,
Clap your hands to honor the pair,

Beloved and pleasant as in tales of yore,
Mistress Pessele and Reb Sheftel Shor,

And in honor of his father by all men discerned,
Our wealthy Master Reb Vovi the learned,

And in honor of the father known to us each one,
Namely the Hassid Reb Yudel Nathanson,

And in honor of their wives whose names I don't know,
And of families and those who have come for the show

From all the world over, from Brod and Rohatin
May they enjoy themselves for ever with their kin.

While he was singing Frummet came in and began crying out aloud at the top of her voice, Has such a thing ever been heard? Here are the bride and bridegroom sitting and fasting, and he stands here rhyming his rhymes. But the marriage jester, paying no attention to her, took the groom by the arm and sang:

O come my love to meet the bride and bid her how-d'ye-do,
She'll be glad for to see her lad, and we'll all be glad too.

THE BRIDAL CANOPY

Have you ever seen the like, cried Frummet, of this fellow whose rhymes stick faster to him than thorns to the hand of a drunkard. Make an end and we'll take the groom to the Canopy. Don't you know that bride and bridegroom have been fasting all day long? Said the jester:

> O Frummet, give ear and let me speak,
>   And, bride mother, list to me,
> Restrain your tempestuous soul awhile,
>   Nor don't think my song too free.
>
> 'Tis not for me nor my father's house
>   I sing sweet song and rhymes do weave;
> And yet like lions you roar at me
>   The whole o' the day from morn to eve.
>
> I was a lad who old am grown
>   And yet for myself no song have sung,
> My own soul's sorrow is stored within
>   The while I bid my soul give tongue
>
> To honor you all and honor your house
>   Do I utter praises and poems weave;
> May two in a family, one in a town
>   Hark to my words and come to believe.
>
> But if that same you do not desire,
>   Between my teeth I shall keep my tongue,
> And if my heart thinks a pleasant thought,
>   I shall tell my soul, let it not be sung.

The jester having finished his Plaint, all those present rose and set the groom in their midst and went forth to lead him beneath the Canopy. Some wondered at the jester who possessed a ready response no matter what was said, and some sorrowed for that after a lifetime spent in rhyming it was doubtful whether, once he was dead, even as much as a single rhyme would be engraved on his tombstone. In brief, all those present rose and accompanied the groom to the place where the Canopy had been erected.

As soon as they entered the cantor began singing, "May He Who is mighty over all bless bridegroom and bride." And the bride made a treble circuit of the groom as it is written, "The female shall go round the male." And three times for the three fashions in which a woman is acquired, and for the sake of the saying of the sages of blessed memory in the Talmud, "Every man who has no wife remains without good, without blessing and without joy"; also for their blessed saying, "He remains without Torah, without a wall and without peace"; and finally for the three times that man and woman are joined. The first is the time preceding birth when, as we have learnt, the Heavenly Voice proclaims forty days prior to the fashioning of the babe that so-and-so is intended for so-and-so, and once one or other is born the two souls go asunder for a number of years until one recognizes its fellow and they rejoin at the hour of marriage. The third time is the one following death, when the souls unite never more to be separate in the World that is all of it Good.

In short, bride and bridegroom were standing under the canopy, and the joy was increasing by leaps and bounds. What shall we tell and what shall we omit? If we tell that they ate and drank and danced, we have already heard the like at the tale of the wedding of that lad which was related by Israel Solomon of Buczacz, and anybody who repeats himself leads to boredom. And so we shall instead tell how the holy Rabbi of Apta, his own honored self, conducted the ceremony, and what was more stayed with the in-laws and gladdened the heart of bridegroom and bride with his tales and exaggerations, as was his holy fashion of pointing a moral by adorning a tale.

Who shall tell of the qualities garbed in those his tales, or make known even a whit of the secrets dread and awesome that were concealed in each and every word. When he had made a wedding feast for his son they had had to send for two waggonloads of straw for the guests to pick their teeth with. He had made his son a fur coat so thick that a mounted soldier with a lance held upright in his arm could be hidden in the fur. But in case you suppose that that coat must be heavy you are quite wrong, for it could all be folded into a walnut shell.

And ere the old man of the water drinkers left Brod he took the holy Rabbi of Apta into an inner room and they had a conversation on their own matters; and he informed him that it had been decided that he should go to Jassy in order to purify the air there; and he promised him that he would have the merit of finding a grave in the Land of Israel. And both things were fulfilled; for he was appointed Father of the Court in Jassy, and he merited to have his body return to the bosom of its mother.

Nor need you wonder because you may have seen his grave at the Holy Congregation of Mezibez; it is known that on the night when the saint died, a noise was heard of a beating upon the windows of the Assembly House of the Ashkenazic community in Tiberias, and a voice crying, Come forth to accompany the Rabbi of Apta; and when they went forth they saw thousands upon thousands of souls following the bier all the way to the graveyard; and in the morning they saw that the soil had been turned. And there is a tale of a certain saint who used to visit his home after his demise; on one occasion he arrived late and they asked him why. He replied, I was busy showing the way to the saints of the Land of Israel, who came forth to greet the Rabbi of Apta when he came just now to let his body rest among them.

But how fine and sweet was the sitting of the fathers-in-law together, both the real fathers-in-law and Reb Yudel Nathanson, the supposed father-in-law. And when folk stood behind them and called out, Long life to you, Reb Yudel, both of the Reb Yudels would turn their heads around together and reply, Long life, long life. And Nuta, the waggoner, in particular did wonders for to gladden bridegroom and bride. As he had accepted the trouble of toiling along the roads with the Hassid, so he merited to sit and to rejoice with him. And you were the one who said that a man should not leave his appointed sphere. But with Reb Yudel it is different, for the Holy and Blest One aided him. And when he came they rejoiced with him exceedingly and said, so you're Nuta who went traveling with Reb Yudel; if it hadn't been for you Reb Yudel would never have come to all this.

But Nuta being modest would not accept all the praise as belonging to him, but associating himself with his horses replied after this fashion, Ivory and Peacock first, and I only follow. When the poor folk saw how affectionately the rich folk entreated Nuta, they almost knocked him over in order to shake him by the hand. But Nuta handled them after the fashion of the wise merchant of whom Reb Zechariah told, in order that his hands might remain free to grab what was going in the way of flesh and fish. When he had eaten and drunk he became more than happy and pretended to be an enlightened maskil and spoke German and danced before the bride calling her, *Herr* Nathanson, meaning Mister Nathanson. Nonetheless he did not forget his piousness, and when he saw the musicians hiding meat in the drum he went and put butter cake into the drum as well, thereby making the meat prohibited according to law; in order that they should not err through eating a stolen meal.

In brief they sat there all night long, eating and drinking and happy and glad, and all those with voices sang; and they danced and sang the songs of Reb Joel, the marriage jester of Shebush, and the songs of Reb Ozer, the jester of Rohatin, and the songs of Reb Samuel, the jester of Zolkov. And the Brod singers made them still more joyful and sang songs sweeter than honey, such as the tale of Weasel and Well, and the tale of the Sweet and Loving; but since these are well known they do not need to be repeated here.

And here we might have made an end, all being for the best, bringing bridegroom and bride to their home and their couch; but in the honor of Jerusalem, of whom the Psalmist said, "Let my tongue cleave to the roof of my mouth if I do not remember thee, if I do not vaunt Jerusalem at all my rejoicings", we shall mention the man of Jerusalem who was present on that occasion, and we shall mention the fine thing he did in honor of the bridegroom.

There was a certain man present who had been born in the Land of Israel, and who, by reason of the straits and distresses of the times, had been forced to depart from the Land of Israel; and he chanced to find his way to the Holy Congregation of Brod, where he lay sick of the fever which pierced his body and burnt him and shook him backward and forward and from side to side; and he came to understand that the Holy and Blest One had brought the sickness upon him only as punishment for departing from the Land of Israel; for as long as he had dwelt in the Land of Israel he had been hale and hearty, but ever since he had departed from thence, each fresh day in succession was worse than those that had gone before. Day by day he sought ways and means of returning to the Land of Israel and prostrating him even upon the dunghills thereof; and he was in and out of Reb Yudel's house, where they conversed at length together on all that concerns the Land of Israel, seeing that Reb Yudel had some knowledge of this matter, his own heart being there although his limbs and members were yet in exile; and he who had

THE BRIDAL CANOPY

eyes wherewith to see could observe round the head of Reb Yudel a great light deriving of the Light of the Land. And therefore Reb Yudel felt bound by powerful bonds of sympathy to this Jew who had been forced to depart from the Land; and they traversed it from end to end in their conversations, backwards and forwards, like princes walking to and fro in the halls of their father, the king.

At the last Reb Yudel brought him to his home to rejoice with him at the wedding of his daughter; and the Jerusalemite sat watching the rejoicing of Reb Yudel and his daughters and all the fine folk of the town, who practised pilpulisms with the groom and tested his wisdom and knowledge of Torah; and at last his heart was roused to give enjoyment to bridegroom and bride. He thought upon the blessings wherein the exaltation of the New Jerusalem is compared with the joy of bridegroom and bride, in the words of the prophets, Isaiah and Jeremiah. And his heart was stirred exceedingly when he remembered Jerusalem in ruins, and all the deeds of his host, the Hassid, who had resided in the tents of the Torah, accepting whatever troubles each day might bring in order not to be parted from the study of the Torah; even when he had made the rounds of the countryside for the sake of the injunction of the Bridal Canopy his heart longed for matters of Torah; and by reason of the Torah he had merited the sight of his daughter's joy with her spouse, that outstanding student of the Torah whom he had found for her. Yet even so he had not reached the half of his joy, which he would attain in the day that the words "making Zion to rejoice in her sons" are brought about.

So stirred was he that he mounted the table, rested his head on his hand and began in a sweet voice singing and rhyming rhymes the like of which no ear had ever heard; even the womenfolk, who cannot enjoy the honey of our Holy Tongue, clapped their hands for joy to hear him; and since his speech was uttered slowly and clearly after the fashion of the Men of the Holy Tongue, it entered the hearts of all who hearkened. He told how the twenty-two letters of the Hebrew Alphabet took on flesh and became the children of a childless pair who had maintained the study of the Torah in a cave despite the decree of the government; of the studies of the twenty-two, each one finding a work of Bible, Talmud and external wisdoms to study, the name of which began with the initial letter of his own name; how each wedded himself a wife whose name began with the

[371]

same letter as his own; and how they all ascended to the Land of Israel and each settled in a place beginning with his own letter.

And indeed it is a most worthy work, and is added in the Hebrew to the tale of Reb Yudel for love of the Torah; yet the translator despairing of retelling it in English, by reason of that greater light of the Hebrew tongue which shineth therein and can be given again in no other of the seventy speeches of Mankind, he has seen fit to omit this Ballad of the Letters. For which omission he craves the indulgence of the reader, suggesting that he who would know more of this ballad should betake himself to the Hebrew. And if he know no Hebrew, let him learn, as Frey Luis de Leon advised the Inquisitors.

So sweet was this ballad that when the Jerusalemite had made an end of singing it, all the fine folk of the city rose and kissed him upon the brow and honored him greatly; and they ordered that the ballad should be copied out as a memorial to the occasion. Thereupon the poet sat him down and copied it out, writing it in the blackest of black ink, so that our righteous Messiah, may he come and speedily amen, might see how black this long and bitter Exile hath made the faces of Israel. When he saw his work in writing his heart was stirred even more, his eyes filled with tears and he said, Lord of the Universe, all my thoughts and all my talk are of nothing save the Land of Israel; this Abraham went up to the Land of Israel, this Tanhum went up, this Baruch went up, this Shalom of whom I wrote went up, all of whom I wrote merited to ascend to the Land of Israel; may it be Thy will

> That just as I now have told of the might
> And worth of the upright who live in Exile,
> The Lord of Hosts will bring me from my plight
> And give me the spirit to write double of them
> When we sing the great and mighty song while
> He returneth the captives of Zion and Jerusalem.

But now to return to Reb Yudel. In brief, Reb Yudel married off Pessele, his daughter, and also found the husbands of Blume and Gittele, wedding causing wedding, as folk say; for there were a number of youths present who showed that the glory of their youth was their power in Torah and wisdom; and they pilpulized and argued with the groom at his wedding address. And the Hassid and his wife saw the children of their daughters, and lived in wealth and honor, all transient successes being united and joined in them; and at the end of their days it was their merit to ascend to the Holy Land to be given light by the Light of Life.

Were we to relate all the happenings that befell Reb Yudel and Frummet his wife from the time they departed from Brod in a waggon until they came to the river Danube, and from the time they took ship for to sail the great seas, we would never come to an end; yet to relate the praises of Reb Yudel we must tell that he accepted all troubles and distresses with joy, and would say that all the misfortunes of the world were as nought against the future joy of being in the Land of Israel. And for many a year ere he went up to the Land he had his eyes covered with a kerchief because he did not desire to use his eyes more Without the Land; and he dwelt before the Lord in the Land of Life, flying in the heights of the intellect and doing all those correctional measures whereby a man shall live in This World and the Next World; and he wrote works in the Holy Spirit.

The story-teller has made an end,
So the poet a little rhyme will lend.
Ended is the tale of the Bridal Canopy,
May the Blessed God our deliverer be,
May the fear of Him remain in our hearts,
And may King Messiah soon come to these parts,

AMEN

Work of translation ended and completed in Jerusalem,
praises and glory to
God the Creator, on the Eve of the month of
Nisan, 5697 A. M. Revision completed
on the Twenty-fifth of Iyyar, 5697 A. M., the day
the Three Martyrs were buried.

GLOSSARY

ADAR: Hebrew month; February or March.

ALFASI: Isaac Alfasi (eleventh century), author of a famous talmudic compilation.

ALSHECH: Rabbi Moses Alshech, sixteenth-century teacher, preacher, and casuist; disciple of Josef Karo; lived in the Kabbalist community of Safed, Palestine.

ARI: *see* Isaac Luria.

ASHKENAZIC: pertaining to the Ashkenazim, Jews of Central European tradition, as opposed to the Sefardim, Jews of the Spanish tradition, from whom they differ in ritual and in their pronunciation of Hebrew.

BABYLONIAN TALMUD: *see* Gemara.

BEHAYA: Bahya ibn Pakuda, Spain, end of eleventh century; religious philosopher; author of *The Duties of the Heart*.

BEMA: platform in the center of the synagogue upon which the Torah is read and certain prayers are recited.

BNEI KEDEM (the Sons of the East): Transjordanian tribes known for their wisdom (*see* I Kings 5:10).

CLOSE (*or* Kloiz): name given from the sixteenth century on in Central and Eastern Europe to a house of talmudic study, usually attached to a synagogue.

COUNCIL OF THE FOUR LANDS: the autonomous central organization of Polish-Lithuanian Jewry, sixteenth to eighteenth centuries.

COVENANT OF FATHER ABRAHAM: circumcision (*see* Genesis 17:1–14).

DEPARTURE OF THE QUEEN: the conclusion of the Sabbath, which is symbolically presented as a queen (or a bride).

DIVINE PRESENCE (Shechina): divine hypostasis indwelling in the world and sharing the exile of Israel.

EIDELS, SAMUEL: *see* Maharsho.

EIGHTEEN BLESSINGS: one of the oldest parts of the Jewish liturgy, occurring in the weekday prayer service.

ELLUL: the month preceding the Days of Awe (roughly, September); a period of preparation for the solemn season.

EMDEN, JACOB: son of Haham Zvi Ashkenazi, 1697–1776; rabbi in Emden; author of many books on Jewish laws, polemical pamphlets (anti-Sabbathian), and an autobiography, *Megillath Sefer*.

ETHICS OF THE FATHERS: a tractate of the Mishnah dedicated to ethics and the glorification of the study of the Torah.

FAST OF THE FIRSTBORN: held on the day preceding Passover, commemorating the sparing of the Israelite firstborn during the tenth plague in Egypt.

FAST OF GEDALIAH: commemorating the murder of Gedaliah, governor of Jerusalem after the destruction of the Temple (586 B.C.E.).

FEAST OF TABERNACLES (Sukkot): an eight-day holiday (in the Land of Israel seven days) beginning on the fifth day after the Day of Atonement. It commemorates the wandering of the Israelites in the desert.

FOUR QUESTIONS: recited by a child at the Passover Seder, beginning with: "Why does this night differ from all other nights?"

[375]

THE BRIDAL CANOPY

GAON (pl., geonim): lit., excellence; title given to outstanding rabbis.

THE GATES OF ZION: a seventeenth-century collection of prayers for various occasions.

GEMARA (completion): part of the Talmud which consists of discussions of the Mishnah. There is a distinction between the Gemara of the Babylonian Talmud and of the Palestinian Talmud.

GENERAL CORRECTION (Ha-Tikkun ha-kelali): a penitential prayer composed by Rabbi Nahman of Bratzlav, an eighteenth-nineteenth-century hassidic master.

GOLEM: a robot in human form, created by magical means, especially by the use of divine names.

HAGADA: the text of the Passover home service.

HAHAM ZVI ASHKENAZI: Moravia-Salonica-Amsterdam-London-Lemberg, ca. 1660–1718; talmudist; was involved in anti-Sabbathian polemics; author of responsa.

HALITZA: a religious-legal ceremony, enacted in order to free an unmarried man from the obligation to marry his brother's childless widow (see Deuteronomy 25:5–9).

HANUKA (dedication): an eight-day holiday (Feast of Lights) beginning on the twenty-fifth day of Kislev (November or December), commemorating the re-dedication of the Sanctuary by the Maccabees (167 B.C.E.).

HAROSETH: Passover Seder dish made of fruits, nuts, and wine, to symbolize the mortar used for brick-making by the Hebrews in Egypt.

HASSID: lit., a pious man; a follower of Hassidism, religious movement founded by Israel the Baal Shem.

HAVDALAH ("separation" of the sacred and the profane): benediction at the conclusion of the Sabbath and holidays.

HOLY TONGUE: the Hebrew language.

HOUSE OF STUDY (Bet ha-Midrash): a place of learning and worship; usually identical with the House of Prayer.

HURWITZ, ISAIAH: Eastern and Central Europe, sixteenth-seventeenth century; talmudist and mystic; author of the *Two Tablets of the Covenant*, and compiler of a prayer book; called *Sheloh* after the initial letters of his work (*Shene Luhot Haberit*).

ISRAEL BAAL SHEM TOV (Master of the Good Name): founder of the hassidic movement (1700–1760).

ISSERLES, MOSES: Poland, sixteenth century; wrote glosses to the *Shulchan Aruch*, adjusting the Sephardic work to Polish and German usage.

IYYAR: Hebrew month; April or May.

JERUSALEM TALMUD: see Gemara.

KABBALA: lit., tradition; Jewish mysticism; its writings pointed to the deeper layers of religion, which it represented as the authentic "tradition" of Israel.

KIDDUSHIN: a talmudic tractate dealing with the laws of marriage.

LESSER PASSOVER (Pesach sheni): the holiday celebrated one month after the "first," or original, Passover and observed by those who were prevented from celebrating the original festival (see Numbers 9:9 ff.).

LURIA, ISAAC (also called the "Ari"): the outstanding representative of the later Kabbala; 1534–72; head of the mystical school at Safed, Palestine.

THE BRIDAL CANOPY

MAHARSHO: Rabbi Samuel Eidels, Eastern Europe, sixteenth-seventeenth century; noted commentator of the Talmud.
MAIMONIDES: Moses Maimonides, foremost Jewish thinker and scholar (1135–1204).
MASKIL (pl., maskilim): followers of the enlightenment movement.
MATZOS (or matzoth): unleavened bread eaten during Passover in memory of the unleavened bread prepared in haste by Israel's ancestors in Egypt.
MAZAL TOV: good luck; greeting extended at festive occasions.
MEIR OF PRESMISLEIN: hassidic master in Przemysl, Galicia, 1787–1858.
MEZUZAH (pl., mezuzoth): parchment scroll containing scriptural texts, attached to the doorpost of a Jewish home.
MIDRASH: exposition; exegesis based on Scripture; also, works recording such exposition.
MINYAN: quorum of ten men necessary for a communal religious service.
MISHNAH: the earliest and basic part of the Talmud. There are six parts (Orders) of the Mishnah.

NATAL NIGHT (or nital night): popular term for Christmas Eve (dies natalis, birthday [of Jesus]); according to custom, the study of Torah was omitted that night and people played cards.
NEW MOON: the first day of the new month is celebrated as a minor festival, and a special meal is prepared.
NIGHT PRAYERS OF PENITENCE: special services held a week before the New Year.
NINTH OF AB: fast commemorating the destructions of Jerusalem.
NISAN: Hebrew month; March or April.

OBADIAH OF BERTINORO: Italy and Palestine, fifteenth-sixteenth century; noted commentator of the Mishnah.
OG, KING OF BASHAN: see Numbers 21:33 ff. He was noted for his giant body.
ORAL TORAH: oral tradition which supplements the "Written Torah." In the course of time the "Oral Torah" was committed to writing (the Talmud).

PASSOVER: eight-day holiday (in the Land of Israel seven days) beginning on the fifteenth day of Nisan (March or April) and commemorating the exodus from Egypt.
PERISHA: commentary on Jacob ben Asher's legal work Arbaa Turim, by Joseph ben Alexander ha-Kohen, a disciple of Moses Isserles.
PILPUL: a dialectic, critical method used in talmudic study, especially in Poland from the sixteenth century on.
PREPARED TABLE: see Shulchan Aruch.
PURIM: the feast of "lots" (Esther 9:25); holiday commemorating the defeat of the wicked Haman. It is observed by the reading of the Book of Esther and by games and masquerades.

RABBI JUDAH THE PRINCE: compiler of the Mishnah (end of second century).
RASHI: abbreviation for Rabbi Solomon (ben) Isaak (of Troyes); classical commentator of the Bible and the Babylonian Talmud (died 1105).
REB: Mister; sometimes Rabbi.
ROSH: Asher ben Yehiel, Germany and Spain, thirteenth-fourteenth century; outstanding talmudic scholar.

THE BRIDAL CANOPY

SABBETHAI COHEN: a seventeenth-century commentator on parts of the *Shulchan Aruch*.

SANHEDRIN: the high council in the time of the Second Temple. Also, a talmudic tractate.

SHECHINA: *see* Divine Presence.

SHOFAR: ram's horn blown during the service for the New Year.

SHULCHAN ARUCH (Prepared Table): code of Jewish law, compiled by Josef Karo (sixteenth century).

SIX ORDERS OF THE MISHNAH: see Mishnah.

SPOILT SCROLLS: scrolls of the Torah in which a scribal error has been found or in which the writing has lost its perfection. Such scrolls cannot be used in worship.

THE STRAITS OF THE TIMES (*Zuk ha-Ittim*): a chronicle of persecutions in the course of the Chmielnicki rebellion, 1648-49.

TALLITH: prayer shawl; worn by male adults at morning prayer.

TANA DEBEI ELIYAH: a midrashic work from the early Middle Ages.

TAZ: abbreviation for *Tur Zahar*, a commentary on the *Shulchan Aruch*, by Rabbi David ben Samuel of Lemberg (seventeenth century).

TEFILLIN: leather cubicles containing scriptural texts inscribed on parchment. They are attached to the left arm and the head during the weekday morning service. They are a sign between God and Israel.

TEVETH: Hebrew month (December or January); the tenth of Teveth: a fast commemorating the beginning of the siege of Jerusalem by the Babylonians (586 B.C.E.).

THIRD SABBATH FEAST: a meal on Sabbath afternoon to which Kabbalists and Hassidim attach mystical significance.

THIRTY-SIX HIDDEN SAINTS: perfectly just people in any given generation; their identity is unknown; their existence is necessary for the security and survival of the world.

TOSEPHTA: parallel work to the Mishnah.

TOSSAFFISTS: *see* Tossafoth.

TOSSAFOTH (Addenda): explanatory notes on the Talmud by Franco-German scholars of the twelfth to fourteenth centuries.

TRACTATE OF THE FASTS (Taanit): a talmudic tractate.

TURIM, OR ARBAA TURIM (Four Rows): legal work by Jacob ben Asher, Germany-Spain, thirteenth-fourteenth century.

UPPER ASSEMBLY: in heaven.

UPPER EDEN: highest rung of the heavenly paradise.

WISDOM OF SIRACH: Book of Wisdom, or Ecclesiasticus, by Joshua ben Sira (*or* Sirach), ca. 200 B.C.E. Included in the biblical Apocrypha.

YALKUT: a midrashic compilation.

YESHIVA: talmudic academy.

ZELIG: published the commentaries of his father, Benjamin ben Aaron.

ZOHAR (The Book of Splendor): chief work of the earlier Kabbala (end of thirteenth century).

TRANSLATOR'S NOTE

The Bridal Canopy deals with a culture, rounded off and complete in itself, which has been forced into the background of Jewish
life, and which, in any case, has been all but unknown to western
Jewry for a century. At the period of the story the culture in question was just commencing to sense the inroads of the modes of life
and thought current beyond the walls of the ghetto; but it was still
powerful enough to feel itself quite secure against any such inroads.
It was a culture based on an absolute and unquestioning religious
faith which did not depend upon any of the contingencies of time,
place and circumstance. This faith provides the entire background
for the story; and so some sketch of the world of a God-fearing Jew
in Eastern Europe (more particularly in Galicia) round about the
year 1820 is necessary in order fully to appreciate the tale.

From the fourteenth century the Jews of Poland had constituted
a middle class between the nobles and the serfs. Certain German
groups connected with the Hanseatic League held a similar position,
but maintained external political connections which the Jews lacked.
Poland was one of the last countries to maintain the feudal system;
the Polish nobility was engaged for hundreds of years in an effort to
prevent the kings centralizing power in their hands as had happened
in Western Europe; and the Jews within the territories of each noble
were his exclusive property. As was the usual state of affairs in the
Middle Ages the Jews entered the territory in question by virtue of
special contract and could be expelled at the expiry of the contract, or
at earlier dates if the lord of the manor so desired. Within such territory they were at the disposal of their lord, who used to lease
mills and inns to them, or had them act as his factors and undertake
all the thousand and one other middle-man duties which might fall
their way. Jews were goldsmiths, bankers and moneylenders, and at
one time all Polish money was minted by Jews; there are still Polish
coins in existence with Hebrew legends upon them.

As time went on and the institution of the Free Cities reached
Poland, it naturally happened that Jews, as far as permitted, settled
in them to be free of the none-too-light hands of their feudal lords.
In opposition, others of those same lords set up their own towns

[379]

round their castles and contracted with Jews to come and dwell there. The presence of Jews in towns immediately led to the growth of a Jewish artizan class. The existence of a large trading class led of necessity to the growth of a Jewish carter class.

In the early part of the sixteenth century the kings of Poland established a special poll tax on the Jews. For the collection of this tax a special council was established, consisting of representatives of Jewry throughout Poland. This council was known as the Council of the Four Lands (these being the four parts of the then Poland), and it was given very extensive rights of internal jurisdiction in Jewish affairs. Each of the Four Lands, again, had its own council. The Council of the Four Lands continued to meet until the second half of the eighteenth century, when it was finally abrogated; but the memory of it was still fresh in Jewish life at the period dealt with in *The Bridal Canopy*.

In the year 1648 the Cossacks, who guarded the then Polish marches beyond the Dnieper against the Turks and Tartars, rose in revolt against Poland. Their originally peaceful revolt coincided with the death of the Polish king, and this led to a complete state of anarchy within Poland on account of the peculiar constitution of that country. The Polish nobles, in an effort to prevent the centralization of power in the hands of the kings, had at a rather earlier period established Poland as a "Republic" ruled by a king who was elected for life. The king was dead; there was nobody to direct the state pending a new election; each noble began acting for himself; and the Cossacks, aided by the Tartars, poured across Poland, burning, looting, murdering Jews, nobles and Roman Catholic priests; but most of all the former who were the least defended, although they stood shoulder to shoulder with the Poles in defending the cities. The horrors of the period are recorded in a number of contemporary Hebrew works and have not yet faded from Jewish folk memory in Eastern Europe. According to one account, over seven hundred communities were destroyed and six hundred thousand Jews massacred. The Cossacks passed through the territory covered by Agnon in the present story; and, since a hundred years ago the tradition was still stronger than at present, it is not surprising that his Reb Yudel knows of all its details; nor that the special fast commemorating the evils of 1648 should still have been kept up. The very whisper of a phrase such as "fleeing from the Wrath of the Oppressor" could still conjure up an extremely vivid meaning, as related in the tale of that name (p. 141).

One of the results of these evils was the growth of the Messianic Movement of Sabbethai Zevi, who converted to Islam at Constantinople in 1666. Many of his followers converted with him, and descendants of his crypto-Jewish sect are still to be found in Salonica; among them were numbered many of the Young Turk leaders executed by order of Mustapha Kemal Pasha (Ataturk) in Turkey soon after World War I. Other Jews, again, remained secret believers in Sabbethai Zevi and in his mission, and are supposed to have passed on the belief to their descendants for several generations. In the first half of the eighteenth century there began a second Messianic Movement within the borders of Poland, centering round the person of Jacob Frank. This movement too led beyond the borders of Jewry, for Frank and his followers accepted Catholicism. By so doing they all became gentlefolk, in accordance with the provisions of Polish law in cases of the conversion of Jews; there are very few Polish noble families which do not now contain a considerable percentage of Jewish blood derived from followers of this sect.

At almost the same time as the latter movement there began the Hassidic sect, which has been the greatest new spiritual force within Jewry the world over during the past two centuries. It is the internal world of this sect which is characterized in the person of Reb Yudel Hassid, the hero of *The Bridal Canopy*. The old Adam of this person is entirely subdued by the highly specialized training he has given his soul in accordance with the teachings of the Hassidic saints; yet nonetheless he remains a human being. But the nature of the Hassidic attitude toward the world and God will be dealt with below.

By the end of the eighteenth century Poland had been partitioned, and Galicia had passed into the hands of His Imperial Majesty, the Austrian Kaiser. This ensured the introduction of certain foreign ideas into the ghetto. At the same time, the end of the eighteenth century was marked by the "Enlightenment" or *Haskala* school of German Jewry, headed by Moses Mendelssohn. This school of thought was already exercising its effect on Galician Jewry by the time of Reb Yudel, though he knows nothing about it and is unaffected by it when he meets it, as related in the account of his debate with Heshel, the "enlightened." It should be mentioned that the Galician stream of Enlightenment was the direct progenitor of the state of mind which produced active Jewish Nationalism toward the end of the nineteenth century.

Such was the external world in which Jews such as Reb Yudel lived. The Polish noble was no longer the sole law in his own domain; but the day was not so far distant since he had been. The average Jew felt that he had escaped the worst horrors of the past, and did not look forward to the future with apprehension; but for the moment he was somewhere out of Past, Present and Future, basking in the light of the Torah as expounded by the particular Hassidic saint in whom he put his trust. Which leads to the spiritual world within which East European Jewry, for the greater part, then lived and moved and had its being.

Jewish tradition postulates a peculiar relationship between Jewry and God. This relationship was established between God and Abraham by the Covenant recorded in Genesis XV, a Covenant for all ages. It was later renewed, and to this day is renewed for every Jewish male by the Covenant of Circumcision, which makes the Jew a full member of Jewry and a participant in the Covenant with God. At a later period God entrusted the Torah, through Moses, to Israel as an everlasting heritage. It is this Torah which has shaped and bounded the spiritual life of Jewry, whatever the sect, to the present day. Despite certain experiments carried out in the teeth of bitter opposition in Communist Russia, the Torah looks as though it will still remain the potent factor in Jewish life which it always has been.

The Torah is more than the Law. It is the entire corpus of Jewish lore and tradition; and as such it is but an earthly manifestation of the eternal Spirit of Righteousness and Truth which preceded Creation. Here on earth it is of necessity bounded and limited by human language, perceptions and thought; but the basic element in Torah is the eternal one, not the manifestations, which may vary from time to time and from place to place. Like the oak tree contained in the kernel, the *entire* Torah can be found in the Pentateuch if you know *how* to look—the entire Torah with all the ramifications and developments which have developed therein throughout the ages. And hence the Talmud states that all the Torah, in all its developments to the very last, was revealed to Moses upon Mount Sinai.

Jewry's feeling toward God and the Torah found expression at every point of life, for the Torah covered them all; and day by day, at the commencement of the Evening Prayers, the observant Jew recites:

"Thou hast loved the House of Israel Thy People with an everlasting love; Torah and commandments, statutes and judgments, hast Thou taught us. Therefore, O Lord our God, we shall converse of Thy statutes when we lie down and when we rise up; and shall rejoice in the words of Thy Torah and in Thy commandments forever. *For they are our life and our length of days, and we shall meditate upon them by day and night.* And take not away Thy love from us forever. Blessed art Thou, O Lord, loving Thy people Israel."

The Torah was holy, and its holiness extended to the language in which it had been revealed. What was more, its holiness extended to all its developments throughout the ages, which were, as said above, in any case implicit in the original revelation. The Pentateuch, and in a lesser degree the rest of the Bible, was considered as the Written Torah, and as such had to be preserved intact; but growing out of it came the Talmud, which was the Oral Torah and was only written down when that step became absolutely necessary to preserve it for future generations.

The basis of the Talmud was the Mishnah, providing the applications of the Torah, on the basis of the letter and the spirit, to daily life according to the scholars who lived in northern Palestine at the end of the second century C.E. This Mishnah was studied in Palestine and in Babylonia; scholars commented upon and discussed it in both countries, their additions being finally collected as the Gemara. There are two Talmuds, that of Palestine and that of Babylon, but both are based on the same Mishnah and frequently serve to corroborate and complement one another. The Talmud which has exercised the greater influence on Jewry is the Babylonian.

Besides the historical and geographical divisions, there is a more important one in the actual text of the Talmud. That is the division into *Halacha* or Law and *Agada* or Legend. Naturally Halacha is far more than Law and Agada than Legend, but the two terms will serve. Halacha has provided the basis for Jewish behavior and social custom throughout the ages, particularly wherever and whenever Jewry enjoyed the local autonomy which usually went with the ghetto. Agada expresses by proverbs, maxims, legends, parables, fables, biblical exegesis and what you will, the spirit underlying the Halacha. What is more, Agada unites with the entire stream of extra-Talmudic homiletic literature dating from much the same ages and parts and known as the Midrashic literature. Rabbinical legal literature expanded the Halacha as the conditions of Jewish life required, and continues so to expand it, along its own lines, to our own times. And in one form or another the same is true of the Agada.

These, however, are the exoteric Torah which comes from the application of the revealed eternal principles to daily life; and, daily life being the common fate of all men, the observance of the exoteric Torah is incumbent upon all Jews. Since the Torah, however, is of external origin it is not surprising that it should also be a guide to esoteric knowledge and to those eternal mysteries which lie beyond the senses and beyond those particular varieties of space and time by which we are imprisoned. Naturally a key is necessary to unlock this esoteric meaning, and that key has been provided Jewry in the Kabbala—which means both "Tradition" and "Reception." The Kabbala was the special study of the Mekubal, the "Received One" or "Initiate." A Jew who refused to consider this esoteric meaning as anything more than a tissue of fantasies was just as good a Jew as any other; in the eyes of the Kabbalists he proved himself to be blind but not, therefore, a sinner.

There are two sides to the Kabbala, the theoretical and the practical. The former is a cosmogony and a philosophical system; a number of systems, rather, all fused into one by a fundamentally identical outlook upon the Universe. Practical Kabbala is the outcome of an attempt to put the theoretical Kabbala to use for the purposes which best suit the requirements of the practitioner. Postulating the existence of Universes and ranges of experience other than that in which we are now so cribbed and cabined; regarding the human soul as an ultimate yardstick and implement whereby all things that have emanated from the Inconceivable Reality we call God can be measured and worked upon; believing in the absolute existence of Good and the relative existence of Evil as an umbra or husk to Good; the adepts of the practical Kabbala were usually intent on bringing back the fundamental unity in our own Universe and those immediately connected thereto. On earth the absence of this unity was symbolized in the Destruction of the Temple and the Exile of Jewry from the Land of Israel, which was accompanied by the Exile of the *Shechina,* the Divine Presence. This absence of the Divine Presence could also be sensed in personal life; and the main purpose of the Kabbalist was to bring back the Divine Presence. In earlier centuries each Kabbalist evolved a system of his own; toward the end of the sixteenth century Rabbi Isaac Luria, the Ari of Safed, together with a number of other Kabbalists, most of them his pupils, a few independent, but almost all resident at Safed in Galilee, evolved a system by which Kabbala for certain ends was applied through the whole range of life. These ends were primarily the re-establishment of that harmony of the spheres which must precede the ultimate redemption of Jewry and the coming of Messiah. The methods consisted of a pure life combined with devotional and intellectual practices. Those who practised them, more particularly during the seventeenth century, frequently took the sufferings of exile upon themselves for a period of seven years, never sleeping twice in succession in the same town or village except on the Sabbath, rising at midnight to weep and mourn for Zion (thereby helping to readjust that disharmony which on earth had produced the loss of Zion); Reb Yudel in the following story is after a fashion true to this type.

Practical Kabbala was tried as an effective factor in Jewish life by the group associated with the false Messiah, Sabbethai Zevi, and Jewry in Europe and Asia actually believed that the day of Redemption was at hand; among others, Pepys mentions the state of mind in the year 1666, when the excitement Zevi aroused reached England. Either Zevi's assumptions were wrong, however, or else Kabbala cannot be applied in politics; for when Zevi was brought face to face with the Turkish Sultan he cast no spells and uttered no Names of Power, but meekly accepted Islam and was given a palace post and allowance. Many of his followers became Moslems with him; but Jewry in general experienced the most serious disappointment which it had undergone in its internal life. The name of Sabbethai Zevi became anathema; practically all the Hebrew literature dealing with him was destroyed; and the mere suggestion that anybody was a covert follower of the false Messiah was sufficient to ensure partial ostracism and a considerable fall in the social scale. All of which will be found illustrated in Agnon's tale.

Such was the effect of the fall of Sabbethai Zevi that sixty years after his death Moses Hayyim Luzzatto, one of the biggest all-round men Jewry has produced in the past three centuries, underwent rather harsh treatment from the Jewish authorities in Venice because they thought that he showed a tendency toward regarding himself as a Messiah. At about the same period, in the first half of the eighteenth century, another Messianic movement started on the borders of Turkey and Poland, centering round the dingy person of Jacob Frank. He too led his followers out of Jewry, this time into the official ranks of the Roman Catholic Church, which welcomed these new sheep to its fold but nevertheless remained rather dubious about them.

Meanwhile something else was happening within East European Jewry. The seventeenth and eighteenth centuries are replete with legends of "hidden saints" and "Masters of the Name." The former were accounted among the thirty-six hidden saints, mentioned in the Talmud, by reason of whose virtues the Universe continues to function. They lived unknown and secluded, usually pretending to be uncouth and ignorant craftsmen, and ascending to the surface of Jewish life only when some great need called for them. They were all practical Kabbalists, and usually they were Masters of the Name; at the least they were "possessors of Degrees." That is, they for the most part were blessed with supernormal powers such as second sight, capacity for communication with other spheres, etc. The Masters of the Name, however, were actually capable of affecting the course of nature; they could "shorten distances," cure sickness by prayer and laying on of hands, perform minor miracles and do a number of other remarkable things, all as the result of the most rigid askesis. They possessed a knowledge of the hidden powers of letters and words, and knew how to construct those groups of sounds and combinations of letters which, by acting in higher spheres, could produce a reaction in our own sphere.

By about 1750 a new movement had already established itself as a force in Jewish life. It centered originally about Rabbi Israel, Master of the Name or *Baal Shem,* but the school of thought extended very rapidly, and any number of secondary, tertiary and quarternary teachers were soon busy propagating the movement. The most essential factor in this movement was the fact that the *Hassid,* the pious, righteous man of loving-kindness, was made the center, instead of, as hitherto, the scholar. Naturally the Kabbalist interpretation of life and of Jewry kept its place and importance; but the center of gravity was shifted from the righting of the universal disharmony to the righting of the disharmony within the soul of the individual man.

What was more, scholarship, which had hitherto been the best manner of demonstrating love of God and of the Torah by the acquisition of the latter, was now called upon to share its pride of place with the joyous fulfillment of the commandments. After all, there was much to be joyful about (and I must confess that in my opinion this particular element in Jewish spiritual life is a very ancient one, and probably the most Hassidic document in the world is the 23rd Psalm); despite all evil, that essentially good thing, life, goes on; whether in your person or in the persons of others, it continues; despite all persecution, Jewry, God's chosen people, are still in existence and are the living proof of an individual Providence; if we Jews are still in the world, says the Hassid, despite all that has befallen us, we even have the right to believe that we shall one day (may it be speedily and in our own times, amen, he would add) return to the land of Israel, a nation saved and redeemed. Meanwhile the great God that controls the universe does not neglect me on account of the, according to our standards, bigger job He has in hand, and His special Individual Providence watches over me and leads me in the proper way. It is true, argues the average Hassid, that my knowledge and faith are not sufficient to ensure my complete trust and faith in God; but these are necessary for my well-being, and I must therefore take as my guide somebody who is better informed than I regarding the workings of the hidden sides of the universe. That person, who has already proved himself by his teachings and his deeds and general foresight, is my rabbi (usually known by the more familiar terms, *tsaddik* or saint and *rebbe* or teacher) and saint. In him I put my trust, for his great personal merits and knowledge of the ways of God will suffice to set me on that manner of life which is best fitted for me. Meanwhile God is good and God is great, and we must put our trust in Him after the fashion indicated by our saintly rabbi whichever-one-it-may-happen-to-be.

And so Reb Yudel, armed with the instructions of his saintly rabbi, Abraham Joshua Heshel, of Apta (a historic person, incidentally), fares forth to brave the dangers of the unknown world lying beyond his own House of Study. There is nothing mysterious in the world which he is about to enter; the gentiles are an unknown and doubtless unaccountable race, who have to be borne with, because, though not of the Chosen People, they are also in the image of God. The authorities or their representatives are dangerous; it is to be assumed that they desire to harm Israel; in times of old they used to levy heavy taxes and permit pogroms now and again. In Reb Yudel's time they are behaving even worse, for they wish to introduce all sorts of outlandish tricks into the Jewish street; they wish to take the young men as soldiers, God forbid, to fight in wars that have nothing to do with them; they wish to teach German; and worst of all there are some Jews who are deceived by their devices and do not realize that these things are only traps meant to ensnare Jewry and entice it away from the paths of righteousness. But when Reb Yudel meets such a person he knows just how he has to be handled.

Throughout his journey, as indeed throughout his entire life, Reb Yudel lives according to the letter and the spirit of the Torah. And who should know what they are better than he and his like? For they live in the Torah and the Torah is their life as it has been the life of all their ancestors, and as it will doubtless be the life of their descendants. The Torah has given Jewish life its content and character in the past. There is no reason to suppose that it will cease to do so in the future.

Before ending, I must thank Mr. Agnon for his unfailing helpfulness in clearing up any questionable points with regard to text, customs or Jewish scholarship; I must also thank my father, Joseph Hayyim Cohen Lask, from the tremendous harvest of whose knowledge in Hebrew literature, Jewish history and Jewish life I have gleaned the little that has made this and all my other translations from the Hebrew possible.

I. M. LASK

Jerusalem, New Year 5697 (1936/37)

PUBLISHER'S NOTE

S. Y. Agnon, born 1888 in Buczacz, Galicia (then part of the Austro-Hungarian Empire) started his writing career as a boy of sixteen. His first poem, "The Little Hero," was published in the Hebrew periodical *Hamitzpah*. From that time on, he wrote numerous stories and poems, first in Yiddish and then in Hebrew. In 1908, Agnon settled in Palestine. In 1909, his story "Agunot" ("Deserted Wives") was published, from which he derived his pen name Agnon; his original name was Czaczkes. From 1913 to 1924 he lived in Germany where he came to know Martin Buber, who published German translations of some of Agnon's stories in his periodical *Der Jude*, and Salman Schocken, who later became his publisher.

It was in this period that Agnon started to write his first major novel, *The Bridal Canopy;* he completed it after his return to Palestine. This novel of epical power and proportions purposed to portray Jewish piety, love of God, Torah, and God's creatures, the perfect inner harmony and the disregard of material gain or loss—a life which Agnon's loving eye found in Eastern Europe in a not too distant past. Reb Yudel, the hero of the novel, personifies such humble, devout, dedicated, albeit naïve existence, immersed in sacred memories and in quotations from holy books. It is a tale of the Jew in exile and his fervent trust in redemption.

Mr. Lask's translation of *The Bridal Canopy* appeared in 1937, and is based on the Hebrew version (*Hachnassath Kalla*) published in 1931. The translator realized the impossibility of reconstructing more than a part of the continuous undercurrent of biblical and talmudic phrases in the narrative. His solution was to reproduce "the scent of an English style of a period corresponding in a way to that which Agnon set out to portray." Today, with the wealth of literary analysis and critical review that have been accorded Agnon's work, a translator would be free to essay a different approach to his task, but it is doubtful whether the joyous quality, the loving tone, the subtle irony of the original—and an undercurrent of alienation—could be better grasped.